Melanie
xxx

BEAUX BELLES
GRIND AND PUNISHMENT

Hi Andrew
All the best

Tim

BY THE SAME AUTHORS:

BIG BEN

TIM BRADY & MELANIE WILLEMS
BEAUX BELLES
GRIND AND PUNISHMENT

First published in Great Britain 2013
Copyright © 2013 Tim Brady and Melanie Willems
Published by Tim Brady and Melanie Willems

Paperback ISBN 978-0-9567919-2-4

Also by the authors: "Big Ben – law and disorder" published 2011

1 3 5 7 9 10 8 6 4 2

Printed in Great Britain by CPI Mackays Ltd
Typeset by Alison Padley

www.melandtimbooks.com
www.melandtimbooks.co.uk

For Adam and Mounir and Tim WJ

"Not a shred of evidence exists in favor
of the idea that life is serious."

Brendan Gill

1

It's B.A.D.

Piers Minister could still remember the first time he had fantasised about his domineering aunt.

It was one of his earliest memories. It stuck in his mind like a barnacle to a fishing boat – and this no matter what else was available for him to think about.

He wondered whether everyone else was as haunted, and what haunted them. It seemed not to matter how full or glamorous his life sometimes appeared. Certain thoughts and remembrances were immune to time's slow burial. Even now, at the height of an exciting social experience, Aunt Diana would occasionally flash up, like a hologram. No wonder some people believed in ghosts.

Yet Aunt Diana was alive. She was, thought Piers admiringly, a powerful presence, and she had been as long as Piers could remember. Family events felt mundane until she glided into the room. She was kind to Piers, but he, like everyone, had experienced her acerbic comments and her look of disapproval. This was her signature, a stage spotlight of imperious intensity that pinned one in place like a hapless butterfly. She was a mistress of ocular communication. Piers recalled her beady stare, bright with intent, eyes narrowing slightly as she focused on her opponent.

As a small boy, this intimidated Piers greatly. As a teenager, those looks made him shiver with delight. There was an odd tingling as Diana dared him to pursue his line of thought, a secret jousting between them that no one else noticed. Piers held his ground, and stared insolently at Diana's plunging neckline, honing in on her string of milky pearls, hard and intransigent, like little bullets on guard, daring his gaze to settle hungrily in their spot.

It wasn't really Aunt Diana's breasts that were the main attraction, mighty resting place for a pearl necklace as they were. It was rather her apparent sophistication, control and mastery of all that she touched that infused Piers with the certainty that, if ever he were touched by her, he would explode.

As Aunt Diana wasn't actually available for sex romps with one of her nineteen-year-old relatives, Piers had to make do with girls his own age.

It never felt quite right. Chatting over coffee was fine. The lampooning of a classmate's fashion-forward faux-pas was fun. Getting drunk and dancing to Kylie was fantastic. When the bedroom beckoned, though, Piers felt lost. He managed to perform. That was the sum of it. The girls were too inexperienced to notice. Throughout, Piers remained painfully aware that he was looking for something else.

In his fashion student days, he started to wonder if he were gay. It would have been convenient. People thought that he probably was. Piers' predilection for the powerful older female figure, his lukewarm attraction to the girls around him, and his fascination for couture and crochet seemed to be needling him towards the inevitable.

Yet there remained one problem. Apart from his own, Piers had absolutely no interest whatsoever in cock.

Piers accepted with good grace the fact that he was straight. He eventually came to terms with what pleased and teased him. At least, he admitted it to himself. He couldn't, however, bring himself to admit it to others.

Peer pressure prevented him from coming out as an aficionado of the more mature woman.

Piers lived with his inclinations, caged by them, occasionally feeling rather wretched because of them. He took care to *clear history* every time he relieved himself by trawling through cougarslut.co.uk. He lived a secret life, yearning for the craggy lioness, but too timorous a wee beastie to actually join the hunt in person.

"*Dica!*"

Piers started. His solitary musings were being disturbed by a surly barista. He smiled to himself. Ah, he thought, the gentle whisperings of the Italian language. The call was followed by a couple of muttered oaths. Sometimes Piers wished he'd never become fluent in the language. It would be nicer to still be able to enjoy Italian as music – so elegant.

The barista slapped down a receipt for collection.

This was one of those Milan bars where you first queued to pay, and then queued again to retrieve what you had ordered. Piers thought that the system showed a profound lack of trust in Italian society. Either suspicious bar owners were expecting the customers to run out with stolen brioches, or there was concern that staff were sneakily planning to fund a holiday home in Liguria on illicit coffee takings. As criminal master plans went, this made no sense. However, the espresso was invariably excellent, and Piers did not fancy himself as a militant reformer of European coffee purchasing habits. If you had to choose your battles, this was not one of the top three.

Fashion Week in Milan brought with it a touch of the same old, same old. The bar in Piazza Castello was overcrowded with noisy self-styled opinion-formers, fresh from the last *sfilata* of the mild February day in the Castello Sforzesco. Piers took another look around. He reflected that at least he had achieved some of what he had set out to achieve. He was a moderately successful designer now. His public image remained lower-key than some, but he was equally obsessed with form, and popular amongst his peers. His runway show earlier in the week had been well-received. But he did tire quickly – as he did every year – of the hangers-on at Fashion Week. They put him in mind of the unwelcome belch that one might have to endure after the pleasures of a pint of lager. On this occasion, Piers had given his own hangers-on the slip. He was enjoying a few moments alone, surveying the crowd and reflecting on the choice of career he had made. It was at that moment that his eye strayed onto something familiar.

What caught Piers' eye was one of his own creations. A brown leather Napier handbag swung on a lady's arm.

It was one of Piers' favourites. He had designed it for the subjects of his teenage obsessions. The handbag was a simple calfskin bag, intended for a woman who would favour the understated, rather than an outfit that made the statement for her. Indeed, a Napier owner would never be upstaged by what was on her arm, be it animal, mineral, or husband. Naturally, the woman was impeccably dressed from head to toe. It was Fashion Week, after all.

The woman looked over. Her eyes flashed in recognition. Piers knew that look. There was no hesitation to be expected when women like her looked at you like that. None transpired. She excused herself from her conversation, finished her espresso, and made her way over to Piers. An engaging smile danced around her carefully made-up face. Piers suddenly felt as if he were on a tight rope. The woman was old enough to be his mother. Her perfume filled the air. He felt faint.

"Tell me, you are Piers Minister! I *love* your work. You are a master." A master. This betrayed the woman as an Italian.

She was exactly Piers' type – attractive, confident, well-dressed, and blessed with a sexy Italian accent to boot. As they engaged in small talk, Piers felt a stab of excitement. He knew that he was storing visual material for a later lonely moment. Would he dare to touch her? That memory often helped at the critical point.

"Thank you so much," he said finally. "I am delighted to see that one of my bags has been matched to one of the ladies that I pictured while I was designing it."

Piers' remark had a noticeable effect. The lady's eyes sparkled brightly, *à la* Diana. Heavens, it was like being bathed in tiny diamonds. This was getting dangerous. The woman looked as if she might linger for some time, and Piers could feel himself weakening. He had to act fast.

"Sadly, signora, I must be going now. It was my pleasure to meet you. I do wish you a very good evening. Arrivederci."

As he left the bar, Piers' legs felt as stiff as the words he had just uttered to the disappointed dama. *Never mind*, he thought. It was essential to protect himself, especially during Fashion Week. Eyes and spies were everywhere. Although there was nothing wrong – in the slightest – in a young man being attracted to an older woman, Piers wasn't quite ready to publicly declare his inclinations. His courage failed him. Anything outside of the norm attracted commentary and unwelcome attention. Piers wanted to remain in the shadows, near the light, enjoying the light, but away from the full glare of scrutiny that was the spotlight's dark side.

He felt slightly miserable. It was an odd quandary. He fully identified with gays who remained in the closet. He felt that he had been loitering in his own for years, between hangers and hangers-on. And yet, so long as the closet was full of designer threads, what better place for a fashion designer to stay?

Distracted, Piers realised that he had turned the wrong way out of the bar and was heading round the west side of the castle.

How exasperating.

He paused to get his bearings. He would need to cross Parco Sempione to get home to his apartment in Corso Como. Still, it was a pleasant temperature for the season.

The walk would do him good. Piers felt glad to escape the crowds. He breathed in deep and walked on, allowing himself to weigh up those potent images of *Lady with Napier Handbag*.

The rain that afternoon had left a heavy scent of grass in the air. Being outside was a welcome relief. Milan didn't have many green spaces in the city centre. Used to the English countryside of his childhood, Piers appreciated the sudden freshness of the air.

Lost in thought, he didn't hear the footsteps padding up softly behind him. He did however feel – and how – the blow to the back of his head which sent him reeling. The next thing Piers felt was a hand on his arm. It turned him round roughly. He just managed to avoid a blow aimed squarely in his face. A fist glanced off the side of Piers' head, leaving his ears ringing.

What the attacker didn't know was that Piers was a trained kick boxer. His reflexes immediately went into overdrive. He brought his knee up hard into the aggressor's chest and managed to free himself from the grasp before any more punches made contact.

Piers was feeling dazed, but alert enough still to realise that he did not know if the attacker had a knife. His self-defence mechanism kicked in, and activated his legs. He was off, running for his life.

He could hear the attacker following him.

It all seemed like a very active dream. Piers was reasonably fit but he sensed the mugger was gaining on him.

He had to get out of the park. Once he got to Via

Legnano there should be traffic. He would be safe. He could hear a few cars in the distance, but he could also sense that his personal criminal representative was gaining on him. Then he saw a figure walking under the trees by the side of the road ahead of him.

"Aiuto. Aiuto!"

Piers desperately tried to get the figure's attention by waving his hands as he ran. He hoped that this might scare the attacker off. His heart sank as he realised that the figure looked like a woman, or at least by the skirt probably not the kind of man who would be of huge use to Piers at that moment. Clearly, the attacker shared the same view, as his pace did not slacken. As Piers drew nearer to the figure, the attack was made concrete. The mugger launched himself at Piers again, knocking him to the ground. Piers was pinned to the grass – and this time there was no escaping the blows which started to rain down on him.

More footsteps, like a light drumming, or heavy rain. Oh dear, thought Piers, is there an accomplice? There was a defiant cry:

"Bastardo!"

It was the woman from the bar.

His attacker momentarily stopped hitting Piers to look up at the unlikely figure who was challenging him. This was swiftly followed by a shriek of pain. The man rubbed his eyes wildly. Sensing his chance, Piers wriggled out from underneath his aggressor, gave him a kick in the nuts for good measure, and turned to face his saviour.

The woman stood there, brandishing a can of pepper spray.

She was still on full alert. She immediately took advantage of the attacker's disorientation and thwacked him round the head with her Napier handbag, rather like Margaret Thatcher might have dreamed of doing to Jacques Delors. There was a loud crack. The attacker moaned again, and coughed wildly, but somehow scrambled up and made off at surprising speed. He seemed to melt back into the park. Piers thought about following him, but as there was blood streaming from his nose, he decided against it.

"Signor Minister, you poor man! Are you alright? Please, let me assist you. My car is just round the corner. Let me take you to Pronto Soccorso!"

"Signora, you saved my life. I think. How can I thank you? I don't even know your name, signora…"

"Barlettano. My name is Mrs Barlettano… but please, please… call me Claudia."

Ben Barlettano leaned back in his slightly bouncy office chair. The chair. One of his favourite things in the office. Damn, it was fine being a lawyer. He yawned as his fingers tapped his keyboard automatically, opening yet another needlessly verbose email. Who were these people? Why did they write to him like this? He leaned in and quickly scanned the accompanying document. Okay. They were using the wrong version.

"Ham," Ben said, not looking up from the screen.

There was a little scuttling noise as Ben's trainee Hamish peered around from the computer screen opposite. Hamish was a curly haired boy who looked about twelve. He was the calmest, sweetest colleague Ben could remember coming across. Sharing an office with him was distracting only by virtue of the fact that one could genuinely forget that he was there. Ben had jumped out of his skin more than once as Hamish had plonked a cup of tea on his desk, or made some other thoughtful gesture that earned him Ben's begrudging liking. He was also smart. Ben liked smart trainees.

"You see this," said Ben, authoritatively swivelling his screen an inch so that Hamish could make out the cross glare on the screen.

No, thought Hamish, *can't see a ruddy thing.* But he nodded quietly and moved around so that he could see.

"Wrong version," said Ben. "They have sent through the wrong version of the document. We could have been at cross purposes for days over this. This is incompetence on a grand scale. These people are arseholes. Remember that, Ham. We are going to have trouble. You know it the minute you see this level of buffoonery on what should be a simple and straightforward exchange."

"Er... Ben?" said Hamish.

Ben turned his cool but not unfriendly gaze on his colleague.

"What, Ham?"

"You have... er... glitter on your cheek. Sort of... here." Hamish poked at his own chubby cheek, somewhere where a cheekbone should have been.

Ben rubbed his cheek ruefully. Last night had been far too much fun for mid-week. He hadn't seen Rubens for so long, and he had showed up with Jamal. Given the infrequency of their meetings these days, they had started the evening in a bar. They had a quiet beer in a manly and grown-up manner. But it had not taken long for the evening to degenerate. Alcohol offered such a welcome release of inhibitions. Ben remembered getting home at two in the morning, wearing a pink boa, a ton of glitter and singing a Lady Gaga tune (so impossible to get out of your head... *Gaga ooh lala*).

"It's the damnedest thing to get off, glitter," Ben said to Ham. "Now. You have reminded me that we need to chat about your first three months sitting with me. Shall we do that now? No time like the present."

Ham thought that he would rather knit a willy warmer for an elderly uncle than be assessed at this precise moment. But he nodded with what could pass for enthusiasm. You had to go with the flow to get on in an office.

Ben had been working at Beaux Aspen for just over two years now. He had joined the firm from SBK as part of a team led by Hartmut Glick, a German corporate lawyer of great distinction. With military and painstaking precision, Hartmut had duly organised a transfer of his team. Law was a people business – you needed the people to carry out the work. Hartmut liked people, although you would be hard-pressed to ascertain this from his impassive gaze and cool demeanour. The transfer had been very successful. Plenty of impossibly dull work had followed them like a bad smell.

Hamish settled down in a chair, dutifully waiting for something that might pass for feedback from his principal. But Ben was already distracted. His eyes had widened considerably. He was staring at his screen in amazement.

"Ham. Have you seen this?"

There goes my assessment, thought Ham. "What?" he asked.

Ben had opened an email. It was addressed to all Beaux Aspen personnel. It was not very long. Ben started to read it in portentous tones:

"Dear colleagues,

We are proud to announce that after careful consideration and productive discussions we have agreed a merger with the firm of Dickerhint Strudel.

Many of you will be aware of the synergies that exist between our two firms' practices..."

Ben's voice trailed off. It really wasn't that exciting demonstrating that he could read out loud.

"We will be more powerful than ever we could have imagined," intoned Hamish.

Ben looked surprised, then smiled:

"Indeed. But this is significant. It doubles our size."

"So size matters. There were rumours that this would happen," said Hamish reflectively.

"Yes, I know. But it all seems so quick."

"Does it say that we will now be a giant client solution delivery machine?"

"No. That is a missed opportunity, because clients would really want that confirmed."

"The new firm," read out Hamish, *"will be known as Beaux, Aspen, Dickerhint."*

He looked up:

"B.A.D? Really?"

"Poor Mr Strudel," said Ben.

Far from the world of dawdling in a law firm, Monique lay on her sofa in Kennington. She kicked off her kitten-heel shoes.

No one was there to see this happen, but had they been observing, they would have noted that in this, as in many things, she was graceful. She looked better than it could be considered healthy to. Her canary yellow shift dress fitted beautifully.

Desirability could be very bad for you. However, Monique of all people did not need a long lecture on the dangers and irritations inherent in attraction and its immediate consequences. She was tired today.

Her head rested on an embroidered cushion, near a charming French table. This formed a pedestal for a large goldfish bowl. She shifted around and tapped the glass, smiling as the little golden fish swam up, mouthing expectantly at her.

"Oh, Sushi," Monique sighed, "what am I to do about all this?"

Sushi the goldfish had precious little to contribute to the discussion, but he remained Monique's favourite interlocutor. He swam around in water all day, and never leaked a thing. He was relaxed about the music business. He liked a nice flake of fish food. You could trust a fish that knows exactly what he likes.

Monique stared at her phone. Jake was a good texter. He used the medium expertly. He was also – evidently – very taken by her. Of course, men were generally very taken by Monique.

"What do I want?" she muttered. "What do *I* want?"

Do I, she wondered, *live in the present? Do I take the view that what is now is all that I truly need to care about? Or should I try to analyse matters further, to a degree that might drive me insane, and that would paralyse enjoyment of the moment?*

If that were to be the consequence, living in the present would be a sensible thing.

Then again, what seems right for now may be cooking up a stew of misfortune for further down the road.

Monique was a rather practical person. She was used to attention and juggling shenanigans. It was far easier to get into romantic scrapes than it was to hold down and work at a conventional relationship.

Sometimes people forget that, she thought crossly. They keep trying to advise you to be like them – but they are not playing the same game.

Monique had only recently emerged from an on and off, surprisingly lengthy relationship with Harry Gumpert. Harry was married, and a wealthy lawyer. The split had occasioned odd feelings. She felt like a castaway for a short while – as if she were marooned on a solitary island of *tristesse* that no one else could land on. However, good-looking people don't generally have to mourn the death of their relationships for long. Monique soon found herself again at the centre of attentions, wherever she went. This was a relief of course, and had helped her to tackle the occasional *fado* brought on by the split up. It had been nice dating sensible, affluent boys for a while.

By an accident of circumstances she ended up sitting, quite single and comfortable with it, at the seafood bar at

Heathrow, lazily picking at some smoked salmon before boarding a plane to Milan. Some rather scruffy-looking youths had piled on to the seats near her.

Monique ignored them. She ignored them even when the young kids came up to them with CDs to sign. She ignored them even as one of them said a little too loudly into his phone: "Yeah. We've just played to forty-five thousand people in Hyde Park." Monique did not care. She was going to Milan to escape a man who was finding her lack of commitment difficult, and to shop.

But she did look over. You would, of course – the seafood bar is simply not large enough not to. She happened to look at the exact same time that Jake looked at her. They exchanged an unduly serious look. She found out later that Jake was terrified of flying, so in an airport, at a seafood bar, his mind was more on swimming with the fishes than on surfing the sea of love. Notwithstanding this, Jake was eye-catching, to say the least. He had the longest eyelashes that Monique had seen on a man. He was handsome, in a dark, smoky way – long, lean and addictive, a cigarette made flesh. She looked at his lips and thought straight away of kissing him. It was quite a jolt.

Jake Le Jones was used to women looking at him in a certain way. Fame brings that – a certain shine of recognition in people's eyes, a suppressed but all too obvious excitement, and eagerness to please or impress. Jake was not very famous yet, but his band were well on their way. The Fondant Furies were making sound waves.

Jake smiled:

"Hi," he said, "where are you flying to today?"

"Milan," answered Monique politely.

"Are you from Milan?"

"No. I'm from Nice. But I've lived in London a long time now. Where are you flying to?"

"We're going to Berlin. We're got a few small gigs lined up."

"Are you in a group?"

Jake laughed. Another teenager stepped up shyly. Jake smiled and signed the CD, then asked the youngster:

"Can I show this to my friend?"

"Of course," came the excited reply.

"Here," said Jake, leaning over. "This is us."

Monique leaned over the gleaming plastic cover:

"The Fondant Furies?"

"Yes."

"The Fondant Furies."

"It's great that you can read."

"I memorised it first time. Don't take this the wrong way. Don't you think it's a bit cake-like?"

Jake frowned:

"It's just a name. It stuck."

"You've got that right. It's a sticky name. I'm not altogether sure about it – although it makes me hungry," said Monique, sweetly.

"You're probably not our demographic," said Jake easily.

Monique shot a look at him. She liked men who were not shaken by her opinions.

"How did you come up with that? Did you think of the Blistering Blinis? Or the Violent Vol au Vents?"

He looked at her:

"Easy now. I'm not looking for constructive criticism."

"What are you looking for?"

"Possibly your phone number. But I'm hedging my bets. We'd have to agree to disagree on the name."

"What is *your* name?" asked Monique.

"It's Jake. Rhymes with cake."

"That will make it easy to remember."

He grinned: "I'm Jake Le Jones. You?"

"Millefeuille McDoughnut. Not really. Monique. Monique Mottin."

Monique caught sight of the departure board. Her flight was boarding. She gestured at it:

"Time for me to go. Sorry for being silly. Here: my card. Don't go expecting anything. I barely know you, and you're not named after anything I really fancy."

He stuck out his hand: "Wish me luck. I hate flying."

Monique took his hand. She held it for a second longer than she should have.

"Flying is the safest form of travel. You will be absolutely fine."

They both suspected that something was going to happen. The conversation had begun.

Amber Bluett shuffled papers on her desk.

She looked around and leaned back in her chair with satisfaction. The chair leaned back with her. What a pleasurable support it was. There had been nothing like this in prison. It was a *proper* office chair. It was ergonomically designed to accommodate a whole lifetime of happy sedentary activity.

This was better than jail, no doubt about it. The kidney-shaped desk was also most satisfactory. She spread her papers out carefully. Such room to position them in.

Does anyone really understand the pleasures of good office furniture?

Admittedly, it was unbelievable to be here at Beaux, Aspen, Dickerhint. Amber still felt a great wave of glee every time she thought of how she had worked the system. After all, it was only two years ago that she had been sent to prison for aggravated assault – as you are wont to be, if you have assaulted somebody in an aggravated way.

Amber had spent her first month in silent rage and despondency. But she was tough, and she knew that sulking would do no good. She had no intention of rotting in a penal institution, when there were other institutions to rot in instead. Amber had considered her options. She was smart. She was not going to let this crush her. She pulled herself together. She knew that there was only one way out.

She reformed carefully, as only a true psychopath could. The prison staff were astounded at her progress. She kept her cell spotless. She was polite and responsive. She studied hard and took a course in human resources. This was against the advice of the prison career service officer, who really did not see a natural fit there. They recommended a career in public relations. But in this, as is often the case with career advisers, the prison service's career adviser was woefully wrong.

Being a psychopath is positively helpful in human resources. How could you possibly stand being burdened with empathy for others, if you were going to last the distance? The management of the hordes of salary slaves is not a skill given to all. Not everyone could convincingly dangle motivational carrots before weak-spirited wage earners, as if before cartoon donkeys. Amber thrived in human resources. She picked up the psychobabble with ease, and learnt how to make everything into an insoluble problem, so that she might be left alone to do exactly as she pleased. She thrived like a mushroom in a cellar where several long lost bodies were fertilising the soil with gusto, and where, additionally, the human resources might have gone for a little privacy, weeping at the impossibility of securing any improvement in their working conditions.

It all fell into place. There was a scheme for rehabilitation set up by a noble-looking barrister. Again, the existence of the scheme was no accident. It was, that barrister knew, an important step in his long-standing desire to be made a peer. Charity is a box that *must* be ticked, and properly ticked, if childish dreams are to be fulfilled.

Humbly, Amber sat through assessments, laughing easily, full of warmth and recognition of the error of her ways. Law firms fell over themselves to give her interviews. Not only did this give everyone concerned a warm and fuzzy feeling, but you certainly didn't have to pay market rate to a blooming ex-convict. It was a win-win all round.

The phone rang.

"Hello, Human Resources, Amber speaking," she said, in a voice that completely belied her murderous tendencies.

"Usual place. And read the email I've just sent you."

"Whatever happened to *hello*, Nicholas. I think you're losing your manners."

"Be there. I have no time."

"I suppose you *didn't* have me at hello," mused Amber. "All right. See you later."

She cradled the phone for a second. This was a manifestation of one of the more unexpected developments in her rehabilitation.

She had wanted to work in a large comfortable organisation where the coffee flowed freely, the offices were respectable and there was plenty of easy pilfering. It had boiled down to two firms in the end – Dickerhint Strudel and Stiller, Boils, Kumpelhauk.

Amber felt nervous on the morning of the interview with SBK. She always thought that there was a risk that people could see right through her in interviews. Or at least part of the way into her. What lay within was too dark and murky to peer through properly – like diving in very bad weather. For her interview, Amber had dressed formally in a pencil skirt, jacket and silky blouse, all given to her by the prison charity. They were good pieces. No doubt some lady barrister had got fat. All that dining – straight to the hips, until you looked like Ken Clarke. Amber dressed her hair carefully and headed out.

SBK's offices were a marble desert studded with green plant oases at regular intervals. They were clean and light and warm. Amber was ushered into a large conference room, dominated by a long shiny table. She felt like an imposter immediately. It was nice, though. She helped herself to a cup of tea, almost scalding herself in the process, and grabbed a bourbon cream.

"I rather like those myself," said a cool voice.

Nicholas Casterway had always borne a striking resemblance to a tall and evil doctor. His shiny head gleamed in the lights. His glasses were little and round. His suit was stunning – Amber saw that immediately. This was the proper stuff, not a hand-me-down. She glanced enviously at the details – the perfect silk tie, the discreet but heavy cuff links, the sober, matt quality of the shirt. Yes, he had the coolness of a skeleton walking to the North Pole – but there was an immediate frisson, before they had so much as finished exchanging pleasantries.

She was not sure what came over them. She still wasn't, even now.

She had sat opposite him. The table lay between them like a visiting parlour.

"So," he asked, looking away. "What was it like in prison?"

He swivelled towards her as he spoke. His eyes bored into her on the word *prison*.

Amber looked back at him insolently. She recognised him. She recognised a fellow bully, with weaknesses as huge and evident as the Grand Canyon. Unlike the Grand Canyon, though, which is beautiful, there was something else about Nicholas – something akin to a gaping, baying hole of darkness that sucked out most goodwill and justice in any space he occupied.

"What was it like in prison?" she repeated slowly.

She stared at him and locked on his gaze.

"What was it like in prison?"

Her hand wandered to her top button, concealed under a frilly silken cravat on the blouse, straining against her breasts.

"What," she asked reasonably, "do you *think* it was like in prison?"

The button popped. His eyes widened.

"There were," she explained, "many things I missed in prison."

She undid another button, very deliberately, locking in on Nicholas like a heat-seeking missile.

"Get over here," she ordered forcibly.

Nicholas whimpered and slid under the table. Before they knew it, his head was bobbing between her legs, her skirt was bunched up and slightly torn at the vent, and she was lying back in the chair and discovering interview techniques that she had long forgotten.

Amber pushed back the chair and dragged Nicholas onto it, fumbling with his expensive belt buckle, which clicked and clattered as it released. The chair leaned back as far as a premium economy seat. Amber unzipped Nicholas expertly and released his quivering cock. She dragged off her sodden pants, hitched her skirt around her hips, and lowered herself onto his tumescent shaft.

"Oooh," she said, almost to herself, "oooh, here we go."

She pumped up and down, first slowly, then quicker. Her hands strayed to her clitoris. There was no way that she was not going to milk this for all that it was worth. It had been a while since she had got laid.

After what seemed a long time but was only half a billable hour, they climaxed, and stopped, like a fairground ride coming to its inevitable and mechanical halt. They breathed heavily. At least they'd followed government health recommendations and got their heart rate up. Nicholas's glasses were twisted. For an older man he was remarkably nimble, thought Amber, as she rose briskly and attempted to smooth her clothes into something more akin to their state in the lady barrister's wardrobe.

She adjusted her stockings and turned to see Nicholas looking at her blankly.

"What," she asked, "are you looking at?"

To her vast surprise she had been offered the job. However, Amber was also offered employment at Dickerhint Strudel, a firm with better biscuits. Dickerhint Strudel appealed to her for other reasons, too. The legal press was awash with rumours that the firm was in merger talks with Beaux Aspen. Amber was well aware that Ben Barlettano, who had been instrumental in getting her convicted, worked at Beaux Aspen.

Serendipity, or what.

All Amber had to do was to ensure that she won the battle of the Human Resources Managers in the planned merger – which itself was the worst kept secret in the business. There could be only one.

This was easy enough. She sent an anonymous letter to her opposite number in Human Resources at Beaux Aspen, telling her it had already been decided that she was the one to go. She signed it *A concerned friend.*

Her rival was already worried. The letter duly caused her to blow up at her partner employers, none of whom could manage their way out of a paper bag at the best of times. The emotional scenes that followed ensured that Amber's rival's card was heavily marked. The partners at Beaux Aspen almost immediately decided that they could do without her. After all, the grass is always greener. Amber Bluett over at Dickerhint Strudel was a shining beacon of rehabilitation, with excellent tits.

Such is life, thought Amber. You just hand your rivals the rope, and point them to the bitter fruit tree. Meanwhile, the two law firms' merger proceeded apace after the usual fashion of blind optimism, with Mr Strudel's name consigned to the bins of history faster than a pastry dropped by a clumsy Austrian waitress.

From then on, things fell into place like a drone's well directed hits. Nicholas and Amber had embarked on a relationship of such toxicity that moths fled any room where they performed. In the world of garish acts for mutual gratification, they were Olympians.

Amber had missed physicality in her prison months. She was making up for it with a man who had interesting habits, including borrowing his wife Britta's silicon kitchenware. Amber sometimes wondered if Britta knew where her rolling pin had been.

Perhaps it was best if she never did find out.

"Hello?"

"Kelly, it's me. Ben."

"Oh, darling. How are you? I miss you so much."

"Yeah, yeah, I'm sure you do. It must be awful for you in Paris."

Kelly Danvers had called herself Ben's girlfriend for a long time now. But, as chance would have it, she had recently been offered a position working in Paris for a year. Paris being a mere two hours away from London by train, it seemed like a wonderful idea.

Kelly gave the matter some thought. She considered whether the increased money, extra responsibility and the thrill of living in the most romantic city on the planet was worth the separation from her beloved Ben. In the abstract, it had seemed a no-brainer. She decided that she had to go.

Ben understood the decision. He didn't blame her at all. Although it wasn't easy managing a long distance relationship, *especially* on the sex front, it was obviously the right thing for her career.

Disappointed nonetheless, Ben tried to turn the state of affairs into something positive, as best he could. This was right for his own development, too, he reasoned. After all, you would not want to get into a rut.

Ben and Kelly had been dating for two years or so in London. They had moved in together, staying on in the building where they had met, The Castle Lofts in Elephant and Castle, just south of the Thames. Although Ben still had nights out with the boys, he had decided that his bachelor life of casual sex with multiple partners (male, female and one or two where he genuinely couldn't recall) needed to be brought to a civilised end. The wild days of his courtship of Kelly – with all of the misunderstandings that only a bisexual could bring to that dance – were now over.

Resisting temptation had been easier than Ben thought, once he had made it into a challenge. Getting out of the club, bar or bathhouse with a pristine, untouched penis was like an endorphin rush after exercise. In fact, public chastity had become rather like a drug for Ben. It made him feel impossibly smug and satisfied with himself. No one ever rejected you if you did not put yourself out there. He compensated with plenty of masturbation in the privacy of his own home.

Telephone conversations were achingly awkward, thought Ben, even when you loved the person you were talking to.

Kelly laughed:

"Well, I'm not going to lie to you. This city has plenty of charms. But, you know... I wish you were here to enjoy them with me. There's a space on the sofa where you should be. How's life in London anyway? Is work good? Is Hartmut still treating you well? Has he found ways of making you draft?"

Ben smirked audibly:

"I actually have some news on that front. It's quite exciting. We're merging. A firm called Dickerhint Strudel. But that's not all. I overheard one of the partners prattling on. Turns out we're taking on one of their HR Managers. I think you'll be entertained by this. She is a woman by the name of Amber Bluett. Ring any bells?"

Kelly gasped.

"Are you *kidding me*? Holy cow! Amber Bluett! What do you know? Hell, I thought she was still locked up. How in the devil's name has she got a job working in a law firm?

Does this mean that that mad bitch is going to be privy to your personal details now? Ben, this is not good. It could be bad. Very bad."

"I wouldn't worry too much about it Kelly. There are eyes and ears everywhere in law firms. There's only so much she could get away with. Anyway, apparently she is a reformed character. She even looks different. I hope she's not a born-again, mind you. I don't think I could take that."

"I don't like it, Ben. We know her, remember? She attacked me. If it hadn't been for you and Hartmut rushing to my rescue, her brothers would have assaulted me..."

Kelly's voice trailed off, remembering the scene of two years earlier, when an attack by Amber's brothers had nearly turned very nasty indeed.

"Listen, darling, I'll keep an eye on her. More importantly, you look after yourself in Paris. I'm sure it's full of all sorts of fascinating guys, who would be all over you if you gave them half a chance."

"Don't worry about that, Ben. I'm not the one who used to wake up in different beds every weekend, remember. I'm all yours, baby. Anyway, better go. I'm on my way to a work dinner. Speak to you at the weekend. And watch out for Amber. Au revoir, ma petite saucisse. Bisous!"

She was gone.

Ben felt the weight of the receiver in his hand, a dull object that was now empty of Kelly's Southern drawl. He leaned back and sighed. He wanted to feel her heavy breasts and make her gasp in delight. The lack of sucking in long distance relationships was nothing to be happy about. Or was it rather that long-distance relationships sucked? It was tough to be philosophical when one felt ready to go.

Ben fixed himself a drink and settled back on the sofa. Feet up, he gazed out of his living-room window. The Shard gleamed, silhouetted in the distance. God, you saw the Shard from *everywhere* now. He knew that Kelly would remain disturbed by the news that Amber Bluett had resurfaced. Ben was wary, too.

But Amber really did seem quite different now. Prison had made her into a babe. Whilst retaining the same marvellous embonpoint as before, she now offered the welcome additions of a slender waist, toned legs, and a peachy butt that strained to bounce out of her skirt whenever she leaned over. Ben had found himself on the receiving end of such a vista when he caught her leaving the secretaries' meeting the week before. Kelly need never know that just minutes before he called her, Ben had happily pleasured himself reliving that exact same scene.

There was genuinely no accounting for taste.

2

Slings and Arrows

"Oh, *darling*. Could you not have given me one of the *china* teacups?"

Eleanor Napier Jones' steaming Darjeeling was sitting on the table in front of her in a large, black mug depicting what appeared to be Catwoman glowering at a handcuffed villain.

Although usually adept at ignoring the distasteful – of which there was *so* much these days – Eleanor couldn't help but stare at the sheer vulgarity of the image.

Cartoons had changed since she was a girl. Eleanor certainly couldn't remember Wilma Flintstone or Olive Oyl bare-breasted, with what looked like a chain linking their nipples. And why did the supposed villain have a large hole where the seat of his trousers should be, and what looked like a large Bramley apple in his mouth? Even more vulgar was the bold lettering emblazoned on the long, curved handle of the mug. It read *PPLAY at home*.

PPLAY, of course, was the acronym for the well-known sado-masochistic club Pain Pleasure Lust And Yearning, where Hartmut and Caroline enjoyed privileged membership. It was, remembered Caroline fondly, where they had first met. *Whip crack away*, indeed. Caroline turned round, an absent-minded smile flickering on her face. She stifled a gasp as she saw what her mother was looking at. Luckily, the addition of Marky and Sadie to the Glick-Napier Jones household had not shaken Hartmut's (admittedly belated) attention to detail. He swooped in and deftly removed the offending receptacle, to the relief of both mother and daughter.

"Oh, Hartmut. *Thank* you."

Eleanor watched as Hartmut smoothly placed a pristine Denby Natural Pearl teacup and saucer in front of her, at regulation distance from the table's edge.

"Two and a half minutes to go until your Darjeeling is ready," Hartmut informed her.

Eleanor still wasn't quite sure what to make of Hartmut Glick. She found him rather disconcerting, and not just because he was German. She knew – didn't everyone? – that Teutons were famous for ruthless precision, with sleek Mercedes sweeping aside the hapless British Rovers. However, Hartmut's perfectionism was on an altogether different scale.

Though Eleanor would never betray even the slightest hint of the thoughts she may harbour in many regards, Caroline knew perfectly well that her mother couldn't quite fit Hartmut into her Weltenschauung.

Initially, Eleanor had been content to label Hartmut a standard, educated European, attempting to rise to refined English middle class norms. However, she quickly realised that Hartmut was not quite from that mould. Eleanor detected something unexpected and rather disturbing in Hartmut. His rational perfectionism was complemented by effortless good breeding.

Her first grandchildren, Marky and Sadie, were the twin products of that good breeding. From time to time, the adults would glaze over as they looked at the angelic twins. Their arrival seemed – even now – to be a magical development.

Despite knowing exactly how it had happened, Hartmut had no idea when it had happened. One Sunday morning, Caroline had announced that there was an irregularity in her cycle. After a frisson of irritation at the disturbance to the order of his weekend, Hartmut realised with a start that this could be the beginning of a rather greater disturbance in their lives.

Save for the unwelcome intrusion of baby-related paraphernalia, including the cutest tiny gimp costumes, and a splendid baby cage, Caroline's pregnancy had passed uneventfully. There were no unusual cravings – everything went very much according to expectations. They experienced nothing but the customary dressing up, whipping, gagging, and much wearing of rubber maternity wear. But those months were behind them now. That was then.

Hartmut remembered every detail of the day the twins were born, as he watched his beloved lover screaming in exquisite pain, about to give birth.

Although he had been surprised by his new found paternal instincts, and the strange warmth they provided at unexpected moments of reflection, Hartmut couldn't help but feel that the situation presented all the trappings of a wasted opportunity. There was Caroline, lying supine with her legs in stirrups, without him being able to take advantage of her unusually vulnerable position. In other circumstances, with the added stimulus of a uniform busily tending to her, the tableau would have proven *inspiring*. He made a note to consider how to develop that idea later.

Hartmut and Caroline had decided on a homebirth, despite the increased risks. It was either that, or leave out all the slaves. There was remarkably little flexibility in the birth plans they reviewed with maternity professionals for exploring alternative presentations around the birthing process. It seemed that anything cutesy or involving whale song was okay. Restraints and chains were not. Frankly, this seemed a little old hat.

However, Caroline and Hartmut were used to encountering a lack of appreciation wherever they turned. They compromised on health and safety, and engaged a professional midwife. In line with their vision, they also engaged half a dozen extras, now littered around the bedroom in various states of leather and rubber undress, as titillating an installation as might befit the arrival of new life. Although not in need of the extra money, Caroline had made sure that those worthless PPLAY also-rans had paid handsomely for the privilege of being humiliated during such an occasion.

"Are you sure you don't want the painkillers, Caroline?" Hartmut's practical side had kicked in.

Caroline's shrieks got louder.

"Are you out of your mind, Hartmut? And miss all of

this? And where are the *fucking* nipple clamps?"

"There, there, dear," crooned the midwife. "It's perfectly normal for your breasts to be tender. Just concentrate on pushing."

Although Harriet Watanabe had been warned that this would be a slightly different birthing experience, she was finding it harder than usual to concentrate on the job in hand. Even the thought of the beautiful three-piece suite this extremely well-paid job would provide couldn't quite blot out the rather large phallus being wielded by a buxom blonde in the corner. *Where* was she going to put it? Oh. *There.* Goodness.

"At least get the buggering handcuffs on me Hartmut!" yelled Caroline, with a look that was daring him to disobey her. "And you in the green mask, whip that little shit harder. Put your back into it! Why should I be the only one in pain here?"

Mercy me! As Harriet stared between Caroline's legs, willing the babies to appear so she could beat a hasty retreat, she couldn't help but notice Hartmut's careful cuffing of Caroline's wrists to the iron bedhead. It's amazing what surround vision will sear into your mind. *Think of the elegant Renoir sofa that this would pay for and how it will look in the sitting room. The deep buttoning. The gently swept arm design. The stumpy feet.*

Caroline screamed again.

"There, there dear, the baby's coming. The baby's coming. Some discomfort is normal, dear," said Harriet soothingly.

"It's not the baby! Hartmut, show that fool how to whip

properly. I'll have your membership rescinded, you limp-dicked excuse of a man. You're ruining my special day!"

Caroline's breathing gradually became more regular as Hartmut's masterful strokes calmed her shattered nerves. The slave's whimpers connected with her own pain, helping her to concentrate on the push.

Harriet was used to staring at vaginas, yet she did not remember another time when she attempted to blot out the rest of the world with one. Unable to imagine what children could emerge from such a woman, Harriet started to imagine her longed-for sofa bursting forth instead, followed by the chairs, and, after today's experience, the footstool that she thought she had more than earned.

Hartmut gave slave number one an extra hard thwack as little Marky appeared. Caroline knew more than ever that Hartmut was her soulmate. No one else could have possibly helped her through this experience. He had even managed to find a use for the damned grapes a friend had brought. She'd always hated grapes. As she mustered her most baleful of stares, she wondered how many of them that pallid, scrawny specimen in the gimp mask would get up his anus before finally having to admit that he had failed his mistress.

"Push them in, you pathetic little wretch! Sadie's on her way, and she's a damn sight bigger that those sodding grapes!"

"I should not displease the mistress if I were you," said Hartmut threateningly, without interrupting his thwacking. "And do not even dream of releasing until you are off these premises."

Much whipping later, and Sadie emerged on to the scene. Harriet was relieved to see neither child had any strange marks on them. In fact, they were perfect. That was not something that she could say about the parents. She would pray for them on Sunday.

It would take Harriet a long time to get the rhythm of Caroline's shrieks, Hartmut's strokes and the groans of the grape-stuffing grovelling gimp out of her head.

She never did get the Renoir suite. She went for the Da Vinci, instead.

The twins were now six months old and bonny babies. They were surprisingly good children, in the way that first-borns often seem to be. It seems that parents prepare for the worst, reliably informed in gruesome detail as to how their lives would not be worth living from the birth on. Lulled into a false sense of security by the better-than-expected first experience, parents found second children to be more like the *appellation contrôlée* spawn of the devil. At that stage, the subtle increase in the lack of sleep that a second child delivers will make anyone interrupting rest seem like a torturer from the Spanish Inquisition.

Everyone has their breaking point.

Eleanor had a sip of her tea:

"Did you hear about cousin Piers, darling?"

She couldn't quite get used to glimpsing her daughter's breast as Marky eagerly imbibed. It was so unseemly, over the kitchen table. Eleanor averted her eyes. She had only breastfed in deepest privacy.

"Apparently he has a ladyfriend. Italian," continued Eleanor, gamely.

Caroline knew her mother well enough to detect disapproval from the faintest of intonations.

She looked up at Eleanor:

"Well, good for him. How did they meet? Is it serious?"

"They met in Milan. During Fashion Week. And yes, it does seem to be serious. I don't know what to make of it, but I suppose we must wait and see. He's bringing her to meet us in a few weeks. He wants to see the twins, so I said you would do one of your roasts. Would that work? I do hope that we can fit it all in."

Although Caroline could baste with the best, the prospect of cooking for perfectionist Piers, his undoubtedly exacting Italian girlfriend and her own perennially disappointed mother whilst all the time keeping Marky and Sadie in check, brought a slight frown to her brow. *Thank goodness for Hartmut.*

She looked searchingly at Eleanor:

"Do we know anything about her, mother? Does she have any particular food fetishes that I might need to be aware of?"

"I'm afraid he's being rather secretive about her," said Eleanor. "He won't tell me a thing."

"Well, mother, given your usual reactions, that's hardly surprising."

Eleanor mustered a look of surprised indignation, before allowing herself a pinched smile.

"Darling, your cousin has a *weakness* for the female form. He also has quite the contrariness of his dear late father.

Let's face it: Piers spends all his days surrounded by those Twiggy women, and then chases after the first Lollobrigida to cross his path. Let's just hope his latest inappropriate dalliance is over well before your wedding."

Eleanor sighed. The wedding weighed heavily upon her. Although she adored the twins, she still regretted that their arrival had preceded her daughter's marriage. The marriage itself remained a sore spot. Try as she might, Eleanor could not bring herself to be thrilled by the prospect of Hartmut Glick becoming Herr son-in-law.

Eleanor had long hoped that Caroline would end up marrying Tarquin Henderson-Smythe. That would have been a fine and acceptable development. Tarquin was such a presentable young man. He was so artistic and elegant. Caroline Napier-Jones-Henderson-Smythe would have been welcomed to so many more functions than poor Caroline Glick might be. If only Caroline had understood that marriages were alliances. Had she understood realities, there would have been Christmas banquets at opulent Harrington Court, the Henderson-Smythe's estate in Somerset. Instead, all dreams fading like lace in an attic, Eleanor's best hope appeared to be for sauerkraut in Stalag Luft. *Muss I denn*, indeed.

Social climbing produces many surprises. Rubens Ribeiro still couldn't quite believe he was being paid without having to take any clothes off.

He wasn't entirely escaping his go-go dancing past. Clubs still availed themselves of his services. He occasionally made a cameo appearance on stage at Intoxication. His luscious skin still elicited the same admiring, lascivious looks from the crowd. But Rubens now performed at Intoxication for fun.

Fun was great. But things had also moved on significantly. Rubens' dancing fees were pocket money, buying him brunches in Chelsea rather than the essential range in Waitrose. Not that there was anything wrong with the essential range in Waitrose. That had once been the very height of luxury. What felt intoxicating now was paying the price of a bottle of wine for some tiny little Mimosa – and not caring. Or purchasing a vanilla-scented candle for the price of dinner for two. For a candle! Oh, he did love London.

The escorting had stopped. Rubens had an easy relationship with sex, but he had had quite enough of people who used money to fabricate an easy relationship with him. Life was so much less stressful now that he had extracted himself from those situations. He had started to dread his phone ringing; now he felt relief, a heightened feeling of freedom. Well, a few seconds after the first ring, anyway – when it dawned on him that the caller wouldn't be a potential client, that Rubens wouldn't have to be Paulo Pauzão, and that the call would no longer lead to a hotel room where delight and excitement would have to be feigned at the underwhelming genitals of an unattractive man, occasionally with suboptimal hygiene. Escorting was not glamorous but Rubens had kept his standards as best he could. He had always insisted that his clients take a shower. Compromise was important in life – and we all compromise for pay – but cleanliness was one red line

Rubens used to adhere to with all the zeal of John Major in Brussels, conscious of the bastards waiting for him back home.

That was all behind him now. Rubens had moved on. Onwards, and upwards. Rubens was now deputy manager of Outrageous Fortune, the hottest new cocktail bar in Covent Garden.

Outrageous Fortune was a stroke of luck. When Alex O'Connell and Jamal Qureshi decided to invest some of the O'Connell money in a new venture in London's West End, they installed Rubens as deputy manager. This was a move born of friendship and trust. Rubens' lack of experience had led to another asset being thrown into the mix. Rubens soon found himself being mentored out of his old life by Siegfried Allcock. Whatever else Siegfried was, he was also an experienced bar manager.

Siegfried and Alex were university contemporaries. University acquaintances find themselves in a small world. At Cambridge, Siegfried had also had a brief Brideshead-style fling with Tarquin Henderson-Smythe. This was well before they had both realised that they were probably each more interested in Maurice's gamekeeper. Whereas the straight majority of the British middle classes seemed quite happy, by and large, to pair off with their social equals and ascend the ramp to their very own Ark with a double garage and – occasionally – room for a pony, the gay minority rebelled. Repelling each other like two positively charged silver spoons, the homosexual privileged cherished a bit of rough.

Siegfried had taken a somewhat different route from

Alex after the time for study and dedicated introspection had passed. Not for him the heady combination of high finance and do-gooding that Alex had juggled. Siegfried disappeared for a while, travelling the world working for hotels. In due course, his natural organisational aptitude led him to management roles. It had been hard graft, and offered little by way of certainty. As lines started to crease his once handsome face, Siegfried realised that he had largely expunged his wanderlust. After years of watching exotic sunsets, he began yearning for life back in the UK. He realised enough was enough when, one autumn, the delights of Bangkok took second place to his weekly highlight: watching BBC clips. He pined for British beer.

His company had offered to transfer him back to London. Siegfried was astounded at this magnanimity, given his latest crisis with staffing, and that awkwardness with the water feature. Despite the trials and tribulations of Siegfried's turn at the helm, management brought him back for exploratory planning. It was on this visit home, one evening, once Alex and Jamal had outlined their plans to cream some pink pounds off the giant prawn cocktail of the gay demographic, that a plot was hatched. Siegfried had had enough of kowtowing to the global jet set. He would *never* forget that evening selling the benefits of his establishment to three Kardashians. Enough really was enough.

However, Siegfried appreciated that the move would not all be a walk in the park. He would now have to kowtow to an even tougher audience: gay London's *A List*.

This, explained Alex, was where Rubens would come in.

The combination of Siegfried's business discipline with Rubens' easy charm and impeccable contacts would be a knockout. Siegfried was tired of the buttoned-up life and wanted to let loose a little, and Rubens wanted to prove there was as much between his ears as between his legs. They hit it off. Alex and Jamal considered that they had found a perfect team. Outrageous Fortune was born.

"How did that new barman work out last night, Ziggy?"

Siegfried winced. He was a proper Wagnerian Siegfried. Yet, after stumbling over the pronunciation once too often, Rubens had renamed him. Although Siegfried sounded a very *interesting* name in a one-to-one conversation, Rubens knew it wouldn't work in a trendy West End bar. It needed to be shorter. Snappier. It had to be either Ziggy or Freda – and, Rubens mused, Siegfried wasn't quite ready for his drag alter ego. Ziggy worked. Rubens bore in mind that the bar served cosmopolitans in Covent Garden, not snakebite in Snaresbrook.

"Dillon is a smart one. The customers love him. What can I say? Even I was mesmerised by that butt of his." Siegfried paused as he visualised Dillon's perfectly formed buns. Realising that Rubens was staring at him and smirking, Siegfried resumed, haughtily:

"He'll need watching though. I don't want him enjoying himself too much."

"What do you mean?"

"He has that look about him. Flirts with man, woman, or furniture. That can be a good thing in this business, but there could be more to it. He has a twinkle in his eye that screams *I'm a bad boy who gets away with murder*."

"That's a very expressive twinkle."

"Huh. I've seen that twinkle all over the world. I'm sure he will be doing our brand no harm at all. He'll satisfy the beautiful people from the clubs. But I just hope he remembers he has a job before he takes his fourth line, bump or snort of whatever at Farfaraway, hmm... probably round about now."

Siegfried harrumphed. His wise man of the world act was sometimes a little too much for Rubens' liking at times, but Rubens was easy going. He could see that it meant a lot to Siegfried to be able to pontificate at times, like a committee chairman who is so far beyond his best that he's actually on his next committee.

Rubens looked at his watch. Twelve o'clock. Lunch time on a Sunday. Instead of overseeing a busy brunch at Outrageous Fortune, Rubens too would normally have been down at Farfaraway, London's newest Sunday morning after-hours club, dancing with the ultra-cute Dillon. Dillon would be leading the way, with that amazing *bunda* that any Brazilian would have been proud of. For a moment, Rubens wished he *were* there with him. A club followed by drug-fuelled sex on a Sunday afternoon was just the *best*. In another time, Dillon's buns would have been the cherry on his cocktail.

Ah, well. Rubens grinned to himself with a little regret, reminding himself, too, of Mondays, Tuesdays and Wednesdays past. They were invariably less fun, even if his *espiritu brasileiro* had manfully tackled the comedowns from hell.

He surveyed his busy room. The decision to be more serious had not been taken lightly. Alex had placed faith in him. That meant a lot. Rubens knew that it also made sense. Although Rubens could still pass for twenty-something, he knew that he couldn't live for the moment forever. It was time to grow up, and pass the baton on to the younger, freshly foolish generation.

He glanced over at the tall, distinguished-looking man he worked with. One could ignore Siegfried's incipient baldness and the slight podgy swelling round his waist. Rubens felt inspired and glad to be working for someone like his new manager. Until recently, Rubens had been Dillon's behavioural twin. Now he, Rubens, had to learn to manage Dillon and his kind. Rubens couldn't just rely on his smile and his looks. He was now relying on his brain.

It wouldn't be easy, but Rubens was smart. Having a boss with fifteen years' experience in a proper job, in a real business, was exactly the support that he needed. Rubens sighed. He would do everything to gain the trust and respect of this new man in his life. Rubens was looking forward to being Siegfried Allcock's right hand.

"Mother, I'm taking the twins up to bed. Coming?"

Pleased to be disturbed from the contemplation of her family's disappointing liaisons, Eleanor rose from the low couch. She broke into a proud smile as her daughter passed a sleeping Sadie into her arms.

From the outset, Eleanor had worried – 'twas the least of her worries, but it niggled – that Hartmut's elegant new house in Hampstead would in no way be suitable for young children. True, it was extremely spacious, but there were so many pristine sharp edges on the glass and marble furniture. Eleanor often pursed her lips at the very thought of Hartmut's décor. *Mausoleum chic*, she thought primly. Young children were definitely not Fabergé egg-friendly.

She was pleased to observe that, although the twins were only six months old, Hartmut and Caroline had clearly decided to take no chances. As Eleanor passed the sitting room on the way to the staircase she noticed that sturdy railings had been installed. Eleanor pretended not to see the two pairs of handcuffs dangling on the railings near the leather chaise longue. As she reached the top of the stairs she found the landing also to be generously protected from any marauding tots. She was quite taken with the attention to detail.

However, not even Eleanor's legendary capacity to smile in the face of the distasteful, and rise serenely above the embarrassing, was able to blot out what she saw next.

"Oh, *I say*, Caroline."

Last time Eleanor had been in the twins' room, it had been remarkable only for the fact that it seemed like a normal children's bedroom. The wallpaper still had the coloured bunny rabbits on it, and the carpet was still the luxurious shag she remembered.

But the little wooden cots had gone. In their place were two large double-sided five-point black leather slings, hanging from thick metal chains attached to large hooks in the ceiling. One sling had a pink and the other a blue cradle, carefully strapped in. Eleanor had to admit they looked extremely well made.

What now? thought Caroline. *Oh – the slings.*

She smiled reassuringly at her dumbstruck parent.

"Mother, these have been the best investment we have made. Marky and Sadie fall asleep so easily. I think it is the rocking motion. They are far better than a conventional cradle. They're all the rage in Berlin, Hartmut tells me. And they are sturdy enough for us to unstrap the cradles and actually get in and lie with the babies for a while. You should try it. In fact, why don't you? Relax and live dangerously for once, Mother."

Eleanor was not at all sure that she appreciated the implication. There was a mischievous glint in her daughter's eyes. Why was it that so many of Caroline's comments came across as gentle taunts? Just because Eleanor maintained certain standards, her daughter seemed to think that her mother had forever inhabited a bubble of restrained decorum, and would remain there until gentility gave way to senility. Well, this erstwhile child of the sixties would show her daughter that she could still do the unexpected. Those contraptions looked jolly comfortable.

"Maybe I will, dear. Put Marky down, and help me unstrap Sadie's cot. I'll get in and then you can pass me Sadie. I'll imagine I'm cruising sedately down the Rhine. Rhine, seamen and song, eh."

Caroline was taken aback by her mother's sudden acquiescence to the ridiculous. This would look funny, though. Caroline wondered whether she could discreetly take a photo of Eleanor in a bondage sling on her phone. It would cheer up the family portraits. There was no time for that. Stepping up to the fashionable cradles, she expertly

45

released the cot's catch. Her mother seemed a lot more agile than Caroline expected. She hopped up into the sling without even taking her Louboutins off. It was a seamless role reversal, completed by Eleanor readily relaxing in the contraption, at ease, while Caroline remained awkwardly at the side, disconcerted at the thought of Sadie watching her grandmother lying in a sling, with those red-soled stilettos screaming for attention.

Eleanor beamed:

"Darling, this is indeed marvellous. Technology never ceases to amaze one. I always found hammocks to be such uncomfortable and inconvenient devices. If only we had had one of these on the yacht."

The front door banged shut. This was swiftly followed by the sound of Hartmut Glick talking, and another man answering. This sociable interaction floated up the stairs, an advance warning of more social interaction in the offing. Although Eleanor had successfully overcome her reservations about the swinging furniture, she most certainly did not want Hartmut to see her in such a position. *Never let a German catch you unawares*, she thought.

"Darling, quick now – please help me out."

Unfortunately for Eleanor, the sling had been far easier to mount than to get out of. Worse, in her sudden, frantic attempts to reach the floor, an awful spasm gripped her left thigh.

"Ow," screamed Eleanor in a most unladylike way.

Upon hearing an unfamiliar female shriek coming from the first floor, Hartmut went into overdrive. He bounded upstairs two at a time, followed by his companion.

He felt rather pleasurably arrested by the scene that greeted him.

Ben Barlettano, trailing in his wake, was even more taken aback. An older lady wearing a red chiffon dress, pearls and bright red high heel shoes appeared to be writhing in a sling, while Caroline Napier Jones held a baby in one hand – and appeared to be massaging the older women's left leg with the other. How very odd. What new arena of indulgence might this be categorised as? Nursery school of hard knocks? Kindergarten torture garden?

"Eleanor, my dear," said Hartmut, "I'm getting conflicting information here. You appear to be stuck in…"

"… Sadie's cradle swing." Caroline interjected firmly.

"I've got cramp, Hartmut! Get me out of this flaming hammock!" screeched Eleanor.

"Of course. Try to gently stretch the leg. Ben, please come and gently hoist my future mother-in-law out of this swing with me."

"It's a whole new meaning to swinging," offered Ben cheerfully.

Not all of Ben's attempts at pleasantries found their audience.

Eleanor glared at Caroline, whilst attempting to relieve her leg. Cramp was deeply unpleasant – and this was so undignified.

Ben smiled to himself. Only Hartmut would find himself in such a position. And only Hartmut would handle it so briskly. Together they hoisted Eleanor out. She came out at some speed, like a very red salmon leaping upwards.

"Walk on, Eleanor, and keep on stretching the muscle."

Hartmut's practical advice did the trick. With the searing pain lessening, Eleanor's sense of propriety quickly reasserted itself.

"Thank you, young man, for your assistance. The thigh *was* the limit. I am Eleanor Napier Jones. Charmed to meet you."

As he introduced himself, Ben too felt charmed to meet the elegant lady with the surprisingly firm thighs and the delicious shoes. There was something in her demeanour that commanded respect, and that was at interesting odds with her screaming and swinging in a leather sling hanging from his boss's ceiling. Then he had the fantasy-crushing realisation that along with Eleanor would come Hartmut Glick – as a son-in-law.

Although stranger things must have happened at sea, it was probably much safer to buy Kelly a pair of Louboutins for her birthday.

3

Old Masters and servants

Harry Gumpert arrived at work wearing sunglasses.

True, there was a pale shaft of English sunlight lightly dappling London's pavements, but it wasn't exactly an Arizona glare. Nonetheless, Harry looked good in sunglasses. They carried off the bags under his eyes.

He walked into work with the confident spring of someone who could leave anytime he wanted to. A couple of people smiled at him. Harry loved tough economic times. Everyone was suddenly a whole lot nicer to anyone within even spitting distance of power. It felt good to be on top. Harry clocked himself in the lift mirror and felt – how should it be put – sexy. *Yeah, sexy*, he thought, as he contemplated his well-dressed figure, and his thick if greying hair.

He was rich too, so much richer than all those people from his Cambridge days who'd gone for "interesting" careers. Architects? Pah. They did not know what *drawings* were. Actors? All theatre administrators now – every one of the poor, deluded crew – apart from the speech therapist. Businessmen, teachers, politicians and accountants – well, some accountants were on a par, but hell. You'd have to be able to live with the job description.

No, Harry, decided. There was no doubt possible. He was great – and clever, too. And handsome. A great, handsome, wealthy, sexy lawyer. How was it even possible that he'd got to his office floor without some random woman kneeling before him to pay homage to his manhood?

It was time, Harry decided. Spring was beckoning and he needed someone to have lazy sex with. Large organisations were a beehive of possibilities, teeming with people trying to have a life that bore some faint resemblance to their pathetic little dreams of accomplishment. Someone, somewhere in this building, was feeling just vulnerable enough, just lonely enough, just tense and insecure enough, just stupid enough to believe that being on the end of Harry's cock would assist in stitching life's rich tapestry. There was always someone who believed in destiny around.

He had in fact identified his prey some meetings before. She was called Lucy. A luscious blonde bombshell of a young trainee solicitor, lips like fresh baked madeleines, a bottom like firm fruity jelly, a complexion like smooth custard. This was no trifling matter. He knew she liked him, because he was one of the least ugly men in the office, and she seemed to be one of those women that needed affirmation with regard to her own attractiveness. Thank goodness, women never learned. Harry dangled his power, partnership, and preposterous paternal interest before Lucy. He had wormed his way into her world, feigning interest, developing an acquaintance, enquiring as to her views on business development and client care. It was like shooting fish in a barrel.

She was conveniently located in an office opposite a coffee point. He paused by her door. She was alone at her desk, frowning slightly as she typed an email.

"Lucy, good morning."

"Oh, hello, Mr Gumpert. How nice to see you."

There it was. Surely anyone could see that her response was a come on, thought Harry. How *obvious* young women had become.

He chuckled in an avuncular way:

"Lucy, I'm sure I've asked you to call me Harry."

"Sorry, yes of course. I think I am the very spirit of contrariness. Bartlett – Mr DeVere – always wants me to call him Mr DeVere, so I call him Bartlett almost invariably. You have so kindly allowed me some familiarity – and yet I can't seem to grasp it."

There! A perfect opening. Harry chuckled to himself.

"Well, maybe we need to work on it. I was just thinking about some of the things you mentioned about the marketing plans for the group. It's always good to get the perspective of the younger lawyers. I'm quite tied up today – but might you be available for a quick drink after work?"

Lucy blushed very slightly:

"Yes, yes that would be lovely. A nice glass of wine goes a long way to breaking up the silly little stresses we have! And I do have some thoughts on the seminar receptions."

"Or we can just get drunk and forget about the world," said Harry, waving a hand loftily.

She laughed a bit too loudly.

He twinkled at her and went off to pretend to work. Harry's day comprised a number of meetings with clients in which his main contribution was to talk with absolute certainty, look manly and offer gravitas. No one ever seemed to grasp that the only people in the room who knew any law were his sidekicks – the shy spotty young lawyer with glasses, who listened carefully and was already thinking a few steps ahead, and the young Asian woman, so short that she almost disappeared under the table, but who would later give the spotty lawyer three ideas that would completely transform his approach to solving the issues. Harry was the ultimate gilding on the lily. But there you have it. If you're clever enough to be able to charge people for nothing, you certainly deserve to sit at the very top of the Christmas tree.

The irony was that the clients simply loved Harry. Had they been left in the room with the true contributors alone, they would have felt that they were being short changed. They might have complained that, without Harry, they weren't getting enough "grey hair". Harry chuckled as he remembered that particular occasion. Clients could be fools! They sometimes took advice from people who had already given them wrong answers *even though they knew this to be the case!* Oh, a lawyer's lot could be a happy one.

The day was broken up by a partner lunch, festooned with fake joviality and closeness. Besuited persons gathered like hungry crows around some token salads, nursery main courses and cheese. Most lunchers dripped snippets of their own superiority into the conversations, from the sons at Eton to the tickets secured for Glyndebourne.

Conversation felt like a helpless inevitability; with the best will in the world, interlocutors were desperately trying to persuade themselves and each other that they were doing something worthwhile, whilst remaining to a man (and to a rare woman) sadly uninspiring traffickers of tedium. Insecurity was etched large, and played out in every story of another slightly adventurous business trip that the teller treasured the opportunity to trot out – again.

Harry was indeed one of the more enviable of the crowd, and not only because his bottom actually fitted into an ordinary chair. He knew the slippery strains of power in the room – who people feared, who people hated, who people liked. He had cultivated his network of allies over the years, and was popular enough. Too many people, within and without the firm, thought Harry was an important service provider. Harry was safe, but always on the lookout.

"This LGBT group, then. What do you make of it, Harry?" Tom Bindman was a large partner with a country estate. It was very nice to go there and drink from Tom's cellar, so partners largely passed over the time when his lack of attention to detail had almost cost the firm several million pounds as a result of negligent advice in a property transaction. Thankfully the client had died very suddenly of a heart attack, and neither his board nor the widow had really understood enough to take matters forward. Well, one could laugh about it now – particularly when Tom was handing out the Chambolle Musigny.

Harry smiled easily at Tom:

"It does no harm, Tom. It's good to see young people feeling free."

Tom grimaced:

"Yes, but do we need to be so obvious about it? I mean, why LGBT? Can we drop the BTs? I think I can get my head around dykes and homos – but why encourage the rest?"

Harry pursed his lips:

"I know, Tom. I know. But we're sort of all in it together now. Every other firm has an LGBT group. If we had an LG group, I think we might look different. And we really, really do not want to be different."

Tom sniffed:

"Well I don't mind so long as no one shoves it down my throat. Honestly. You'd think that we spent all our time in the office thinking about sex."

Harry inclined his head non-committedly. He thought of Lucy's breasts, and of her smooth creamy thighs. Would it take one drink, or would it be a longer pursuit? He hoped it would be sudden. He wondered distractedly whether the LGBT group members were having more sex than he was. The thought slightly annoyed him. But he also chuckled inwardly at the thought that the LGBT group thought it could change anything. *We're not holding you back because you're gay – despite occasionally wondering uneasily about what you get up to at weekends. We're holding you back because you're easily replaceable assets and are making us more money if we don't promote you!*

It all seemed so distinguished and glamorous on the surface, yet Tarquin Henderson-Smythe was under no illusions. Despite the erudite conversations in the opulent gallery in Mayfair, he was really just a salesman in a Savile Row suit, trying to make a decent margin in order to keep the business afloat.

Of course he loved his work. Renaissance art was his passion, and he was blessed to be surrounded by what he loved. But it seemed no job was without its hair shirt. Some of the collectors Tarquin dealt with had to be seen and heard to be believed. They disturbed his refined world, rather as if Jedward were performing at Last Night of the Proms.

Wesley Nest typified the cash-rich culture-poor type of client that Tarquin could only stand by setting himself a target of how much he would overcharge for the work of art they wanted to buy. As he never tired of informing Tarquin, Wesley had made a fortune selling handmade jewellery to the lower middle classes of the Home Counties. Sadly, he wore plenty of his own jewellery, and sadder still Tarquin had to admit that some of it was really rather good. Some only, mind. This meant that there was still an awful lot to lampoon.

But it wasn't Wesley's crassness that rubbed Tarquin up the wrong way. What got Tarquin's goat was that Wesley compensated for his unctuous manner with his own clients by expecting fawning servility from those who served him in turn, all delivered with a dose of high camp familiarity.

Worst of all, Wesley had somehow found out that Tarquin too had Dorothy on speed dial.

"Now, dear, seeing as I don't want you to have to run out to the shops, how about we discuss the Scorreggio further at my new favourite bar? You know I only drink Veuve and unfortunately you don't run to that here."

Tarquin winced. If he had told Wesley once that the painter's name was Correggio, he had told him a dozen times. He winced again as he realised that he would have to spend time in public with Wesley if he wanted to make the sale. He knew the drill. Wesley would need to parade the fact that he was able to spend a small fortune on a painting, all the while quaffing champagne surrounded by gold-digging courtiers. *Champagne! Champagne for everyone!*

You think you have life organised, sometimes. You have your friends, your family, your habits and your surprises. You expect the unexpected but it lies neatly within manageable parameters. Someone remembers your birthday. The weather turns out nice again. And everything continues as it should.

The French would call it a *coup de foudre*. When Kelly stepped into the Parisian café, she saw Morten, and then saw nothing else.

Morten was tall, and blond, with neat hair, good eyelashes and deep blue eyes to throw yourself off a pier for. He looked like a beach landscape in perfect, blissful conditions – the deep cream gold of the sand, the brilliant blue of the sea, and not a cloud in the sky. His skin was the colour of pale honey.

Morten looked well, energetic, and sporty, but relaxed at the small round table, like a leopard in repose. He was reading a book with a concentrated look. His fitted dark shirt hinted at an athletic torso. His jeans were dark too, at odds with the bright Parisian weather. As her eyes coursed over him, Kelly found herself approving his boots, as if it were important that not one thing about him should fail to meet her standards, galloping away with *yes, yes, yes* as they already were.

She remembered later feeling overcome in an unaccustomed manner. It was a fleeting feeling and she vanquished it using logic. She reminded herself that instant attraction *is* usually a fleeting thing. When the object of desire opens their mouth, attraction often vanishes, like snow in late spring.

But what a fine sight Morten was. A fine, fine sight. Kelly felt a flash of relief that she was wearing presentable clothes. Her fresh well-cut shirt, an interesting and flattering skirt and heels were serving their purpose. Thank goodness for the heels. One can't walk in them, but they do enhance a first impression.

Kelly scanned the café for Morten's companions. She imagined a foxy redhead in a black polo neck, or a dark serious girl whom Kelly might feel more attractive than, through sheer weight of vitality. Kelly's guess was that she might only score an appreciative look from Morten, but she was a competitive sort, and hoped for more.

Nothing. There was nobody. He was on his own.

His phone rang and he answered it. Oh dear. He had a lovely voice. Kelly could not quite make out what he was saying. She had only come into the café to buy a Rocher Suchard Noir – a rich dark chocolate praline lump that said it was from Paris and that it did not care about crapulous preconceptions about what might be good for you. She changed her course, her mind and her plans, and settled at a table near Morten.

The waiter came over.

"Un grand crème, s'il vous plait."

"Bien sûr, Mademoiselle."

She sensed Morten looking up and turned with a smile.

"Excuse me," she said. "May I borrow your phone? It's for a local call."

He looked at her:

"Of course. Why not."

She dialled, and listened. From the depths of her handbag came a ring tone.

"Oh good."

Kelly smiled apologetically as she returned the handset:

"It's buried in there. I had a horrible feeling I'd left it behind. Thank you."

He smiled with a look that made Kelly glow.

"No problem," said Morten, and Kelly knew he meant it. There, she thought. He has my number now. If he hasn't got the brains to use it, I'm not interested. Although I am. I really am. I can't help this.

As she left the café, she turned back. Yes, he was looking over. She waved confidently, with a smile. He raised a hand.

He called two days later.

"Wesley, darling. Oh, we've missed you. Dillon, Wesley's here, please get his table ready."

Rubens dusted off his best iron-on smile, and slightly flexed his biceps as Wesley's hands held his bare arms midair kiss. Wesley leered as he hung on to Rubens' arms for longer than he should, like a fat baby greedily grabbing at a lollipop:

"Have you lost weight, dear? You really should get down the gym, dear."

Wesley's beaming grin signposted the fact that he thought he was being really funny. But then it was easy to make that mistake when a pro like Rubens Ribeiro always laughed just enough, and then seamlessly led into a flattering butter-wouldn't-melt observation about Wesley's latest timepiece.

"Gostoso – the watch. Wow."

"Do you like it, dear? I picked it up on a trip to Zurich, but I added the diamonds to the face myself. You have to know what you are doing of course, and be able to afford *both* the watch *and* the diamonds! But enough about me. Let me introduce you to Tarquin, one of my art dealers."

Where did one start cringing? Where did one stop? There was so much to cringe at. Tarquin decided to float above it all. He shook Rubens' hand with a surprisingly relaxed smile. Rubens immediately intrigued Tarquin Henderson-Smythe – not least by the way he had dealt with Wesley. He had not let him get remotely under his skin – all whilst capably commencing a drinks-in-pounds-out pumping exercise for the maximum return on the bar visit. It seemed so effortless. Maybe Tarquin could compare notes, and get lessons. Rubens seemed to deal with Wesley masterfully.

Wesley wittered on as they headed for a booth:

"Rubens, Tarquin's advising me on some ridiculously

overpriced work from the sixteenth century that will look lovely above the Chesterfield in my drawing room. The house is neo-Tudor so it will fit in perfectly. I'm feathering my nest, dear."

Putting all his concentration into smiling as if he actually were entertained, Tarquin thought how he would like to tar this particular Nest before it was feathered. How did Rubens keep his equanimity, faced with such drivel?

Tarquin determined he would get to know the Brazilian better.

By mid-evening, Tarquin had been introduced as Wesley's art dealer to Dillon, Federico, Vito, Leandro, Robson, Lincoln and half a dozen other young men with dazzling white teeth, perfect olive skin and a taste for Wesley's champagne. Tarquin was starting to wonder if there was a town called Stepford just outside São Paulo. However, at least Outrageous Fortune attracted a better class of boy wonder, when compared to some other venues where Tarquin had had to compel himself to enjoy an evening with Wesley. Glancing over at Rubens as he glided around the room dispensing the favour of his attention to the eager clientele, Tarquin noticed that the champagne-quaffers all seemed to know Rubens. Rather well, by the body language.

As Wesley was now busy telling his latest courtier, Denilson, about the custom interior of his Bentley, Tarquin decided to wander over and ask Rubens about his technique.

Rubens was taking a short pause at the bar. He looked up with the tiniest flash of irritation – but softened when he saw it was Tarquin.

Tarquin was taking his courage into both hands. He was better accustomed to old and unattractive gay men. It was odd to be talking to an objectively beautiful and independent party. Tarquin had consumed three glasses of champagne. It took that much for him to approach strangers. He wasn't drunk, but the world around him was now viewable through a Vaseline-coated lens. He fixed upon Rubens with some earnestness, and not a little desperation:

"I like your style," he said conversationally. "I think your friends must have drunk ten of Wesley's bottles of Veuve between them. Wesley likes boasting to the boys, they like free champagne and you do great business. Everyone's happy."

Tarquin hadn't intended to be quite so direct. It did not bother Rubens, who smiled genially at the elegant Englishman.

"You're very upfront for a dealer, gostoso. But I don't know what you are talking about. Brazilians and Italians are very friendly people. Wesley is a lovely, funny guy. Well, you must know that, as you have spent the last hour and a half drinking with him. Maybe you managed a bottle of Veuve yourself."

Rubens' warm smile and innocent brown eyes belied the fact that he had just accused Tarquin of being a gold-digger too. Instead of telling him to back off – as was his first inclination – Tarquin decided that he should instead relax a little. Rubens had worked out how to play the situation, so why shouldn't he, Tarquin, find a way, like Rubens had, to *rationalise* it all? There was obviously a way to spend the time necessary for business with Wesley, without hating every single second spent in his company. After all, Tarquin reasoned, he had enjoyed the champagne. It was perfectly chilled, and served professionally. This was one of London's coolest new cocktail bars, and Tarquin had met a dozen of the finest specimens of Latin manhood. He knew that in ordinary circumstances he would not have the courage to speak to such creatures. He would probably have spent time admiring them from a distance, through the medium of some art film or photography exhibition instead.

"Gostoso? What exactly does that mean?" Tarquin decided he too would glide above comments that he didn't want to acknowledge.

Rubens laughed:

"Well it basically means sexy. I'm surprised you never heard it. You're not really on the scene, are you?"

Was the Cucinelli pullover such a giveaway? Tarquin had realised that no one else in the bar was dressed as he was, not even Wesley in his Champagne Charlie guise. He also twigged that Rubens had implied that he was sexy. Tarquin was certainly distinguished-looking, although he flinched at the term, feeling it was but a short step to *debonair*, and then it would be downhill all the way to the dreaded *spry*. This man who looked as though everything you could ever want to know about him lay right there in the confines of his perfect surface, this glorious Brazilian, played Wesley more easily than Tarquin had ever been able to. Rubens ran his little symbiotic ecosystem smoothly, dealing flattery for large bar bills, peppered with witty rejoinders, and he had now just called Tarquin sexy. Tarquin didn't care if it was just Rubens being smooth. He was going to take a risk for once.

"I may be upfront for a dealer, Rubens. That's why I am inviting you to the gallery. I'd like to take you on a personalised tour of my artworks. We have considerable delights on offer, and we can discuss technique some more. Here's my card. I hope you use it."

With that, Tarquin gave Rubens what he hoped was his most enigmatic, yet inviting look, turned on his heel, and returned to sit next to Wesley.

Wesley was still regaling Denilson with details of how much various items in his house had cost:

"… and then we decided to make thirteen of them, which set me back fifty odd thousand pounds. So *extravagant*, but you know, so indispensable. The effect is as good as I hoped. Tarquin, there you are. Well dear, thank goodness you finally summoned up the courage to go and talk to him. I can't take any more champagne and I've *certainly* had my fill of Rubens' sidekicks, lovely as they may be. And don't worry – he'll call you. Now if you could please get me the bill, I'll call Roger. Can we drop you at home?"

Somewhat bemused, Tarquin went to the bar and asked for Wesley's tab.

So the sly old fox was fully aware of what was going on. He had actually been setting him up. Maybe there was slightly more to Wesley than first met the eye. Of course he was still a crass bore, but it seemed he was a rather observant crass bore. What a cunning stunt. Tarquin would have to be careful with the price on the Correggio.

She was late. What a tardigrade that woman was. How dare she believe that she could survive insulting him like this. Nicholas Casterway took a dim view of lateness. He was a busy man and did not have time to waste waiting for any woman, however compliant. A slack attitude to punctuality was something that made his nostrils flare.

The phone rang. He answered.

"There's a Miss Jonquil Perrin from Offices of Distinction to see you, Mr Casterway."

"She's late. Send her up."

The woman came in purposefully. She looked business-like. Her manner, however, indicated that she was well aware that her appearance formed part of her sales proposition. The clothes were pristine. The cut of her dress, and the precise quantity of cleavage and leg revealed, were essential details of the tender, second only to her research on the potential customer and knowledge of what she was offering. Nicholas deemed her judgement on his tastes to have been exemplary, a fact which slightly distracted him from his annoyance.

"Miss – er – Perrin, I had thirty minutes of which twenty-seven remain, so I suggest we make a start." He smiled curtly.

They faced each other over a coffee table that the eager sales executive was using to display the brochures. As she indicated the first range of mahogany inlay desks, she deliberately leaned over as much as possible, in the hope of erasing her time-keeping mistake with a bird's eye view of her rather large breasts, straining at the leash of her perfectly fitting top.

As the woman had been late, and the first range of furniture she was showing him reeked of nouveau, Nicholas ignored the proffered brochure and stared down her cleavage instead, all the while lazily sipping a glass of still water.

The shamelessness of his action told the young lady that this sale was not going to happen unless she changed tack. Obviously, the mahogany was not to his taste. She needed her biggest guns. Leaning back slightly she reached for the most expensive range she offered.

"Mr Casterway, maybe you might feel this is more suitable to the image Stiller, Boils, Kumpelhauk wishes to... oh, goodness!"

In her eagerness to redeem the situation she had waved the new brochure at Nicholas rather too enthusiastically, almost hitting him on the nose, but actually catching his glass of water. Nicholas started, and managed to throw its contents all over her bust. It seemed inadvertent, but it was – of course – anything but. The fabric of the top immediately clung sheerly to the skin, revealing just what an amazing pair of large, firm tits the woman had. *Don't call me sheerly*. After staring, transfixed, for a moment, Nicholas slowly reached out and took a breast in each hand.

It was the usual place. It was the usual time. It was the usual outcome.

Nicholas Casterway had been having "business meetings" in the same hotel in Victoria for a number of years. Some of the meetings had even, from time to time, concerned business. Most, however, were arranged purely for pleasure. Although "Jonquil Perrin" was a newcomer to the Handford House Hotel, the magnificent breasts currently being seized and squeezed in Nicholas' greedy hands as he took her, doggy style, were quite the hotel regulars.

The breasts belonged to Amber Bluett. Her performance during her interview for the Human Resources role at Stiller, Boils, Kumpelhauk had opened up more opportunities than LinkedIn. *Opportunititties*, as Amber liked to joke. Nicholas had known immediately that she would be a natural at the role playing he needed to get his kicks. She acquiesced to his mises-en-scène, and so it had proved a fruitful pairing.

To date, she had been a client, a supplier, a takeover target, a caterer, and even on one occasion a minor Royal who wished to remain discreet. All to no avail, as she would inevitably end up with a glass of something or other thrown all over her breasts, Nicholas jumping upon her, followed by fifteen minutes of hard shagging in the bedroom. There then remained ten minutes for her to shower, apply make-up, dress and vacate the room, until the next time.

Nicholas found his experience of sex to be much the same as that of eating a curry. As long as he was still hungry, he could not stop grabbing the delights around him and stuffing them into his mouth. However, as soon as he was sated, he wanted what was left removed immediately. Ejaculation meant expulsion. It seemed natural to him.

Nicholas would not have cared much for any analysis of his preferences. He wanted his Handford hook-ups, and could not contemplate eliminating them in favour of love-making in the family home with his hard-skinned wife, Britta. Although a most suitable partner to have at his side for formal dinners where she could be relied upon to belittle other guests with the barely concealed glee of a bloodthirsty dictator beheading dissidents, she had long ago ceased to be the object of his desires. Besides, the ghastly woman had been denying him sex almost since their wedding night. She was always tired.

The breasts that had been so alluring just minutes earlier, although now freshly washed and even perfumed, now had all the appeal of week-old mackerel Madras. Struggling not to wrinkle his nose, Nicholas wondered if that common little tart was really going to go out into the street displaying them as she was, like a proud patissière with her fresh cream puffs.

More importantly, why exactly was she still there?

The dark-rimmed glasses, pouting cherry lips and platinum blond bob that made up "Jonquil Perrin" finally seemed ready to vacate Nicholas' personal space. He was already anticipating closing the door behind her, opening the window, and breathing again. But then a most unexpected thing happened. The woman had the temerity to talk.

"What do you know about Ben Barlettano?"

Being a lawyer of many years' experience, Nicholas was used to being asked difficult questions to which he did not wish to give a truthful answer. Britta said his ability to deliver preposterous falsehoods whilst under scrutiny was one of the traits she most admired about him. This simple enquiry, however, caught him off-guard. Nicholas Casterway was of flexible sexuality, and, provided there was a degree of control or humiliation associated with the act, he could and did occasionally eke out satisfaction with members of either sex. A couple of years earlier, a male sex worker, highly recommended by a confidante of his, had brought along a third man and they had performed a whole charade for Nicholas' gratification. Although the third man had performed his duties in the Handford House Hotel in a more than adequate way, it had been rather less satisfactory when he had reappeared to challenge Nicholas at a Stiller, Boils, Kumpelhauk meeting.

That man was Ben Barlettano. A dirty little slut – well, a lawyer – but also a libertine, a sexual deviant, a free-loading monster who had no place in a civilised organisation.

Remembering the scene still provoked an icy rage in Nicholas. Nicholas could harbour a grudge for a lifetime, masking his desire to destroy with courteous cold handshakes and meaningless smiles. Ben Barlettano would pay for daring to cross him, and he would not see it coming, for in Nicholas' opaque and chilly world, revenge was a dish best served frozen.

Having researched Nicholas Casterway, Amber was well aware of the meeting room incident where Ben had made a speech which had foiled Nicholas' plan to remove Hartmut Glick from the firm. She sensed that there was slightly more to the story. She saw in Nicholas a potential ally for her own desire for revenge.

Nicholas eyed her with equanimity:

"He was an associate at SBK, until Hartmut Glick took him over to Beaux Aspen. But I imagine you knew that."

Amber realised that she would have to work much

harder to get any information out of this particular stone. Having just seen the effect on Nicholas of the mere mention of Ben's name, she decided her cards must now take her place and be laid on the table.

"I believe Ben Barlettano is a fundamentally dishonest person, who peddles lies as a stock in trade."

She hesitated a moment, weighing her words:

"He cynically portrays an image of a clean-cut, regular guy with a supposedly glamorous, successful girlfriend." Amber suppressed a shudder as she thought of how she hated Kelly even more than Ben. "However," she continued, "in actual fact he inhabits a very different world outside of the office. Judging by the company he keeps, and the rumours I have heard, it seems that straying from the straight and narrow is a major part of his life. He is clever, I grant you, but also intrinsically duplicitous."

Amber crossed her arms. If Nicholas did not realise the potential in combining forces, he had the strategic know-how of a mouse planning to steal bait from a mouse-trap with no extra precautions.

From Amber's description of Ben, Nicholas could not help but think that the younger lawyer had the fundamental attributes necessary for a long and successful career in law and, most irritatingly, he even reminded him of himself. Where was she going with this?

"Having my own history with Ben Barlettano, I have an interest in the matter, and for the good of everyone I think the cheat should be unmasked. I want him to feel some of the pain that he caused me."

Nicholas' interest was suddenly piqued. This could lead

to new duties for his sexual partner. Excellent! The woman was to be encouraged in her revenge fantasies.

He pursed his thin lips:

"The boy is rash, and the rumours swirl. He is a loose cannon. It is distressing to hear that he is up to his old tricks. Everyone must have hoped that he was an altogether more reliable sort now. Dear me. What would the clients think?"

"Quite. I do not believe that the majority of B.A.D. employees know about Ben's secret seedy gay lifestyle, and I am sure that some may be upset to find out. Of course, it's not just the fact of being gay – although that is *revolting* – it's the fact that he pretends to be so perfect and regular. I have decided that if Ben insists on hiding his extreme deviancy, then I shall have to be the one that shines a torch into the sordid barrel of his life. It is my duty to winkle him out. A man like him should not continue to just sail forward in life as if everything were *okay*."

Listening to Amber, Nicholas felt a shiver run down his spine. This rarely happened after sex for him. After sex, the world usually returned to a grey shade, its tedium only relieved by the constant ratty feeling of still being ahead by a nose in some imaginary race. Although the woman's plan hardly contained any substance likely to truly sink the American, if a campaign against him were carefully executed, it could at least take off some of the sheen from him. With a bit of luck and a fair wind, it could be the foundation for a more sustained long term character assassination, especially if combined with some sleuthing by Nicholas' reliable private investigator, Felix Skink.

Nicholas looked at Amber without feeling any trace of the post-coital disgust which normally oozed into his soul. This instrument of Beaux, Aspen, Dickerhint could indeed become more than a mere sexual fancy. She might be a catalyst for his revenge, possibly achieving the definitive ruin of Ben Barlettano.

That would be something to give the days a little more purpose.

4

Delayed gratification and other preposterous ideas

Monique sat in her meeting. It was another waste of time. It was so pointless that she ate a jammy dodger in crunchy protest. She remembered Kelly telling a story once about jammy dodgers. In an interview with two lawyers, one fat American and one slim Englishman, Kelly told how she had sought to break the ice by commenting on the welcome presence of a jammy dodger on the biscuit plate. The Englishman had smiled agreeably, acknowledging the perfect inanity of the small talk. English people are never happier than when talking about anything other than the pressing topics at hand. The American had smiled, too. However, he then reached over, grabbed the jammy dodger and stuffed it whole into his fat face. The Englishman's face froze in a tableau of embarrassment and awkwardness. But it had not been a problem. Kelly had realised immediately that the American had simply no idea what a jammy dodger actually was.

"The person who would partake of our services is an urban dwelling silent revolutionary," said the meeting chair, waving a hand at a power point slide that had so many pie charts upon it that it made you think of lunch. "A thinking individual, astute – and fleet of finger..."

How much more of this nonsense could Monique take? A lot, she decided. If you had little idea how people functioned, you needed to have budgets set aside to pay others to tell you this largely recycled stuff about consumers and target markets. It was the packaging of the pretty obvious and its onward sale, right through to the website and the high street. It paid her. Long may the edifice be polished. Long may we all live off the illusion that what we are doing is useful, and push the pots of money around until we die.

Her phone vibrated. She looked down, frowning. So long as you looked concerned enough, it was acceptable to be taking calls in meetings. In fact, if you did not have a device handy in a meeting, it conveyed the impression that you were not concentrating – rather than the other way round.

The name of the caller flashed up.

Jake Le Jones.

Monique's heart leapt. After meeting him, she had investigated him. There was plenty of easy access information about his surprisingly successful career in the music business. She had even listened to a few of his tracks. She had discovered that he appeared to be an intelligent man. In fact, some of his observations were downright erudite. Could you really live a life outside of offices, conference calls, facilities management, office passes and canteens? And actually make money? And live? And breathe? Did some people not commute to offices, but studios? What on *earth* did they do all day?

She was keen to find out.

She stood up and nodded seriously at the meeting chair, lifting an authoritative finger. As she said "Hello?" she was already well on her way out of the room. There was almost a frisson of approval at her obvious need for ubiquity. It's all in the performance.

Outside of the conference room a rush of freedom overcame her. It was glorious to escape for a while, to take a call from what seemed to be another world, to open a window, to throw the email circulation lists away.

"Hello," she repeated, more softly.

"Monique? It's Jake."

"I can say "hello" for a third time – but I'll move on. Your plane obviously did not crash."

"No. In fact, it was pleasant all round. You don't have time to think, to be honest. Late nights, a lot of meetings with the press, a sound check, the odd bit of filming… it's quite nice to be back."

"Glad you made it back."

"How was Milan?"

"I loved it. How could I not? You probably know all this, but there are splendid people hiding in Milan, cultivating lovely little courtyard gardens. I love the language, the fashion, the buildings, the weather, and the food. I love the relative proximity of the Great Lakes, and the friends that I am making there. I still haven't seen the Last Supper – the queues are always horrendous. Until I have seen it I shall of course be obliged to return."

"What are your plans this week? I was wondering if we might have a drink."

Monique hesitated for a moment:

"Let me buy you dinner. I won't take you anywhere extravagant, but I am French, and we French don't drink without food."

It was Jake's turn to hesitate:

"Okay. What do you have in mind?"

What Monique had in mind was Rubens' bar.

"A friend has opened a bar. Outrageous Fortune. I think it's called after my bank account. It's pretty central. It serves food as well as proper cocktails. It'll be relaxed."

"Will your friend be spying on us?"

That sounded unexpectedly intimate. Monique felt a stab of pleasure at the thought. Control yourself, she told herself. He probably just wants a quick shag. No, said her hormones, he's in love with you. He wants to bond and be in love forever. Nonsense, retorted her sterner Gallic self. Control yourself. They're all the same. All very keen so long as you give them *nothing*. But even if that were the case, reasoned her hormones, wouldn't it be better to just enjoy this man's sheer unadulterated lust and bathe in the warm glow of deeply satisfying sexual relations? What is the alternative, after all? He has a pleasing face and a body you'd like to see naked. Her Gallic self considered this, with pursed lips, but with a soft hungry look in its eye. *Hormones, you have a point*, it conceded. Nothing ventured, nothing gained.

"I rather think he'll have better things to do," she said crisply, "like mixing me my next drink."

"Oh, joy!" snorted Alex, "just what I needed for the perfect night out. A dozen Eurotrash-on-steroids *mariquitas con plumas* in faux golden leather jockstraps pretending to dance to yet another *superstar* DJ. Honestly! Does nothing ever change around here?"

Jamal gave Rubens his *see what I have to put up with every time we go out* look. Being dancers with skin like bay Arabian thoroughbreds rather than Gloucester Old Spot pigs, Jamal knew that he and Rubens were frequently mocked by the pale gay Brits who pretended not to love all things tanned. Such envious melanin-free freaks tried – and failed – to mask their intense displeasure that Jamal and Rubens could actually carry off primary colours.

Alex sighed impatiently as he looked around the room. He put an arm around Ben's shoulders:

"London clubbing was *so* much better in the '90s. These days, all these Spanish imports serve up inflated stage shows that can't mask the fact that the music is just *crap*. I mean, how are we supposed to say no to drugs, when that's the only way one can actually put up with more than thirty minutes of this repetitive rubbish?"

It was an oft-rehearsed rant. Jamal expected that Alex would now continue by comparing the size of promoters' egos to the Spanish housing market, and move to explaining how he was looking forward to the inevitable crash when simpler clubbing would make a return, when good music would be the reason for going out, when it wouldn't all be about six per cent body fat and having biceps bigger than most people's calves. Gratifyingly for Jamal, the rant usually ended with Alex getting completely distracted by the latest gym-addicted Eurotrash import from Napoli, São Paulo or Beirut. The circle thus complete, one could move on to the next predictable speech. *O tempore, o mores*, Alex might say, with a sigh.

Alex could have been talking Greek for all Rubens cared. He never saw the point of analysing the finer points of a club. He was out partying with his closest friends, and that was a special event these days. Locura Total certainly was an event worthy of the name. Anyway, what was Alex *doing*, admitting that he remembered clubbing in the '90s. Alex sounded *so old* at times.

Easily distracted, Rubens caught sight of a pair of tight white jeans. They framed a surprisingly pert pair of cheeks. He blocked out the irrelevant chatter around him and gave the butt the attention it deserved. As he was taking in all its contours, the butt turned around. Had Rubens been the kind of person that one could embarrass, it would have been a perfect occasion to do so, as Dillon Lloyd caught him in full ogle.

"Hey, boss! Eyes front. I didn't know you were coming here tonight."

"Dillon, baby, you have to wear those jeans to work. Jamal, we should cancel the advert in QX, give Dillon a T-Shirt with our logo on the back, and send him out round Soho with those jeans on."

Thankful to have a reason to avoid another exposé on the malaise afflicting London's muscle mary scene, or – worse – an Economist-inspired treatise on the Eurozone crisis, Jamal turned his back on Alex and gave his cutest employee a flamboyant kiss on both cheeks.

Behind Dillon, clouded in the mists of a mediocre appearance garnished with forty-something spread, and thereby practically invisible to the hot-seeking missile that was a clubber's gaze, stood, by way of contrast, Jamal's least cute employee.

Dillon had completely forgotten about Siegfried Allcock. He was thoroughly enjoying the attention being lavished on him (and his butt) by Jamal and Rubens. Fortunately, Alex recognised his old friend. Siegfried stood hesitantly, waiting for an opportunity to join the conversation. Alex grinned at him:

"Oh my God, come here, you!"

Rubens looked round, wondering why Alex was sounding so enthusiastic about such an *ordinary* gay.

Siegfried was grateful to be acknowledged:

"Alex. Hello."

A few months ago, Siegfried's modest English looks and the free-spending habit of an overpaid ex-pat would have assured him the company of at least some of the boys in DJ Station in Silom. He hadn't cared if some of the *potato queen* Thai boys saw him as a drinks ticket, or were just convinced that he must be loaded in another way. What mattered was that he was never alone, and always felt popular. Now, he didn't seem to matter, ever, in the slightest. He felt like Nancy-no-friends' less popular sister. But rather than accept the fact that he had reached the age where the neighbourhood bar would be the apogee of his social life, Siegfried remained determined to find his niche in the London clubbing scene.

Alex hugged Siegfried enthusiastically. Siegfried belonged to his generation, and was a university chum. Alex was sure that he used to read the Economist, too.

"I had no idea you were coming tonight, Siegfried. Good to see you. So – how do you like London's A-List at play? Have you seen the amazing stage show? More Barbie can't dance than Barbi-can, but we don't care, we're all so out of it, they seem fabulous to us. Anyway, how are you? How was the bar tonight?"

Siegfried pondered for a moment whether it was the right time to broach the subject of diminishing takings with Alex. In his previous career he had found that sowing ideas in his bosses' heads was often more effective out of the work environment. Colleagues took things on board more readily when their minds were uncluttered with the daily grind, rushing to the next meeting, avoiding the company bore, and of course hitting one's target. On the other hand, bad news at a party was about as welcome as Sarah Palin at a MENSA meeting. *Sod it*, he thought, it was better that Alex found out from him.

"It was very busy tonight. Very busy. Takings were up on last Saturday, but not by as much as I would have expected. I'm concerned there may have been some pilfering. I think I need to keep a very close eye on Milo, our new barman. I'm not going to mention it to Rubens just yet. I don't want him to think I am questioning his judgement in hiring the man."

Alex frowned. This was not the best news. Money missing from the bar was a classic problem in a business with transient employment. It was never pleasant to deal with. Despite the warnings, they had resisted putting CCTV into the bar, as they did not want the customers to feel watched, nor for the staff to feel they were presumed guilty until proven innocent by the all-seeing eye. Besides, they had a system. Two of their closest friends were on hand pretty much all the time, and there was a strict rule of a receipt for every sale. Alex wondered if he was being filmed at that very moment. He probably was. Clubs were slaves to Big Brother these days. Involuntarily his abs flexed harder, and his mouth fixed in a cross between a pout and a sneer, much as if he were the vain offspring of Billy Idol and Victoria Beckham.

Siegfried ignored Alex's pouting. It was all too familiar. Siegfried had seen Alex attempt this many times over the years. Observing Alex trying to look alluring, yet manly, was a necessary evil of them both growing older. *At least Alex still carries it off – just*, thought Siegfried. He continued:

"Milo is a cute, friendly guy. There is no doubt about that. But when Rubens suggested him for the job, the very first thing he mentioned, before even telling me about his relevant experience for the role, was the fact that Milo had a huge cock. Oh and that everyone knew this, as Milo was a total shower show-off in the gym, forever proudly parading around with a semi."

Indeed. Alex was well aware of the *Penis de Milo*. The situation should be monitored – not yet electronically, mind you, as what was the point of a principle if one doesn't stick to it. Alex also remembered the glory that was Milo nude. His mind wandered to thoughts of what jeans Milo would be wearing to the bar. Alex would need to see how he looked. Maybe Rubens hadn't erred in hiring Milo, after all.

With a holler, Ben came back from the bar clutching

three bottles of water and a Vodka Red Bull – Sugar Free, of course. As he approached, a random girl, chattering loudly in Spanish and desperate to get wherever she was going, teetered on her platforms, lurched into the drinks and knocked Ben's nine pound drink over Dillon Lloyd's otherwise pristine behind.

Utterly oblivious, the girl was off to annoy the next person, leaving Ben staring horrified at the light orange stain spreading over the seat of Dillon's white jeans. An orange arse was not the best clubbing look. Feeling the clamminess on his skin, Dillon turned to have a go at the idiot who had just soaked him. Maybe it was the mortified look on Ben's face, or maybe it was Ben's face, or Ben's body or... *wow, who was that guy?*

Ben was genuinely embarrassed:

"I am so sorry, this girl just sort of fell into me, and... well, I am really, really sorry! I'm sure it'll wash out, but... may I at least get you a drink?" Ben was blushing hotly, as he handed the bottles of water he was carrying to Rubens.

Dillon looked at Ben:

"I've just had a drink, thanks. What I do need though, is a hand to get this..." Dillon paused as he theatrically rubbed his wet bottom and sniffed his fingers, "... Red Bull out of my jeans. Bathroom is that way. If you're sorry, come and help!"

Stifling a giggle, Rubens grabbed the remnants of Ben's drink from him. "Well go on, gostoso, it's the least you can do. Oh, and please behave yourself with my employee. Danvers has spies everywhere, you know."

Not for the first time in his life, Ben found himself

following a cute butt into the toilets of a premier London gay club. Embarrassment had been superseded by irritation at losing the drink he had queued ten minutes for. Irritation, meanwhile, was being given the heave-ho by lust. Lust intensified as Dillon placed his butt over the washbasin in the bathroom, undid his belt, unzipped himself, and then pulled the back of his jeans towards the tap to reveal a pair of Chelsea buns a master baker would have been proud of.

"Babes, I can't see the stain, so you do it. Don't pretend you haven't had your hand down a guy's pants before. And please do it properly. Orange jeans are so last year." Dillon flexed his glutes, and looked sideways at Ben with a lascivious smile. The toilet attendant smirked and tried to sell them both lollipops.

Against his better judgement, Ben gingerly put his hand down the back of Dillon's jeans. His hand made contact with Dillon's soft, smooth skin. He tried rather feebly to stretch the fabric of the jeans to give the stain a good scrubbing. Ben could feel an unwanted semi buoying up inside his own jeans. The throngs of clubbers impatiently waiting to take their drugs in the cubicles under the *drug-free zone* signs dissolved into a haze as he concentrated on restoring Dillon's trousers to their former state of perfection. However, under the bored gaze of the attendant who was ensuring no toiletries were spilled or stolen, Ben's incipient erection faded away, along with the stain on the jeans.

Dillon had observed the rise and fall of the Barlettano baton, and decided he had to go in for the kill.

"Thanks, babes. That'll have to do where that's concerned. I've got some K. Come with me."

Ben had been trying to avoid drugs, but it had been a tough few weeks at work and he suddenly thought *screw it*. Waiting in line with the horde, Ben wondered how Dillon was going to give him the stuff. *Did he have two bags?* Everyone knew it was one person to a cubicle.

However, Dillon knew that Locura Total was one of those clubs where capitalism had conquered bureaucracy. The fiver he pressed into the attendant's hand opened a toilet door for two.

Locked into a private space with a bump of K up his nose, the inevitable happened. Dillon's lips touched his. Grabbing the hand that was grabbing him, Ben had to decide whether he should give in to get what he wanted, or resist so he could keep what he really wanted.

It used to be so simple. When Ben had first followed Rubens to one of London's Saturday night club extravaganzas, everything was up for grabs. There was so much to see, so many boys to do. The ghosts of Saturday nights past swooped gleefully through Ben's memory. But the kid in the candy store could so easily become a bull in a china shop. There was more at stake now. Now Ben had to be extremely careful. By all means touch the merchandise, but one clumsy move and something would get broken. And he would have to pay.

Ben's rules were really quite simple. Kissing on the lips was an honest show of affection – at worst it evidenced restrained desire – but a tongue was duplicity itself. A hand on the butt was merely a compliment, whereas a hand on

83

his package was an insult. An insult to the relationship he had with his girl in Paris. Kelly Danvers.

Ben pushed Dillon's hand away. With the briefest of apologies, he opened the door and made his way back to the safety of Rubens. Ben's penis had got him into many a tight spot, but tonight, other than alcohol, a few cigarettes, a lorry load of lust and a bump of K, Ben had successfully resisted temptation.

Temptation, however, has time on its side.

Something aromatic and spicy was arousing Alex from his somnolent Sunday afternoon suffering. He unwillingly opened an eye. Jamal was carrying two bowls of something steaming.

"You'll feel better after this. Great on an empty or delicate stomach."

Jamal had faithfully recreated his mother's Shorba with all the spices that he brought back every year from Algiers. It seemed the most appropriate dish to break the fast after a big night out. They had been living for about twenty hours straight, on nothing but potions, powders and pills.

"Is there any reason we are watching Five Star's Greatest Hits, Jamal?"

"You know there is. They were my favourite band when I was a kid. I used to learn all their dance routines. I so wanted to be Stedman. His clothes were so cool at the time. So shocking – and yet not that surprising – when he got caught in that toilet. Shame Five Star didn't come back with an *Outside* style video à la George Michael. Anyway, I saw Denise Pearson on TV the other day, and thought they deserved an outing. Oh, look. *If I say yes* is next. That's my favourite."

Alex chuckled silently to himself, wondering what Jamal's admirers would think if they knew that their muscle-bound hunky go-go dancer's first role model was Stedman Pearson, shoulder pads and permed coif and all. Still, it could be far worse. It could have been Barbra.

Alex sighed, and ran a hand through his hair:

"Siegfried mentioned that we might have a problem in the bar. He reckons that there is some money missing – and he suspects that Serbian guy that Rubens hired a couple of weeks ago."

"What? Mad Milo from Mitrovica? I would be very surprised about that. I know the lad. He can be a bit crazy. I think I'd be too, if I were a civil war survivor. But he really doesn't strike me as the dishonest type."

Alex noticed the deliberate way that Jamal mentioned civil war, challenging him to cast aspersions on a fellow traveller from troubled lands.

"You know him?"

"Sure. He's done some stripping. How do you think he got his nickname? The other one, I mean."

"Well, there must be something going on. Siegfried wouldn't just invent a story like that. Maybe you should ask Rubens if he has noticed anything?"

As he chewed the last bits of meat off his chicken thigh, Jamal weighed up what Alex had just said. Alex was open-minded, but Jamal knew that Alex considered that men who were relaxed about getting naked in public for money could often be nakedly relaxed about how they got their hands on the public's money. He also knew Alex thought civil wars led to a general brutalisation of society, institutional breakdown, and a loss of respect for accepted norms in the communities that had suffered. In short, although not judging every stripper from a troubled third world country as a manifest embracer of different moral values, Alex could often be quick to judge in the face of flimsy evidence. This tendency sat awkwardly with a man who had spent most of his career working for charities.

Jamal sighed:

"I'll speak to Rubens. But let's not jump to conclusions, Alex. There's probably a simple explanation that does not involve poor Milo at all. Maybe Siegfried has just got his sums wrong."

It was time for Alex to beat a strategic retreat from the cliff edge of prejudice:

"The Shorba's a triumph, as always!"

"I don't believe it!" Amber was practically spitting down the phone. "Ben Barlettano! He has only gone and outed himself by becoming the head of our flaming LGBT group. Because he is *bisexual*, the women still fancy their chances with him, and the men can still take him to strip shows. Now he seems to be more liked and respected than ever as he has taken the *gutsy decision* to come out at work. What a complete *bastard*!"

"I had wondered why you were using this number on a Tuesday." Nicholas gave no further reaction. She had disturbed him of an evening where there was no sexual encounter to arrange. His irritation swirled around him like dry ice.

"I'm sorry for calling out of the blue like this, but I had to tell someone. I have spent the afternoon congratulating Ben and praising him to the partners. I've even drunk tea with the LGBT group. Now, I can put up with a show of hypocrisy with the best of them, but such sustained pretence takes it out of you – *especially* when you have to put up with self-righteous lesbians. Lezzers always make me feel a bit sick at the best of times. Ever since Francine, my first cellmate."

"Such admirable sentiments. I would expect nothing less from HR."

"I implement the rules but it doesn't mean I have to believe in them, does it? For that matter, I'm not a fan of poofs either. Who cares what they get up to in their private lives, but it isn't natural when all you want is a big prick up your arse, is it?"

"You seemed to enjoy it the last time we went for extras at the Handford, my dear."

"Yes, but that's different, Nicholas. I am supposed to like cock. Thankfully I do. Provided it's attached to the right man, that is."

"What about when a cock is attached to a woman?" Nicholas had not yet presented Amber with his strap-on. It was still early days and he was as yet far from tiring of shagging her back and front whilst playing with those amazing breasts. But there would come a time when his prostate would need a good tickle. He could foresee that he might be hanging on to Amber's tits when it happened.

He enjoyed sex with men, but he only really enjoyed being penetrated by a woman. Nicholas liked tradition, albeit with his own twist.

"Pre-op trannies! Are you trying to shock me, Nicholas? That's pretty disgusting. And stop changing the subject."

Nicholas sighed. Whilst he was now rather keen to be on the receiving end of Amber's thrusts, he was concerned occasionally that maybe the girl was a little too conservative for him. The working class, thought Nicholas sagely, always had been and probably always would be *conservative*. Even broaching the subject would be a risk, given that the more important task – more important than his own sexual gratification – was the gratification of his desire for revenge, and the opportunity Amber presented to help him achieve that. Better to call a lady of the night for the strap-on, and keep Amber for Ben. He decided that it was time to direct Amber, rather than let her go off on another well-intentioned, but ultimately futile, attempted act of vicious vengeance.

"Amber, your news about the boy's private proclivities was only ever going to be a little amuse-bouche. Let's consider it a starter for ten. Everyone has secrets. I'm taking a longer view here. I would wager that young Mr Barlettano has more than one rattling skeleton in his closet. Remember the privileged position you hold over him. You have access to certain information, and although I would of course deny ever suggesting it, the power to *alter* certain information, especially if aided by an expert in the field. You need to be patient. You seem to be doing a fine job of lulling him into a false sense of security. Befriend him further. Wait for any sign of weakness, a crisis. Be his rock. Then store up every shred of data gleaned and use it to eviscerate the man. Kicking a man when he is down is not only easier, but is usually a more complete victory, from which they rarely recover."

Nicholas could tell from the uncharacteristic silence at the end of the phone that his words had hit home. Confirmation of his assessment duly came. Amber spoke slowly:

"You are right. As usual. I have waited for two years to get out of that prison cell. I can wait a little longer for the right opportunity."

"Excellent."

Nicholas afforded himself a mean little smile of satisfaction. "Now, as we are already speaking on the telephone, let us kill two birds with one stone. Wednesday 26th, 6.30pm. You are Tatiana Koklova, the battered wife of a Russian oligarch who needs legal support to protect her from her brutal husband. Wear something expensive, even if it is only the perfume. Usual place."

5

Rubens me up the wrong way

"Allo?"

Ben was at his most cosmopolitan:

"Bonjour, could I speak to Kelly, s'il vous plaît?"

"Hello darling, how are you? Is my French getting so good that I sound like a native now?"

Ben thought that it was actually rather difficult to judge this from the word *hello*. But since Kelly sounded genuinely pleased that she may have sounded French on the phone, he decided not to spoil the moment.

"Wow, Kelly, you have picked up the accent so quickly. So what's up? Work okay? Making friends? You managing to keep the hordes of Frenchmen at bay?"

Ben hadn't intended on mentioning other men so early on in the conversation. Oddly, though, now that he had given up playing the field and placed all his eggs in Kelly's basket, something rather unexpected had happened to him. He was feeling jealous. He needed reassurance.

Kelly had been equally surprised at the change in Ben. Finding him in bed with Rubens when she had turned up at his flat two years earlier in search of their first date had rather set the expectation that she would always be the one chasing him.

"Mon chéri, the city is great. Work is fine. Monique and Cornisha are coming to visit – so I've got that to look forward to. I have made friends here, but it will be nice to see some properly friendly faces from London – especially as you seem to be too busy at work to visit me. And as for you being concerned about Frenchmen, what about me? In the daytime you have a bevy of beauties at Beaux, Aspen, Dickerhint trying to get into your pants, and then at night you have boys taking you out to God knows where. And remember, I have seen what you get up to."

Ben couldn't see the amused look on Kelly's face. Playing on Ben's feelings of guilt was the easiest thing in the world. After all he had put her through, she figured that she still had a little more credit stored up in that account. He fell for it, and worried away:

"Kelly, work is really hectic at the moment. Hartmut has required me to be available every weekend if needs be – so planning is a challenge just at the moment. You know that I have changed, though. I can't stop being who I am or seeing attraction in both sexes. But I can stop acting on it. And I have. Definitively. All I want is you. I love you and I want to be with you and only you. For ever."

After those words some women might have felt an uncontrollable urge to rush to the Gare du Nord. To her surprise, Kelly found that she was not one of them. Ben had always had something of the adoring Labrador about him, but this had been perfectly counterbalanced by the risks inherent in his bisexuality. All that Kelly could think of, hearing him speak like this, was that he sounded more needy than romantic. Sadly, there was no greater turn-off than sounding needy. The legal profession may have been moulding Kelly into a hardened cynic, but she loved Ben, and did not want to stop loving him. However, his words had had precisely the opposite effect that he had intended. She needed to change the subject.

"And I love you too darling. Now, how are other things at work? You still being mean to poor Ham?"

"I'm never mean to Ham, or anyone for that matter. But I do have some news from work. I've finally made it official. No more consorting with coat hangers for me. I am out and proud. You are talking to the new head of the B.A.D LGBT group. The whole firm knows I am bisexual, whilst happily in a long term monogamous relationship with some woman. I am striking a blow to change people's attitudes."

Better. Although he did sound a little *worthy*, this was definitely preferable to needy. Kelly wondered what that would make people think of her. Dating the head of the LGBT group was not the first thing that she would normally highlight on her resumé but it did sound fun. Especially for people as outwardly conventional as most lawyers were.

"Ben that's great. I'm proud of you. How has it gone down in the office? Does Ham now come into your office with his back firmly against the wall, making sure he never drops anything in case he might have to bend over and pick it up?"

"I'm not even going to answer that. Ham! Poor little sausage. You're as bad as Lynne Glackett. She's one of the group's newer members – a walking cliché generator. She gifts us endless ridiculous fishy references to lesbians. But to come back to your interesting theory about Ham – no, it's not been like that at all. With one or two exceptions, people have been great. Amber sent round a really positive, upbeat email to all staff, urging them to support us, and informing people that fostering diversity was a proven method of attracting and retaining the best people. Believe it or not, she even wrote me a little card, saying she thought I was marvellous, and how she was so sorry for all the awful things she had done. I really think she has changed. She is starting to remind me of that sweet girl I met at your party on my first day in London."

Kelly shivered. She would never forget what Amber had come so close to doing to her. Whilst she would like to believe in the reformed character fiction, she had seen the look in that woman's eyes once too often to believe in a fairy tale ending.

"Really? I would be very careful if I were you Ben. She might have changed – but I doubt it. You need to be cautious with HR at the best of times. One unwise step and your card is marked. They carry weight."

Ben reflected that actually Amber was carrying a lot less weight than she used to. More importantly he knew how to handle himself:

"I'm a bit too senior now for that to be a really scary prospect. Kelly, give the woman a chance! She is still shy round me. I think she feels dreadful about what happened and just wants to make amends. I told you, she even looks different now."

Suddenly the boot was on the other foot. Kelly felt a pang of jealousy. She knew how Ben's head could easily be turned by a pretty face, big chest and narrow waist, regardless of the genitalia beneath. Surely he couldn't...

"Why, you're attracted to her, aren't you! And she's playing you. This is to get back at both of us. The little bitch!"

"Kelly, what the hell? Yes, she is attractive, but I would never go there. In any event, do you not remember the *m* word? Monogamy, in case you have forgotten. Jeez, this distance thing is harder than I thought it would be."

Kelly blushed red, realising how stupid she had just sounded.

"Sorry, Ben. You're right. I guess not seeing each other is hard for both of us. I will be over in a few weeks' time. Let's not argue. I love you and I miss you."

Although Ben wasn't impressed with Kelly's outburst, part of him was rather happy to have been on the receiving end of a jealous reaction for the first time in a while. Kelly might have a point about Amber, but he doubted it. He would be cautious, but he would never stop believing the best in people, despite all his legal training.

"Cornisha, do you have five minutes?"

Cornisha Burrows turned round to see Pam Shank and Lynne Glackett bearing down on her in the corridor. Pam looked as though she were about to summon Cornisha to a hearing on war crimes in Syria. Lynne looked like she could be after more of those pink paper clips.

Cornisha nodded:

"I have a conference call in ten minutes. Is it private or can we chat whilst I make myself a cup of tea? I do find that a conference call without a hot beverage is rather like having a tooth extracted without anaesthetic."

Pam gave Cornisha what she hoped was a winning smile, which filled Cornisha with foreboding.

"I think the kitchen would be the perfect place for our chat," said Pam.

As they stepped into the kitchen, Pam winked at Lynne:

"I love your dress, Cornisha. Green suits you so well."

Lynne winked back at Pam.

Cornisha ignored the winking and sighed to herself. They obviously wanted something. Knowing Pam she would find out in five, four, three, two…

"Cornisha, we want you to join the LGBT group. As I am sure you know, we have just launched the group. We think it is important to have the transgender community represented in order to highlight all and any issues within the firm. We will also have meetings with other firms' LGBT groups in order to ensure we stick to best practice and learn from others' mistakes. We feel you would be a valuable member of the team, and would like to make sure that you suffer no discrimination."

Pam smiled regally. She was used to getting her way, as most people were either scared of her, or knew they could not match her for what she described on her CV as tenacity.

Cornisha shook her head:

"That's very nice of you, girls, but I think I'll give it a miss, thank you. I wouldn't want all those meetings distracting me from my job and leading to a breakdown in the supply of stationery. Imagine if we were to run out of glue sticks."

Cornisha was tempted to wink at Lynne, who was stifling a giggle. Lynne was very easy to entertain. But it wasn't the time to get Pam annoyed.

As if summoned by oestrogen, Ben came into the kitchen. Pam eyed him. As LGBT group leader, he should probably assume responsibility for recruiting Cornisha. Thankfully she, Pam, would take charge while he was being flaky. Pam could get a lot of meaning into a look.

She continued, briskly:

"Cornisha, this is an official, company-sanctioned body, and as such has importance alongside our day jobs. Beaux, Aspen, Dickerhint is making serious efforts to ensure that the kind of discrimination that has held us back for generations will be consigned to the wastebin of history!" Pam fixed a steely gaze upon Cornisha, daring her to resist.

"Well, that is marvellous, Pam, but I'm afraid I have never actually felt discriminated against at Beaux Aspen, either before or after the merger with Dickerhint Strudel. And you must know that I am a very private person. I don't really like to be in the spotlight, and certainly don't feel at ease representing people. I'm not a lawyer, my dear."

Pam understood Cornisha, but she thought that she was missing the point. Pam was convinced this was the right thing to do, and Cornisha just wasn't getting it. Besides, ancillary staff were needed to show just how diverse B.A.D had become. They needed Cornisha. Pam took a sharp intake of breath, drew herself up to her full height, and looked over to Lynne for help.

Lynne had known Pam since their very first week at

university. They had both been dreading the fresher's event, renowned as they were for men and women coupling as if a well-known technology firm were on the verge of launching the iChastityBelt. As lesbians, they weren't relishing being made to feel different, again, on their first night out at college. Miraculously, however, they found each other. Well, to be precise, Pam had made a beeline for Lynne, and a couple of cheap bottles of plonk later, they were exploring each other's tonsils, tits, toes, and everywhere in between. The night was long, torrid, and beyond either of the girl's wildest dreams of how college would start out.

Although the people you meet in your first week at college are rarely the ones you will stay in touch with, Pam and Lynne became good friends. Pam's take-no-prisoners attitude to life had led easily into activism at university. Lynne had been dragged along for the ride. The full-frontal approach was the one Pam rarely abandoned, even when it came to a student charity calendar for women's rights in Bosnia. Whilst Lynne had declined to flash her clam in the service of Balkan equality, she had accompanied Pam driving a lorry load of knickers and sanitary towels from Newport Pagnell to Sarajevo. On another occasion she was alongside Pam, and half a dozen other die-hards, in front of Zimbabwe House with placards supporting disabled lesbian single mothers in Harare. Not that it wasn't a worthy cause, but just how many of them could there actually be? It didn't matter a jot to Pam.

Although Pam's direct action approach had notched up many notable victories, both younger women sensed that this would not work with Cornisha. Cornisha had a rock solid serenity about her, and would not be bludgeoned into changing her mind. In stark contrast to Pam's bulldozer ways, Lynne liked to listen. She would burrow under people's skin until she understood just what made them tick. Pam and Lynne made rather a good team. Lynne would calmly manoeuvre the person into talking. She would listen, file away, analyse, and then home in on the weak points. Responding with the most delicate of observations on that precise aspect of their resistance would loosen the bolts holding all their arguments together, until it just required a smart little hammer tap from Pam to bring the whole edifice crashing down.

Looking over at Ben as she spoke, Lynne entered the fray:

"Oh, Cornisha, if only everyone were as strong and capable as you. Apart from doing a marvellous job of looking after the office, you are also our big sister. You're always there for us when we get stressed out with work, or go slightly off the rails for a day."

Cornisha had seen the girls in action, so was not going to be taken in by Lynne's honey. Or at least not yet.

Lynne continued, smiling:

"I was so nervous before starting here. I remember being worried about whether I would be accepted as a lesbian. Not that it has any bearing on my effectiveness, but law being such a conservative arena... well, I was worried about having to pretend, or just having to keep quiet. Not being yourself is so tiresome. It takes too much energy, to say nothing of flying in the face of breaking down barriers with colleagues. Pam was totally different. I think her exact words to me were *Fuck homophobes! Don't they know it's the 21st century? If they give me any shit they'll be sorry!* But that still didn't help the nervous young woman inside of me."

Lynne paused. Cornisha politely waited for her to continue. Ben, meanwhile, was pretending to be taking forever about making a cup of tea, but was actually rather interested in where Lynne was going.

"Of course, now I am here, I know that I needn't have worried too much," mused Lynne. "Apart from the inevitable jokes about how much I like cats, and *have I tried the vegetarian pie-shop in Hackney Wick?* we are actually allowed to walk around freely – imagine that – and get on with our work. We don't even have to wear regulation Doc Martens to warn off the straight male partners. But – and this is my point right here – if I don't tell other nervous young Lynnes who are thinking of a law career about all this, then I haven't really finished my journey, have I?"

There it was. Without even mentioning her, Lynne had thrown down a gauntlet to Cornisha. *You may now be fine, and all very comfortable, but what are you doing to help others?* In fairness, Lynne did have a good point. Like it or not, Cornisha was a role model, and it would be somewhat selfish not to use the influence that she had. And if she agreed now then at least she would spare herself the inevitable Shank attack.

Cornisha was moved. And she knew when she was beaten:

"Fine. No more. I'll join up. Send me an email with the details. Now, I really do have a conference call to get to."

Pam beamed at Lynne.

"Excellent. Well, that's our transgender box ticked."

"You do love like tickling boxes, don't you, sweetie."

Lynne turned to Ben:

"Ben, never mind all this. How are we faring on the good old classic homo front? Last time I looked they were still either all in hiding or pretending to be bisexual. I mean it's all very well getting our "T" lady, but now we're in a bit of a "G" spot, aren't we. We don't want to be known as the BLT group."

"We're getting there," replied Ben. "The Dickerhint side seems to be quite fruitful. Do you know Axel Schwanz?"

"Of course," Lynne could hardly contain herself. "How could we forget Frau Marlene?"

Ben winced. But then, as it seemed was standard for many a minority, nobody mocked the LGBT crowd quite like the LGBT crowd did.

It was a perfect English scene. The enormous gingham table cloth nestled gently into the closely cropped lawn of Bessborough Gardens, providing enough space for a large plate of cucumber sandwiches, a Victoria sponge, copious amounts of chilled Pimms and lemonade, and seating for four.

Helena and Angela had insisted the men wore whites and boaters. The ladies had gone to town, festooning themselves in summer dresses under the shade of parasols. A few stray tourists from Tate Britain, passports in hand searching for Pimlico, and eager to capture a genuine snapshot of real England, were getting them to pose for photos.

100

"More Pimms, Helena?"

"Thank you, Rubens. Now please turn round, and give a big smile to our visitors. Show the lovely people from Osaka what beautiful teeth we English have."

As he grinned at the camera alongside Rubens, Jamal wondered if the shutter-happy party suspected that Rubens and he were not genuine English gentlemen, hailing as they did from Rio and Algiers instead. However, at least they were *British*, as their documentation and tax returns now proved. Jamal's brother in Paris never knew whether he should consider himself French or not, even after twenty years of life there. Jamal, by contrast, was quite clear on this. He would never be English, nor indeed wanted to be – but he felt very much British by now, which to him defined a way of acting rather than an accident of birth. As for being a Londoner – well, he was its very embodiment.

Helena Handcart ticked all the boxes regarding English credentials, being the scion of a rather genteel family from Tunbridge Wells. However, lacking a box herself, she failed on the *lady* front. As for Angela Merkin, or Uwe, as he was known out of drag, being a man in a dress from Dresden, he rather failed on both counts.

They had all been friends ever since Rubens and Jamal had been extras in the show that Helena and Angela used to do weekly at the Royal Vauxhall Tavern.

Rubens hadn't found out what Helena's real name was, or even if she had one. Even out of drag, a state which she rarely let anyone except Angela see these days, Helena was the consummate lady. She was forever bewailing the decline in moral standards and lamenting that the world was going to pot – and then being smoked. For her part, Angela thought Helena was half Dame Maggie Smith and half Dr Evadne Hinge. It all depended on how much gin had been consumed. Angela was Helena's younger, sluttier alter ego. They had been a hit when Rubens had brought them in to do a regular Thursday night slot at Outrageous Fortune.

The ladies were agog with the prospect of scandal:

"Now, Rubens. Spill the Brazilian jumping beans. What is this nonsense I have heard about light-fingered activity at work?"

Rubens paused mid-sip of Pimms, eyed Jamal, and then looked over at Helena, who fluttered her eyelashes at him and looked appropriately concerned:

"I'm afraid the gossip has spread all around the bar, you know."

Jamal snorted:

"And that's all it is, Helena. Gossip."

Jamal's airy tone belied his niggling concerns:

"There *may* be a small issue," he conceded, "… which could equally well just be an error that Siegfried and Rubens will resolve."

Helena eyed him with amusement. She knew how bad for morale such problems could be. She did not want to make things difficult for Jamal. Angela had fewer qualms about expressing herself:

"Oh, come on, Jamal! Seriously? Everyone knows that Siegfried thinks Mad Milo has been helping himself to your money, by not putting all the drinks through the till. Well everyone, except Milo that is, as we are all far too scared of him to tell him."

Jamal narrowed his eyes, and looked at Rubens. He hadn't realised things had gone this far. If that's what the staff thought, then he and Alex needed to act fast, or at least make sure their management team did. Part of his management team, however, had different thoughts. Rubens made an expansive gesture:

"Angela, minha querida, it is just an unpleasant rumour. There is no proof." Rubens weighed up what he was about to say: "I think there is some jealousy going on. One of the other barmen is worried that Milo is getting better tips than he is."

More news. Jamal had not had this conversation with Rubens:

"Who, exactly?"

Rubens didn't really want to discuss this in front of Helena and Angela, but by now there was no way out.

"I have no proof, but I can see that there is not exactly a warm relationship between Dillon and Milo. It is not like the slightly surprising friendship between Dillon and Siegfried. Dillon and Siegfried hang out together. You saw them in la Locura the other night yourself."

"Goodness, what a ripping yarn." Helena rolled her eyes slightly, as was her wont when she intended to say something slightly risqué. "So, young Dillon is afraid that the *Penis de Milo* is earning more money than his own *Chelsea Buns*. Would Dillon be doggedly cultivating the boss and filling his head with nonsense? Do you think Siegfried is *fornicating* with the little trollop? That Dillon is a sharp one, and I wouldn't put it past him to go all helium heels for the sake of filthy lucre."

Helena paused for effect. Then she waved a hand dismissively:

"We may never know the full story, but I'm sure the truth will out. Come on, everyone. Do smile! It looks like Naoko has sent her friends back for more photos."

That evening, Monique wore the canary yellow shift dress that set off her slender figure and dark bangs. When Jake stepped into the bar, and saw her sitting at the counter reading a Thomas Mann novel, he knew he had made a good move. He slid onto the bar stool next to her, and leaned over to kiss her on the cheek:

"Hello again. I love that dress."

Monique's mind was already made up:

"Hello."

She leaned over and kissed him full on the mouth. She tasted slightly of oranges. Cointreau, or Grand Marnier, wondered Jake.

"How hungry are you?" she asked, looking down at Rubens' freshly minted menu.

"Very," said Jake. This was true. He had rushed around all day, and felt very hungry indeed.

He looked around the bar. It was nicely done up. Plenty of clean white, with lively splashes of red, fuschia, and orange. It looked and felt impeccable. Monique followed his glances:

"I think it works well, this décor. It's crisp and elegant for the day and early evening, but you'd be surprised how dim it gets later."

"Sometimes I get pretty dim later, too," said Jake.

Monique shot him a sharp look:

"In my view, we have some of our best ideas when rip-roaringly drunk," she said. "Maybe some of these ideas don't fit into the shackles and constraints of our everyday life. They're still great ideas."

"You don't need to be drunk to have a good idea," reasoned Jake.

"No, but when in Rome…" Monique gestured at the customers around her: "We're possibly all here to throw off our binds."

"What are these binds?" asked Jake.

Monique shrugged:

"Social conventions. La méfiance mutuelle – mutual suspicion. Fear of the consequences of actions."

"You sound as if you have a theory. Go on."

"Not really – just a few thoughts that pester me. You see, we always try to tell people that actions have consequences. But that should not constrain action. We all end up lamely worrying about what might happen. Sometimes you have to get through the immediate consequences of an action – putting up with someone's displeasure, say, when you have pointed out that they are a fool – to reach the result that you want to achieve. Sometimes you need to be masterful, in order to make progress."

"There's nothing too absurd about that."

"No – but what I feel I mainly observe is people *not* pointing out when people are fools, or incompetents, because it's easier not to. The reason is that we are fearful of the consequences. It is easier to do nothing. And so we all slide into mediocrity, together." She paused and looked at Jake: "I envy you, I think. You're in a very different place to me."

"I'm not. I'm right here. And I think we all battle with others to achieve what we want. For the time being, I want a beer. And a steak sandwich."

"You pick the right battles. I think I'll have the same. The meat here is great."

She signalled to Rubens, who came over and said a brief hello. He was respectful of the intricacies of heterosexual courtship. He couldn't fathom it, but he knew that it was slow food.

Several strong beers later, Monique ordered an espresso martini.

"I think it's time to move on from Outrageous Fortune."

Outside, Jake kissed her. It felt like a kiss that had been a long time coming. And it was painfully good. Monique realised she had all but forgotten how dazzling the right kiss was. But then Jake stopped, and stiffened.

A photographer with a beer gut appeared, his camera at the ready like a well-used gun. He was grizzled, with stubble that could mate with a porcupine. He yelped cheerful-sounding comments as he took a series of flashing shots, which felt as if they were exploding into their faces. Jake expertly raised a hand and stood so as to conceal Monique as best he could. A cab appeared and they hailed it. All Monique remembered was Jake's calm, measured tones as he managed to get her into the cab, whilst avoiding the worst of the exposure.

"Sorry about that," said Jake. "Occupational hazard. We've been lucky. I don't think he got anything too useful on you."

Monique felt shaken. It felt a lot more intrusive than she had ever imagined that such interest would.

Gallic control took over:

"This was lovely but I'm going home now," she said.

Jake looked at her:

"Okay. You know I'd like to have another drink."

"I know. But it's a little overwhelming. It has been fun. We can meet up again."

The cab dropped her at the foot of her building.

She kissed Jake quickly again:

"Goodbye, rock star."

He smiled:

"Are you around next week? You said you wanted to see that gallery I mentioned."

"This is all a bit strange for me," she said. "Let's talk. But yes. The gallery's a definite. I want to see London through your eyes while I can."

Tarquin Henderson-Smythe stared at his watch. He had not felt this excited for a long time – not since he had identified the Caravaggio in Lady Barbara's closet. She had identified the room as a closet, for reasons best known to herself. It was a lonely little room off one of the landings in her large house. She had ushered him in there and disappeared off to summon some tea.

Time stood still. The room was clean, but the air was leaden with lack of circulation. There should have been a ticking clock on a wall, or a slowly swinging grandfather pendulum, to break the silence, to give it a semblance of connection to life. It was simply quiet, and abandoned.

Yet there on the faded wall he had seen the painting – a delicate scene, grimy with lack of care, but unmistakably interesting. Of course Lady Barbara had interrupted his silent scrutiny with the distant rattle of fine china, coupled with a fog horn command to "come out of the closet". *I have done, dear, so very much so*, he had thought.

Tarquin was excited that Rubens was coming to the gallery. He still could scarcely believe that he had enticed him over. Tarquin's elegant looks did not entirely sit well alongside the bursting vitality and animal sexuality evident in the likes of Rubens. It was like contrasting a Jackson Pollock with a Da Vinci. Or a Watteau with a Picasso. But Rubens had plainly wanted to see some of the treasures of the gallery. And why not? Tarquin was all for people breaking out from the chains of stereotype. Especially if it gave him the chance for some cock.

The gallery bell went. Tarquin smiled. Heavens. He was in his thirties, and a handsome professional. He did not need to get nervous about showing somebody around paintings. Even if that somebody was *some body*. Oh, who was he kidding? He was as excited as a dog at dinner time. Tarquin ran a hand through his hair and headed for the door.

"Hello, gostoso."

Rubens was an unframed picture. He was tightly fitted out in black jeans and a vivid red hooded top. Seeing him away from the bar only emphasised his singularly healthy and toned looks. Pallid English faces passed to and fro in the street behind him. Goodness, thought Tarquin, let me have a piece of that. *Red velvet beef cake.* He felt an urgent need to compare and contrast this physical specimen with the precise anatomical studies of which the gallery held a considerable library. Tarquin hesitated, slightly giddy. But Rubens was at ease. He wrapped Tarquin in a bear hug.

"So, my English gentleman. Teach me something I don't know about art. I'm going to canvass your opinion on everything here. Canvas, eh?" Rubens laughed at his own joke.

"Five out of ten," said Tarquin briskly, leading the way into the gallery's main room. "Don't worry," he added over his shoulder, "I've given up on jokes. Such an English way of breaking the ice. Let me see if I can get you interested in what we have here anyway."

"We do have art in Brazil," offered Rubens. "Maybe I can tell you something about that some time."

"I'd love that," said Tarquin earnestly. He turned to face Rubens, his blue grey eyes burning. "Sometimes, I feel that art is all that there is that is worthy and good and that has a chance of survival in the long term."

Rubens looked at him:

"I know what it is like to feel things are more short term, that's for sure. Life is very cheap, sometimes."

They paused. Rubens looked around. The gallery was wood-panelled with careful lighting and a wonderful high ceiling. The paintings hung with precision on the wall, positioned for size and subject. Rubens nodded:

"This is magnificent, gostoso. I feel as if I am in a chapel of good taste."

Tarquin took him to a Breughel.

"Look at this," he said. "This is painted on panel, in

the early seventeenth century. Look at these figures. Look at them skating, so free and easy, wrapped up against the frost. Look at them playing, and loving. We can feel the exhilarating rush of cold air on cheeks as we spin on the ice. We are alive today, and they were alive then. This painting has passed through many hands but above all been gazed upon by thousands."

"Ice, ice, baby," said Rubens, appreciatively.

Tarquin took him to some religious pictures, pointing out the skill manifest in the depiction of textures and fabrics, and the way light played upon the figures. "You need to know your myths," he said. "One golden apple here, one infant there, one fleeing maiden, or warrior. It's all communication of thoughts, ideas and storylines. It weaves the fabric of civilisation. Paintings flatter, and depict, and deceive."

"Then photography came and killed it," said Rubens, thoughtfully.

"Steady on. Painting is not dead. Drawing is not dead. There are subtleties you can show in these media that you can't really achieve with a camera. Photography has its own canvases, anyhow."

"Everything changes, though. I think we should all have to do art," said Rubens, expansively. "It focuses the mind."

"Let me show you something that will focus your mind. Follow me."

Rubens was intrigued. Tarquin took him through an elegant corridor and up some narrow stairs. It felt as if one were burrowing into the past. Tarquin's office was surprisingly large, and was on any view a very pleasant room. A large polished carved wooden desk dominated the space. The computer screen was thin and discreet. There were lampshades on decent stands, and a rather exotic looking carpet decorating a more practical floor covering beneath it. There was a lovely sofa. Tarquin led Rubens to the wall:

"Now look at this."

It was a Rubens. A gorgeous, vivid Rubens, bold and beautiful, on the wall of a private office. Rubens was astonished:

"Wow. I could steal this."

"Not really," said Tarquin easily. "It's wired up. And you'd probably find it hard to sell on without the necessary contacts in the underworld. It's for sale – but for the time being, it's almost mine."

"*Increível,*" said Rubens.

Tarquin stood softly behind him:

"I think there's something else that's almost mine."

Rubens did not need asking twice.

6

The Stag Queen

Sylvie van der Sloot had no strippers at her bachelorette party. She knew of the risks of these tawdry little affairs – the desperate celebration of the end of singledom, which people marked by calling old flames, or pulling their own pants down, or going crazy in some shape or form, because goodness, you need to show that you are *not* in control of the animal that is your sexuality. Sylvie was as determined as a dung beetle that no unpleasant surprises would leak forth from her fiancé's stag do. Her Dougal was precisely the kind of clean-cut, hard-working man she had planned on marrying all her life.

Dougal was trim, handsome, and, best of all, ready to accept that she was the leader in the relationship. His gay brother, Dillon, added spice to the mix. Dillon was a perfect shopping companion. This was quite the opposite of Dougal, who would marvel at how his little brother was able to tell *she who must be obeyed* what to do, what to wear – and even what not to wear. Sylvie adored Dillon, laughing when he lampooned her occasional crimes of fashion. How gay it was indeed to skip along on his arm, hoping that people would believe that she was the apple of his eye, rather than him being the fruit of the pair. At those who muttered "cougar" she would have responded tartly with something amusing about big cats, had she been able to think about it in time. Alas, she never did.

But the delightful yin of gay brother Dillon unfortunately had a malodorous yang in Dougal's other passion in life: his rugby. The very thought of Dougal's rugby team made Sylvie shudder. Not only did the players make up what they lacked in real talent with the ability to bore any trapped onlooker to beyond breathing with dull glory stories anchored in and around the odd-shaped-ball game, there was also no compromise to be found about the smell of used rugby kit. You needed a room in the house for it. No wonder rugby was the preserve of the well-to-do, she thought.

Sylvie loathed sport. She loathed the sweat and tears, the scratches and scrapes, the mess, and consumption of whole afternoons as if they were but mere minutes. Dougal's friends were generally a well-heeled, respectable crew, but they congregated in an area of her beloved's life over which she had no control. This disconcerted her. It disconcerted her yet more when she discovered that many of them would be attending the stag night.

She naturally did what any woman in her position would do to protect her future husband. She decided to organise the stag do.

It would be on a Tuesday, precisely so that it could not go on too late. She booked paintballing in the morning, golf in the afternoon, a curry in the early evening, and then drinks in a fashionable London cocktail bar. Egged on by the bar event organiser, as Dillon had styled himself for the occasion, she even booked a show at the bar for them.

Dillon had been very helpful. Some of his brother's rugby friends were extremely cute, and he had heard that the difference between a rugby player and a bisexual was about eight pints of lager. He was determined to try his luck at the first glazed eye.

It was going to be a night to remember at Outrageous Fortune.

"So who exactly are we entertaining tonight?"

Angela Merkin looked up from the mirror illuminated by multiple light bulbs, satisfied that her fine-featured face was now perfectly adorned. She looked questioningly across the touch-up room at Helena Handcart. The room was one of those essential all-purpose spaces so common in bars, fulfilling the functions of storeroom, private meeting room, staff changing area and – of course – make-up HQ. The key's whereabouts were frequently a drama, and the cleaners were forever denied access, as the room would usually offer at least one flat surface strewn with remnants of *face powder*, from which a seasoned hand could eke out a decent freshening up.

"My dear, the stag is the brother of darling little Dillon behind the bar. Apparently the stag's rather proper bride-to-be considers our performance to be the most respectable of all options available to a group of young bucks."

Helena tweaked one of her outsized lashes:

"What a sensible woman she is."

Outside, the evening crowd looked up in interest when a large group of beefy men walked in noisily and headed towards the reserved tables near the stage. Dillon rushed over to greet his brother and his hunky friends, trying hard to swagger, but fumbling his way into a fast sashay instead. In trying to be straight, he looked rather tortured. This was fitting – which is more than could be said about his jeans today. These were so tight that Dillon was sure he spotted at least a couple of alarmed glances as he rounded the bar. He told himself that these were *admiring* glances, and tried to erase from his memory that dreadful moment when his beloved white jeans had burst on him, exposing his tender-skinned bottom, on the one day that he had gone commando. *If I ever do therapy*, he mused, *we'll be talking about that for weeks*.

"Gentlemen. Welcome to Outrageous Fortune."

Siegfried watched nervously from the other end of the bar. He was grateful for the probable influx of money that Dillon's initiative would bring. But he had an instinctive dislike of groups of straight men in a confined space, especially when it involved team sports. Probably a hangover from being abysmal at rugby himself at school, and always feeling left out of all the fun and games. That, and being rogered with a cricket stump.

As Dillon greeted the guests, and took the first order, Siegfried relaxed slightly. They seemed pretty subdued, and had more the air of the school physics society than the rugby club, despite their physiques. Maybe tonight wouldn't be so untoward after all.

Dougal's friends weren't quite sure how to react to

going to a gay bar. On one hand, they told themselves, *so what*. They explained to each other that they were chilled about it. They were twenty-first century men who had left behind the stereotypical Neanderthals of the recent past. Yes, *recent* past – everything is relative in the history of the world. Time's arrow, *innit?* As it seemed that every other rugby club in the land had done, they were even talking about getting naked for a charity calendar this year. So what if amongst the female admirers there were also some gay men who would buy it and ogle their bums? Charity was charity, and they did have rather fine bums. There was nothing gay about recognising the fact. Nothing gay at all about hanging out together and having a man-crush on Prince Harry. And yet, it still didn't seem quite right, that there would be no women to flirt with as the night progressed and the drinks started to take effect. And... could all those gay guys really be trusted?

Feeling outnumbered, in unfamiliar territory, and without yet having imbibed alcohol to bolster their confidence, the group stuck together. They had circled the wagons. The group lay low like a huge shy bison, hoping not to attract the attention of any marauding homosexuals. They would, and should, stick together. They must, as they did not want to be picked off one by one, defenceless in the face of so much gaiety. Most importantly, they should go in groups of at least three to the toilets. They may check out each other's cocks in the showers at the club, but that was normal. It was just comfortable familiarity. However, neither they, nor anyone else, would check out their cocks at the urinals in this bar. That was a wholly different proposition. They didn't want their poor penises to be subjected to any visual sexual abuse by some pervy poof.

However, the first marauding homosexual that slipped through their defences brought a drinks menu. That was sneaky, but finally welcome. He then returned with lager, spirits and the first of many rounds of shots, this one on the house, that one strangely delicious. Dillon didn't bite, didn't touch any of them, and – although camp and wearing ridiculously tight jeans – he seemed to pose no immediate threat.

Unusually for midweek, Rubens was working alongside Siegfried. Rubens had been informed that he needed to learn how to handle groups of straight men. Although Rubens had never had any problems, that he was aware of, in handling men, gay or straight, he took Siegfried's instruction at face value, and turned up eager to learn. He didn't know that Siegfried had in fact a different reason for having him there.

Milo watched proceedings with his usual air of ennui, efficiently producing drinks for customers at the bar, and cocktails for Dillon to serve at the tables.

"Another round of tequila shots, please, mate."

The group was now wasting no time in getting the party started. Milo appreciated the courtesy they were showing, and also the generous tips. He didn't go for trying to turn straight men himself. He was satisfied with his fair pick of gay men. It amused him to see Dillon buzzing round them, and even Rubens and Siegfried letting their managerial façade drop when the better-looking guys approached. Milo was there solely to make money, and so treated the men as nothing more than the paying customers that they were. They were soon treating Milo like one of the lads. The sight of this infuriated poor Dillon, who couldn't help mincing when he was annoyed.

"Straight, are we, Milo?" he muttered, slamming empties on a tin tray. "Born that way, were we, Milo? Leave those kids alone!"

You can't keep a good scrum of rugby men down. There was a group. There was drink. With staggering originality, Dougal's group were now playing a drinking game. They were slowly owning the bar. Inhibitions dissolved like sugar cubes in champagne cocktails, in the mix of tequila, beer, chasers, and competition. The regulars were annoyed and fascinated by the antics, silently criticising the boorishness, but clearly fixated. This was fantasy made real. Straight men were drinking with them. All sorts of possibilities were taking root.

A drum roll interrupted the proceedings.

"Ladies and gentlemen, please take your hands out of your trousers, and put them together for the stars of the evening! Tonight we have something truly special for you all. We have the scintillating talent of London's Wasted End. We have the music of the fright. We have the merged beauty and the beast. Here to put on a special stag night show for Dougal Lloyd, who will be getting married next weekend, I give you... Helena Handcart and Angela Merkin!"

Another drum roll and a puff of dry ice kept up a semblance of theatricality.

Helena walked on stage alone, looking as if she were

expecting to take tea with Mussolini. She looked backstage expectantly, with a slight air of concern:

"Where are you my, dear? I'm *never* going to find you a husband if you insist on being late for every social occasion. Potential fiancés do not like to be kept waiting. Oh, do hurry up!"

Turning to the audience, Helena surveyed the men in front of her, drew a sharp intake of breath and brought up her hand to clutch her pearls:

"Oh, my, what a fine group of gentlemen we have here. Let me have a closer look. I see Dunhill jackets, I see a Montblanc watch, expensive shirts, no tattoos… One of this lot must have a house in the country."

Helena paused for breath, and aimed her most engaging smile at the group of men, before directing a look of disdain at the rest of the bar:

"My step-daughter, Angela," Helena pronounced the name with a hard "g" as the Germans do, "yes, Angela, is a rare beauty. She has the visage of a lady, the form of a classical nymph, and the manners of a common slut." Helena's face fell slightly, before brightening up as she remembered a more cheery thought: "But she has such a forgiving character. She is forever ready to turn the other cheek if slapped, which is what she should get for being so late. In fact, I'm minded to get one of the gentlemen to teach her a lesson and administer the punishment for me. I'm sure there must be some slappers amongst you who would enjoy punishing my Angela's cheeks."

A slightly nervous laugh went round Dougal's group. Helena's double-entendres were admittedly weak, but the drinks were strong and plentiful, and the boys were waiting to see what manner of old trout this Angela could be. Although they would have preferred lap dances in Prague to an old drag queen with tired repartee, they could smell that there was fun to be had that evening, especially if it could be at Dougal's expense. He would be made to pay for denying them strippers.

Dougal was also being made to pay for rather a lot of shots. Rubens and Siegfried had been keeping a close eye on the group. Of course they were making sure that everything was above board, but it didn't do any harm that the rugby boys were easy on the eye, and hopefully getting easier as each round went down.

Maybe the old maxim about drinking until they were pretty was working, but when Angela Merkin strutted out on to the stage, jaws dropped. She was wearing what had once been a wedding dress. The garment had survived intact from the wide shoulder straps, through the modest high neckline down to an inch below the breast, where it had been cut off revealing a remarkable flat stomach, the hint of a heptathlete's abdominals, and a diamante stud in her navel. The bottom half of the dress had been utterly savaged until it was no more than a scarf around her groin, which did not even attempt to conceal the lacy white knickers into which she had somehow managed to tuck her admittedly small and ladylike genitalia. Angela had a sumptuous pair of legs in those skin-coloured tights – yet it was her perfect peachy behind, the lower half calling peek-a-boo to the audience which demanded and received the attention of the men. Little did they know, or care, that the improbably spherical curves had been surgically enhanced by the man they called Dr Buttmeister of Bonn.

Angela was most definitely one of the more beautiful drag queens. As a boy, she had been forever bullied for sounding and looking so feminine and delicate, but now the curse had turned into a blessing. A light layer of foundation, dramatic mascara and shocking pink lip gloss was all it took. She looked like a china doll.

"Well, you weren't expecting this, were you boys? You may close your mouths now. How funny, it's normally the rugby team saying that to my Angela." Helena kept a perfectly straight face as a ripple of laughter went round Dougal's friends. Although they knew Angela had to be a man, she was sexier than most of the women they knew. She looked available and a swift ladyboy fling could even be blamed on the excessive quantity of alcohol.

Helena could see she now had their full attention.

She turned to Angela, and waved a hand expansively:

"But, my darling, what are you wearing?"

"Mother, you said I was looking for a husband this evening. Well, my analyst says I need to visualise success. I saw a gorgeous white wedding and a honeymoon on a Caribbean beach. I thought I would combine dress and bikini into one. I think some of those young gentlemen rather like it."

Angela smiled coquettishly. Helena raised an eyebrow:

"Do you know, my dear, they like it so much, I think they want to see more."

Helena paused dramatically.

The boys fell suddenly silent, thinking that they could see just enough and didn't want to spoil the illusion by seeing any more of Angela.

"And so, thanks to Dougal's darling little brother, Dillon, we have a treat in store. Now, who would like to see Dougal dressed as a bride?"

A huge boozy cheer went up as Dillon led his brother off to the touch-up room, where Justin, a.k.a. Donna Rear, was waiting with his mascara wand.

Dougal had known the boys wouldn't let him escape the night with just a hangover. There had to be humiliation somewhere along the line. He was now stripped to the waist. A rather overweight, camp man was applying thick slap to his face. He was about to be dressed as a bride and paraded in front of a bar full of people. And there would be photos.

The room was hazy. How interesting it was. Full of all sorts of items.

What would Sylvie say? Dougal was sure she couldn't have planned this part. He took another slurp of beer through the straw that he had been provided with to avoid spoiling Justin's work, and surveyed the mask that was appearing in the mirror in front of him.

Outside, Helena and Angela had been putting on quite a show for the rest of the boys, who were now finding it all simply hilarious, and wondering why they didn't go to drag shows more often. Alcohol was indeed a transformative drug. Helena decided to see if she could take the boys just a little further:

"I have just heard from the backroom, that a little extra

help is going to be needed to turn Dougal into a real Stag Queen. Angela, my dear, please could you go and finish him off backstage?"

As Angela walked off stage to a boisterous round of applause and exhortations to check out Dougal's knickers, Helena put the next part of the plan into action:

"Now, whilst, we are waiting for our visions to reappear, let's not leave them having all the fun. Thanks to a little inside information from the brother of the groom – and yes, I do mean the little slut who's going quite spare watching you real men effortlessly resist his supposedly irresistible derrière – I have a number of questions to determine how well you know your friend. If you get the question wrong, you shall have to down one of our Felching Fudgepacker shots. Don't ask what's in them. Or, if you don't fancy a Fudgepacker inside you..." Helena paused and looked round at the slightly nervous group, "you may elect to take off an item of clothing. If you get the question right, then you pass this choice onto another member of the group – who shall comply, without question. Rules are rules, boys, and there will be no second chances. We'll go round the group. All clear, gentlemen?"

The group roared unsteadily.

As Dillon and Milo arrived with a couple of trays of shot glasses filled with an evil-looking concoction of green gloop, and the rugby boys cheered in anticipation of some more humiliation in store, Helena turned and smiled at Siegfried and Rubens. Not only was she bumping up the rugby boys' spend, but the prospect of them losing clothing meant that none of the regular crowd was going anywhere.

They were keeping Milo and Dillon busy with their orders. It was going to be a bumper Tuesday night at the till.

Dillon had one more surprise in store for his big brother. With Siegfried in tow, he went to the touch-up room, where Angela was applying the finishing touches to Dougal's make-up, ensuring there was as much physical contact as possible whilst she did it.

"Break time, ladies!"

Dillon shook the little plastic bag of white powder at them with a grin on his face.

"Oh, crap," moaned Dougal, "Sylvie is going to kill me for this."

"Relax. How is she going to find out? This might be the last night you can get away with it. Let's face it, if you are going to go out into the bar with that get-up on, alcohol won't be enough, darling brother."

Although Dougal knew full well that it wasn't big, clever, right, or recommended by the Surgeon General, the whole evening was turning into a litany of things Sylvie would disapprove of, and somehow that felt like a kick in itself. Dougal decided to go with the flow. He wasn't programmed to lead or resist, after all. That's what Sylvie most valued about him. And so it came to be that he followed Dillon and Siegfried in snorting a line of coke.

"Okay," croaked Dougal, "I'm ready for the dress, now."

The line had flattened his inhibitions. He watched Angela deliberately bend over to get his costume out of her bag, and marvelled at her arse. He wondered if taking her from behind would feel just like a real woman – so long as he was careful where he put his hands, of course.

The others had left the room by the time Dougal stood up and allowed Angela to ease off his trousers ready for the costume to be completed. Unfortunately for the groom, he had thought a little too much about how Angela's behind might feel and it showed. Angela needed no more encouragement, and quick as a flash the pants were off. Dougal found out that Angela's lips felt as good as any he could imagine.

Racing to serve all the customers, alone now with Milo, Rubens was wondering where the hell everyone had gone. As he watched Dillon and Siegfried return to the bar from the touch-up room, Siegfried rubbing his nose as he did, Rubens immediately realised what they had been up to. He felt an uncharacteristic twinge of irritation. Cocaine during working hours was one line Rubens would not cross, especially as the night had turned out to be busier than they thought, and given that they were short-handed to boot. Worse yet, it looked as if Siegfried, his supposed mentor, had taken one of his barmen to indulge with him, leaving Rubens powerless to discipline his own staff. And then there was the developing situation over by the stage to monitor.

As the questions came and went, and shots were drunk and barely kept down, the clothes had started to come off. Truth be known, the rugby boys were relaxed about being naked. In their state of inebriation they even quite enjoyed the attention they were commanding, even if it was from a bar full of gay men. A compliment was a compliment. It was good practice for that calendar. *When dressed I look like a barrel. You need to see me naked to capture the lines my muscles carve into my body, the firmness of my limbs, the definition I have strived to achieve. Look at it. Look at me. I exercise in front of a mirror for a reason. Love me now, for that reason.*

Sylvie van de Sloot, unable to resist checking on how her plan was going, walked into Outrageous Fortune just as Owen, the team's scrum-half, lost his last piece of clothing, jumped on stage and launched into his version of a butt-naked haka.

Dillon saw her, and flipped:

"Oh damn, damn, damn! Milo, vodka tonic and a JD diet for the blond guy here. Sorry, my colleague will be with you in a moment, I need to rescue a bride."

Dillon rushed out from behind the bar, imagining that his slight frame might block out at least some of the exhibition behind him, leaving Milo to deal with the bemused customer.

"Sylvie, *darling*, how are you?"

She wasn't at all happy and it showed:

"I said no strippers. I organised no strippers. So the bloody rugby club turns themselves into their own sodding strippers. And where the hell is Dougal?"

With the rest of the bar now giving the boys all the encouragement that they had no real need of, Outrageous Fortune was no place for a bride. Sylvie needed rescuing. Dougal in drag would lighten her mood. Dillon brightened up:

"Sylvie, come to the backroom. There's something I need to show you that will make you feel a lot better."

There is no nice way to express this. Dillon and Sylvie opened the door to the touch-up room just in time to see

Dougal shoot his load all over Angela's face.

It took Sylvie a moment to realise that the person in front of her, wearing a blond wig and tiara, far too much make-up, a sparkly bikini top and naked from the waist down was her husband-to-be. They stared at each other in silent disbelief. Angela got up and discreetly sidled off. Dougal was left on the far side of the room. He tucked a blond strand of hair behind his ear:

"Darling, it's not what you think! He's a man."

As soon as the words escaped Dougal's mouth, he knew they were not helping. This was a sticky situation. His relationship was either over, or his punishment would be on a scale of severity as yet unprobed. Sylvie glared at him, unable to say a word. She managed a strangled noise, and stormed out of the room, leaving her fiancé rooted to the spot.

After the initial shock of the situation, Dillon had been staring at his older brother's cock, fascinated, as if he were a doctor examining an exciting new disease:

"Yours is completely different to mine, you know. I've never seen you, well, you know, like this, before. It's completely different! I think you should probably go after her, by the way."

It was the order he had been waiting for. Dougal pulled his trousers up and ran after Sylvie, as fast as his trembling legs could carry him.

It took a lot for the clientele of a gay bar to be distracted from a naked rugby player performing on stage for them. And yet, a woman rushing through the bar shrieking "I'm going to kill the stupid fucker!" being chased by a crazed demon of a creature with the head and shoulders of a rather unfortunate bride and legs encased in crumpled chinos easily did it. As Sylvie made it out the door of the bar, and Rubens managed to stop Dougal from running into the street looking like a cross between Rick Santorum and Miss Piggy, the bar was suddenly quiet, with everyone listening to Dougal's sobs of how it was an accident, and how he loved Sylvie with all his heart.

Siegfried decided that the evening had gone far enough. The stag group needed to get dressed, pay the rest of the tab and leave before someone called the police. He told them this quietly but with authority born from years of handling closing times. *Better to quit now with a good night's takings under my belt*, he thought. He didn't want any trouble.

As Rubens started cashing up, he considered his discovery. His boss was almost certainly doing drugs at work, and doing them with Dillon. Rubens was worldly enough to know that this was not as uncommon as one might think. In the catering industry, there were widespread, ready-made excuses: long hours and fast pace, creating pressure that weak-willed people succumbed to. However, he hated the mood swings that drugs brought, and was less than thrilled to think that his mentor would be subject to them. *Can't I even pick a decent mentor*, he wondered, irritatedly? *What sort of a numbskull am I?*

There were only two of them left in the bar. Dillon and Milo had skedaddled. For a moment, Rubens wondered if he should speak to Siegfried about the matter, before immediately realising that this was a very bad idea.

Siegfried would undoubtedly still be under the influence.

And besides, there was potentially an even bigger problem. Considering how many people there had been in the bar, the printout from the till seemed distinctly low. Rubens was hoping that somehow, some of the money had been placed in the till without a receipt, but as he finished the cashing up, he found that unsurprisingly it matched to within a couple of pounds.

Something was definitely up. He looked up, and called over to his boss:

"Siegfried, I think we've got a problem. The takings are, I'd say, at least a few hundred pounds down on where we should have been with the business we did tonight. I know you have had some suspicions before. Tonight, we are too far down for there to be any doubt. It looks like somebody has been taking drinks money and not ringing it into the till. With all the confusion we had with the group tonight, it would have been fairly easy to do. I doubt anyone was insisting on a receipt."

Siegfried's eyes narrowed. No one likes having a thief on the staff. Siegfried took pride in being in control of all aspects of his business, especially the money.

He spoke decisively:

"We need to deal with it. I've been asking Dillon to keep an eye on that Serb you hired. Milo may make a very good adult performer, Rubens, but I thought it was a risk when you took him on. I wanted to let you have some responsibility, but you must also learn from your mistakes. As it happens, Dillon told me earlier tonight that he suspected that Milo was not ringing up all the drinks.

It's a good job that he is still on his trial period. I'm afraid we'll have to let him go, Rubens, and until then watch him like a hawk. But we can't only blame the staff, Rubens. You should have spotted this sooner."

Siegfried's look brooked no challenge. Rubens felt chastened. It was an uncomfortable situation. Nothing indicated that Milo was the thief. Rubens found him very reliable and he had made himself indispensable. But what did Rubens, or for that matter anyone, really know about him? *Someone* was almost certainly stealing, and there had only been the four of them working that night. Should he, Rubens, have been keeping better watch on Milo? Firing him was going to be unpleasant. Milo was sharp. He would ask what was up. Rubens didn't know what he was going to say to him. He had so much to learn about this job.

Although Siegfried could be harsh at times, Rubens thanked his lucky stars that he had Siegfried Allcock there to guide him through the tricky waters of management.

"Order, order," said Ben.

Pam looked over at him:

"Why on earth are you saying that?"

"I don't know," said Ben mildly, "it just seems conducive to everyone getting their backsides on chairs and their thinking caps on."

"Good point, well made, then," said Pam, taking her coffee firmly in hand, and sneaking a biscuit onto her saucer.

"We should up our game, people," she said, munching

pensively. "Do you know that at some law firms they offer these fuckers wrapped individually in glass jars?"

"People who offer individually wrapped biscuits in glass jars shouldn't do law," said Ben firmly. "They should go and open a cupcake shop. That kind of nonsense softens people's brains, and expands their seats. It's Professional Obesity Britain."

Ten people were standing around slightly awkwardly. Chairs eventually scraped back and people sat down gingerly, as if they might need to run off at any moment. Ben waited until they were settled.

"Well," he said, smiling. "This is it. The first meeting of the LGBT group at Beaux, Aspen, Dickerhint. Welcome all. This is an exploratory meeting. I remain slightly worried about the concept of groups like these. But I've been persuaded by Pam and others. Even though my first thought was that I was singling myself and others out, and thus facilitating further discrimination, on balance, I've come to the view that there is a purpose to standing up as a group, and making sure that the ton of prejudice levelled at prospective group members the world over is not allowed to seep into office carpets any more than it already does."

Lynne broke in:

"I think it's great! I'm as excited as a blind lesbian in a fish shop."

"Lynne," said Pam, patiently, "you can't say that in an LGBT meeting."

"Why not," said Lynne, "I'm reclaiming the words fish and shop."

"Again?" asked Ben mildly.

Pam looked exasperated:

"But, Lynne, you're just playing into the hands of a world that… oh, never mind. Women and fish. Just think about it. It's a stupid thing to say. There are many old and ignorant jokes being perpetuated right there. Women don't smell of fish."

Ben slapped his papers down on the table:

"Ladies, I am pretty sure that the aromatic quality of lady parts was not on the agenda for this LGBT meeting. Can we focus on what we need to discuss?"

"Yes," said Cornisha gently. "If this were to be the quality of discourse why don't we all just shoot ourselves, and save others the pain of doing it for us?"

Pam agreed:

"Yes, let's move on. I think we need to set some targets. What are we looking to achieve?"

Ben looked down at his notes:

"I think we want to encourage people to be open and comfortable with their sexuality in the workplace, and to feel wholly accepted by others there. We look to achieve change. We ought to deny prejudice based on sexual orientation a place at any table. How do we achieve that? We'll need to think about it. I'm for small but focused steps. Action, rather than discourse, indeed. My suggestion is that we do not seek to change the world overnight. We provide a forum for people to exchange views. This group should be a source of support and advice. I'd also like to target others within the firm and break down common misconceptions about LGBT."

"For some of the partners in this firm, that's exactly what we all are: living misconceptions. Are we sure we're not just signing up to early redundancy at the first available opportunity?"

"I dare say that's a risk. But together we are stronger. We might otherwise find ourselves on exactly that same list, with less recourse than we might have otherwise."

"Can we also make sure we have the best parties in the firm? Nothing breaks down misconceptions quicker than a fine night out."

"I think there is everything to be said for that approach. But let's also think on how we can network across organisations. Gay and proud – not just here, but giving clients who happen to be gay a proper service."

"Ben, you're a naughty boy."

Ben sighed:

"Why don't we just call the minutes of meeting *exhausted innuendos*? It would be quicker that way."

Pam clapped her hands:

"Action points. Let's meet monthly to start. I'll start thinking about a corporate networking LGBT party. We can play up to some clichés – I don't know, have some pink drinks, maybe? Have a giant pink pound sign hanging in the room? Hang some pictures of famous gay people around the room to inspire us? Have a well-known guest say a few words?"

"All that might be good," agreed Ben. "Let's also get group membership up. Strength in numbers, people. Strength in numbers. I'll try to write up some sort of mission statement."

"I'll contact other groups in other firms," offered Lynne.

"Fine. Just go easy on the fishy analogies."

"I'll be the *sole* of discretion."

Hartmut Glick thrust his key into the heavy front door and clumped through into the shelter of his entrance hall. His face was a picture of a grumble.

What a day. He was annoyingly damp. He felt as if he might start to steam gently. The rain had not been fulsome enough to warrant fumbling for his umbrella, but it was sufficiently persistent to splatter his fine leather coat.

Schweinhund! What more did the skies have in store for him?

"Caroline, my lady, ich bin da."

The house was surprisingly quiet.

"Ha," Hartmut continued aloud, "have you gagged the twins? I'm still not convinced that it's a sound part of their routine. But if the cap fits…"

There was music drifting in from the den.

"Was ist das?" he muttered.

He took his coat off and adjusted his collar. He caught a glimpse of himself in a gothic angled mirror and smoothed his hair. No doubt Caroline was in need of punishment. She had probably deliberately stopped the direct debit payment of the council tax again.

Hartmut moved up the stairs. There were lights flickering through the door, ajar.

He opened the door and caught his breath. The den was glittering with what seemed like a thousand candles. Caroline lay in the corner on the couch, clad in a diaphanous gown, her hair languid about her shoulders.

She moved upright as she saw him, putting her finger to her lips:

"Hartmut, my love."

"The children?"

"They are with my mother. They've been rather naughty today, so they deserve it."

Hartmut gestured at the room:

"What is this all about?"

"Ich habe ein Frage."

"*Eine* Frage. Please. We have been through this. It corresponds with the noun…"

"Hartmut. Everything is so good that I should like to take a chance on wrecking it. I know you don't like surprises, so surely I shall pay for this dearly. But, my love, will you marry me?"

She held out an open box. In its velvety depths nestled a fabulous bejewelled cock ring. Hartmut was entranced. It glittered with a large number of exquisite, bold gems, sparking off the light.

Hartmut loved beautiful things:

"Meine Liebchen."

He took the box and picked up the jewellery. It was perfect. It stirred him.

Caroline came over to him:

"It may feel sudden. But I've never been so sure of anything in my life."

Hartmut smiled:

"As if you had not been punished enough by two small children."

He looked down and paused, before smiling again:

"Warum nicht? My answer is yes. I will marry you, Caroline Napier Jones. For pain, for pleasure, forever."

"Wait a minute," said Caroline. "It cannot be a proposal until someone gets on their knees."

She sank down like a drowning mermaid.

Hartmut looked at the cock ring again, before his face hardened into its usual granite appearance.

It was all pretty wunderbar.

Kelly was conscious that everything about her feelings for Morten was too much, too soon, too fast and too intense. She also knew that, when Cornisha and Monique visited, there would be nothing but wise advice and sensible suggestions about making sure of this, and being careful about that. None of that cut any ice. None of that mattered. Whenever she saw Morten's tall figure striding towards her, she felt an urgency that simply took precedence over other considerations.

She thought about it a good deal. The collective ability of others to see what was best, what was good for you, and to recommend an appropriate course of action was well established. It also felt as stifling as a Mexican sauna. Obviously, this was all wrong. In the abstract, it seemed clear enough that having more than one lover would lead to emotional turmoil. But having Morten and Ben was necessary. She loved Ben. She wanted Morten. Kelly could not bring herself to care about much else.

Every day a person walks past hundreds – thousands –

of people. As they wander by, they all seem nice enough. Some were very attractive. Others, less so. They were at different stages of life, and swung in the arms of different moods. Life was sociable in urban societies. But how rare were those people who made you catch your breath. Where were the people that caught at the pit of your stomach with strange, urgent, ruthless claws, who twisted your thoughts and desires with the precision of a mathematical equation, whilst throwing reason to the floor like a bone licked clean after a carnivore's feast?

It's easy to condemn and comment, thought Kelly. *But my body wants him. Only I know my body, and its inclinations. My peculiarities are my own.*

Morten made her dream. She woke each morning in the arms of lascivious thoughts, closing her eyes to capture some of the last feelings of satisfaction as she drew him close to her in her mind. Dreams could not be enough. The yearning was unfulfilled. Yet fulfilment was close at hand. It seemed madness to deny it. *How many people will I walk by? How many people will make me feel this way – five? Ten? Twenty? I may not meet many who do*, thought Kelly. *I am fussy. I am strong. I dominate others. Morten matches me punch for punch. I want him.*

When he asked her over for dinner, she said yes.

How our intentions reveal themselves in our actions, thought Kelly, as she prepared every inch of herself. She chose simple, sexy clothes. In the local Nicolas, she picked chilled champagne and a bottle of intoxicating red wine. The time for value sparkling wine had passed. *If I indulge, I will do so in style*, she thought.

She refused to think in terms of sin. It was not for nothing that "sin" meant "without", was Kelly's view. By all means deprive yourselves of everything that life has to offer. Please don't welcome me into your austere, untouched, unloved existences. I want to feel Morten. I'm not looking for anyone's approval or understanding. The shop assistant smiled at her as she paused over the burgundies. He nodded with approval as he packed her purchases. She added a packet of nuts, and paid with a large note.

Morten lived in a quiet Paris street. Cars and motorbikes were parked in orderly lines. The heavy wooden doors to the building swung open easily and she ascended the winding staircase to the second floor.

He opened the door. He was so perfect that she felt like kneeling there and then and ripping his trousers off. *Best to shut the door first*, she thought, as she came in. The door closed and she kissed him. The kiss lingered and grew passionate. She searched his mouth, questioning, yet absolutely certain of what she was saying. His hands found her breasts and her body.

They parted, slightly breathless.

"Hello," said Morten.

"It's a lovely place," said Kelly, moving into the living room. She looked out of the window, at the twinkling Parisian lights. The rooftops looked exactly as they did in the Aristocats. Morten was kissing her neck and slipping his hands under her top. She raised her arms and stoked his neck and hair, arching against him.

"Would you like a drink?"

"Mmmmm."

She led him into the bedroom. It was pristine. She allowed the ghost of a smile to play around her face as she took in the Scandinavian feel – minimal but clean-lined furniture, and a crisp, beautiful bed. The urgency returned, unexpectedly violently. She slipped off her shoes and pulled Morten onto the bed.

She had not seen him naked before. His torso was lean and long. She traced every contour. His legs were stronger than his frame suggested. She touched his thighs, and felt around his body to his toned buttocks. He was stunning. His eyes were closed, as she took him in her mouth and sucked his beautiful cock. It was the most incredible turn-on. Kelly wished she could have felt this way when the time for the smear test came around. Wait. Focus. The most incongruous thoughts pop into your head at the wrong time.

"Have you got a condom handy? Mine are in my bag," she said softly.

Morten smiled at her and reached towards the side table. Kelly expertly dressed him, and then kissed him hard. He took control of her and stroked her. She felt her mind dissolve. It was the most blissful feeling of escape. He was now moving inside her. Everything vanished. It was all about here, and now, and the release, the welcome release of climax.

Only half an hour had passed since Kelly rang the doorbell.

They lay there, in a warm glow. Morten drew her to him, and played with her hair:

"Thank you," he finally said. "That was pretty much as good as it gets."

She laughed:

"Boy, I needed that."

"It had crossed my mind too," he said. "For me," he added, hastily.

"What's for supper?" asked Kelly.

7

Bolognesi and Battersea

"And so for once it was *me* marvelling at Rubens' naked flesh as I reached orgasm!"

Ben appreciated as much as the next person the coincidence of Rubens Ribeiro having had sex under a painting by Peter Paul Rubens. Ben was also amused at the casual way in which the Brazilian acknowledged that men *marvelled* at his body. Obviously, this was true. They did. Indeed, Ben had marvelled himself at Rubens' all and everything, all those months – or maybe years ago – when they had been together.

Ben knew by now that this grade of admiration was something that was earned through mindless toiling in the gym. Going to the gym as intensively as was needed to achieve the requisite appearance was a worthy yet incredibly dull task. It was only made bearable by repeatedly seeking out small results in the omnipresent mirrors, with the gift of music to drown out the conversations of the gym bores. Then there was also the possibility of seeing something sexy in the locker room afterwards.

Ben tried sometimes to speak of himself with unerring

confidence, just to see if he could imitate the neutral, natural way that Rubens did it. It never quite worked out. When Ben tried to sound self-confident, he wanted to slap himself as soon as the words were out. Mind you, it could be something to do with the fact that being something of a master in Excel spreadsheets was not the sexiest thing to sound proud of.

Ben smiled at Rubens:

"So, are we going to this reception so that you can further your appreciation of Old Master techniques? Or is it Master Tarquin's techniques that you're looking to further explore?"

"Both, actually, Ben. I'm pleased about this. He's cute. I've spent my time in London at work, chasing men, dancing, having sex, partying with friends. I've never bothered to wonder what lies behind the walls of galleries and museums – except of course for the famous ones that you have to visit once, when friends are over and insist on going. I love my life. But, you know, when I was with Tarquin, surrounded by all those old paintings, I felt something, Ben, and it wasn't just the usual excitement at the prospect of sex. I think I am changing. I'm going to broaden my horizons. Just think, we're going to go to a cocktail party, where I am a proper guest looking at a collection of paintings. I'm not the topless waiter who has to make small talk to self-important queens, all getting more deluded about their chances, the drunker they get. I might be able to experience the other side of what London can offer. A cultured guy like Tarquin can maybe help me get there."

Rubens paused. He really meant this. It could be a new phase in his life. He might be shedding his skin. Perhaps fortunately for the preservation of his epidermis, he noticed a tall, dark shadow which managed to look both threatening and reassuring in the doorway of a boutique on the other side of the road:

"Oh *bija*, look at that security guard in there. Meu Deus, do I have time to go and get searched by him? Full cavity, you say, sir? Yes, please!"

Ben silently thanked the stars that although Rubens may consider that he were changing, he would in fact never change, and that was a most joyous and natural thing.

They were heading towards the Bolognesi Art Gallery in Old Bond Street where Tarquin Henderson-Smythe was hosting an event. Fine art galleries competed with designer boutiques to strip the world's über-wealthy of their spare millions. In this part of London, even the impeccably dressed and handsome security guards looked as if they could buy and sell the average Briton ten times over. Not that the average Briton often made it there. Ben thought that Mayfair had virtually given up being part of the United Kingdom. It had seceded and become part of the Plutocratic Republic of Everywhere, along with Davos, seven star hotels and all yachts over a certain size. It was a sea of Arabs, Russians, and Chinese, stepping out of their Bentleys and Ferraris to pick up diamond-encrusted trinkets. The BRICs may be reshaping the world, but it was the ARC of prosperity which was keeping Mayfair afloat. The nation of shopkeepers had lost an empire. Now it was their turn to bow and scrape to rich and powerful foreigners in search of assets to strip and locals to command.

Although, Ben consoled himself, to be fair, none of them could probably draft a sale and purchase agreement for toffee. There was still a little more time before the bowing and scraping became overly universal.

Without Rubens, Ben would have completely missed the entrance to Bolognesi's. An unmarked black door with a discreet brass nameplate and bell to its side contrasted with the screaming opulence of the jeweller to its left, and the ropes outside the boutique to the right, ready to corral a queue of impatient tourists, eager to get their hands on a new range of limited edition handmade bags.

Rubens gave their names through the intercom, and they were duly buzzed in. The heavy door swung open. It revealed a small antechamber with a glass door and a darkened corridor beyond. Their shoes clicked satisfyingly on the marble floor. Ancient drawings adorned the walls. They reached the reception desk where an attractive red-haired woman gave them a welcoming smile and informed them that drinks were to be partaken of up the stairs, on the first floor.

As they padded up the carpeted stairs which creaked authentically at every step, Rubens turned to Ben with an earnest look.

"This is so much better than the usual guest lists I get on. So chic!"

Rubens had a point. He was without a doubt a hallowed member of the desirable subset of gay London's A List. He was usually called by promoters and asked whether he wanted *guest list*. But, all in all, once you arrived as a supposed VIP at a London club, the experience was often rather underwhelming. First of all, you usually had to queue. This was because, more often than not, there were so many people on the guest list that they could have quite happily held a party all on their own. Then, you had to work out which of the queues to join. Any indications or use of traditional directional indicators such as *signs* would of course make it too easy for amateurs.

Once safely ensconced in the correct queue with the various other VIPs and hangers-on, it was a nervy wait watching the *paying* queue move more quickly. This had a faint logic to it. After all, they paid the highest prices, and the promoters had not yet stripped them of their money. By the same token, at least the VIPs could feel superior to the *advance purchase* queue whose members were neither important nor so profitable, and most significantly had already sent their cash to clubland via the Internet.

When you finally got out of the horizontal rain, the flustered door whore would ask you three times whose list you were on, and then still wouldn't be able to find your name on the handwritten list stuck to his clipboard, despite the fact there were only a dozen names on it. Lastly came the final humiliation, namely the discovery that guest list only meant a *reduced* entry price, *another* queue for the coat check, and four pounds more to leave a coat and a bag.

The Bolognesi gallery would never make guests wait. The boys swished through the double doors into a delightful high-ceilinged room, where a genteel crowd was sipping champagne, nibbling on canapés and occasionally looking up from their conversations to gaze at a work, like cows in a field watching a train go by. Ben was reminded of a lawyer's event, albeit with slightly more expensive art on the walls, and slightly more expensive accents in the air. An expensive accent was the first to greet them. Tarquin stepped towards them with a warm smile:

"Rubens, I am so glad you could make it. And this must be your friend, Ben. Welcome to Bolognesi. Allow me to introduce you both to a dear family friend. This is Eleanor Napier Jones."

Ben was surprised to see Eleanor, otherwise known to him as the lady with the firm thighs that he had rescued from a sling a few weeks earlier. Eleanor, by contrast, was the very model of decorum. She greeted the men with a slight inclination of her head and the merest hint of a smile.

"Rubens, delighted to meet you. Ben, charmed to see you again. I trust you have been keeping well and that my son-in-law is not working you too hard. What a small world, Tarquin. Ben works with Hartmut – who, as you may remember, is my daughter's fiancé."

Tarquin noted Ben's confusion. It seemed to be tinged with embarrassment, but Tarquin was far too polished to pry. Rubens was struck by Eleanor and thought what a good thing it had been to bring Ben rather than one of his less presentable friends.

"An honour to meet you, Mrs Napier Jones." His tone struck the right balance between friendly familiarity and respect for a lady who obviously merited it. Or so he hoped.

"So are you in the art world as well, Rubens?"

Tarquin needed all his poise not to spill his Moët.

He should intervene before Rubens said something inappropriate. Not that Tarquin's sexuality was necessarily a secret – but he liked his privacy, and considered it a personal matter – not something he wished to broadcast.

He continued the introductions:

"Rubens is the manager of a marvellous new cocktail bar in the West End, Eleanor. One could say that their concoctions are works of art themselves, perhaps with a more modern twist than the offerings we have here at Bolognesi. In fact we do have certain clients in common, which is how we came to know each other."

One of the wonderful things about Eleanor Napier Jones was that people generally assumed that her exceedingly proper exterior meant that she was incapable of conceiving of anything unseemly. But as it happened, Eleanor could generally detect a half truth from the next room, and her exposure to the earthier side of human nature was quite extensive. Tarquin had been a little too eager to explain how logical it was that he knew Rubens. This indicated to Eleanor that there was an altogether more primal logic at work. Attractive young men who clearly enjoyed each other's company were often just friends – where there were women in tow. Yet – there never *were*, with Tarquin. She had given up any lingering hopes of Tarquin making a move on Caroline some time ago. The chemistry between Tarquin and Rubens hinted at something more. No, those two were definitely buggering each other. She smiled sweetly, graciously accepted Tarquin's mendacity, and surveyed Ben.

He must be good with documents. Eleanor would

gladly have put a frame around him and hung him on the wall with the other beautiful objects, but he seemed rather awkward for an advocate. Maybe he was embarrassed due to the circumstances of their meeting at the Glickhaus. Goodness knows why. It was she who had been trussed up like a Christmas goose. At that moment, Ben looked over and met her eyes. His awkwardness appeared to vanish. He looked as if he were unable *not* to look. *Oh, my*. Eleanor almost recoiled under the strength of Ben's gaze, before he looked away. Heavens. He was more difficult to categorise, that one.

It reminded Eleanor of how Piers used to behave around her elder sister, Diana. *No, surely not!* Poor Piers had seemed awestruck by Diana. Although used to commanding respect wherever she went, Eleanor dearly hoped she did not have quite that effect on young men. It would be a little unseemly, somehow. Yet, there seemed more than awe in that look. Something quite at odds with the fact of his turning up with Tarquin's lovely new bit of exotica. Who was who's beau? All most queer.

Eleanor's musings on Ben were interrupted by a loud and shiny irruption:

"Oh there you are, dear. Oh, and Rubens too – well, well, well. I wouldn't have expected to see you here, dear. Are you staff tonight?"

Wesley Nest grinned at the group, preening like an over-adorned seal. He considered this was the perfect conversational gambit. Tarquin winced. Eleanor pretended not to hear or even see the unwelcome intruder. Ben thought *Twat*.

Rubens brushed off the remark. He knew Wesley didn't mean any harm by it. He knew exactly how to handle the Wesley Nests of this world.

"Wesley, how lovely to see you! Actually, I am not working today. Do you know, this must be the first time when I am not being paid to be in your company."

Eleanor pricked up her ears. Rubens delivered this barb with effortless charm and a warm smile. There was obviously more to this piece of exotica than met the eye.

Wesley simpered:

"I'm not sure I like that, Rubens. I've only got Tarquin to boss around then. Now, that reminds me, we are having a little soirée to celebrate the Scoreggio. How much would it cost to get you to come and serve cocktails?" Wesley turned to Ben and added: "Maybe you could bring this one to help. Do you make drinks, dear?"

Rubens was enjoying putting Wesley in his place, unlikely as the jeweller was to ever remain there for long:

"Oh, I don't think you could afford him, Wesley. Ben is an important lawyer. Be careful what you say, or he might sue. And where are your manners? You haven't even greeted Mrs Napier Jones."

Wesley directed a look of asinine joviality at Eleanor. His business side immediately kicked in. Would she buy his jewellery? She looked somewhat haughty. And a little too understated for his taste. But it was always worth a try. Nothing ventured, nothing gained.

"Hello, dear, pleased to meet you. I'm Wesley. I'm a bit of a naughty boy, and I make handcrafted jewellery. The boys should bring you along to my party in Leatherhead."

Eleanor smiled graciously at Wesley. She had already had an ample sufficiency of the man's company, and had no desire to see his handcrafted jewellery.

After wondering if there really was a place called Leatherhead, Ben decided that it was time to escape. He would go and look at the Bolognesi offerings. It was a gallery after all. However, just as he was about to make his excuses, he noticed a familiar shape just behind Wesley.

"Mamma?"

What the…?

Ben's mother was standing less than six feet away from him, accompanied by a dark-haired, fashionably-dressed man, little older than Ben himself.

Claudia Barlettano turned round like a shot at the unexpected word. A look of joy flashed across her face at seeing her beloved son. She then realised she was holding the hand of a man that her son had no knowledge of. The hand quietly freed itself. A look of panic flashed across her face. *Che figura di merda!* Drawing on all her experience of ignoring inconvenient truths in Milan, she conjured up her look of joy again, and rushed over to her son. It was her Benedetto, after all!

"Figlio mio! Give your mamma a kiss!"

The group looked on questioningly as Ben hugged the well-dressed woman he had just called "mother". Rubens alone had already been surprised once before by the unexpected arrival of Claudia. He knew just what to say:

"Mrs Barlettano, how lovely to see you again! And what a gorgeous outfit you are wearing!"

"Oh, Rubens, hello again! Thank you, the pleasure

is mine. Ben, I am so glad you are still friends with this beautiful man. How is the football going?"

Eleanor noticed the look of complicity that flashed between Rubens and Ben. There was obviously something Ben's mother didn't know about. More buggering probably. Eleanor appreciated the elegance of Claudia, both in her impeccable dress, the understated handbag which looked strangely familiar, and the warmth with which she was greeting the group. Such a welcome contrast to that buffoon from the sticks. She seemed refreshingly refined for a European.

"So, mamma, what in the name of tortellini are you doing here in London? When exactly were you going to tell me that you were in town?"

Claudia had had a few moments to prepare for the inevitable question. She gave Ben her best mothering smile and gestured towards the man who had been standing unobtrusively behind her:

"Ben. I want to introduce you to someone that I have recently met. Piers, please come and meet my son."

Before Ben could process the fact that the man his mother had been standing next to had been described as *someone she had just met*, with all the coyness of naïve hopes and dreams captured by this description, a champagne flute crashed to the floor and shattered into shards on the unforgiving wooden surface.

Piers! Eleanor froze like a bag of sausage rolls from Iceland as she heard Claudia pronounce the name and simultaneously recognised her nephew. So this meant that *this* Claudia was the Italian slattern that her beloved

Piers had met in Milan. Eleanor's previous admiration for Claudia evaporated as quickly as the fawning words of a sports commentator upon discovering a champion athlete had taken drugs, to be replaced by condemnation of the most self-righteous kind. *The woman was old enough to be his mother!*

"Auntie Eleanor! What a lovely surprise. Why, Tarkers didn't tell me you were going to be here." Although Piers wasn't expecting his aunt to react too well to his new love, he also knew that Eleanor was not the type of woman to cause a scene, no matter how irritated she was. Victorian values could still be surprisingly useful in modern British society.

"Mamma? Auntie Eleanor? Anyone else got a family member here? Ooh, is that second cousin Maud over by the vol-au-vents? Oh, hello dear." Wesley eyed up the waiter who had come over to clear away the evidence of Eleanor's uncharacteristic slip, his eyes resting longer than decorum counselled on the backside of the man's trousers. "Where did you hire this one, Tarquin? Would he work bare-chested at my soirée if I paid him extra?"

Seeing Ben's look of utter disbelief, and noting the freezing disapproval fit to restore the Greenland ice sheet emanating from Eleanor, Tarquin was quite glad of Wesley filling the stony silence with one of his *funnies*. The waiter with the matador-tight trousers efficiently swept away the glass, coolly ignored Wesley, and yet somehow ensured that his behind stuck out to its full advantage until the job was complete.

Not having been in Britain in the 1980s, Rubens was

wondering what a vol-au-vent was. His instinct told him that keeping quiet was a far better move than either asking what one was or – worse – trying to mediate in other, more delicate matters. Mediation depended always on the consent of the parties. Tarquin glared at Piers, silently urging him to do something. An *atmosphere* was not what he wanted when he was supposed to be charming clients.

Piers deliberately took Claudia's hand as he faced his aunt and his lover's son.

"Ben, I am delighted to meet you. Your mother and I met recently in Milan. She has told me so much about you that I rather feel that I already know you. My name is Piers Minister. I hope we'll have a chance to meet properly, rather than by surprise. Auntie Eleanor, I have been dying to introduce you to Claudia. She is the woman who has put a smile back on my face. She brings warmth to the plastic life of a fashion designer. I am looking forward to you two becoming firm friends."

It was a valiant effort. However, Ben could not get over seeing his mother with a man his own age. How the hell would she feel if he presented Eleanor Napier Jones as his new amour? Or Rubens, for that matter? Holy crap! The things he had put himself through to keep Claudia blissfully unaware of his own sexual exaggerations! He may as well have bummed the waiter clearing up the glass from the floor. How could she do this to him?

Eleanor's composed exterior was in danger of suffering the same fate as the unfortunate flute. She had had a bad feeling as soon as she had heard of Piers' latest affair. The decision to disapprove had long been taken and duly recorded – but to see Piers with such a creature... well, rather like the orange tint to Claudia's complexion, it was simply *beyond* the pale. And this elderly harlot was carrying one of Piers' bags. She was besmirching the very name of Napier. *How dare she carry my namesake bag!*

Unlike Rubens, Wesley Nest rarely thought silence to be the best policy, especially when there was an embarrassing situation to exploit.

"Oh, I adore Milan. Women there really know how to wear jewellery, and lots of it too. I'm thinking of opening up an outlet there, actually. Maybe I could interest you in one of my handcrafted necklaces or bracelets, Claudia? You're going to need something special for the wedding after all."

The *w* word almost caused Ben's champagne glass to suffer the same fate as Eleanor's. Piers' aunt, however, was not one to be caught out twice. Her resurgent sense of decorum could wield outrage like an exquisite scalpel, and there was to be only one victim. She forced out her haughtiest smile:

"What a splendid thought. Claudia, you really should visit Wesley's showroom down in Leatherhead. Or visit him at home. He has a marvellous pad."

Wesley nodded enthusiastically:

"Yes, I most certainly do. Bluebell End, in Leatherhead."

Eleanor ignored Wesley:

"I am certain you would feel at home. Some people turn up their noses at provincial fashion, but I'm sure you would be far more comfortable there, my dear, rather than in one of the London boutiques. They can be so challenging when one is a beginner. I mean, you wouldn't want to look like one of those dreadful nouveau riche creatures who merely judge an item's merit on its price tag, and on how shiny it is."

"Cara Eleanor, how kind and thoughtful you are. Do you know, Piers had warned me that you could be a bit of a... Ben, how do you say *stronza* in English? Oh never mind, let's just say that a poor woman like me who rarely gets out of Fifth Avenue or Via Montenapoleone is so grateful to receive advice from one who has obviously so many, many years of experience."

Eleanor did not need to see the look of alarm cross Piers' face when Claudia uttered the word *stronza* to know it was not a compliment. She expected vulgarity from one of that woman's ilk. It merely confirmed her in her opinions. She smiled victoriously:

"What a delightful language Italian is. I'm sure that if I had the time to spend in your captivating company, I would learn all manner of choice phrases. Sadly, however, enthralling as the conversation is, some of us are here to enjoy the exhibition. Tarquin, it's time you and I were elsewhere."

"Eleanor, we will have plenty of time to get to know each other now that Piers and I are together." Claudia pulled Piers close: "But now we must leave and look for *shiny* things to buy. Ben, I will call you. And please be respectful to your great aunt Eleanor. Oh, that makes you so sound *so old, cara*."

Great Aunt Eleanor! How could his mother do that to him? Jeez, he had even been thinking about her surprisingly firm thighs! Ben was in shock. And that Piers seemed a real creep. He had to be. There could be no truth in that relationship!

Piers' fashion industry-trained gaydar had spiked as soon as he had seen Ben and Rubens together. Wasn't Claudia's son supposed to be seeing a beautiful American girl? Just as Eleanor had had her suspicions, Piers Minister would have bet his bottom that Ben was more than just friends with Rubens.

Although as surprised by Claudia's announcement as everyone else, Rubens had seen far too much in life to be phased by an unexpected relationship. Why judge? It would be difficult for Ben, but he should learn to just relax and accept it. Wesley had been funny. The champagne was nice. And Tarquin looked adorable, with that hot flush on his cheeks.

Wesley meanwhile was determined to get as many of this crowd as possible down to his soirée. Claudia would buy some of his handcrafted jewellery. He was almost certain of it. She'd probably root out the nice pieces amongst the slightly less successful attempts at adornment. He would make sure Tarquin dragged them all down. He must. Wesley's commissions had bought half of Tarquin's wardrobe. To Leatherhead, and beyond!

Tarquin had feared the worst when the glass had smashed. At the end of the evening he had recovered. Interest had been high, and sales had actually been rather good. That was, after all, the principal reason for mingling with these devilishly irritating egos, as they wandered round his beloved gallery getting their Canalettos mixed up with their Campagnolas.

The women parted with decorous, venomous smiles. They were now determined to detest each other, but they both worshipped at the altar of propriety. A gallery in Bond Street was not a font to be sullied. There would be other occasions. With a start that momentarily fractured her frozen smile, Eleanor realised that the next occasion would probably be her own daughter's wedding.

Exercise was a godsend when it came to overpowering unwelcome trains of thought. An express train had steamed into Ben's station when his mother had announced her relationship with that Piers Minister. Yet, with Ben's legs pumping like pistons and hot blood coursing through his veins as he flew towards Vauxhall, exercise came and whipped the offending course of considerations out of him, like a kind and considerate angel.

When Ben first arrived in London, he had thought cyclists were mad. They were idiots who belted through red lights, thinking their helmets would somehow protect them from a truck, and inconsiderate oafs who thought dodging pedestrians on zebra crossings was acceptable, because bicycles were emissions-free. However, after a while negotiating London transport with all its points failures, staffing issues, overrunning engineering works, snarled up traffic and noisy teenagers eating fast food on the seats next to, in front of, and behind him, Ben had decided to sup with the devil. He invested in a bike himself.

With all the zeal of a convert, Ben only ever seemed to use his Oyster card on his way to an airport these days.

Every journey seemed quicker and more pleasant by bike. His Orwell-inspired motto was now: *two wheels good, four wheels bad*. Ben had considered purchasing a motorbike, which would have been fast and made him feel extremely cool, but, unlike a bicycle, it couldn't help him stay in shape, a perennial concern of his. A motorbike was also surprisingly costly, unless one went for those little scooter things which Ben thought looked silly when one was six foot four tall. So the motorbike was rejected. Ben was lean, mean and green.

This Saturday morning, Ben was particularly glad of his bicycle. Like almost all of South London, Battersea still didn't have the Tube. North London had lines going out to Zone 9, which Ben had struggled to believe actually existed – until, that is, he had needed to go to Amersham for a meeting one day. South London barely got out of Zone 2, and even then the line that made it all the way to Morden was named the Northern Line, as if to underline the fact that it was there solely to take those poor unfortunates to a better place above the River Thames.

As he cycled past a few scrubby bushes some enterprising marketing folk had named Embassy Gardens, he thought about how long it would take for his compatriots decamping from Mayfair to finally revamp the area. Would other countries follow the US in relocating their consular staff down here? Maybe Nine Elms would become Nine Elmbassies. Vauxhall was awfully convenient for all those gay diplomats. There was even the promise of a Northern Line extension going all the way to Battersea Power Station. Endless little boxes with sideways-on views of the Thames, with a few luxury penthouses for non-doms, were sprouting up all along the south bank, west of Vauxhall Bridge.

Idle musing and furious pedalling had carried Ben to the Rosery Gate of Battersea Park where he crossed another triumph of marketing, one of London's Cycle Superhighways. Ben liked the idea, but painting blue stripes down the side of busy roads which then disappeared at difficult junctions didn't quite seem like the M1 for cyclists to him.

The sight of the tree-lined lake brushed away annoyance with inadequate cycle lanes. It almost made Ben forget that he was in the centre of London. Almost. There were some very serious-looking guys working out and grunting in the open-air gym outside the athletics track, and a number of very distracting lycra-clad young women jogging and bouncing their way around the park's perimeter. As he arrived at the rather bizarre Peace Pagoda overlooking the Thames, the military fitness class, mustering its slightly overweight bankers and slim PR consultants, barked its way into his musings on the Hobbiton-esque English countryside. Not content with competing for the best jobs, best schools, parking places, spouses, nannies and interior decorators, Saturday mornings saw Londoners competing against themselves, battling the bulge, and determined to wheedle some praise out of Steve who had actually served in Afghanistan.

Ben now had a regular Saturday morning jogging appointment with Bertha Cheung and Amber Bluett from work.

Amber Bluett.

Ben could not believe he was seeing her socially. Voluntarily. When he had first found out that Amber was to be installed as one of his new Human Resources managers at work, he had dropped a cup of coffee. The keyboard succumbed, but Ben survived to wonder about it all another day. The memory of what Amber had tried to do to Kelly Danvers a couple of years earlier still made him shiver. And yet prison seemed to have transformed the woman. Not only had she dropped several pounds, but she was all sweetness and light at work. She couldn't do enough to help.

Amber had become firm friends with Bertha, an unquestionable belle of Beaux, Aspen, Dickerhint. Although Ben did not stray from Kelly, Bertha tested his resolve to the limit. Not only was she a stunning, leggy brunette from Beijing with a surprisingly large chest and tiny waist, she was also clever and equipped with an evil sense of humour. The fact that Bertha flirted with Ben made him feel even better about how his resolve was standing up to temptation. He puffed out his chest as he thought what a *man* he was now.

As he was bending over to lock up his bike, Ben's bottom received a firm spank, the hand lingering more than was strictly appropriate.

"I'm sorry, I just couldn't resist. Amber, you should feel that boy's glutes. You can tell he's a cyclist. It's got me right in the mood for a good session! Morning, Ben. Thanks for helping me warm up."

Ben turned, gratified, to meet Bertha's provocative smile. He kissed her on both cheeks, and briefly fantasised about throwing her to the ground and ripping off her lycra. *Bellissima,* certainly – but strictly off limits, even when she did touch his butt like that. Today, Ben courted attention by deliberately wearing his old, worn-thin sweat shorts that hugged him in all the places he would like Bertha to hug him. There was no harm in looking good, as long as he understood the touch-and-go situation that he was in. Everything would be fine until Bertha touched him, and Ben would have to go into hiding. Thankfully Amber was here today, as he couldn't very well hide behind a tree.

"Good morning, Ben." Amber Bluett shyly raised her eyes to meet Ben's.

Amber and Ben had never talked about what had happened two years earlier. Ben couldn't decide whether Amber's timid, respectful manner towards him meant that she was truly the reformed character that a B.A.D Human Resources manager needed to be. Amber, for her part, was very conscious of maintaining her façade. She was wary, though, of testing her acting skills any further than she had to. Teary contrition and remorse were hard to keep up when laced with insincerity. And little of this was possible to do whilst jogging round a park.

Ben hadn't been the only one to spend some time on his choice of wardrobe. As Bertha unzipped her tracksuit top and peeled it off, Ben was momentarily transfixed by what emerged. The bright pink Victoria's Secret sports bra struggled to hold Bertha in. It somehow made her breasts look even larger than usual. The garment helpfully said "VSX Sexy Sport" on its front, clear enough to be visible, but not clear enough to read without looking quite hard, which Ben was now doing, much to Bertha's glee. Although not many women would probably appreciate sharing a nickname with a large World War I cannon inspired by Bertha Krupp, it rather amused the buxom lawyer from Beijing. She found it quite appropriate. The original Big Bertha had also had an explosive effect on a great number of men. Fort Ben was still holding out, but Bertha was prepared for a siege. She had time. She could probably wait until she was guaranteed a direct hit on his supplies of resolve. And if she didn't, so what? The pleasure was in the chase.

"Look Ben, we match!" Bertha grinned as she put her arm around Amber's shoulders. Amber, who had also removed her outer layers, was wearing the same pink top as Bertha. Below their midriffs, both women were wearing white, skin-tight running shorts. As he had been invited to look, Ben examined these thoroughly:

"Wow! Do you two often go out like this?"

"We have been known to cause more than one cyclist to ride into a bush before now. We tend to avoid busy roads."

Bertha's grin widened. She sensed that Ben was aroused. Lord, did he arouse easily. She had definitely found a weak point. She decided to test the defences a little more:

"You know, when men see the two of us like this, they seem to go off on these lesbian flights of fancy, imagining that just because we like to dress up like this, well, you know, we must be... I mean, can you believe it, Ben?"

Suddenly aware of his tumescence, Ben turned crimson, and looked away, pretending to check on his keys whilst desperately trying to adjust himself. *Think of Nicholas*

Casterway quoting Chitty on Contract. And – why in the name of dancing bears didn't I wear that longer, looser vest?

Amber looked a little impatient:

"Why don't we start the run, guys?"

Although enjoying Ben's embarrassment, and pleased to be part of its cause, the woman who achieved orgasm every time she rode Nicholas Casterway's cock found a semi-aroused Ben Barlettano disgusting and rather pathetic. Losing control just because he was with two women wearing matching running kit? How contemptible. It only emphasised that Ben was essentially an overgrown teenager. This made it even more maddening that he had eluded Amber's attempts at revenge thus far.

Although relieved to start the run, Ben was painfully aware that Nicholas and *Chitty* had not worked their deflating magic yet. Ben was doing some bouncing himself as he started his jog. A woman pushing a Maclaren stroller couldn't take her eyes off him and almost pushed her daughter right into Amber. Enough was enough. Ben stripped off his vest, ignoring the comments from Bertha, and hung it carefully from his waistband, so that it draped down and covered his embarrassment.

Ben concentrated on the park as he settled down into his rhythm. Battersea Park was one of Ben's favourite green spaces. It was beautiful, with swathes of mature trees, as well as a lake which would half freeze over in winter, leaving all the birds sliding about like mercury on the loose. Tourists didn't usually get this far south. Yet the surrounding areas were reassuringly middle class. It was more Labrador than Pitbull, which was particularly comforting when one's shorts were as threadbare as Ben's.

After a couple of circuits of the park, they stopped at the outdoor fitness area by the running track. Ben was able to put his vest back on. He knew that doing pull ups bare-chested did rather single you out as an attention-seeking knob.

"So, Ben," ventured Bertha, "I hear you are heading up our new LGBT group. I was rather surprised when I heard you were one of the *B*'s. I guess that makes you Queen Bee. Oh, dear, is that homophobic? And in front of HR as well! Or should I say bi-phobic? Does that even exist? It sounds more like a pair of spectacles."

Although Ben in his wilder moments had rather fantasised about taking advantage of multiple, muscled-up gym drones, he wasn't sure he liked being called a Queen Bee. It didn't feel very sexy. In fact, it seemed rather insulting to his manhood. Yet, given how his manhood seemed to misbehave wantonly and embarrass him, maybe it deserved an insult or two to keep it in place. He would roll with it. He smiled neutrally:

"Bisexual, and foreign. We are very open-minded in the LGBT group. We're a perfect reflection of Beaux, Aspen, Dickerhint itself."

Amber ignored Ben's sarcasm, and pretended to be fully occupied panting for breath.

Bertha continued:

"And what about the *T*? Does that stand for *tarts?* Are we finally recognising those poor lawyers, who, lacking the necessary legal ability to get on, try to sleep their way up to partnership? Should they also be covered by our diversity programme? Now there's a fun minority group for all the family."

Bertha gave Ben an impish grin, and looked at Amber with a solemn, enquiring look on her face.

Amber pursed her lips. There was something about that in her training notes somewhere. She had to step in:

"Bertha, darling, you shouldn't speak like that. A joke's a joke, but as you well know, things can get hairy if you go too far. If you do want to make fun of such things, please make sure that you do so out of my earshot. Our diversity in the workplace policy involves combating any form of discrimination to ensure that we have a pleasant, trouble-free environment for everyone whilst hiring and nurturing the best talent available. Underpowered *tarts* would not fit into that category, and neither do I think that they are particularly needy. As you very well know, *T* is for *transgender.*"

Having recently been dragged along by Alex O'Connell to see the *Sing-a-long-a Sound of Music* show, which revolutionised the whole concept of singing along to movie scores, Ben couldn't help thinking that *T* was actually a drink with jam and bread. Maybe the song was ripe for an inclusive update?

Bertha, whose family had lived through an altogether more serious Cultural Revolution, had grown up accustomed to being told that she couldn't say this or couldn't say that. Training to be a lawyer also had its fair share of learning what not to say. In her free time in London, Bertha revelled in saying exactly what she wanted to. As long as she was not hurting anybody, she would not be told *you can't say that*.

"Transgender. Of course! Now, that must be why Pam Shank and Lynne Glackett were practically forcing poor Cornisha to join the club. You need a *T*. Otherwise you'd just be an LGB society, and who's ever heard of one of those? Goodness, we'd make B.A.D a laughing stock in *The Lawyer*. Gosh, this club just gets more and more fun. Amber, maybe you and I should pretend to be having a torrid affair, so that we could join? Think how we could tease Pam and Lynne. Anyway, what do you do in the meetings? Do you discuss burning issues of diversity and tolerance in the workplace, or do you just get together for Graham Norton evenings and sip cocktails?"

For a moment Ben was mightily distracted by an image of what Bertha and Amber teasing Pam and Lynne might look like. Four rather hot women. Together. Shame he was neither single, nor the right sex to join in. Nor that they actually were ever together for that matter, outside of Ben's fertile imagination.

"Bertha, cocktails are always good. I know you may find this tough to believe, but we are actually trying to achieve something useful. LGBT groups may have suddenly spread across law firms like the latest must-have app on your iPhone, but unlike the case with most apps, there is clearly an underlying issue that LGBT groups have been formed to address. Some people are still worried about losing promotions if they come out as gay, as *the clients wouldn't react very well to it*. Speaking of which I hear you're working on that new Arab deal that came in the other week?"

Mention of work always changed the look on Bertha's face. She was extremely ambitious. The playful sex kitten could easily switch to a coldly calculating predator. Bertha assessed every detail and possibility in any work situation far faster than almost anyone Ben knew. She had a killer instinct which showed no mercy for the weak.

"It's an interesting case, Ben. I'm looking forward to sinking my teeth into it."

Bertha reflected for a moment that she had heard that Ben had been in line to help on the matter, until one of the senior partners pointed out that maybe having the head of the LGBT group doing leading work on a case of this nature *might* be taken as foisting western ideals on a conservative Middle Eastern society. In other words, as he had pointed out grimly, it was unlikely to go down well. At some point she would tell Ben this, but not now. Instead, she kept her off-duty Bertha hat firmly on.

"Come on Amber, let's go and do some sit-ups. Ben, please do something sexy to give us something to watch whilst we're crunching."

What a woman. She was as mean as they came. Ben realised that it was always going to be tough resisting the Berthas of this world. Flirting followed by casual sex had been such a good recipe for general contentment. But a steady relationship had worked wonders in a different way. Ben was happy in his choice. He repeated this like a mantra. A praying mantra. It had to be true. It was just such a shame that Kelly Danvers lived in Paris.

8

Sex, lies, but no videotapes

Stewing was something Rubens usually thought should be reserved solely for feijoada. But, ever since he had realised that he would have to fire Milo, he had been mulling the fact with an increasing sense of unease.

Having never been a manager before, he had never fired anyone in his life. To make things worse, although the evidence seemed clear, Rubens felt some sympathy for Milo. Rubens had wanted to give him another chance. Siegfried remained adamant.

Of course Rubens did not condone stealing, but sometimes he felt that these comfortable Brits had no idea what it was like to have grown up in a place where normal life meant trying to stay alive. Rubens had lost his brother to the drug gangs in Rio, something he was sure had hastened his beloved mother's early capitulation to cancer. His best friend Jamal had had friends shot in the head because some crazy with a Kalashnikov thought they were decadent for going to university. For his part, Milo had been a kid during the Kosovan war. Before the family escaped to Mitrovica, they had had a farm somewhere. Somewhere they never went back to. It was on the wrong side of the line. Milo had grown tired of the tension, the fear, and the stasis of the city trapped by history and geography. He had to get out – and he had done so.

London had opened its arms and let Milo start afresh. London didn't judge people – well, not too much. It paid less attention than was sometimes thought to people's backgrounds. It would generally give a chance to anyone who worked hard, obeyed the law and paid their taxes. Yet it was also at times cold, calculating and callous. It didn't judge you on your past because it didn't know anything about your past – but it also frankly couldn't care less in most cases. Two sides of the same coin. *Leave your problems at immigration, you're a Londoner now.* Very few people in the city had any idea what demons Milo might be struggling with, or what situations he still had to manage back home. All that the punters knew about him at Outrageous Fortune was that he was a damn good barman, and that he was a stripper with a dick the size of the pints he pulled. That was all that was relevant. Perhaps it was enough. Milo had found his place.

Yet now Milo had broken his contract with London. Milo had not obeyed the rules. Money had been taken. The business, and the city, needed revenge. Recompense. Rubens had to fire him. Dillon would probably tell tales that would tarnish his reputation. The city was about to spit him out.

It was the end of the shift on a quiet weekday night. Rubens cleared his throat and called Milo over. Siegfried was no human resources expert or employment lawyer, but he had nonetheless given Rubens a steer in terms of what he should and should not say. Rubens must try to keep things general, and in no way directly accuse Milo of stealing – because they did not actually have any proof that he had.

"So, is this the part when you tell me I am an excellent barman and you give me a pay rise?" Milo grinned confidently at Rubens. Milo was not going to make this easy, thought Rubens. Better to get straight to the point:

"Milo, I'm afraid this isn't working out. I am sorry, but we are going to have to let you go."

Rubens forced himself to look Milo in the eyes as he got the words out. Awful as the situation was, Milo at least must have known this was coming.

If he did know, then Milo was a fine actor. He stared at Rubens in disbelief, shock etched on his face.

"It isn't working out? Seriously? Rubens, I can run this bar on my own and have frequently done so, as well you know, when everyone else disappears for a while. Have you seen the tips I get? What have I done wrong?"

There it was. The question Rubens had hoped to avoid. Thankfully he had an answer prepared.

"Milo, there are a number of skills which a barman here needs to master. We have been assessing your performance over the past weeks. Unfortunately you have not demonstrated the competencies required for the position to a level high enough to justify your employment in this establishment on a permanent basis."

Phew! Rubens had managed to deliver it. Human resources jargon did not come as naturally to him as it did to Amber Bluett, especially when it was of the firing sort. But it did not seem to have the desired effect on Milo. The disbelief was turning into something else.

"*I have not demonstrated the competencies required?* What is this crap, Rubens? I serve drinks. I serve them fast, and I get them right. I keep the bar stocked. I cover for my colleagues. The customers, they love me. What am I not doing right? And who is "*we*"? You and I have known each other for long enough. Please have the decency to tell me the real reason you are kicking me out of here."

Milo had indeed turned out to be a really great barman. Rubens was sweating now. He went for the line that he and Siegfried had decided should put paid to Milo's resistance.

"Milo, we are looking for our barmen to demonstrate their performance at the till, basically to help us raise our takings. But we are not seeing that on your shifts."

Milo couldn't challenge this, and Rubens thought it sounded plausible. It was obliquely true, too. The missing money had been depressing the takings. The bar wasn't hitting its targets. If Milo hadn't been stealing the money, they wouldn't be having this conversation now.

Milo's eyes narrowed as he gazed at his soon-to-be ex-boss. So Rubens had finally told him why he was on the way out. He decided to play along and test Rubens' resolve.

"OK, I get it. You need your barmen to be more aggressive salespeople. You need me to try actively to sell more drinks, talk to the customers more, and behave as if it was my till in the bar. I can do this more. Just give me a chance. I can show you."

"Listen, Milo, I appreciate you wanting to improve, but

171

we don't think that it will work here in this bar for you. This was a trial period. Thanks for your work, but we don't want to take you on permanently. We don't think you are right for this place."

Rubens was feeling slightly sick. Milo was perfect for the bar. This was all the complete opposite of what Rubens really thought. However, Siegfried had told him not to say a word about the thefts. Is this what management was about? Having to avoid the truth and invent nonsense to navigate around situations? Although Rubens respected Siegfried and his indubitable years of experience, it was hard to believe that lying was the way to progress in the business world. The serious job Rubens had wanted for so long was making him feel sordid, in a way he had never felt when he supplemented his personal training earnings with go-go dancing, stripping and escorting. The only lies involved there were telling clients that they were starting to look in great shape. Go-go and striptease brought a spark to a night out. And escorting – well, that had a happy ending, practically by definition.

Milo rubbed his eyes:

"Rubens, is there anything you are not saying here? I get it that my time here is finished. But it is bullshit what you have just said about me not being right for this place. I can't believe that you, of all people, are saying this crap to me."

For the first time Rubens' discomfort at performing a difficult task was tinged with something else: a sliver of doubt. Milo did not look guilty. He looked outraged and angry. Disappointed, even. Rubens hid behind another sentence he had rehearsed with Siegfried:

"I'm sorry you feel that way, but I'm afraid it doesn't change the position of the management team."

Milo's appeal for honesty from his friend had elicited nothing. He stared Rubens down:

"Listen, my friend. You and I both know that I am the best barman you have here. I know the cocktail menu by heart, which is why I sell more of them than all my *permanent* colleagues put together. I make more money for you than any of them! Then you say I have to go because I am not good enough? Bullshit! I think I know what the real reason is. Is there money missing, Rubens? Do you think it is me?"

Milo could see that Rubens was in acute discomfort and was not sure what to say next.

"Okay, Milo." Rubens knew Siegfried would not be happy with him, but he could not keep up the pretence any more. He was not going to completely compromise who he was for career progress alone. If he'd wanted to do that, he'd have taken a night class in law. Milo deserved the truth at very least.

"We have noticed that on certain shifts we are making a lot less money at the till than we should, given the number of people in the bar. I'm afraid we have noticed that it always seems to be on your shifts that this happens."

Although Milo was relieved Rubens had finally stopped lying to him, he also understood that the man he had considered his friend had just accused him of being a thief.

"You bastard, Rubens. We have known each other for years. Have you ever known me to be dishonest? What have I ever done to you? Do you have any proof that I took money, apart from the fact that it's Milo the stripper, Milo the escort, so who can trust the guy who sells his dick for money anyway? Oh, but wait – that used to be you too, didn't it, my friend?"

Milo's eyes looked as if they might well bore a hole through Rubens' head to pin him to the wall behind. The fact was that Rubens had no proof. Outrageous Fortune was one of the few places in London that did not have CCTV monitoring people's every move. Alex's liberal instincts had overruled that prospect. Alex did not wish to be part of the fascist surveillance state. At times like this, however, it would have been useful.

Rubens was now completely lost for words. Everything he said had seemed to make matters worse. He sat there, with nothing to add, hoping that Milo would eventually unpin him from the wall and just leave.

Milo was not finished yet. Other than realising that his friend had accused him of thieving, he also noticed the use of the word *we*. And Rubens' silence told him that they obviously had no proof.

"Fine. Don't say a word, Rubens. But I didn't take the money. I know you don't believe me now, but when it happens again, and another ex-stripper gets the blame, well, don't say I didn't warn you, my friend. See you around."

Kelly skipped towards the Gare du Nord to collect Monique and Cornisha from the Eurostar. It was an ugly old Gare, really – yet full of the lightness of friends and lovers meeting. Hand-made signs, some gleaming from iPads, were joyously held up to greet those arriving. There were squeals of delight as people reconnected, and warm smiles from those observing the antics, as they strode by to their own destinations, shouldering the light bags that gave them away as frequent inter-city travellers.

Kelly found herself jumping up and down in her cute polka dot dress, with snazzy red shoes.

"My girls! My girls!"

Cornisha wore a forest green suit with black trim, and elegant stilettos. Monique sported a short pleated navy blue skirt with a white and navy top, and elegant sun glasses. She looked as if she were heading out to sea and – oh, thought Kelly, catching her breath, Monique may as well be, given the news that I have to share.

I must tell them. I must tell them. I need their advice. But I really don't want them to despise me.

"It's so good to see you! Welcome back to Paris! I've missed you so much!"

"London misses you too, Kelly. And look at you. You've caught French style! Why, I feel positively dowdy next to you."

"Cornisha, as if! A couple of gentlemen are already staring your way. I'm sure they'd wink at you, given half a chance."

"I'm sure they would, dear. If Arthur were here, he'd give them a piece of his mind. It's true that the French look at women with considerably more interest than the English do, as a rule. But the French would also be considerably more horrified at my life history, so I suppose we're all even."

"Depends on whom you're telling your story to," said Monique.

Cornisha nodded:

"I suppose that's true. But who lets the truth stand in the way of an excoriating generalisation?"

"Men here are quite… inspired," said Kelly thoughtfully.

"Inspired?" questioned Monique.

"Let's get a move on and discuss the creativity of the Paris-dwelling male over dinner, shall we?" interjected Cornisha.

They companiably surfed the Paris metro, swaying together as the train rattled through shallow tunnels. The days of Parisian tube tunnels being adorned with *Dubonnet!* and *Ça, c'est Paris.* appeared to have long been swept away by new marketing waves. French advertisements retained a nostalgic air, though, from Dior new wave skirts to the art deco influence detectable in the campaigns for department stores. In the middle of the invitations to consume ran the busy trains, packed with people who did occasionally smile if you smiled at them, alongside those as walled in by their headphones and ear mufflers, as Edgar Allen Poe could not in his wildest dreams have anticipated or hoped for.

Kelly lived in some splendour in the 7th arrondissement. The flat was rented long term by her firm. It was spectacular, for a relatively junior lawyer. Monique and Cornisha were to share a charming second bedroom, and they cooed with pleasure over the view from the wrought iron balcony and the roof tops disappearing off into the horizon.

Kelly mused that the last time she had taken that view in properly was while being taken vigorously from behind by Morten, on his finest form. She tensed slightly at the memory of the wild abandon. She really needed to talk about this with her friends. It seemed like a subject for a conversation far, far away. It would be discussed – yes, it would – but not now. Then. After…

"Dinner," she said firmly.

They sipped on kir vin blanc in a bistrot not far from the Hotel de Ville. It was warm and pleasant, as busy and humming as one could wish for. Monique chose a salad and a steak tartare. Cornisha went for soup and osso bucco. Kelly had snails and lamb. Cornisha looked at her with some surprise:

"I did not have you down as a gastropod-vore."

Kelly nodded:

"They're delicious with fresh crusty bread. I think it's mostly the warm parsley and garlic butter that I enjoy – but I'm sort of in love with them now. They're a bit like sex – faintly disgusting if you analyse it over much, but hotly fabulous if you just go with the flow."

"Is sex ever faintly disgusting?" asked Monique, arching an eyebrow.

"Oh yes," said Cornisha firmly, "half the ills of the world are caused by people getting stuck on the details of a properly fanned out sexual life. If people worried more about being clean and healthy, and less about the shape of their genitals and where they wished to stick them, we'd all be a lot more comfortable."

"Oh dear," mused Monique, "I'm missing out on faintly disgusting sex."

I'm not, thought Kelly. Her stomach had butterflies again

177

at the mere thought of Morten, naked, gloriously ready. She frowned. She used to feel this way about Ben. She remembered the anxiety, the fierce rush of possessiveness as she glimpsed Ben's tall frame across a room. That love, where had it gone? It still glowed faintly when she thought of it, like a night light. But Morten was the sun, blinding, burning, and terracing her. How could she stay indoors, on such a glorious day? Certain Americans from the Deep South like herself were manifestly joining forces with mad dogs and Englishmen, and running outside at high noon.

"This is a lovely red," said Cornisha, peering into the depths of her glass.

"It would make a perfectly dramatic evening dress, this colour," mused Monique.

Kelly nodded:

"I'm probably kidding myself, but I'm getting better acquainted with what I like in wine." *And what I like in men*, she thought. *Make that what I need in a man. Oh dear. Will they understand anything at all about it?* Kelly and Monique dug into chocolate mousses born from the whipping of eggs into submission by strong and dark chocolate, allied with the twin culinary essentials of butter and sugar. Cornisha had zabaglione, and swooned over the Marsala wine. Kelly decided that the time had come to say something.

"So, Monique. What's up with Jake?"

Monique smiled:

"Oh, it's very good. I'm in love – but I also see him for what he is. I think he's very talented, and he's gorgeous. I'm very aware that he has the world at his fingertips. But

I know that no matter how many people apparently adore you, there are only ever very few that you want to get close to. I don't know if I ever come across as lacking in confidence – but there is one thing that I am very confident about. This is my conclusion: he may as well adore me as adore anyone else."

Cornisha laughed:

"That's a wonderful way of putting it. You are smart, clever, attractive and funny. And we do enjoy seeing you in the gossip rags."

Monique acknowledged the compliments thoughtfully:

"It took all that confusion – and some pain – over Harry, to finally feel as if I am now the woman that I should have been all along. Ultimately, none of it is ever wasted."

"It took me a lot longer than you," said Cornisha, "I think we all look back and wonder why it takes us so long to learn simple lessons of life and love, when clues are all around us, should we ever bother to look for them."

"We never learn," said Kelly abruptly.

Cornisha blinked:

"Well, we sort of acquire an inkling…"

"No we don't," said Kelly, with some passion.

"Well…"

"Oh shut up! Shut up, the pair of you! There is no bloody Cinderella ending!"

Kelly buried her face in her hands.

An uncomfortable silence descended. Cornisha looked most thoughtful, and concerned. Monique was open-mouthed with astonishment.

Finally, Monique gestured over to the waiter:

"I think we need a bottle of champagne over here."

"Morten," said Cornisha carefully. She looked at the unfamiliar figure on Kelly's phone.

"He's Scandinavian?"

"Yes, Cornisha."

Monique was intent on the image:

"He's very good looking. Kelly, he is lovely. He is tall, I see. And look at those twinkly eyes. But if he looks stern, then a shiver goes down your spine. Yes, I would go for him in a flash. I love Swedes. Definitely part of my five a day."

"What is he doing in Paris?" asked Cornisha.

"He's a doctor. He works for a humanitarian organisation. He organises teams to go into emergency areas. He's hands on in the field – but he's currently involved in some project which means he's based over here while they do whatever it is that they need to do. We don't talk about work much – mainly because I just can't compete. I'm a lawyer. He's saving lives."

"We all do useful things sometimes," said Cornisha briskly.

"Yes," said Monique, "I actually think much of what Jake does is utterly pointless, but we all look up to him. I think I bring meaning to his life, rather than the other way around. It's not a very fashionable view."

Kelly looked at them both and drank deep from her glass:

"I know we're all skirting around the point here, ladies."

"Mmm-hmmm," said Cornisha.

Monique raised an eyebrow.

"I know," said Kelly loudly, "I have a boyfriend."

"Oh, that," said Monique. "Ce petit detail."

"Ben. Ben Barlettano? Remember him? Tall? Good-looking chap?"

"Is he your boyfriend?" quipped Monique.

Cornisha placed a placatory hand on Kelly's arm:

"We know. We don't judge."

"We don't judge," said Monique, suddenly fierce, "not just because we love you, but also because we do understand. This guy is hot."

Kelly groaned:

"No one talks about it. No one really talks about how hard it is to be faithful, and how – on balance – we're not. I'm not. I've been unfaithful, and do you know what the worst thing is? I can't wait to be unfaithful again. It just sounds awful. But I love them both. I'm sorry, I don't care how confusing it sounds. I love them both. They're very different."

Monique frowned:

"I slept with Harry Gumpert for – ooh, was it two years? On and off? Never caring about Sarah, or the kids? So I'm not going to be judging you. But do I think that it was a good idea? Manifestly not. He was not worthy."

"But it's odd, isn't it," reasoned Cornisha. "Even someone as unimpressive as that – he got you through times. He... met your needs."

"Yes," conceded Monique simply.

"I am glamorising Morten more than that," said Kelly thoughtfully. " It's all about the excitement, and the newness of it, and the promise that he might be a better catch – more fulfilling, more interesting, more of a match sexually. I'm very well aware that these are the feelings we always get at the beginning of relationships. We can't help nursing almost impossible expectations that we hope against hope will be met. There's the sheer bliss of unreasonably extravagant emotions that one can finally surrender to. I have that orgasmic lightness in my heart at the very sight of his name. I've lost much of that with Ben. And I know it's unfair on him. These things are not meant to last for ever."

"Is Morten magnificent in bed?" asked Monique.

Kelly rolled her eyes:

"Amazeballs."

Monique sighed:

"It may all sound tragic – and I do understand the moral dilemma – but can I just say how very lucky you are? How very lucky we are?"

"We've never talked about Jake in that way."

"No we haven't. But everything works there too. And it is very, very, very important that things work there, too."

Cornisha nodded:

"I'm not sure what you should do. I think it's not as cut and dried as people would like to think. You're unmarried and young. You know full well that this could blow up in your face. But you also know what you're doing. No condemnation. No encouragement. We love and support you."

"Can we just get drunk now? And please keep it to yourselves."

"It's private. I'm just glad you're not asking me about Arthur."

"We're not. It's fine. Champagne. Fast."

"Hi. It's me."

"Ben… hello, how are you?"

This sounded forced even to Kelly's own ears. To Monique and Cornisha, sitting opposite her at the kitchen table and who had just been listening to breathless tales of Kelly's illicit Parisian romance, this was as cringeworthy as discovering your skirt tucked up into the top of your tights after walking through an open plan office.

Cornisha topped up the brandy glasses. She sensed they would need it.

"Napoleon," she said to Monique. "Now, there was a little man."

"Apparently not," said Monique. "Some reports put him at one metre seventy-three. About five foot eight. The height issue was exaggerated for satirical and other devious purposes."

Ben was chatting away happily. Monique and Cornisha could just make out the cheerful chirruping of the telephonic connection.

"So," Ben asked Kelly, "have you had a nice night with the girls? Lucky them. I wish I were there too. I'd be touching you up when the others weren't looking. I want to make love to you all night long. You look so beautiful when you've been working from dawn to dusk and have those adorable panda bags under your eyes…"

Ben could be surprisingly romantic, thought Kelly. He had never disappointed her. These were all the sorts of sweet nothings that had persuaded her that Ben's dalliance

183

with Rubens was just a passing phase, and that, ultimately, no one could fill the love-shaped hole in his life the way she could. But tonight, this was acutely uncomfortable. He felt like a pair of shoes that had been outgrown. Not only did nothing fit, but it actually pinched.

"Oh. I wish you were here too," she said, lamely.

The lie filled the kitchen. Both Monique and Cornisha winced and squirmed.

Ben was oblivious, naturally:

"At least we'll be together for a whole week when you come over to London for Hartmut and Caroline's wedding. I've got a couple of things planned, but you'll find out soon enough about those. I need to keep some secrets from you."

He laughed.

Kelly shut her eyes. She knew how much stock Ben placed on honesty. She knew that he had a code. Relationships were open book to him. No secrets. She had his word and she trusted him implicitly. He could laugh. His was the laughter of the righteous.

She attempted a chuckle back. It sounded the most unconvincing titter that she had ever uttered.

Kelly caught Cornisha's eye. They both looked away. This was exemplary embarrassment. Kelly swallowed hard:

"Ben, I can't wait to see you and have a proper talk face to face."

This was another lie. At least Ben knew that she was with the others. Small mercies: she did not have to talk about sex with him.

This was untenable. She had to finish the call, and deal

with the situation when she was in London:

"Anyway, darling, I'd better go. Monique was regaling us with another story about her popstar boyfriend, and we're screaming at those photos in Sizzle! magazine. There's bound to be a bit coming soon about tossing plasma screens over balconies. I'll fill you in. Anyway, I'll see you in London. 'Bye, Ben. Love you…"

Kelly just managed to squeak the last two words out. Ben repeated them tenderly, so she quickly pressed the red disconnect button as if it were the off button on an out of control appliance, and recoiled from the receiver.

Silence remained.

"I'm sorry," said Kelly, "I'm really sorry. I am a terrible person."

"Yes, you are, rather. But you're a lawyer, so we knew that already. It may yet pass."

Monique wordlessly held out a ballon of decent cognac. Kelly looked askance at it. Monique swirled it at her with insistence:

"Here, Kelly. It's only because it's you. Let's have another drink. You make me feel like brand new. After that performance, my own virtue is freshly restored to previously unseen condition. It seems we can put this out of our heads if I tell you more about my fabulous life with Jake Le Jones?"

9

Wham Bam Thank you Man

"Habibie! Come and give your favourite girl a hug."

Ben looked up from his conversation with Jamal and Alex. A woman in an electric blue cocktail dress sashayed towards their table. She had curves like hairpin bends, long curly jet black hair, fine features, full red lips and stunning green eyes. Oh, he missed being single so much at times.

"Kasim, look at you! You really are the belle with the balls." Jamal embraced the vision.

Kasim? The belle with the balls? Ben felt foolish. Now that he was paying attention, he could see an Adam's apple. How had he failed to join the dots, given the surfeit of gold jewellery, and a hat that even Princess Beatrice would have drawn the line at?

"Habibie, you are a bad, bad boy. Alex, you are wasted on that Maghrebi. If only I had met you first…"

Kasim turned to the rest of the group for dramatic effect, and noticed Ben sitting there:

"Oooooh. Who are you, habibie?"

Still perturbed at not having recognised a drag queen, Ben stood up awkwardly and stuttered a greeting:

"Hi, I'm Ben."

"Oh, Ben, how handsome you are. Oh, I knew it was worth leaving my beloved Palestine and coming to this dreary, cold, grey town. I am Lady Gaza, and I am delighted to meet you."

Lady Gaza? Surely not. It was all too predictable – but Kasim carried it off so well. So well, in fact, that Ben only now noticed, trailing in Lady Gaza's wake, a dark-skinned fine-featured man, whose black hair and piercing green eyes matched those of his companion, but who was filling a white T-shirt and plain blue jeans, instead of a padded dress.

Moving swiftly on, Ben's butterfly libido abandoned Lady Gaza and darted off to buzz around yonder dark prince.

Lady Gaza followed Ben's gaze with amusement:

"I think you will want to meet my friend. Ladies, this is Zahoor. Yes, I can see your questioning eyes and surprised ears – and yes, he really is a whore. The name is perfect for him, habibie. Don't be taken in by those innocent eyes of his. They will be undressing you as I speak. He has a rare gift of being able to tell the size of a man's penis just from a glance at their jeans. It's his little X-Men superpower thing. Not exactly Wolverine, granted. But it's very useful for a size queen in a hurry."

Zahoor ignored Lady Gaza and smiled at Ben. He did not bother denying the assertion. Instead, he raised his hands to his eyes, imitating a camera. He looked through the hole made by his adjoined fingers, twisted his right hand as he pretended to focus in on Ben's jeans, and made a loud clicking noise as he mimed taking a photo. He then made a play of pointing his imaginary camera at Lady Gaza's crotch, which earned him a shriek and a smart thwack on his shoulder with her clutch bag.

Oh, how Ben loved London. This was the place where the world met up, and, if it was lucky, sometimes managed a shag, followed by an exotic breakfast. This had been the London that Ben had adored and briefly revelled in, before the monogamous relationship with Kelly swung into play. He sighed. Things were as they were now – regardless of how sexy, talented or available Zahoor was.

Lady Gaza was enjoying herself:

"Can you big boys move up and make room for us?"

Ben shifted his seat along, ensuring he did not end up next to Zahoor and his X-ray eyes. Doubtless his hands would be equally skilled. Ben felt strong, but there was no point in littering his path with easy temptation. Besides, the B.A.D LGBT group meeting was about to take place. The others would be arriving soon.

The bar was filling up. A scruffy blond guy walked over, making an unwelcome beeline for Kasim. She parried with grace:

"Hello, habibie. What a delight to see you. And of course your faithful jacket, that you never seem to tire of. Now, if you are here for a lovely chat with us then please pull up a stool and join me. But let me inform you that Lady Gaza is not in the market at the moment. You should know it is my time for the month."

The scruffy blond looked awkwardly at Kasim for a moment. A confusion of thoughts seemed to race behind his eyes. He said that he had just come over to say a quick hello. Kasim held her smile as he shuffled shiftily off:

"If it is one thing I learnt in the souk, it is that a good salesperson should always know her customer. That guy totally lacks the personal touch. Has he never heard of the holy month of Gramadan? Neither a bump nor a line shall pass my nostrils for the next four weeks. Not even after sun down! I need to find a new dealer when fasting is over, darlings."

Ben suddenly imagined a Fox News exposé on Lady Gaza. What would they make of her and her noble abstinence for the sacred month? She would terrorise them. In their defence, she was not exactly state fair family-friendly. For a start, her stilettos would get stuck in the mud. She also seemed unlikely to be able to have her head turned by a warm cinnamon bun.

Before coming to London, Ben had not known many Arabs or Muslims. Media reports had led him to believe that such persons were constantly angry, usually offended at something, probably waving a placard, and allergic to anything resembling fun. Additionally, they were not fond of smiling. Their main hobby was prohibiting anything and everything because it insulted their tradition or religion. Lady Gaza presented an example of how Ben had come to change his views. It was not just her cheerful ministrations that impressed him. Ben had met others, a whole continuum of personalities, and some of the more liberated souls were still able to catch Ben by surprise with their views and ideas.

The Muslim centre of gravity was certainly on the

traditional side – but did it really differ so much to swathes of the United States? Ben wondered about this. Alex had once said to Ben that if evangelical Christians and fundamentalist Muslims ever realised just how much intolerance they had in common and allied against their real enemy – the Godless – then there finally would be a properly defined clash of civilisations.

Almost on cue, a cabal of women appeared in the bar:

"Are we in the right place?"

Ben's ruminations were disturbed by the commanding tones of Pam Shank. She strode into the bar, followed by Lynne, Cornisha, and a gaggle of assorted legally qualified lesbians and gay men. Rubens swished into view from nowhere, gave Pam a smile that softened her, and showed the group to their immaculately prepared table in the quietest corner.

Lynne gave him a lascivious look:

"He's a bit of all right, isn't he? Is he the one that Ben got it on with? If I hadn't swapped fun sticks for lady gardens, I'd have a bit of that myself."

"Lynne Glackett! May I remind you that we are ladies who munch? For heaven's sake, we haven't even started and you are already making a mockery of this event. This may be a social occasion, but we also have a couple of serious issues to discuss tonight. Please avoid the stereotypical references for one hour? It's not much to ask, you predictable fanny monkey."

Pam admonished Lynne further with a prolonged glare. Lynne really did need to up her game. It was precisely by being complacent that the world found itself going backwards – sometimes appearing to be on the verge of losing the very rights that people had fought so hard for over centuries. Lynne knew exactly what Pam thought about all this. Pam was very clear, very frequently, about the ills of the world. Lynne dutifully feigned sheepishness for a moment, before she turned to Cornisha and winked.

Ben decided he should make a start:

"Distinguished colleagues, I am delighted to welcome you to Outrageous Fortune. Aside from being a great bar, which contrasts most agreeably with our conference rooms, it is a very fitting venue for tonight's meeting. The owners, my good friends Alex and Jamal, know something about both of the topics we will be discussing tonight. They have been together for longer than most marriages last. Yet of course, in today's world, many gay people all over the world do not have the option of actually getting married themselves."

Ben paused:

"We may have won some of that battle. But it is far from over. Alex has spent years on various charitable projects in some of the more difficult places on earth. On those trips, he always took the time to try to understand just what it was like to be gay in such societies."

Ben paused again. He would ask Alex to tell the LGBT group more about this later, after a few drinks:

"Jamal, on the other hand, grew up in Algeria. As you know, most Muslim countries are not the easiest places for young people struggling with their sexuality. The nineties saw a brutal civil war between the army and the Islamists. Jamal experienced all this first hand. So, to the agenda for the evening. First, we wish to formulate our response to any government who does not propose to legislate for gay marriage. Secondly, we shall address the issues faced by the LGBT community in places where discrimination, and indeed criminalisation and violence, are the norm."

"Do you only have good-looking friends, Ben?" Axel Schwanz, a tax lawyer, was managing to mince even while sitting down. How *did* he do that? Ben decided to ignore his comment. He looked over to Pam, who picked up the thread:

"Any government proposing civil marriage for same sex couples can be sure that there will be those who will oppose this policy – hazarding a wild guess, probably on the religious right. It is important, therefore, that both as a group and individually we do our part to show support for this overdue measure of equality worldwide." Pam glared at Axel, daring him to interrupt. She was good at glaring and made excellent use of that proficiency: "Now, is everyone aware of the differences between civil partnership and civil marriage?"

"No verb."

Lynne Glackett had been jousting with Pam Shank for too many years to be put off by one of those professional glares.

"Pardon, Lynne?"

"Well, one of my friends invited me to her civil partnership ceremony. Instead of telling me that she was getting married, she told me that she and Carrie were getting the civil partnership thing done. Rather than being married, she's now *in a civil partnership*. You *marry* – verb –

but you don't *civil partnership*."

"That is very inconvenient. English is usually such a flexible language, always spawning neologisms."

Axel enunciated the word carefully, showing off his English vocabulary, much as he would a new D&G suit on a trip to Italy.

"There's also no courtesy title for the spouse of a peer or a knight." Lynne looked at Pam. "So if Axel should enter into a civil partnership with a man who was or became a peer of the realm, he would be entitled to call himself neither Sir Axel Schwanz nor Lady Axel Schwanz."

Axel nodded:

"They say marriage. We say civil partnership. Oh, let's call the whole thing off. I'm so glad we have started to move this forward."

Cornisha leaned forward:

"You see, this was one of the reasons that I didn't want to join the LGBT group."

Ben and Pam swivelled around, alarmed, to look at her.

Cornisha continued:

"You LGBs have the best of intentions. But most of you can't help forgetting that the transgender community has a whole load of other issues that go beyond a missing neologism and a disappointed dame. In most places a marriage is defined as being between a man and a woman. Thus, if a person changes sex, by definition they have to end their marriage – regardless of what the two people in the marriage actually want. It can be heart-breaking. And it certainly underlines many people's attitude to us – that we are seen as, somehow, fundamentally wrong. How *dare* they?"

She had said her piece. Calm returned to Cornisha. As tends to be the case with those who maintain a serene exterior, when something angers them enough for them to speak out, other people listen. If it was bad enough to get Cornisha to speak up, then she must be furious.

The rest of the group were quelled into silence for a moment. Axel and Lynne felt guilty for trivialising the issue.

Pam took charge:

"Thank you, Cornisha. You have raised what is possibly the principal practical reason for supporting this initiative. Axel and Lynne – remarkably, given your track record on participation – your points also have relevance. Civil partnership guarantees by law all the rights and privileges of marriage. What is different is the form, the style. Coming back to your point, Cornisha, the issue is the implicit judgement that is being passed on the true worth of our unions. Our own society took the big step of admitting that the LGBT community stood to be accorded the basic rights of everyone else. However, it still took what feels like a legislative miracle to finally be awarded the distinction of being able to marry. Has society at large truly admitted that same sex couples are as valid as those comprising members of opposite sexes? In too many places, and in too many ways, we are still second-class citizens. Aside from remedying the cruel treatment of the transgender community, this is why support of gay marriage worldwide is an important step for all the LGBT community."

This time, no one interrupted Pam, nor did anyone reply with a facetious remark. Ben disclosed that a letter had been drafted for the group to send to governments, and that everyone in the LGBT group should support it. He suggested mildly that people might also consider asking LGBT-friendly straight friends to participate. This was vital, too.

Ben continued:

"In the UK, along with most of the West, our community has been fighting for decades. The advances we have made would astound people from only fifty years ago. Each generation has passed the baton on. New causes have been identified, argued for, and are being won. Attitudes are changing. But, if it may occasionally feel that we are approaching the last lap in the battle for true equality over here, some societies are still waiting for the starting gun to be fired. We should be trying to influence the government to help the LGBT community in countries where practising homosexuality is still punishable by victimisation, jail, corporal punishment – and in some cases, death."

Keen to keep the conversation going, Pam jumped in:

"The Government's announcement that it would cut aid to regimes that implement anti-gay laws was a good start, but what has actually happened? Do we know of any change?"

"What about another letter-writing campaign to the Department for International Development?"

Ben looked round the table.

General murmurs of assent were heard. They were in sharp contrast to the guffaws of enthusiastic laughter coming from Jamal and Alex's table as Lady Gaza recounted another of her experiences.

Lynne was the first to air her views:

"Don't worry, Pam, I'm not going to carp on about grammar again. I only thought the conversation was floundering and you know I am a dab hand at sparking things up. Let's mull it over before we take any decisions."

Pam narrowed her eyes. Ben groaned. The rest of the table tittered. Beyond them Lady Gaza rose and headed for the ladies. Lynne continued:

"Aside from my campaign to reclaim every fishy word going, for us and us alone, I do actually have conflicting feelings about this issue. The message of cutting foreign aid to governments who abuse the LGBT community would be a positive one, on the face of it. However, given that all governments do business with serial abusers of human rights, do we really think that they are going to become ethical when it comes to us? Maybe I am a cynic, but is it just a coincidence that this is being suggested at a time when we are desperately trying to reduce our deficits? Should we ask ourselves if we are not just a fig leaf for treasury bean counters, keen to reduce expenditure?"

Lynne had a point. The group listened carefully to her words. Even Lady Gaza had paused on her way to touch her face up, and was surveying the group with an interested look.

Lynne wasn't finished:

"Let's assume for a moment that our glorious governments are indeed being high-minded about all of this. What effect do we really think that the withdrawal of our meagre budget could have on recalcitrant regimes? Do we think, for example, that Uganda will suddenly become a homo heaven because some patronising white ex-colonialist withdraws their pennies? China is already a more important investor and will for sure be ready to step into the gap, without all those pesky conditions. Then the poor gays will be branded carriers of a Western disease, and there will be zero influence left over the government to mitigate even their worst excesses. We could end up exacerbating the problem."

"Might I make a comment? I know I am not part of your group, but I did grow up in a territory not well known for its welcoming attitude to gays and lesbians."

The group turned to face the speaker. Ben saw that Lady Gaza was having the same effect on Pam and Lynne that she had had on him when she entered the bar.

He waved a welcoming hand:

"Everyone, this is a friend of Jamal's whom I mentioned earlier. Kasim, please go ahead. We are having an academic argument here. We would love to hear what you have to say from a practical viewpoint."

"Thank you, habibie. Hello, everyone. I was born in Palestine. I lived there until I was eighteen. I am gay, and always have been. I was not able to hide it. Everyone gets harsh words, and I got very good at coping with them. The beatings were harder to endure, but I became tough, a lot tougher than I might look. But flesh cannot resist a blade. It was my mother who sent me here, where, thanks to your systems, I was granted asylum. My life was genuinely in danger back home. And so a scared, damaged young man called Kasim blossomed into this vision before you. I am Lady Gaza, as sure as the sun sets and rises, and

I'm free to be fabulous every day of the week."

She paused and bowed her head in recognition of the attention. Ben wondered where she was going with her argument, or if it was just an excuse to come over and make pulses race.

"I am sure you are aware that the European Union is a major sponsor of the Palestinians. The EU has given around five billion euros to various Palestinian groups over the past twenty years. The EU qualifies the protection of minorities as a fundamental right. So where *were* they when they were funding the very people who were oppressing *me*? Why did they not do anything to try to help people like me? Was this ever raised in meetings? What of all of my gay friends who still have to hide on a daily basis or go about their business in constant fear of being discovered and punished? And we all know how many of those Brussels bureaucrats are gay themselves. Hypocritical queens!"

"So," reasoned Ben, "you agree with our proposals that we should be trying to influence where aid goes and withhold it from regimes who do not respect lesbian, gay, bisexual and transgender rights?"

"I did not say that, Ben." Lady Gaza eyed him quite seriously. "You see, habibie, those hypocritical queens are also pragmatic queens. They know that there are other sources of funding available to the Palestinians that come with quite a different set of strings attached. We are next door to one of the greatest concentration of riches and religious fervour on earth. If the EU were replaced, I hardly think life would become better for the likes of poor

Kasim. I am afraid I am in agreement with the lovely lady who spoke just now. Better to stay in there and at least try to head off the worst of what they might try to do to us."

"So, are you then saying that, in your opinion, we should just leave things as they are?"

"I did not say that either, Ben. Really, you are very good at trying to put words into my mouth. You should know that it is not your words that I would like in my mouth, habibie."

Lady Gaza pouted deliberately at Ben, as Axel and Lynne giggled into their Martinis.

"No," she said, "there is definitely something that you should be doing. There is something that I think is quite simple that you should be doing to influence your government. If you had been listening, you should have picked up on what I am about to suggest."

"Asylum."

Lynne's single word caused Lady Gaza to smile in her direction.

"Exactly! You are beautiful and brainy, if I may say so. I think the EU should relax their asylum policy for gays, lesbians, transsexuals and bisexuals coming from countries where we can have no real life. You Europeans are terrified of being invaded by us brown-skinned hordes, but the beauty of the gays is that you only get *us*. Relatively few of us have children. When we do bring up children, we are usually helping you by offering homes to children in desperate need of a comfortable, supportive and loving home. We arrive, we do the jobs you don't want to do, we set up companies and we don't overburden your schools or social services. Gays don't usually live on benefits. I mean, could you imagine trying to look this good on a jobseekers' allowance? Impossible, darling! Do you know the price of a good lipstick? Another thought: you certainly don't have to worry about us on security grounds. When did you last hear about a gay trying to blow anything up with their handbag? Au contraire. The EU should roll out a welcome mat for the gays. We come here, we get on and then we go back home and show the guys who have been stuck there how well we have done. Our family and friends who supported us are happy for us – and the ones who didn't, well, at least they shut the fuck up. Because, darlings, *now* we have money. Everyone benefits."

Ben couldn't help but think that what Lady Gaza was proposing sounded far-fetched, but her argument was interesting.

"Oh my God, I think you are on to something." Lynne jumped up from her seat. "Pam, could you imagine it, a whole smorgasbord of lesbians and bisexual women to pick from – and we could feel virtuous at the same time."

As the group erupted into an animated discussion of the merits or otherwise of Lady Gaza's views, the lady herself decided her work was done. She strutted away to freshen up. Ben found himself looking at Zahoor and imagining thousands more like him. From a selfish point of view, how wonderful that might be. Catching Ben's gaze, Zahoor gave him a conspicuous wink. Ben gathered his wits, and remembered that he needed to speak to Kelly to confirm arrangements for the Glick wedding.

He decided it was time to wind up the LGBT meeting.

*

"The trouble with the law is that we are losing all these Latin terms. All these lovely, lovely Latin terms," said Lucy pensively.

Harry coughed gently, and gulped down some wine. There was something off-putting in the extreme about Lucy tonight. If he'd wanted some nancy nonsense about Classics from a blonde chubster, he'd have tried to cop off with Boris Johnson. Harry could not put his finger on exactly what was troubling him, but then realised that it was her calm that was the very issue. Good God, the calm! There was no sign of the neediness, the eagerness, the slightly over-enthusiastic tendencies, and other slightly *annoying* characteristics of the stereotypical female that Harry had safely stored in his prejudices. Lucy wasn't even angry. She was calm. It evoked a horror film just before the ghost suddenly appears. The tension was building. She was in control of her thoughts, and her feelings, and – oh Christ – she probably had a plan.

Harry blinked. Was she no longer in thrall to him? Did she no longer see him through worshipper's eyes?

"Latin," he mumbled. "Yes."

"Of course," Lucy continued smoothly, "losing the Latin is far better for the provision of legal services to the customer. In a complex analysis, it is as well if you understand all the words. But there are three little words that *you* need to understand, Harry."

She took a long sip of the delicious white Burgundy, her eyes upon Harry like headlights:

"Quid pro quo, Harry. Quid pro blooming quo."

Harry attempted a hearty laugh – the sort his clients liked to hear as he reassured them that he was in charge, rather than the smarter lawyers beneath him, whom he used and discarded like expensive condoms.

Lucy remained composed. She picked out the cashews from the complimentary mixed nuts:

"Harry, Harry, Harry," she said evenly.

Harry snapped:

"Lucy, I'm really not quite sure that I'm following you."

She leaned forward:

"Follow this. You're not just going to discard my career just because you've discarded me."

"Dear Lord, Lucy. Is this some kind of... blackmail?"

"That's a very emotional response, Harry. You disappoint me. Remember what you told us in negotiation training? You said that emotional responses are simply the thermostat of the meeting and have no more significance in the negotiation than the weather. You specifically mentioned that one person's blackmail is another person's use of legitimate commercial pressure."

She sat back, and smoothed her skirt:

"We're grown-ups here, Harry. And it's time for you to sit up and listen. Waiter? Yes. Hello. This gentleman is kindly buying me a bottle of champagne... Yes, it's a special occasion. I've just had some good news from work... Why, thank you."

Harry stared at Lucy in some confusion, but waved a weak confirmation at the helpful young man serving them.

Lucy cast her eyes skywards, gathering her thoughts:

"Let me explain this to you, Harry, because I think

you've misread the position. Let's be clear."

She offered a half incredulous grin at him:

"*You* came after *me*. I was happily minding my own business. Now, I appreciate that we all have issues and urges. I know we ask ourselves questions that make us ripe for therapists to make fortunes out of – as if it were ever possible to truly understand another human being. But *you*, Harry – you wanted a fling in the office, and you very deliberately chose me."

She raised her shoulders as if to say that all this was extremely self-evident:

"You may very well have believed that you could pick me up and set me down. That's not inconceivable, Harry. But what I'm curious about – what I'm curious about is that you appear to be finding it difficult to understand that I may have had some conditions too. Perhaps I, too, come with standard terms and conditions, Harry? Now, how about that? There *is* a quid pro quo, Harry. Actions have consequences. Now, you may call it blackmail. *I* call it self-defence. What's in a name? I'm sure we could, in reality, compromise. We might call it deferred blackmail? It's not the real thing. It is but a pale shadow of blackmail. *Palemail*, if you will."

She waved a hand, almost as if to hurry her train of thought along:

"All you had to do, Harry, is *weigh up the consequences*. Life is full of risks. I'm not some silly little insecure woman who will slink away heartbroken. I'm not a bunny boiler, either, unless you make me into one. But – and here's the rub, Harry – I have contributed significantly to your happiness and on a couple of occasions I have even felt something for you. The way this works in my world is that I get something in return for that. If you think that that is morally deficient, may I simply point out to you, you big, superior, Oxbridge numpty, that people in glass houses shouldn't throw stones. In a nutshell, my dear leader, I am no better or worse than you. I am no different to you – and – just like you – I shall profit from the spoils."

The champagne arrived. The waiter popped the cork. Harry's good manners came on like an automatic watering system. He poured the drinks and snaffled a few nuts for himself. Lucy took a long sip and continued happily:

"It's not as if your decisions are usually that well-founded, anyway. In fact, observing you, it has become clearer and clearer to me that the running of anything at all at SBK should be prised at the earliest opportunity from the lazy, assessment-incapable, judgement-flawed men around the higher echelons of the organisation, and given over with no small haste to those of my sex. I may have all of your flaws, Harry – and perhaps some more besides – but I also have capability on my side. With me around, things get done properly."

"Jesus," said Harry, "Lucy, you are bonkers."

"Aren't we all, dear boy, aren't we all. We're lawyers. If others haven't driven us nuts by the end of the first few years of practice, we surely do a great job of finishing ourselves off."

They drank some more, in silence, as Harry considered the position:

"Well," he said finally. "What do you want?"

Lucy nodded thoughtfully:

"I'm glad we're getting to the crux of it. I want nothing that should prove too difficult for you to acquiesce to. First, please may I have an excellent assessment? That's nothing much. My work deserves it anyway. The point is that I shall get to review whatever drivel you produce in advance of you submitting it. I shall take great pleasure in stripping from it all the patronising guff that those of your ilk always manage to insert when reviewing women. This will be a learning process for you, Harry. You will get a taste of proper objectivity. Second, I want a guaranteed job. Again, I would have been given that anyway – but I'd prefer nonetheless to have someone on the inside fighting for me, instead of having to deal with the politics of the thing. I don't fancy faking admiration for some sporty beer drinker who reminds *you*, Harry, of what you fancied yourself to be when you were young. There'll be some other pointers. I'll let you know."

"And if I don't comply?"

"No one is committing any crimes yet, Harry. We'll consider what to do if you don't come good, so to speak. I doubt that we'll ever have to come to such an unpleasant pass."

They drank in silence under the dimmed lights.

"This is romantic," said Lucy, thoughtfully. She giggled suddenly: "I expect many people here might think we're beginning an affair!"

Harry passed a hand over his eyes:

"God damn it, Lucy. I'll do it. But I need you to know that you are a disgrace to your sex."

Lucy laughed quite loudly:

"We've tried doing it the easy way, Harry. Believe you me. I've spoken to several senior women. The poor dears are littered all over the city. They all sing the same bird song – tales of their like careering all over the place, punctuating the landscape of failure like raisins fallen from a toddler's snack box. I know, Harry. I know about the making women redundant shortly after their first child – or after their second. The bullying, and the unpleasantness. The disregard, the easing out, the lack of respect. I know that the law should protect us, but it is as much use as a papier maché shield on a rainy battlefield. Did you really think that my generation would let you dinosaurs win?"

She downed the last of her glass:

"If I don't singlehandedly win the war of the sexes – and I know that I can't – I will at least ensure that my life tells a tale of me going down fighting. I go forth knowing that if your sex won't play fair, some of us will have the balls to play dirty. Because, Harry, you started it."

"Let Me Rent-ertain You. Seriously?"

Ben looked at Rubens who nodded encouragingly. Ben continued reading the double-page ad in QX magazine:

"For one night only seven top studios present their finest pornstars, performing on stage. *Cockstars*, *Garçons du Monde*, *Macho of the Day*, *Prize Pig*, *Abdomination*, *Männer Männer*, and *Buffalo Sweat* present the hottest of the hot, doing things on stage you never dreamed you would see. Special prizes include entry to the studios VIP rooms where you can meet a pornstar and go home with a baddie bag for your personal Rent-ertainment later."

Rubens clapped his hands:

"Doesn't it sound fun, Ben! It's tonight, I've got tickets, and we are going. No discussion. We need a good night out."

"But Rubens, for God's sake, this is a bit full-on! You know I have moved on from this. I don't do all that slutty stuff anymore."

"Pish. That's why I thought it would be the perfect place for us to go to today. It's just a show. It's like going to the theatre – except that the acting will be dreadful and the sex scenes should be excellent. Actually, according to Tarquin, that's just like the theatre these days. He says it's all very progressive. Tarquin always says that it's not a play until someone has come out as nude as a newborn, epilated in full-on twenty-first century-style. But coming back to tonight – come *on*. You *know* you want to. Plenty to look at, but no touching. Perfectly safe, for a perfectly good boy like you."

Ben couldn't argue with Rubens. It did sound as if it might be a spectacle worth seeing.

This is how, at midnight that Saturday, he came to be dressed in a borrowed pair of black leather trousers and a harness, walking up to the Plasma Club in London Bridge. In the time that he had been living in London, the Shard of Glass had been erected as a destination monument to the exuberance of the Noughties.

Ben was amused to see how his outfit attracted stares from gawping tourists. Maybe they thought that he was an extra from a late night at the erstwhile London Dungeon?

Now that Ben headed up an LGBT group, he felt more secure in showcasing all facets of his identity. He even allowed himself to pose for a picture with a group of tiddly middle-aged women from Canada, who thanked him very politely and wished him a lovely night, wherever he was going. He waved a cheery goodbye at them and hurried off to the club.

It was already busy. Ben liked Plasma. Apart from the decent sound system – essential, but so often overlooked – someone had actually thought about the layout of the place. The centre of the club was a massive space with a high roof and a large stage. So far, so sensible. Off this space were three smaller rooms, each with a well-manned bar and their own toilets. Facilities. It was all about organising the facilities. Most importantly, the corridors joining all these spaces were about fifteen feet wide. It was the only club in London where you didn't spend most of your night queuing to try to get into another room.

Ben never used to notice architectural features when he was high, but since clubbing sober had become the norm, he had taken more time to observe venue layouts. He came to realise just how badly designed most of them were. As he was musing on interior design, he was interrupted by a familiar voice:

"Careful with your drink, big boy. Remember what happened last time we met in a club?"

Ben turned to see Dillon Lloyd smiling up at him. Siegfried Allcock, like an old penny, was standing just behind.

"Can of lager's a lot safer. You're in no danger, bud."

Despite the music and the crowds, Ben sensed that Rubens wasn't his normal self around Siegfried. Subdued was a word Ben never normally associated with the Brazilian. Ben didn't like seeing him like that. Ben wondered what was up. He didn't really want to spend time with Dillon. There was an attraction, but it was a dead beat one. Like a mosquito bite that you scratch, all the while knowing it does no good at all to scratch it. It was kind of irritating having to resist a specific piece of temptation when he was just out for a bit of clean fun at the porn party.

The atmosphere was awkward – strained, and a bit tense. Sexual desire can do that to an ambiance. Fortunately, a muscle-bound man with a face that looked as if it had been hacked out of a slab of granite happened to strut past. He possessed a neck wider than his own head, and was wearing nothing but a pair of tight green army shorts.

"Oooh," shrieked Dillon. "That's Attila the Hunk! Siegfried, give me the pen and follow that pornstar. I need him to sign my butt. See you later, boys!"

The relief that Ben felt on watching them walk off was mirrored in Rubens' face.

"You okay, Rubens? You didn't exactly look pleased to see those two. Is everything okay in the bar?"

"Sure, gostoso, everything's great. Listen, the show's about to start. Let's go and watch."

Although Rubens was perfectly capable of telling barefaced lies when it came to protecting his interests, he sucked at telling untruths to close friends. However, Ben knew better than to challenge him. He would find out what was troubling Rubens when Rubens was ready to tell him.

In the meantime, the stage was filling up with the stars of the evening. Dozens of almost naked men – black, white, Latino, Asian – were posing and preening in identical white *Bunda-Wear* briefs, the latest must-have label from Brazil. It was a porn cocktail.

Rubens sucked his teeth:

"It reminds me of Miss World. They all pretend to be so macho, but half of them are strutting as if they were wearing high heels."

Ben had to admit it was true. He could understand why the Brazilians called their muscular gay men *Barbies*. Objectively, many of the men on stage were fine specimens of manhood, but – with a few honourable exceptions – most of them didn't quite pull the look off. Despite the muscles, they appeared singularly underpowered in the masculinity department. It was like getting into a Range Rover and finding it had a Mini Metro engine under the bonnet. Or – as Rubens once said – "He looks like the King of the Jungle, but he acts like the Queen of Sheba."

Maybe this sense of exasperation was similar to that experienced trying to have a conversation with a model and realising that she genuinely could not talk about anything other than what had featured in gossip magazines that week? Finding out clichés are true is one of the more dispiriting experiences of growing older.

Ben reminded himself that straight men also presented badly on this front. It went deeper than mere appearance. How many straight men had he come across that he genuinely looked up to? How often could the words *fair and decent* be applied meaningfully to men of his acquaintance? So few to admire, to emulate. An individual can look like a man, and act like a leader, all the while being as inconsequential as a pile of jelly. Actions should matter so much more than appearance. Many men's actions presented a pitiful roll call when properly appraised. Ben understood why women felt let down by men. You want something that inspires you sexually to be worthy of the attention you lavish upon it. It's hard to accept that many men are more Gollum than Gandalf.

Do straight men feel that way about women, wondered Ben. Are we all on a carousel of hopelessness, repeating past mistakes and wishing people were better?

If Ben closed his eyes, it sounded and felt just like a regular club on a Saturday night. But with that much flesh on display, the crowd was turned to the stage. The music elicited the merest of sways or tapping of feet. Ben felt like a dance, so he hoped the boys with the pert butts would hurry up, do their thing, leave and let the club start up.

It didn't look promising on that front. As the men filed off, half a dozen broke ranks and took up positions on podiums at the edge of the stage. Ominously, a set was wheeled on centre stage. Ben didn't feel overwhelmed by the artistic director's imagination. The first of the compulsory porn sets had made an appearance: the locker room. Oh, who'd have thought?

A couple of chipboard benches set off by rows of gym lockers did the trick of evoking the damp surroundings of a locker room. The props were completed in an equally wooden way by the hunks in rugby kit. In fairness, seeing as how posing for a naked calendar was an almost compulsory part of the game in rugby clubs these days, this scene looked almost realistic. *Sporno*, thought Ben. That was an exasperating take on things, too. At least it had the welcome impact of starting to level the playing field. Women had been objectified for ever and now men seemed to want in on that action. Goodbye Victorian values, hello prancing peacock.

Rubens spoke up:

"There's something bothering me at work, Ben."

Ben looked away from the naked rugby player he had identified as a profitable image for later to see a troubled look on Rubens' face.

Ben sighed. He had guessed from the atmosphere when Siegfried and Dillon had made their appearance that something was up:

"So, what is it?"

"I had to fire Milo the other day."

"As in Milo with the… that used to do that helicopter thing on stage? Made a mean mojito as well?"

Rubens nodded. The rugby players now formed two neat lines, one lot of beefcake standing in front of the bench, the others seated admiringly, about to lurch in for the first strike. It all seemed *very* realistic.

"So what did Milo do? Was he getting too fresh with the customers? Don't tell me he was escorting from the bar?"

The performers had obviously rehearsed. Four heads were now bobbing up and down, synchronised perfectly. Well, it was important for teams to rehearse set pieces. Each of the standing men had one hand on a head, the other tweaking a nipple. Their own. After a short time they moved down one, resuming the exact same position with their new adorer. This happened twice more. The routine was exemplary, although lacking in spontaneity and believability. Ben knew he shouldn't be admiring it, but it was strangely hypnotic. It somehow reminded Ben of one of those Steps videos that gay Brits seemed to adore.

Rubens shook his head:

"It was nothing to do with that."

Rubens was reluctant to talk – yet, at the same time, he needed to. Ben thought he should give Rubens some time. He would get there. In the meantime, Ben was keen to see if rugby Steps were going to be able to get to the climax together. *Five, six, seven, eight.* In the event, three of them actually managed it, the fourth shamefully giving up. Nerves. They all took a bow, exited stage right, and it was time for a change of set.

Rubens leaned closer to Ben:

"You've heard about the problems we've had with money going missing from the bar?"

Clubs are not the best place to have a conversation. Each exchange had to be shouted into the other's ear so as to be heard over the music. However, Ben saw that Rubens was eagerly awaiting his reaction.

Meanwhile, a doctor's waiting room was wheeled on to the stage, followed by an improbably perfect medic in scrubs and a naked blond guy with the body of Tarzan and the face of an X Factor boy band member.

"Everyone has, Rubens. The gay scene doesn't really do secrets. So it was Milo then?"

As Rubens considered exactly how to answer, Ben

watched the inevitable check-up turn into an in-depth examination of all and any issues related to X Factor Tarzan's various orifices.

"Siegfried is convinced that it was Milo. Dillon had noticed things more than once. Milo was still on trial. We just let him go."

Ben looked away from the stage:

"That was convenient. So what's the problem, then?"

Two shaven-headed men had appeared on stage to the side of the clinic. They were a bit older, still buff, but considerably less attractive than those who had passed before. They were also butt-naked. This collection of facts indicated as evidently as a puffer fish ballooning that they were going to veer from vanilla into something a bit harder.

And so it was.

One of them immediately mounted a box, positioned himself on his hands and knees, and proffered his exposed butthole to the four winds. His companion wasted no time in spreading plenty of lube around it, looking to the audience for encouragement as he did it. The crowd declined to clap.

Rubens was engrossed in his thoughts:

"The conversation I had with Milo was as difficult as I expected it to be. He denied it. Forcefully. He seemed disappointed that I could believe he was capable of stealing. He felt as if I was betraying him. I was just like the others, ready to believe the worst of him, because of his background."

A weird contraption had joined the unattractive older

pair on stage. It transpired that it was a rotating dildo on the end of a pole. Presumably, that was why a lot of lube was required. It was presented to the audience as if Beyoncé herself had graced the party. The crowd seemed underwhelmed. The business end was getting closer to the lubed-up bottom as the standing baldie got ever more excited. But, sadly, as it was about to enter the expectant cheeks, it stopped rotating.

Sensing that there was a problem, its operator pulled it back and gave the box a thwack. Nothing happened. Then the dildo fell off, rolled down the stage and off on to the dancefloor.

Bummer. Or not, as the case may be.

The operator looked at the audience with obvious confusion. He ran off to the back of the stage where one did not need to be a lip reader to understand him shouting *the machine's broken, what do I do?* Not seeming to get a response, he decided to improvise.

He grabbed a common-or-garden dildo from backstage, lubed it up with the relish of a connoisseur who had just discovered a bottle of 1870 Chateau Lafite, and then delightedly started to apply it to his patient colleague.

It was the least sexy sex scene Ben could ever conceive of seeing. Finally, people were drifting off and beginning to dance.

"What do you think, Rubens? Did you ever see anything? Do you think he took the money?"

Just as Rubens leaned in to shout into Ben's ear again, there was an almighty bang on stage, and floodlights started circling the roof of the venue. Three trapezes were lowered from the ceiling. The two outer ones each had a man sitting on them, completely naked, gently swinging back and forth over the dance floor. The trapezists were playing with themselves. The middle trapeze remained motionless. A tall black bodybuilder with a dick of death stood upright upon it, as if taunting the crowd and the very use of the equipment he was stranded on. A fourth man, Latin-looking, was lowered from the roof, upside down, tied by his feet. The bodybuilder grabbed him on the way down and firmly positioned the man's mouth on his cock.

Upside-down man was now swaying back and forth with his master and the trapeze. Ben didn't think it looked particularly satisfying in terms of receiving a decent blow job, but it was an impressive feat, and a huge improvement on the broken dildo machine. Even Rubens was momentarily distracted, before continuing:

"The thing is, Ben, I have never seen anything. I am taking everything on trust from Siegfried who seems to trust Dillon. They always seem to be together. What if Dillon is lying to Siegfried? I just don't know."

By this time, the bodybuilder had turned the roped Latino around. He had obtained a condom and lube from somewhere, and was preparing to move to the climax. As upside-down man was lowered into position, the music went up a notch.

It was now impossible to hear anything, and those present wanted to see how the Cirque de So-Gay was going to conclude. Even Ben and Rubens put their conversation on hold. The bodybuilder was somehow managing to control the swaying of his trapeze as he pumped the upside-down Latino. The music was raised to a fever pitch. The bodybuilder then withdrew, his trapeze now motionless, and all four pornstars masturbated furiously, seemingly to the beat. This time the choreography was perfect as music, men and even accompanying lights all crescendoed in unison, the bodybuilder releasing an improbably large amount of cum all over the Latino hanging below him. As they were lifted away to a round of applause, the two performers sitting on the trapezes hoisted themselves gently up to reveal that they had been aided in their act by built-in dildos attached to their trapeze seats.

Ben gawped:

"Jeez, I've really seen it all now. I think I need another drink and then a cigarette. Come along, Rubens, and we'll finish this conversation outside."

Plasma's outdoor smoking area was one of the few in London that looked as if it had been created for people to enjoy. Even non-smokers had come to get some air and a chance to talk.

Ben lit a rare cigarette:

"So, getting back to Outrageous Fortune, you think that Siegfried might be wrong on this one, and Dillon could be working him?"

"I just don't know, Ben. Milo was really upset, though. He warned me to be careful. It made me feel really uncomfortable."

"You need to be all eyes and ears, Rubens. I guess you can't completely trust anyone other than yourself. 'Twas ever so."

Rubens looked thoughtful, again, before brightening up:

"Okay. Enough about this, gostoso. I want to have fun tonight."

He chuckled appreciatively:

"Here we go. Looks like fun is already coming up."

The four trapezists from the show were approaching. The Latino looked even cuter the right way up. Just Ben's type – in another world, of course.

"Ai, papi, why wasn't I doing a scene with you tonight?" The Latino grabbed Ben's harness with both hands and pulled him closer.

"I'm not actually one of the porn stars."

Ben smiled confidently. He knew that no matter how much he fancied the guy, tonight he was in complete control. Kelly would be back in a few days and there was no way he was going to spoil her homecoming with inconvenient feelings of guilt:

"You've cleaned up well. He gave you a real soaking."

"That's why he calls himself *The Sperminator*. I'm Desiderio, by the way, but everyone calls me Desi. You better remember when we wake up tomorrow morning."

Desi flashed a smile that indicated that he was used to men falling at his feet and asking when they should call the taxi. Ben had to admit that, if Desi could have sex hanging upside down with his feet tied together, he would like to see what he could do when in full control of his limbs.

After explaining to Desi that he was with someone, a girl, and that he was actually faithful to her, a fact which made poor Desi want Ben even more, Ben glanced over to check on Rubens, concerned that he was still sweating the bar situation.

Rubens had his tongue halfway down the Sperminator's throat. Ben decided that – maybe, just maybe – Rubens would probably manage the situation, one way or another.

10

Something borrowed, something blue

The ceiling soared above Caroline. Tall ceilings were good for the soul. Converted warehouses, cathedrals, arenas, or grand old railway stations thrilled people – and always had – as they stretched to the heavens. There was something about very tall ceilings that lifted the spirit. She stood by a window that stretched upwards like a bright beam of light, tastefully framed by elegant curtains that politely refused to take precedence over the dazzling view through the glass.

The hotel had been a wise choice. It was spotlessly clean and refined, and skirted by gardens that were well-maintained, yet delightfully relaxing. Nothing was too clipped or too stiff or too formal. But, thought Caroline, as she stood gazing at her last garden view as a single woman, it felt like the home you always imagined you might live in one day, in a world where one were gifted with excellent taste, good furnishings, and a supply of ex-lovers, friends and fine foods on tap.

She sipped cold champagne from a heavy cut glass flute. She took another, longer draught. It felt good. She was grateful. Even champagne could sometimes be a disappointment. It sometimes was nasty, acidic drinking, whose only merit was its precipitous lunge into the blood stream, like a Greek diver launching recklessly from a cliff top. She was drinking, however, her favourite brand of the tipple, and it was perfect. A mellow, rounded flavour with no hint of sourness, it danced on the tongue. This fizz heightened the senses, sending endorphins hurrying up the body's VIP lane with red velvet-roped access to the brain.

Happiness is induced in so many ways. It is like a fat smiling baby gurgling in the wings of life's parade, poised and ready to experience its first enthusiastic rush. Caroline wondered abstractedly how that was, for children. When did they first get that rush consciously, the feeling that causes you to grin wide, long and ecstatically, the sheer leaps of sensations that came from all being right in the world, just for a while? What was it like to experience that for the first time? She wished that she could remember. You *don't* remember your first time, it seems. In any event, can you really experience something if you don't know that you're experiencing it? How did babies feel – about *anything*?

No wonder people took drugs. Caroline imagined that chasing that feeling of relief could become a preoccupying pastime.

She drank a little more, and looked out at a pretty bird. It landed on a thin branch that dipped and swayed gently, as the bird full-throatedly sang, calling to its mate.

She was getting married in a moment.

How on earth had that happened?

Was she quite sure? Was she mad? Was it wise?

Another deep draught brought with it some reassurance. If it all brought pain, she could control it. Did the pain even matter? Nothing could be perfect for ever. At some point, you always have to leave the dungeon.

Nothing lasts – but you do know if you love someone.

The wonder of being in a suite was that one could get away from one's own party. Caroline could hear Kelly and Monique chattering away animatedly in the other reception room. They seemed both close and far away. Caroline had asked them to leave her for a moment. She wanted to walk alone for a moment in her dress. She smiled, thinking that one did sometimes have to walk alone.

She was getting used to the gown. It felt very unusual, a glorious cream column of heavy silk, draped in classic Grecian style over her lovely shoulders. Sparkling long silver earrings set with tiny diamonds rained from her ears, like spiders' webs holding captive shimmering drops. Her hair was swept up, set off with a delicate filigree tiara. Her red lipstick was deep and inviting. She was a breath-taking sight, even to herself. She felt incredibly sexy. She felt powerful. This all boded very well.

Over in an ornate hotel reception area, Hartmut unscrewed a hip flask and presented it to Stefan.

"For my best man," he said.

Stefan accepted the object and looked at it curiously. Stags with enormous horns were finely engraved into the flask. It weighed pleasantly in his hand.

"It's an honour. I can tell you, I will remember this. So

tell me, Hartmut. What are we tasting here?"

"Brandy. From the Napoleonic era. Some of the last bottles in the world, no doubt."

Stefan almost choked:

"That is a gift indeed. Be still, my beating Hartmut. I am now almost too nervous to drink."

Hartmut smiled genially:

"Stefan, I cannot think of a more appropriate moment for us to indulge. Besides, I have two other bottles. The one we have started here is concealed upstairs. I intend to polish it off over the course of today, with close friends. And you, my friend, in coming over here to support me in this most moving occasion, deserve a taste of history. Who would have thought that I should ever marry?"

Stefan had known Hartmut since school days in Germany.

"I never thought you would marry, Hartmut," he admitted, his colour already rising both from the drink and from the excitement of the drink. "I thought you were too otherworldly to even consider such a practical arrangement."

Hartmut arched an eyebrow:

"And yet here I am being most conventional. Of course, the taxation advantages have not passed me by."

"I am sure the Government will be delighted when it realises that its family-friendly policies are paying off."

"The good organisation of one's worldly affairs is very important to the order of one's private affairs," mused Hartmut. "Freedom, my friend – I feel that this is about *freedom*. I sense that I am on the verge of acquiring enormous freedom – space in my mind to dedicate to our quest for pleasure. The mistress of my heart will march me through the last vestiges of my conventionality, through and beyond it to the limitless territory of who I really am."

Stefan pondered this. He was a school teacher. His conventionality was sturdily constructed – a little chalet of practicality and shelter.

"That could get very exciting," he offered. "Many would love to have your force of character."

Hartmut gave a tight smile:

"I have been weakened by true love, but it is also lighting a number of beacons towards the future. This brandy is delicious. I am inspired to say many more things. But I must be careful not to be so inebriated so as to lose myself in the moment and do something unexpected like weep."

Stefan smiled confidently:

"If you weep, I have a clean handkerchief. If you pass a dusty corner I have a small clothes brush. For all other eventualities I have some wet wipes. And I have the rings."

"Wunderbar, my dear friend – wunderbar. Let's ring in some changes around here."

"Is it time yet?"

"Caroline, you look incredible," said Kelly quietly.

The bridesmaids' dresses were a deep lustrous red. The women carried posies of red and cream roses, with tiny buds woven into simple floral headdresses.

Monique looked at her friends:

"I think we will not disgrace the photographer's lens."

Caroline smiled:

"I agree. We all look good. Weddingy enough. I have the most amazing cream latex playsuit for the after party, too. It has silver go-faster stripes down the legs. And the usual zips. It is my man in Amsterdam's wedding present. I am so thrilled with it, I can tell you. There will be suffering in the dungeon tonight."

"Shoes?" asked Kelly.

"Some incredible silver laced thigh highs."

"Whips?" asked Monique.

"Butter cream softness on the leather, a woven gripping handle, and several tails."

Kelly and Monique looked at each other, and shrugged.

"Our work here is done," said Kelly.

"Not quite. We need to navigate the ceremony. Peace must be maintained between the guests. No one should leave who has not been humiliated as he or she expected."

Caroline sighed contentedly:

"I think as a bride I'm supposed to feel unready. But I'm not sure I've ever felt more ready in my life."

It was a cosmopolitan gathering – and not only because the guests were all greeted with strong pink cocktails as they arrived. Guests were politely barred from entering the room where the ceremony was taking place until they had downed the concoction. Some rather large gentlemen were murmuring soft encouragement to that effect. "Yes, you may have another to take in – but you are unable to access the room until I have seen you drink it all." Order was maintained, and ritual imposed.

Taking guests by surprise works wonders. For once,

people were doing as they were told – a matter of great
satisfaction to Hartmut and Caroline. The happy couple
had taken the view that there was a definite advantage to
taking the edge off any social awkwardness right at the
outset. This seemed a wise plan, given that guests ran a
gauntlet that started and finished with Eleanor Napier
Jones.

The gathering was certainly a sight for sore eyes. Harry
Gumpert wore tails. Sarah Gumpert sported a buttercup
yellow ensemble with cream gloves, and one of those
expensive hats that looked like a frozen child's sneeze.
Tarquin Henderson-Smythe was clad in a pale blue suit,
with a patterned orange shirt. It looked incredible – as
did he. His blue eyes were flashing, taking in every detail
around, and wondering whether the hotel knew about the
possible provenance of the small picture to the left of the
piano. Ursula Himmelfarb and Gertrude Plassnik were
talking to Cornisha Burrows, who wore belted green velvet,
with a discreet leather cuff in honour of the occasion.
Arthur wore his best suit. He looked as shiny as it did,
and beamed with happiness. Rubens, Jamal and Alex were
bursting out of shirts and jackets that strained over their
well-exercised bodies. This was making them all feel very
horny. Weddings – well, it's all about union, and fertility,
isn't it? And dancing! And food!

The family members took the lead into the ceremony
room. Hartmut positioned himself at the front of the room,
under a bower of cream and red flowers. The celebrant, a
tall hooded being, waved a hand to start proceedings. The
music started.

Do you really want to hurt me, sang Culture Club, *do you really want to make me cry?*

Caroline entered the room, accompanied by Kelly and Monique. There was a gasp at her beauty. Hartmut turned and looked at his bride. A look passed between them – a look of trust and love, a look that assured Caroline that Hartmut would smash a Fabergé egg for her, and that she would give up champagne for him. They knew that they were the most important thing in the world to each other. This was not about sex. They each took sex by the scruff of the neck and shook it until it yielded to them. This was not about power. They were both powerful and had been powerful and brave for years. This was about understanding, and commitment. I am your castle, you are my rock, and we will survive the perils and fears of the world together, as long as we can.

The reception was held in a drawing room. Delicious drinks flowed, and the canapés were plentiful. Guests could not move for splendid delicacies, served by staff of no less splendour.

Matters were going well. Caroline's best friend from school was already indulging her appetites with another guest in the hotel library. They were being quiet enough. Caroline smiled wryly at Juliet's endeavours. It was better than the wedding where Juliet had welcomed home a member of the Armed Forces on a gravestone, in a cemetery. A fitting tribute to escaping death, and a good story to tell – but nonetheless, not quite enough grind and punishment for Caroline's own taste. Speaking of memorials, at one end of the room stood a glorious tiered cake. On closer inspection, motifs of handcuffs and masks were picked out in white icing – but you might have missed them, had you not looked closely.

Caroline saw Juliet reappear, smoothing her hair with one hand and her skirt with another. Perfect timing, as usual. Juliet looked so lascivious and happy. Her companion looked dazed. Juliet's conquests always seemed to. The quartet played merrily as Hartmut took a long sword. After posing briefly with Caroline for the sheet lightning of flashes, he expertly and deftly sliced the cake.

He calmed the applause:

"Liebe Freunden – dear friends, family and beloved hangers-on. My heart is full, and I am privileged to welcome you. We are always supported by you. For you to share this joy with us is everything that we would have hoped this day to be."

He paused:

"My Caroline. Meine Liebchen. You make me catch my breath. You inspire me to dream. You are my gilded cage, my diamond fetter, the very shackles of my humanity. With you, I can go on. Please… let us all raise a glass to my beautiful wife!"

They drank long.

Caroline stepped up:

"Darling Hartmut. Before all our friends, I tie myself to you, willingly and gladly. Our bonds will be those that last. Our love is not blindfolded. Together we are stronger. And that goes for everyone in the room. Thank you for joining us. To Hartmut, to health, to love, and liberty."

The guests cheered. The music picked up its pace.

Hartmut turned to Caroline. He took her hand, and looked at the band there:

"Caroline. My Caroline. You are everything that I have ever wanted… and I really, really do want to hurt you, some time."

Caroline's blood red lips curled into a carmine smile:

"Hartmut, my master, my love. I think we are going to nail this marriage lark."

"Isn't this amazing?" said Ben.

Kelly started. She turned and looked at him. She hesitated. She wanted to tell him that it was as if she were seeing him for the first time, but it sounded very blunt and obvious. There he was, indeed. Tall. Dark curls softening his masculine face. Deep eyes. Such excellent features, and such manliness. Every girl's dream.

"It is amazing," she said.

Kelly's mind raced. Mixed feelings, she mused. That's what weddings give you. Of course she could not be happier for Caroline and Hartmut. Of course – and most importantly – she believed in their union, in their suitability, in their love, all of which had had to come together rather magically, to give them even half a chance of lasting the distance. But now as she, Kelly, stood there, flowers in her hair, a posy of blood red, cream and baby's breath in her hand, in a pretty red dress, waiting for her bride as any good maid should, the memories of her Parisian adventures posed many more questions than they answered. Marriage? Monogamy? Were we designed for monogamy? If not, is it a good, workable compromise? How does one *exercise* the compromise? Might a good work- out be in order – nay, necessary?

Was it not the case that a good sex life needed more than just two participants, like any good party does? And if that were the case, and the strongest and best of us alone resisted that call to the floor, then does that not lead to social disorder, in the form of unhappy, ill-suited couples tottering about, picking up their children, falling apart, and grimly hanging on – sometimes all at the same time?

In truth, for better and for worse does not sound that great a deal.

The problem was, thought Kelly, I love Ben. I do. But I'm thinking of Morten all the time. I probably love him too. With a fair degree of wariness, admittedly. But the feeling is there.

Why do I have to choose?

It is one thing not to cheat if you have no opportunity to, thought Kelly. It's very easy to fancy distant pop stars, or Alexander Skarsgård. But what was one to do when someone as real, as appealing, as interested as Morten appears on the scene? What then?

Some people live whole lives without meeting anyone that they can really relate to.

"Kelly, you seem a few light years away."

Kelly passed her posy free hand over her eyes:

"Ben," she said, "we have to talk."

For Ben, it was as if the party had vanished. He stood there in shock, as Kelly explained quietly that things had moved on with Morten.

"Do you," he asked suddenly, venomously, "do you have any idea how many men and women I have passed up for you?"

"Ben, it's not a competition. I know you have your chances. I think we all do."

"Oh yes! You manifestly do! Oh, you've really been keeping up with all the chances on your side! Don't you see, Kelly? You make me feel sick! I gave up everything for you."

"Ben, you have given nothing up for me. Everything has always been there, all around you, and it still is. I'm sorry. It's only the shock speaking. Whatever we do, let's not say anything we're going to regret."

"I'm regretting quite a lot already," said Ben loudly.

"Well I don't. I don't regret being in love with you. I don't regret the way life is. I don't regret that you don't understand that someone else has made me feel safe and excited – and sometimes safe and excited simultaneously. It's not an either/or. But I have been away, and lonely, and confused. I've needed the strength of an arm around me. I've needed some attention. It's not against you, or against what we have. I just wanted it all to be simple again."

Ben closed his eyes. Oh, simplicity.

"How simple this is," he said.

They stood quietly.

"Well," said Ben, "I think we've come to the end of our particular cul-de-sac."

"If that's how you want it…"

"What do you mean? How else could I possibly have it? I don't want to share you with Morten. I'd be Morten-fied!"

"That's not even faintly funny."

Ben looked wildly around. His heart pounded sadly. Maybe it was genuinely about to break. Its beats felt like the stabs of throbbing pain.

"This all feels entirely surreal."

Kelly nodded. She had tears in her eyes.

Ben caught his breath, and passed a hand through his hair:

"Let's – let's just ease through the options. We could – er – split up, or have a ménage-à-trois. Or go the full hog and have an open relationship. But, as I recall, you could not even cope with Sanjay flirting with me! What has happened to you? What has happened to us? We won't always bloody have Paris! Paris has bloody well had us."

Kelly looked miserable:

"Let's just have some time apart, and think."

"Think? Think? I know what I think! I think you'll be off having sex with Morten, bouncing all over him like an oestrogen-fuelled rubber ball! What am I supposed to think about that? Is that supposed to be a good thing? I mean, he's from frickin' Scandinavia! Hasn't he got enough liberally-minded people up there to contort with? Why mess us up? Why mess up the one thing… that I even half believed in…"

Ben turned away.

"Ben!"

He waved a hand:

"Just leave me alone. Let's do what you want. Time apart, and thinking. I hope what I think of you improves."

He walked away, but paused a moment, and half turned:

"I'll give you this, Kelly. You've picked a very beautiful place to break my heart."

"There, there."

Caroline patted Kelly.

"He just won't think of the bigger picture..." gulped Kelly.

Caroline smiled ruefully:

"Not sure what the bigger picture could bring here. It's as I always said, Kelly. There is no pleasure without pain."

"I... I had to tell him."

Did you, thought Caroline, *of all the times and places and events...*

"There, there. Don't cry. You'll smudge on me. Not in the bridesmaid's duty manual, that. Life is full of pain and misunderstanding. Always has been, always will be."

"It's not a misunderstanding," sobbed Kelly. "I love them both."

Caroline stared into the mirror of the elegant ladies' powder room at the slightly odd sight reflected there. She moved Kelly to a rather nice soft velvet chair in a corner of the boudoir, and knelt before her, like an extravagantly overdressed maid servant.

"We'll need to think about all this some more, and see what transpires. As far as I know, Ben is still here. You know that Hartmut means the world to him. This is not going to be resolved today."

"I'm not sure I know what to do," confessed Kelly. "How do I even face him?"

Caroline shrugged:

"Dear girl, you're only human. We're all going to die. Humiliation is only as bad as you let it be. It was courageous – if, potentially, a little stupid – to tell him. You're still the same person, and none of us should be judging you. Maybe you do love them both. Maybe Ben should stop thinking in terms of exclusivity. But for now you must fix your face and come and dance. Monique will have some gallic-tinged thoughts on this – and given all of our shared history, Ben and you both need to think things through."

"We're asking a lot of Ben," said Kelly with a slight hiccup.

"No more than we ask of ourselves," said Caroline briskly. "Tell me," she added. "This Morten. Is he worth it?"

Kelly smiled sadly:

"Maybe."

Some warmth crept back:

"Yes. Yes, he might be."

From beyond the scented retreat came the strains of the Fondant Furies breaking into a spirited cover of Depeche Mode's *Master and Servant*.

Caroline hugged Kelly:

"Kelly, we'll talk some more in due course. But just here, just now, your morality is getting in the way of *everything*. You're going to grow old, and die. Sleeping with people is a blessing. One day we may be less desirable. I'm not marrying Hartmut so I can sleep with him. I'm not even marrying him to have children. I've done that. I'm marrying him because I want to be with him. Does anyone get that distinction anymore? So, what this comes down to is this: you need to figure out the answer to one question. Who do you want to be with?"

Kelly pushed her hair back:

"It's fine in theory, Caroline. But who really knows the answer to that question, long term? I'm the practical test subject here, and it's not as clear-cut as that. I know what Ben is thinking, and I've hurt him so badly, it makes me want to scream. If I sleep with someone and they sleep with someone else, not only does it hurt but it makes me want to rip their eyes out and play marbles with them."

"What?"

"With the eyeballs. Play marbles with the eyeballs."

"Oh, I see. I'm not sure they'd be firm enough... Anyway, this can and should be simplified. There is not enough time in the world to sleep with every person that you're attracted to. All you need to get by is a degree of sexual continence, taking a moment to figure out your shortlist of people worthy of your attention. You'll make the odd glaring error. But overall it's a short list. You've got to fit a lot into life as well as sex. That being said, it's easy to see how for the vast, overwhelming majority of us the list must *surely* be more than just the one."

Caroline stood up:

"Above all, what's done is done. Onwards. You'll need to take things one step at a time. There'll be a lot more talking about this before we're done."

11

Bare with me

"She's been screwing a fucking Viking!"

Rubens knew something was up. He'd watched Ben storm around at the wedding like a tornado and leave with suspiciously shiny eyes. Ben insisted that everything was fine and that he did not want to talk to anyone about anything.

He had finally agreed to meet up.

Siegfried was late for his shift, and the bar was quiet. Rubens knew that this was a good time to listen to his friend. They would head out once Siegfried finally showed up – but for now Outrageous Fortune hosted man talk about a girl.

"What exactly did she tell you, Ben?"

Rubens had had a fair amount of experience comforting his friends when a gay man had turned out to be playing the field, or had just upped and left. But this was his first time dealing with a friend who had been betrayed by a woman. Not just any woman, either. It made it considerably more awkward that the betraying party was another friend. Rubens had been close to Kelly Danvers long before he had met Ben. And Rubens liked Kelly.

The bar filled up slowly, but they were left in peace.

Ben lowered his eyes to his drink:

"She told me that she had met someone in Paris. Some Swede or Norwegian or something. That it had gone to her head like too much wine and that they had ended up in bed."

Rubens wanted a description. Like many Brazilians he was a sucker for blonde hair and blue eyes. Rubens suddenly thought, excitedly, that Kelly would not have fallen for a minger. But he contained his excitement. Ben looked as if someone had taken his puppy away. O *gostoso*, thought Rubens. Life isn't easy, and matters of the heart never quite work out as expected. You just have to laugh and dance and sing! Yes, maybe better to ask Kelly herself for juicy details about the blond Nordic God. Ben might not be in the right frame of mind just yet for a good gossip about the other lover's looks. Rubens mused as to how easily he himself ended up in bed with sexy Scandinavians. He dreamed of Stockholm the way children dream of Disneyland. Definitely best not to mention that, either. Yes, empathy must somehow be invited to the table. Rubens told himself that he should be comforting Ben, not thinking about catching up with the woman who had just chewed up Ben's heart.

"Oh, that is terrible, Ben. Was it just the once, then, or...?"

"They've been at it for weeks. I thought there was something different in her voice. But I was too stupid to even think for a minute that..."

Ben's voice drifted off. He could not believe that, whilst he had forgone temptation, she had utterly failed to do the same. Theirs had been a relationship of equals, based on trust and mutual understanding. How wrong he had been about that. What a complete simpleton he had been taken for.

He frowned to hide his pain:

"Once, I could possibly – *possibly* – have forgiven. But more than once? That is premeditated. It is a relationship. This is not just an impulse. So I told her. It's over."

"You did what, Ben? But you two are *perfect* for each other. Is that what she wanted?"

"No. She begged me not to go. She says she needs to work out what she wants. But, Rubens, she betrayed me. If we had had an open relationship then that would have been playing by the rules, but we agreed to be monogamous. And I have been. One hundred per cent. It's been difficult for me. This city is *full* of opportunities. I have wasted all those because of her. I'm furious."

Rubens sought to lighten the tone:

"Well, it is not like that for everyone, you know. There are people out there who have very little sex. It seems incredible, but it's true. They tell me so. Some people are not getting it more than once a week. It's a wonder their bits don't just fall off. If they did, on the information I have, the city would be absolutely littered with… Anyway, I think it helps that you still feel a bit as if every weekend is a short and brilliant holiday. Also, you are a very good-looking twenty-something bisexual, with the libido of a rotting rhino."

For the first time Ben smiled gingerly:

"Rutting, Rubens, rutting. Although, having a *hunk o' spunk* from Sweden steal my girl away, makes me feel about as attractive as a rotting rhino. But, seriously, screw her, Rubens. I'm not depriving myself anymore. In fact, I'm going to take a leaf out of her book. I'm going to be easy-peasy, come and squeeze me. I'm going to line them up like pints I'm about to sink. Never mind the weekend – every night is going to be party night. This weekend, you, my friend, are going to take me clubbing. You're going to get me so off my head that I won't even remember the faces of all the people I screw. Just make sure they're hot. Anyway, we start straight away, right now. You're taking me to the boots-only party you keep telling me about."

Ben sounded very sure of himself, but Rubens was not convinced. It seemed obvious that Ben still loved Kelly. These instructions had revenge written all over them. On the bright side, it would be really good fun revenge. This was better than something grim like throwing someone's clothes in a wheelie bin, or scratching their car. It would be good to have the fun Ben back for a while. Rubens decided that he should speak to Kelly, though. He wouldn't tell Ben that.

"Hello, Siegfried's here. Rubens, here's our cue to leave. Wait a minute, who is that guy he's with? He looks familiar. In a good way. Not so much like Hungry Eyes over there."

Hungry Eyes was a rather tired-looking middle-aged man. His long blond hair looked a little the worse for wear. It's so difficult to keep long hair in check. Hungry Eyes couldn't take his eyes off Rubens and Ben. He had even managed to stumble into their table as he walked past on his way to the bar, steadying himself rather unsubtly on Ben's knee, and almost kicking his bag over. The steadying took longer than necessary. Ben half expected him to try to lunge in for a kiss. He was relieved when the man hoisted himself away, muttering an apology.

But the man behind the bar was plain old-fashioned good-looking.

"That's Zahoor. You met him with Lady Gaza the other night. He's our new Milo."

"You see, Rubens, another one of my missed opportunities. I bet Kelly would have been straight in there. What time does he finish his shift? Maybe I should give him my number."

Rubens sighed. He didn't like all the endless references to Kelly as if she were a bad person. In fact, Rubens disliked it intensely whenever friends were fighting. He must definitely speak to Kelly about the whole situation.

"You stay here a minute, Ben, I'm just going to do the handover with Ziggy."

Ben smiled at Zahoor as Rubens went to speak to Siegfried. *Sod it* thought Ben. He stood up and went to the bar. He noticed the lustful straggly blond perking up. The man stared at him like a dishevelled pet sighting its partially-filled dinner bowl. Ben was wearing jeans and a T-shirt so tight that they looked as if they had been painted onto his body. Dressed that way he shouldn't really complain about getting attention. But he still shuddered at the thought of being in Hungry Eyes' spank bank.

Ben forgot about Hungry Eyes. He's not in my league, he thought confidently. Unlike Zahoor.

"What can I get you?"

Zahoor had practically shoved the other barman aside in order to serve Ben. Not that he had needed to. Ben would have demanded to be served by him.

"Your phone number and availability. And four shots of tequila. Please."

Ben smiled warmly, staring into Zahoor's big green eyes. He didn't want confidence to be mistaken for rudeness. The line had to be walked precisely to get the best results and he did not have time to waste. In fact, he had considerable catching up to do.

By the time Rubens returned, the telephone number was stored, a time the next day agreed, and four shooters awaited, to wish the boys well on the road.

"Gostoso, really? You know I am not that much of a drinker. And it's midweek. You do have a job, remember?"

"Rubens, if I am going to my first boots-only party, then I need some Dutch courage. Here it is – readily available, one shot at a time. There are no worries. Anyway, how is Siegfried?"

Ben leaned in conspiratorially, thinking of something other than himself and his hurt and needlessly starved libido for the first time that evening:

"How are things with the money here? Have things sorted themselves out now Milo has gone?"

"Thanks to God, no more problems. Everything has gone back to normal. It looks as if Milo was just lying to me. Ziggy was right. He usually is when it comes to the bar. I really need to learn from him. He is a good influence. He hasn't tried me to make me feel bad about Milo, and he let me do the hiring of Zahoor. I feel a bit bad about having suspected that Dillon was up to something. I've tried to be pleasant to him to make up for it. Management. It's a bloody nightmare."

"I could help out there, if you like, Rubens. I could be very nice to Dillon, especially certain bits of him."

The thought of what Ben might like to do to Dillon to show vicarious contrition led his thoughts on to the boots-only party:

"Ok, next shooter down. We need to go."

As they left the bar, Zahoor gave Ben a smile that Ben just wanted to dive into and lose himself in, there and then. However, that was tomorrow night's sex, and Ben had to get to tonight's. Planning was all very well in life, but jam tomorrow should never be allowed to stop one from getting a whole array of potted conserves today.

Alex had whetted Ben's appetite in recent months by describing his adventures at boots-only events. Apparently, this experience would make saunas look like a place one goes for commitment. Boots-only was the ultimate in convenience – the McDonalds of mating. The moment you tire of whatever it is you are doing, you simply walk away and sample the next. Ben imagined it to be like Internet porn, but with a super effective 3D touchscreen that touched you back. He shivered slightly with anticipation.

At this hour, the British Museum was closed and free of the hordes that made walking past it such an inconvenience for those in a hurry. Although Ben loved the fact that theatres, galleries and museums practically littered the streets of London, after his first few months living in town he had stopped visiting them as much as he used to. It seemed so much easier to go to a bar or restaurant to meet friends. After all, the landmarks would still be there the following weekend, and the weekend after that. Glimpsing the museum, though, Ben resolved to start picking up Time Out again.

As he looked around, he saw a couple leaving a little restaurant and stepping into a pool of light, laughing, arm-in-arm. He briefly stopped to observe them. They had that happy, adoring look that made other people in love feel warm inside as they recognised the aphrodisiac of simply being close to him or her. Ben, however, had been unceremoniously dropped from the lovers' team. He was now the star striker for the bitter opposition. Accordingly, he felt like going and kicking them both in the shins. They grated like chalk screeching on a blackboard. At this very moment, right now, the woman who was staring pathetically into her partner's eyes was probably having a torrid affair with some randy Scandi who had swept her off her feet. That poor sap of a boyfriend – how little he knew about the knives that women thrust into unsuspecting hearts. Ben looked at him with contempt as he walked past, and made a note to start looking at the *Musts and Maybes* of QX again.

Rubens called him on and Ben caught up with him wordlessly.

Ursa Major was a bar designed for the hairier, more masculine gay man. Although Ben was not a particular fan of bears, Alex had assured him that on the boots-only nights, the place attracted a goodly mix. Its location in Fitzrovia meant that the bar was exceptionally convenient for both the horny of Soho who were tired of merely showing out, and for those tourists who were unsure of venturing south of the river or east of the City. After crossing Tottenham Court Road at the point where the electronics shops gave way to the home furnishings stores, Ben felt another thrill run through him. They entered the street where the promise of sex should become reality again.

It was not the location that Ben expected for a sex club. Dark, disapproved-of activities should take place in dark, disapproved-of corners of the city, such as one of those leaky arches under the seemingly endless railway tracks lining London's skin. Ursa Major, by contrast, could be found in a pleasant Georgian street, well lit, with clean pavements. It even sported a laminated notice in the pocket park opposite, urging dog owners to clean up after their pets and to curb excessive barking. There was a pretty little church a couple of doors down, as well as a florist, and an organic café specialising in produce grown in the Home Counties. All that was missing was a sign over the door of Ursa Major saying *as recommended by the Daily Mail*.

Maybe this was why Alex had insisted on calling the bar Norma Major.

A handsome panelled front door reminiscent of a downsized Number 10 for retired PMs led to a small darkened vestibule. A security guard handed them each a bin bag, and then opened an altogether different type of door. The forbidding fire door was painted black and yawned into a room where a few men in various stages of undress were busily stuffing their bin bags with clothing, like charity workers after a jumble sale.

Rubens pulled his T shirt off:

"Gostoso, remember to keep your money with you. And cigarettes if you really have to smoke, but beware. If you do, you will have to go outside in one of the bar's tracksuits that they save especially for the addicted. I'm not sure how often or even if they get washed, so it could be quite an experience."

Ben decided he could resist, no matter how much he enjoyed a sneaky cigarette with a beer.

"Rubens, where do I keep my money?"

"I told you to wear long socks. You do have proper socks, don't you? When you pay the entrance they will give you a little plastic money bag which you stick down the socks. Unless, of course, you are one of those professionals with a leather man bag. I hope not. I don't like them. It looks as if you are too fashion. Either that, or you are trying too hard – or too much of a regular. None of these are good for picking up."

Ben hadn't realised that there could be a dress code even in a place with no clothes. One should never underestimate gay men when it came to sartorial critique.

"Come on, Ben, you're still not ready."

Rubens was stark naked, and had tied his bin bag in a neat knot. Ben felt a little coy. He told himself that he was in the locker rooms, about to go for a shower. That helped. Of course it was natural in such circumstances to see other men naked.

But unease still flitted around him. It did all seem strange, and Ben felt rather nervous. He suddenly remembered that he was a *grow-er* and not a *show-er*, and that presently Little Ben was decidedly shy – and hence on the diminutive side. That would never do. Ben had a sense of pride after all. He glanced around. The few men around him fell into the *best seen with clothes on* category. Rubens was gorgeous but *been there, done that*. Ben desperately tried to imagine an American Football team. All clean cut, well presented, shiny eyes and teeth… no, it wasn't working. He would have to be brave and pray for some stimulation, before anyone interesting saw him and judged.

As he took Ben's twenty-pound note, the man at the cash desk smiled and asked Ben for his initials. He duly wrote these on a ticket which got sellotaped to Ben's bin bag. Ben then received a voucher for a free drink, and a little plastic bag. This contained his coat check ticket and change. It was all very sensible. Ben made a mental note of his coat check number, given that its loss would be more than a little inconvenient. He carefully stuffed the slender bag down one sock and kept the drink voucher in his hand. He wanted that drink immediately. It was time to go in.

After entering through two sets of double doors, which Ben felt was a little like being swallowed by some industrial version of a whale – Moby Dick, he thought suddenly. Dick! Ha! – the boys were hit by a wall of sound and dim reddish lighting. It was still early. Just a few bared souls clutched pints, waiting for the crowds to arrive.

The bar had a workspace feel, with dark walls, a rough concrete floor and what looked like oil barrels in place of tables. A doorway to the left led to an even dimmer corridor, down which Ben thought he could make out what looked like cells, complete with iron bars across their fronts. A big square archway on the other side of the room revealed, in the space beyond, an improbably parked rusty old Ford Transit. Tyres were stacked in the corners. Old car jacks and various other tools adorned shelves bolted to the walls. Stone steps led down to the mechanics' pit beneath the vehicle. A second arch was half-draped in camouflage netting. Ben could just make out a row of metal bunk beds and what looked like an old US Army jeep.

The bar owners obviously believed in selling the sizzle rather than the sausage. Ursa Major catered for pumped-up prisoners, muscle-bound mechanics and the essential sex-starved soldiers, all classic homoerotic fantasy material. Ben noted with a wry smile that there was no door leading to a dance studio, nor a third arch with a hairdresser's salon, decorated with hairdryers, curling tongs and bottles of frizz-ease. Funny, that, he thought knowingly.

The bar area boasted four large screens. These featured hard-core pornographic videos. But the lack of intimacy deprived the pornography of much of its impact. Improbably buff men having sex writhed around in close-up. Although the sound was muffled by the competing music, Ben could readily lip read all the *yeah man*s and the satisfied grunting. The bar itself took a more pragmatic view to pleasure. Condoms and lube were freely on offer, under posters extolling their virtues, and the dangers of barebacking. Posters boasting Tom of Finland designs advertised the different nights of the week.

Three muscled barmen clad only in Ursa Major square cut briefs and workmen's boots, lolled round the bar, looking available and waiting to serve. Although Ben couldn't really make out much of a smell, save for a faint whiff of cleaning products, an atmosphere of sex and anticipation hung heavy in the air. It had to be said, everything about Ursa Major was focused on sex. Everything, that was, except for one thing. In pride of place on the black back wall of the bar was a large pink poster advertising Mamma Mia.

"What can I get you?" The cutest of the three barmen gave Ben and Rubens a cheeky smile. Ben suddenly remembered he was naked, unlike the barman, and felt at a slight disadvantage.

"Two cans of Red Stripe, please." Rubens turned to Ben. "Beer is better, gostoso, doesn't spill from a can. And they don't do Piña Colada here."

As Ben handed over his drinks voucher, the barman's hand touched his own and lingered just long enough for it to be noticeable. The touch and the accompanying smile sent a pulse of energy through Ben's body, which Frankenstein-like finally jolted his inert member into life. Ben smiled back at the barman, and now with far more to show off, backed away from the bar just to make sure the barman got an eyeful. He was finally putting the cock into peacock. He felt much happier, even quite magnificent, in full display.

The bar was quickly filling up. It was a week night after all, and this was one of the only places to grab a drink where one was sure that it would not be filled with suits. The extent that one has to go to sometimes to achieve this simple aim beggars belief. Sadly, the new arrivals looked nothing like a football team. In fact, some of them looked too old to play football without a doctor's note. Within seconds of spotting the clientele, Ben felt and looked deflated. Not unexpectedly for someone who actually thought about things once in a while, Ben had a pretty sensitive erection. What he hadn't thought about, however, was how attending a boots-only party meant that everyone else would know exactly what was happening as well. And given that he was looking to impress, what if the man he really wanted to be with should walk round the corner, just as his dick was at its most blushingly modest? Would he be dismissed out of hand with no second chance on offer?

This was an interesting paradox. His dick needed to be like a fire-fighter, always on full alert, ready to go if eyes sent the most subliminal of signals. But, on the other hand, surely walking round with a full erection was a bit desperate. Wouldn't it imply that one were partaking of Viagra, or something? Just what was the done thing in a place like this? Glancing over at Rubens, Ben noticed that Rubens seemed to be in the perfect state of semi-arousal. He could have been shown on telly with the best of them, angling as he was almost scientifically to the TV forty-five degree rule. How did he do that? It certainly was showing it – and him – off to the best effect.

Ben cleared his throat:

"Rubens, how do you keep your cock like that? I seem to be going from trying too hard to Tiny Tim."

Rubens laughed:

"As I may have mentioned to you before, my brother, I am Brazilian. It just kind of happens. I'm always slightly aroused, even when I am not. Just relax. Maybe forget you are an American tonight? Or remember that you are, if the right to bear arms arouses you? You don't always have to be Mr Perfect, you know. When the time is right, it will happen. Until then, just stand behind a stool, gostoso... I'm joking," he added quickly, seeing Ben looking around for furniture.

Ben squared his shoulders and thought *to hell with it*.

Half an hour later, he had done around twenty laps of the bar. In that time, he'd identified half a dozen potential targets, downed two more beers, and received his first blow job in one of the cells down the first corridor. Although technically proficient, it had proved mildly unsatisfactory, so he had taken advantage of sex club etiquette. With nary a look, never mind a hollow promise to call the next day, he had patted the guy on the head, extracted his penis from the anonymous throat and, via the washroom, disappeared off in search of Rubens and another beer.

Just as he was passing the auto repair shop arch, the cute barman came by picking up empty beer bottles. Quite suddenly, the beer bottles were deposited on an oil drum, and Ben was pulled under the arch. Olive skin, tight, taut body with black hair cropped to regulation gay length and a smile that would melt chocolate, the cute barman flashed his grin and went straight in for the snog. He was an expert and knew it. After a couple of minutes, Ben gasped for breath:

"What's your name?"

"Dionisio. What's yours, gostoso?"

Jackpot! As far as Ben knew, this almost certainly meant that his conquest was Brazilian. He was bound to be superb at sex. He was also helpfully named after the God of wine and ecstasy. Whatever one might think of what is in a name or otherwise, Dionisio is more inspiring than Derek.

"I'm Ben."

Before Ben could add anything else, the door of the transit van opened, nearly hitting them, and a familiar figure got out. Rubens strolled by without a care in the world. Recognising Ben, he put his arms round them both, and whispered to Ben:

"Don't take him inside the van. The gear stick is a big black dildo. The guy sucking me off seemed to be having more fun sitting on that than with me. How rude!"

Rubens winked, and was off.

Dionisio was kissing Ben again, his hands exploring Ben's body. It felt good until Ben realised that, talented as the Brazilian wonder boy was, no man could do all of that with only one pair of hands. Ben opened his eyes to quite an audience, some of whom were avid believers in participation. To Ben's disappointment, there was still no football team lookalikes. His antics had attracted the decidedly less attractive, older crowd, the ones that earned the bar its other nickname of Hearse-a Major. He pushed away the extra hands, and then shuddered as he came face to face with a scrawny creature in a gimp mask and thigh-length rubber boots. Gimpy had been tracking him all night. A hand came in from that direction that was also smartly rebuffed.

"Ben, come through here."

Ben had thought that the barriers were just part of the decoration, but as Dionisio pulled open a rough door, he realised that they were masking some building work going on. He stepped inside a separate room with a half-built brick wall, real workmen's tools and plenty of concrete dust everywhere.

"Don't make any noise, we shouldn't be in here. And we must be quick."

With another smile, Dionisio whipped off his briefs and jumped on Ben. After the months of resisting, followed by this porn-set situation with a Brazilian Greek God, being quick was not likely to be a problem for Ben. They came together, in a silent embrace, Dionisio arching his back against Ben's chest. It was the first time Ben had had sex with anyone but Kelly for a long time.

Although it felt simply perfect on a physical level, Ben felt a momentary pang.

Just then a commotion of something being knocked over and voices being raised filtered through the door. Ben hurriedly but carefully withdrew, making sure the condom was still intact.

Dionisio frantically searched in the half-darkness for his briefs:

"Where the hell are my underpants? I need to get out there now. It sounds like a fight."

Ben joined him, but the pants had disappeared. Meanwhile the voices got louder and angrier outside.

"Shit, I have to go. Stay here and don't make a sound."

Dionisio shoved open the door and went into the main bar area. Ben closed the door behind him, listening intently as Dionisio ordered people to calm down or he would throw them out immediately. It seemed to work as the noise abated. Dionisio reappeared wearing a fresh pair of Ursa Major square cuts:

"That is the first time I have ever broken up a fight completely naked."

"What happened?"

"Two guys who are together, both cheating on the other, surprised each other in the club. I had to take them to the exit. The manager has banned them. I mean, since when did gays fight in clubs? We leave that to the straight people. Or the lesbians."

Dionisio gave Ben another cheeky grin:

"My manager did ask where my pants were, and why I had a hard-on. Luckily he had a spare pair. Now I do not want to lose these ones."

Round two passed without interruption.

The post-coital beer at the bar felt particularly satisfying to Ben. Rubens had disappeared again, but Ben was feeling mellow and happy to be left alone. One of his earlier targets, a Saudi Arabian named Mahdi, had returned to chat and this was keeping them both amused. Since both men had done what they had come to the bar to do, they ended up talking about politics. Mahdi explained that he felt irrationally guilty every time he went through airport security and saw a little old lady having to take her shoes off. It was an unexpected point of view. This was not the kind of conversation Ben had anticipated in a gay sex bar – but then, what did he know. In fact, Ben enjoyed the talk so much that he was a little disappointed when Rubens finally turned up and said it was time to go.

Ben's first time in Ursa Major had been quite an experience.

An experience that had been noted in all its details by the scrawny man in the gimp mask. Now that the boys had gone, private investigator Felix Skink was enjoying his first drink with neither a gimp mask nor a wig of long lank blond hair to irritate him. His eyes were no longer hungry, his hands no longer grasping. The tracking device that he had dropped into Ben's bag as he had pretended to fall into his table in Outrageous Fortune had led him straight to Ursa Major. There, yet again, his concealed camera had done its work. Not for the first time in his insalubrious career, Felix was looking forward to making the call to Nicholas Casterway. The material was better than Felix had thought possible, and he should be paid accordingly.

12

Seeds of destruction

Amber Bluett sighed.

Unlike the majority of office drones, Amber was highly skilled at ignoring the emails that relentlessly besieged her mobile not only within, but also outside of, office hours. After all, why should Amber pollute *Amber time* with the often pointless prattle emanating from Beaux, Aspen, Dickerhint? *Do this – try that – why don't you – can you –* If anything were truly urgent, then they should ring.

She had once given a colleague an earful after he had sent her an email comically marked *urgent* at 11 am on a Sunday morning – and then had had the *utter* presumption to be cross when he didn't receive a reply until Monday morning.

Amber smiled with satisfaction as she recalled how she had let the mask slip long enough to terrify him out of his pallid skin. There is nothing like responding to petulant complaints with the cold hard steel of bullying – bullying that will stop at nothing. Although the poor unfortunate had never troubled her in *Amber time* again, one bleating challenge from him had been enough to goad her into ensuring that his queries had generally been given short shrift thereafter. For good measure, she also snipped the odd day off his holiday allowance – just because she could. Given that he was somewhat lax in checking his entitlements – the poor, trusting fool – it was all child's play.

Systems are fabricated to be manipulated, mused Amber. *He* never realised how true that was. He just continued scurrying around the office like a little rat in a suit and tie, persuading himself that he was having a blissful experience at B.A.D.

Work – the saving grace of the human race. One simply had to persuade the masses that they should be organised in this private, hierarchical way. After that, it was a simple matter of throwing them enough crumbs to keep them in check. Pop around and let them drive your expensive car once in a while. It's amazing how grateful they will be.

The downside to Amber's steely defence of her personal time was that her first job of the day always remained sifting through the endless mails that found their way to her, sent by a world that never sleeps. On this particular morning, it seemed worse than usual. Admittedly, Amber had had the temerity to take a day off during the week. There were therefore thirty six hours-worth of emails to be clicked through.

The inbox of joy. Amber stared glumly at all the bold type on her screen. Doubtless head office had been busy rearranging the deck chairs on the doomed liner with even more wasteful energy than before. It seemed to Amber as if a volcano of technological diarrhoea had erupted, showering everyone with reports, orders, directives and spread sheets – all to be checked, filled in, analysed and scrutinised. Before Amber could even attempt to get to the emails that actually had to be dealt with, she would have to hack her way through the thicket of company spam that people thought it would be good to copy to Human Resources, *just in case*. There was a rich seam this morning, too, of incredibly tedious company-wide emails telling her with surreal enthusiasm of the successful exploits of Marcia Boggle-Stott at the *Women in Arbitration* conference in Stockholm, or – the absolute pits, this – the new baby pictures of the latest mewling ex-foetus to emerge out of the nether regions of someone who was now enjoying six to twelve months off whilst she, Amber, had to carry on working.

As she first picked out the obviously unimportant emails, repeatedly banging the delete button as if it were the head of that first cellmate in prison she had disliked so intensely, Amber reflected that her inbox was rather like a garden. It sprouted an awful lot of weeds that really should be uprooted and moved to the trash, before she could tend to the plants which required her attention. The existing threads were the ones that she usually gravitated to at the outset, silently cursing the unhelpful replies that were a blight on her shrubbery, and those that all too frequently killed her good ideas with a passive aggressive flourish. Or perhaps there was a steep hill to climb revealed, in the shape of needing to procure some uninterested partner's support?

After the first cull, she would deal with the new seedlings that had appeared from nowhere. These were minor miracles of life, usually spawned from the overactive busy-bodying nature of power drones in New York. Did people not think of the implications of their emails in terms of the time needed to fulfil their oafish requests? Head office seemed to inhabit another planet, a weird parallel reality of priorities, a strange universe where people shaped the world around them to fit with their own perceptions, ignoring all evidence that their perceptions were – well – just plain wrong.

On a good day Amber tried to protect the London office from as much of the HQ lava as possible, so that they could get on with the real job of accumulating billable hours. Much of the time, however, providing this cover proved simply impossible. Amber's person may once have been locked up in prison, but now she felt that her mind had been clapped behind the iron bars of B.A.D management whims.

Rather like democracy being described as elective dictatorship, Amber felt her sole remedy for liberating herself would be the nuclear option of walking out the door.

She sighed again.

Then, quite suddenly, her mood lightened as she discovered an exotic flower blooming on one of her favourite plants in her inbox. There it was, all green and tempting: an invitation to meet Nicholas Casterway. A long lunch break incorporating a swift shag was just what the doctor had ordered.

The anticipation would definitely help to get her through the first meeting of the day. She checked her diary, hoping against hope that work had somehow been cancelled. No such luck: there the meeting loomed. The agenda remained the discussion of the results of the Staff Commitment Annual Target. This was a measure of staff satisfaction across the global firm. It was known as S.C.A.T. The survey had thrown up an interesting find: the London office had the lowest score of all offices globally.

Head office had a S.C.A.T obsession, and had accordingly demanded an action plan in order to raise morale. Or, if not to raise it, to destroy it once and for all, thought Amber grimly. Whatever result would be achieved would soon be qualified retrospectively as the stated aim from the outset.

It was rather like corporate reorganisations. They were usually undertaken to further the careers of the managers in place. After that came reverse engineering, to fit results into some strategy that was supposedly going to provide endless benefits to the company and a contribution to the bottom line. This Franken-strategy gradually took on a life of its own, as more and more managers elaborated it and spun it out. By the time of the presentation to the staff, most of the Stepford management team actually believed that what had been bolted together was really going to lead to business benefits, and couldn't help feeling disappointed when the staff greeted this latest restructuring with a weary shrug. Inevitably in eighteen months' time the new organisation showed itself to be as fit for purpose as any structure built on the sand of an executive's ego could be, and the process started again. That was the way these things worked, in a strange, self-justifying parody of cause and effect.

So a meeting had been set up. It was the only way to go. Some lawyers had been drafted in to contribute: a partner or two, and some associate representatives – including Ben Barlettano. Amber's lip curled. *The day she needed to take heed of that bender's views would be the day she fried his testicles for breakfast and offered him a taste.*

In his office a floor above Amber's, Ben's morale was certainly in need of being lifted. He was feeling decidedly the worse for wear. Could it – possibly – be attributed to the consumption of alcohol the previous night? Ben was surprised that any alcohol-related consequences haunted him after all the cardiovascular activity that he had so rigorously and conscientiously undertaken.

Last night, the no-strings sex with Dionisio had been amazing. It was exactly what his body needed. It crushed out feelings and moved Ben's evolutionary decision-making forward. No more bloody women. That had all seemed very clear last night.

But now, Ben was feeling decidedly alone. In normal times, after an adventure of any kind, Kelly would have been the first person Ben would have emailed. He would have spent some time crafting the story, too, giving her all the juicy details of his night out with Rubens, making her smile, perhaps even laugh, as she read her morning mail. Ben might then have called Kelly to tell her about matters that could never have got through their firms' firewalls. There was also so much more of the wedding that he would have wanted to discuss with her. Throughout the day, Ben would have IM'd Kelly to laugh at funny typographical errors, mistakes and anything else that peppered his daily work.

All that was gone. The inbox suddenly seemed a grey place to stare at.

A meeting reminder pinged up. Ben felt tired just thinking about all the inaction to come. He headed off to the conference room, hoping that an overdose of coffee might save the day.

The S.C.A.T gathering was taking place in the Frankfurt meeting room. Company policy had long dictated that meeting rooms should be named proudly after points on the globe where B.A.D had a presence. Ben wondered if there would ever be, anywhere, a meeting room named Basildon or Elephant & Castle. There had to be a more innovative way of naming these spaces – something less predictable than the perennial Frankfurt, New York and Zurich.

He saw Amber march in, as confident as if she owned the place. She was wrinkling her nose:

"What's that dreadful smell?"

Frankfurt was frequently the last meeting room to be booked as it often had a fusty smell to it, a little like a bag that usually contained festering sports kit. This morning, however, this was overlaid with a sweet, almost sickly smell, like an accident in one of those cheap scent shops on the Walworth Road.

Bertha Cheung looked up brightly:

"Oh, hi, Amber! I saw we were in Frankfurt, so I bought an air freshener. It's jasmine, orange blossom and black pearl with a hint of vanilla. It has one of those vaporiser things that lets off a puff when someone passes by. Rather good, isn't it?"

"It's a bit strong, Bertha." Amber wondered if she would be able to get through a whole meeting without being ill.

"Well, it's quite a transformation," commented Cornisha. "This room is transformed from a teenage boy's room to a teenage girl's room. It's quite an olfactory adventure."

"Well, you'd know something about that, wouldn't you, Cornisha."

Amber tried to bite her tongue where Cornisha was concerned, as it didn't seem very appropriate for a representative from Human Resources to allude to Cornisha's sex change. But when a chance as apposite as this was offered up was for a snide comment, it could not be left begging. Besides, Cornisha had always been in Ben's camp. *Let that green velvet-wearing ginger transgender twat eat my dust.*

Amber shuffled her papers and twiddled her pen:

"Now, then. The reason we are all having this meeting is to discuss the results of the S.C.A.T survey in the UK. We are tasked with coming up with an action plan for the senior partners to review and approve, in order to ensure that staff morale is lifted in time for the next survey."

Amber fiddled with the laptop before her and eventually had it whirring to itself like some ancient transportation contraption:

"The results from the survey are illustrated on these slides I have prepared. Let me talk these through with you. We can then move to discuss ideas on how we can make B.A.D London staff happier."

As Amber demonstrated that the UK's numbers were consistently below the international average and that the

UK one of only three countries to fail to hit the lower minimum target of 73% satisfaction, a number of her audience could feel their eyelids drooping. Remembering a college trick, Ben surreptitiously dipped a finger into his glass and carefully rubbed a little cold water underneath his eyes. Hopefully this would get him through a few more charts.

He could see that Bertha was also finding the meeting hard going. This comforted him somewhat. Why had they both scored the role of associate representatives for this particularly vacuous exercise? Oh yes. They had thought it might enhance their standing in the firm. Fat chance of that.

Although ploughing through her presentation like a farmer sowing potatoes, Amber was fully aware that her audience seemed bored and listless.

Oh dear. She was going to have to yank someone's chain. Audience participation it was, then:

"So why would you say this particular statistic is so much poorer in the UK, rather than the rest of Europe – Ben?"

Amber gave Ben her warmest smile. He visibly started from the state of semi-slumber that his water trick had only briefly held at bay. He embarrassedly sought to see the slide which Amber had helpfully now concealed, finding only the projection of the title – *Suggestions* – illuminating the screen.

Once it had become completely apparent to the others that Ben had been half asleep, Amber jumped in, almost as if she were embarrassed for him and trying to help him cover up:

"Maybe the fact that the London office used to be the main European office before the Dickerhint Strudel acquisition has left the UK feeling as though its voice is listened to less within the firm?"

Ben seized the opportunity gratefully:

"For what it's worth, I certainly think that any frustration that may be felt by staff in London is not directed at the management here. It is more likely a simple reflection of the office's reduced influence in a significantly enlarged organisation. The US has had to pay more attention to our new German colleagues this year in order to get the merger to deliver results."

It was a valiant effort, and yet everyone in the room had noticed that he had been away with the fairies. Ben seemed groggy and knackered. This was not acceptable. Most attendees were now glancing slightly askance at Ben. In truth, he wasn't everybody's favourite person. He was generally perceived to be too colourful. He was a little too *exciting* to properly fit with the general tedium that carefully shielded most other employees' creeping careers. Even with tired eyes, a number of those present found his face unnaturally perfect – too pretty to be counted as one of their own.

Satisfied at the initial result of her little attack, Amber pressed Ben some more:

"Head office has suggested a motivational teambuilding day out with our Berlin office. Apparently, they use a team building consultancy in the States and, as luck would have it, these *professionals* have a branch in the UK. What about a weekend of hiking and white water rafting in North Wales?"

Before Ben could respond, the token partner attending the S.C.A.T meeting, Bartlett DeVere, jumped in. It had been far too long since he had heard the sound of his own voice:

"This sounds like an excellent plan, Amber, especially if it is suggested by our colleagues in New York. They really have a handle on how things are done internationally. A fun weekend out would do us the world of good. After all, not all of us enjoy such an action-packed social life as Mr Barlettano here evidently does. Maybe some social activity that leaves one feeling invigorated rather than wanting to catch up on some sleep in company time might be of benefit to you, Ben?"

Ben winced under the broad smile laden with disapproval and false bonhomie. Ben had been in the legal profession for long enough to know that working sixty-hour-weeks complemented by a demanding family life could suck the youth out of Peter Pan. It seemed clear enough that the last thing Bartlett DeVere wanted was to be reminded of the ghost of his social life past. That sacrifice was expected to be made by all – and the bags under Ben's eyes had definitely smudged his page in Bartlett's good books.

Amber gave Ben a comforting smile of support. But she was happy. Every little helps. What a pleasure it was, leading Ben onto thin ice, and then applying a hairdryer full blast at his feet.

Nicholas would be pleased.

All in all, the present was a low point among many highs and lows that Ben had lived through in The Castle Lofts. This was misery. Break-ups involving loved ones are the saddest canvas of all. No matter what colour you flung at them, it all came out as grey. After a miserable day in the office, Ben was now lying in bed, still exhausted from the night before, but unable to rest. Kelly was on his mind – a smiling, happy, beautiful Kelly, who seemed to have it all, and was so far away that she may as well have purchased a condominium on the moon.

Ben felt like a squash ball being thwacked from wall of anger to wall of tears to wall of revenge by the memory-laden racquet of his mind. He had been dating Kelly for a good two years. It had seemed the most worthwhile thing in his life. But the woman with whom he had shared so much, and who had accepted him for exactly who he was, had now had an affair with another man.

It mattered not that she said that she was sorry. The pain was debilitating. Ben felt dizzy. How could he not have foreseen this? How could he not have realised that he obviously wasn't enough for her? Knowing the strength of the impulses he had been suppressing all this time and the opportunities to stray that had presented themselves like obedient little slaves over the last few months, it crushed Ben to think that Kelly's love for him had not been strong enough to suppress hers.

Last night, the wild drinking and sex in Ursa Major had seemed to be the perfect antidote to his state of mind. But now, it just seemed rather sordid and sour. What Ben really wanted was simply to be alone with Kelly. Everything conspired against that. *We'll never have Paris again*, he thought, again.

Endless repetition of the same thoughts, on loop in

his mind, did nothing to shift the mood.

He picked up the card he had left on his bedside table, wondering whether he should call Zahoor as he said he would. Would filling up a couple of hours with casual sex with a cute stranger really help him out of his hole of despair? Or was it not self-evident that spending a night with Zahoor was simply swapping one hole for another? Ben sighed. As he was not in the mood for a wank, he would have to turn to his other reliable escape valve: physical exertion of a different kind.

Showering after a session in the gym downstairs at the Lofts, Ben was beginning to feel better. That was until a bodybuilder with flashing green eyes and natural-looking blond hair came out of the steam room and started showering next to Ben. Ben had always had a thing about locker rooms, and under normal circumstances he would have either had to make a very quick move on the guy, or an even quicker move to shelter under a towel in the steam room. Yet today nothing happened. Even when the bodybuilder flashed him a smile, Ben just smiled politely back, grabbed his towel and walked off. What was the point? It wasn't what he really wanted. He could feel his gremlins returning.

He should eat something. Millie Myers' gym café beckoned.

Millie was writing up the next day's specials on her blackboard. She looked over at her sad-faced customer:

"Ben, cheer up! It might never happen. You don't look your normal self. I know what will iron out that frown. You need a plate of my fresh made Kedgereegoogoo. It's a herby fish and rice dish in a delicious creamy sauce. It's quite my best effort today."

The dish looked like lumpy rice swimming in green-flecked yoghurt, but Ben knew from long experience that Millie's dishes often tasted far better than they looked. He paid and took a seat at the counter. He felt less alone than if he had taken a table for one.

Millie leaned over:

"A cent for your thoughts?"

She prattled on:

"Amber was here last night. She told me that you are being very brave."

Great. Ben's life had just hit a new low. He was being offered sympathy by Millie Myers and he actually felt grateful to her.

Millie leaned on the counter, and looked critically at Ben. She had always been one for ladling out advice:

"Well, sweetie pie, this is what I think. Although Kelly Danvers is a lovely girl – and nobody here would deny that – you, my ardent cavalier, need to get back on the horse and do some extensive riding before you get hung up by saddle sores. There may no longer be plenty of fish in the sea due to overfishing, but there are lots of fish in London for a lovely boy like you. Go play the scales! Just so you know, my Kedgereegoogoo ingredients do come from sustainable sources. Mark my words, Ben, because I'm intending that they will be ringing in your ears and drowning out that funeral dirge you're obviously listening to. You need to stop moping about and find yourself a nice sustainable relationship to blot out all that overfishing unpleasantness."

Two years of listening to Millie had not really helped Ben understand her use of language any better – but she did have a point. Whether or not he liked it, he was now young, free and single. He had an excellent opportunity to whore his way around London without feeling any guilt. Sex would be like having a whisky for medicinal purposes.

He would call Zahoor, after all.

Nicholas Casterway tutted to himself. He was profoundly irritated at being disturbed from his work by a knock at the door. He decided to ignore it as he was sure he had put up the *Do not disturb* sign and so it was unlikely to be staff. It must be a guest trying to get into the wrong room.

"Hello, housekeeping?"

They always spoke so loudly. It was like a trumpet played by a lucky beginner. Before Nicholas could respond, the door opened wide, and a cleaner walked in, carrying a bag and brandishing what looked like a can of Mr Sheen and a duster.

"Oh, señor, I do apologise, I will return later. I did not know you were in here. You did not put out the sign."

He detected a Latin American accent. At least these women knew how to be servile. She was also attractive with just enough make-up to show off her full lips.

Maybe he needed a moment's distraction:

"No, no, it is quite alright. You may work around me – er – Conchita."

Nicholas caught his breath as the maid bent over low to polish the low coffee table. He caught an eyeful of slim, shapely legs topped off by a skirt that was so short Nicholas could see the pink panties riding high underneath. Eye-catching, indeed. Most stimulating. He thought he would rather like to strip the panties off her and maybe even put them on himself.

"I am so sorry, señor – may I empty the waste bin under your desk?"

Nicholas looked up from the document he had been pretending to peruse. His mind's camera was firmly projecting the image of Conchita's beautiful behind in those pink panties. This was *excellent*. Without saying a word, he swivelled round on his chair, legs apart, and lazily dared Conchita to try to squeeze between the gap he had left between his left knee and the edge of the desk. As she gamely bent down and stretched her arm under the desk to reach the bin that Nicholas had pushed right back to the wall, her back arched slightly in order to maintain some distance between her head and Nicholas' crotch. This made her ample breasts threaten to burst out of the delicate restraint offered by her lacy low-cut blouse. The faux modesty coupled with the glorious tits, red lipstick, and his prior knowledge of that perfect derrière in those little pink panties was suddenly all too much for Nicholas. He took hold of her head with both hands, feeling the softness of her hair in his fingers, and gazed deliberately into her eyes as he brought her face slowly and deliberately closer in between his legs.

"Oh señor, what are you doing?"

Conchita pulled back her arm from under the desk and gripped Nicholas' leg, feebly trying to resist the pressure being exerted on the back of her head:

"Señor, you are so powerful."

Despite the frozen tundra that his sex life with Britta Casterway had become, Nicholas could still have an effect on women. Conchita resisted no more. Her left hand found his zipper and before he knew it those lips were servicing him, as he released her breasts from that pointless prison. Conchita's previously shy gaze belied a natural ability with buttons and belts, as, before Nicholas even knew it, and without even removing her lips from his cock or hardly taking his hands away from her breasts, they were both suddenly naked.

Being at heart very much a traditionalist, some would say indeed a pillar of the establishment, Nicholas pulled the chambermaid that he had just molested through to the bedroom, and pushed her firmly onto the bed:

"Keep your heels on. Legs up. Spread them. Eating out is the best form of room service, you know."

Although Nicholas was a master with his tongue, being so much more generous with a clitoris than he ever could be with words, it was not long before she was begging him for the grand finale. They somehow reached a simultaneous climax, the thrill of the orgasm being accompanied by the relief at being able to stop feigning that silly accent.

Amber lay back and enjoyed the last moments of Nicholas' cock inside her, before jumping up and going for a speedy shower before Nicholas tired as usual of the contact with another human being. A few minutes later she was washed and fully dressed. The last vestiges of "Conchita Suarez" were firmly stashed away in her bag.

Unusually, Nicholas was interested in a short bout of communication:

"So, the boy is presenting us with an opportunity."

He was wrapped in a bathrobe, his cold grey eyes glinting as they did whenever he started talking about one of his favourite subjects: revenge. Getting your own back, getting your own back completely – the most joyful tune of all.

He was keen to fill Amber in:

"It is all exactly as you surmised. Skink has been shadowing Ben Barlettano. After months of bottling up his sundry desires, all for the dream of his supposed one true love, the boy found out that she has been shagging another man. It has hit him hard. Although the photographic evidence that Skink has obtained is rather graphic, that will be a mere corollary. Sexual peccadilloes are ten-a-penny these days and even lawyers can get away with being caught with their pants down in strange places. However, heavy drinking and late nights may impact performance and *that* is indeed unforgiveable. What was he like in the office today?"

A cruel smile flirted with Nicholas' lips as Amber told him how she had drawn Bartlett DeVere's attention to Ben's somnolence in the S.C.A.T meeting.

"*Excellent.* Then the boy himself has sown the seed. We merely need to nurture the plant. This is where you come in, my dear. Your position in the firm gives you access to certain data. Your recent past has given you certain experience."

Amber nodded. Her CV could not possibly list all of her talents. Whilst inside, she had learnt to pick locks and all sorts of other skills that were useful for bringing others down.

Nicholas nodded thoughtfully:

"Together with some monitoring and a degree of encouragement by Skink and his crew, we shall steer the boy's downward spiral to a thoroughly disgraceful exit. It will be simple and effective. The law can be so unforgiving."

Amber felt a thrill of excitement. Plotting an enemy's downfall was so much more rewarding than all that worthy Human Resources nonsense that she had to simulate most days. Managing an underachiever out of the business through the *Performance Improvement Management Process* was good. *P.I.M.P* had been successfully employed to great effect in the regular rounds of cost-cutting that had served to preserve the partners' earnings at their pre-economic crisis levels, rather than reflecting the needs and requirements of clients and the business. But plotting someone's undoing through sheer brutality and underhand action offered even greater pleasure and job satisfaction. This almost matched Amber's sexual greed.

Amber was always disappointed that rules had to be obeyed, and transparency upheld. She could combine the two exercises to great effect, she thought. Ben would now be subjected to a particularly vicious *P.I.M.P* review. He would not realise the direction it was taking at first. He would be so trusting and unknowing at first. She could then sabotage his chances of redemption whilst all the while professing to be his friend.

Working with Nicholas, Amber felt like a Bond girl – one of the evil ones, who preferred shagging the villain. Why didn't those splendid villains ever win on film? They did in real life. It was time to settle old scores.

Zahoor lived a few doors down from the Dalston Superstore. Its edgy cool was part of the DNA of that part of East London just north of Shoreditch. Ben loved the place. As he weaved his way through the consciously ironic fashions of London's new trendsetters, he reflected on how Dalston had changed in the couple of years that he had been in London. How had it taken a fast train to *happening*, when poor old Elephant seemed to be forever stuck in the station? Was it attributable to the wrong sort of leaves on the Bakerloo line? It must be. The only Superstore in SE1 sold cheap carpets to the impecunious indigenous.

He buzzed Zahoor's entry phone. *Entry phone*, thought Ben.

"Third floor. Come up."

Creaking stairs with a carpet that had seen better days. Yellowed paint on ancient woodchip wallpaper. Lights that came on as he reached each floor.

The door was ajar.

Ben wondered if he would find Zahoor nearly naked. He felt a shiver of anticipation run down his spine.

"Habibie, don't you look lovely! Come in! Let me fix you a drink."

Ben stopped in his tracks. A boy with beautiful fine features and jet black hair stood before him, wearing nothing but a pair of Calvin Klein underpants which showed off the curve of his behind to perfection. The boy in question, however, was Kasim, who was applying Lady Gaza make-up, clearly half-dressed.

"Don't worry, habibie, I am working tonight and will be

leaving soon. Zahoor is in the bedroom. He's running late. He had a hard day at work."

Zahoor appeared. It looked as if he had been crying.

This was not the fantasy Ben had been hoping for:

"Have I come at a bad time?"

Kasim snorted:

"Habibie, you could never come at a bad time. You are just what this poor boy needs tonight."

"Ben, I am very glad to see you. I was accused of stealing money at the bar today and they fired me."

Ben felt as if he had been slapped with a large wet herring. What *was* going on at Outrageous Fortune?

Kasim clucked sympathetically:

"My Zahoor is the most honest boy you could meet, habibie. As is Milo, who I know very well, and who told me about what went on in his case. Zahoor is not the first to be set up in that place. He will not be the last, either. You should talk to your friend, Rubens. There's something not quite right in the state of Outrageous Fortune."

13

Blame it on the bubbly

A trip to Wesley's party in Leatherhead was proving as excruciating as Tarquin had anticipated it would be.

He had never seen a Correggio displayed against a background of floral flock. In fact, he hadn't seen such chintzy wallpaper anywhere since about 1987.

His host had already told him how much it had cost per roll, and how difficult it had been to find. Like a professional drag queen, Wesley's home was proof that it took a lot of time and money to look properly cheap.

His host bustled cheerfully forward to greet him:

"Oh, there you are, dear. I thought you had taken your Brazilian barman to meet the fairies at the bottom of the garden."

Sadly, Tarquin had not disappeared anywhere with Rubens. He wasn't at all sure where the Brazilian was. They had arrived together. Ben had then appeared with his mother and her junior boyfriend in tow. Rubens had seemed fine on the way down to Wesley's. However, once he clapped eyes on Ben, a change came over him, like clouds blowing in from the sea. They must, surmised

Tarquin, have disappeared off together.

He wandered through the nightmarish décor until he chanced upon them sipping drinks, merrily looking out of place. They looked engrossed so Tarquin wandered off to try and find a splash of good taste somewhere to soothe his fevered eyes.

"So, Rubens, spill the beans," said Ben. "What the hell is happening at Outrageous Fortune?"

Ben hadn't been able to make head or tail of the position from his conversation with Zahoor a couple of nights earlier. Zahoor had merely offered a tearful description of being fired by Rubens because money was missing from the till. That seemed far-fetched and arbitrary to Ben.

Zahoor had refused to say anything other than he had nothing to do with it, and that he was devastated that Rubens could think him even capable of such a thing. Obviously, Ben felt Zahoor's pain, but he also felt the pain of his own expectations. His primary concern had been that all these feelings would have led to considerably less feeling-up in the grander scheme of things.

Ben had worried needlessly on that score. The comfort of sex was exactly what Zahoor had craved. Ben could do comfort. In fact, he did it four times that night. He had barely slept. This had not served him well the next day, where he had displayed all the art and alacrity of a comatose sheep. Amber had delighted in regretfully bringing his ovine disposition to the attention of Bartlett DeVere. Again. It was so easy to blow it at work – as easy as it was outside of work.

Rubens scowled:

"To tell the truth, I have no idea what is truly going on, gostoso. Everything had been fine for a while after Milo left – but now Ziggy has noticed money missing again. Dillon says that he thinks it is Zahoor. Ziggy gave me no choice. As it was me who hired Zahoor, he made me fire him too."

"Do you think Zahoor did it?"

Rubens paused. He finally answered:

"Zahoor seems honest to me."

"Do you know for sure that money is missing, or do you think Siegfried might have made a mistake?"

"I don't think Ziggy made a mistake. He's too experienced. He's been in business for years."

Rubens stopped again. Such serious talk about business. In the distance, at the end of the garden, he espied Dillon stripping off to a pair of Ginch Gonch briefs and diving into Wesley's heated swimming pool. Siegfried, alongside him, was manifestly unable to stop himself from gawping at the younger man's taut physique and excellent glutes. As Rubens watched, Siegfried drained his glass and beckoned a waiter over for a refill.

Rubens sighed:

"Dillon is not a really serious person. I would not be surprised if that idiot forgot to charge someone or gave the wrong change to a customer. He would blame someone else if he did. This is what I truly suspect. But I have no proof, Ben."

Ben stood shoulder to shoulder with his friend, watching the cavorting in the pool. Siegfried may have had the ringside seat, but they all enjoyed watching Dillon strip off. Ben felt a stab of regret. He had resisted Dillon that night

in the club because he was in a committed relationship –
but now of course, all that was in the past. Now he was free.
Maybe he should get to know Dillon a little better and do
some probing. The swimming pool sure looked inviting.
Wesley must arrange to have it cleaned with a toothbrush
for it to be so sparkling. Then Ben saw the other woman
in his life – the permanent version. His mother, in all her
glory.

Damn! He still hadn't told his mother about his
bisexuality. Could he ever possibly tell her?

Ben sighed. This was a sighing sort of day, really. He
imagined explaining to his mother the reality of his life
and desires. He had to immediately turn down the volume
in his mind, and that was just the start. The drama would
be untenable, and Italian in the extreme. There would
be exhortations, tears, and calls upon religious figures at
various levels of accessibility to assist and provide succour.
It would be operatic. Ben never felt quite ready for that.

However, as Claudia walked up with her new companion,
he reflected that maybe now was the right time. There
might never be a better time. She was happy, yet surely
on the back foot, flouncing around as she was with a boy
half her age. *What would the Pope think of that?* Maybe
letting her find out about Ben's penchant for penis at last
– quickly, precisely, by Ben diving in after Dillon – would
be well-deserved payback for her taking up with a toy boy.

Claudia extended a hand to her son's face:

"Figlio mio. You look beautiful. I think I have had a
little too much of Wesley's champagne. I nearly bought a
pair of his earrings. They were actually lovely, but then I

remembered what Piers' horrible aunt said, and I do not want to give her any satisfaction."

Claudia turned to Piers and gave him a reproachful look:

"I cannot stand people who live for appearances and judge you in such a way… Oh, excuse me."

Ben could not remember having heard his mother belch in public too often. Although it was an obvious consequence of too much champagne, Ben considered that it followed on naturally from her self-indulgent hanging around with this fashion designer. Truly, there was loss of dignity all round. *Piers had seen his mother naked.* It was all too horrible and unnatural for words.

Piers smiled at his innamorata:

"Eleanor's not that bad, Claudia. She's overly protective, that's all. I think we should arrange dinner so that you can get to know each other better. You might find that you have a lot in common."

Claudia spluttered indignantly into her glass:

"Darling, the only thing we have in common is you. But, Piers, if you think it will help then I will do it. How can I say no to a man who is fabulous, cultured, and who makes the best handbags in Milan?"

Ben found it impossible to see his mother as anything other than a parent, despite assuming a more equal role in his dealings with her these days. He had been encouraging her for years to move on from his father and find her own way in life. Ben had become more accepting of others' foibles, since discovering his own bisexuality. These days, he could attend an S&M ball and not blink an eye while a young bare-breasted woman hit an old man on his wrinkly exposed bottom with a paddle. Ben could participate in a drug-fuelled orgy at a chill-out party on a Sunday lunchtime, and feel at ease. He was thorough and even-handed in his approach to sexual gratification. In pursuance of that, Ben had mentally undressed both men and women in his office that were attractive to him, and taken care to imagine all the positions he would like to be in with them. Singly. And all together. This was all fine and dandy. He was tolerant, after all. This counted as *normal*. Ben would have advocated hotly that it was the most natural evidence of a healthy sex life.

But seeing his mother actually kissing a man made his stomach turn. The fact that this man was his own age, and someone whom in the right circumstances Ben might even have gone for himself, just made it even more eye-wateringly, bum-clenchingly awful. Did she realise how *cheap* she was making herself look?

Ben couldn't bear it. It was not right. *This was not as nature intended.*

"I'll see you later, Mamma. Rubens, I need to talk to you about something. Come with me?"

As Ben walked off, he could feel Piers' eyes upon him. *Damn it!* Piers was at home in fashion circles. He could sniff out gay from a hundred paces. This was all piling up like a motorway crash on a foggy day. Ben wanted to tell his mother in his own time, on his own terms. Was that going to turn out to be wishful thinking?

Rubens had barely had time to give Claudia a quick peck on the cheek. He followed Ben meekly towards the swimming pool. Goodness, things were not what they used to be. There was too much tension. Rubens did not like this kind of seriousness.

He bounced around Ben, and cocked his head. It was time for a subject change:

"So, Big Ben, how was work this week? Did you actually make it to the office at all?"

"Don't ask. But you have, so I'll tell you. It started out fine, but the second half of the week was a struggle. I wonder why? I'm sure the booze and sex had nothing to do with it, though. You know how it is: I didn't exactly impress one of the partners with my alertness in meetings. Then I managed to somehow lose a ton of work on an important document. I had been working on it for hours, too. When I went to complete it and send it out, there was only half of it saved. It was awful. My heart just sank. It's odd. It has never happened to me before, and I always despised people who did not back up their documents properly."

Ben sighed ruefully:

"I guess I should have listened to you when you warned me about drinking on a school night. Anyhow, Hartmut has got my back. I'm not going to worry about that stuffed shirt Bartlett bloody DeVere. He wouldn't know a good time if it slapped him in the face. Actually, he could do with a good punch in the nose. Many of them could. I'm not sure they realise that imagining them holding a broken nose is the only thing that keeps me going through these pointless meetings."

This wasn't like Ben at all. Rubens had always been impressed by Ben's ability to keep his career on track. He invariably seemed to land on his feet, and control things more than was supposed possible. It was disconcerting to hear him sound dismissive of his work, as if there were other more important things going on.

"Violence is not the answer?" hazarded Rubens.

"They do say that," agreed Ben. "But what about imagined violence? I swear it helps."

They reached the pool area:

"Oh, that's a shame," said Ben, noting that Dillon and Siegfried had disappeared off. "I rather fancied playing around with the little slut. Shall we have a swim anyway? We need to do something to liven this party up."

Rubens assented. They stripped off to their underwear and dived into the pool.

A slim figure appeared poolside, his silhouette shimmering on the surface like a Turner sky:

"So that's where you got to."

Tarquin Henderson-Smythe was standing at the edge of the pool, accompanied by an attractive woman with a tight blond bob. She was wearing a black mini dress. She was sexy. Tarquin seemed rather put out to find Rubens cavorting with Ben in the pool. He looked jealous, even. Ben thought it was understandable. He was surprised, however, to see Rubens looking sheepish. Rubens? Reacting?

"Tarquin! Ben and I were just talking about things. Why don't you join us in the pool, gostoso?"

"Rubens, I don't have my swimming trunks. As you know, Wesley is my client and some of us do have to keep up appearances."

"We don't have trunks either, gostoso, yet we think our appearances are definitely being kept up."

With that Rubens hoisted himself up onto the edge of the pool, his dripping Calvins presenting a dazzling strip of white against his olive-skinned body.

The woman laughed at Tarquin:

"Oh, come on Tarkers! I hardly think Wesley would be upset to see you in your underpants. He's probably been dreaming of that for ages. I think it is a perfect idea."

She reached down, gripped the hem of her dress and pulled it straight up and over her head.

Ben could not take his eyes off her. He objectified her with a vengeance: perfect Wonderbra breasts, the flattest of stomachs and legs that looked as if they had just walked off a Victoria's Secret catwalk. Enchanted, Ben backed up to the far edge of the pool and hoisted himself out, following Rubens. He couldn't take his eyes off the woman.

This was a change.

What a great thing change was.

"I'm Vicky, by the way."

She gently lowered herself into the pool, shivering slightly despite the heat of the day. She disappeared under the water, swam along the bottom and emerged just by Rubens and Ben, water dripping off her now slicked back hair, her breasts lapped by the water like two very reassuring dinghies.

Ben realised what was happening in his pants and there was only one thing for it. He lowered himself speedily into the water. *Nicholas Casterway masturbating. Nicholas Casterway masturbating.* The cold water and Ben's concentration stopped danger in its tracks.

Vicky smiled as if she were interested:

"So Tarkers, aren't you going to introduce me properly? Such a shame all the best looking men are gay."

The mixed spa in the Bellinghurst was one of London's best kept secrets. Nicholas Casterway knew that late on a Saturday evening he would have the place practically to himself. From his vantage point in the Jacuzzi, he had been watching a lone woman swim twenty lengths in the pool. She emerged dripping, obviously keen to treat herself to the caress of some bubbles.

The swimsuit struggled manfully to contain her as she gingerly entered the Jacuzzi where Nicholas lay like a sea slug. He refrained from stretching his legs out and *accidentally* touching her feet.

All things came to those who waited.

"What a gorgeous place." The visitor smiled over at Nicholas. "I told my husband he should have come down with me – but he insisted on watching the match on TV in the room."

Perfect. Nicholas flashed her what he thought was a warm smile as he felt a stirring below. Foreplay was such an important part to any experience. Anticipation. He visualised her lips satisfying him.

She was smiling warmly, but not specifically at Nicholas:

"I told him if he gets bored watching a load of overpaid men run round a field, then I would be down here waiting for him. I was rather hoping for a neck massage after my swim. He's awfully good at them."

Unexpected. Still, the woman seemed rather rueful. Should Nicholas offer up his own stringy hands? He'd always felt his hands would probably lend themselves better to strangling something. Giving gentle sensual pleasure seemed a little pointless – like having your meat chewed for you. But who knew. Maybe there was enough patience in his bony joints to relax the lady after her swim. She did seem to be rather egging him on. Perverse little piece!

Just as Nicholas was contemplating making an offer, the changing room door banged.

His companion brightened:

"Ah, marvellous. Maybe Justin's reconsidered?"

As she moved about to get a better view of the door opening, her foot brushed against Nicholas'. Was it just an impression, or was she in no rush to break the touch? Was she deliberate, or clumsy? Maybe she was one of those swingers he had read about. Might this be some sort of prelude to a ménage-à-trois? Nicholas hadn't indulged himself in that manner for some considerable time. He felt thrilled as he contemplated spit-roasting the woman while kicking her husband around like a dog. The simple things in life were what Nicholas really took pleasure in. The husband had better be decent-looking, though.

His eager anticipation was quickly dashed when, instead of the good-looking Justin with the expert hands, a woman walked in. It was Amber – for once, being Amber. She made a beeline for the shower, showing off her slim, hard body, clad in a bikini more appropriate for a Mediterranean beach pose than for the Bellinghurst. She seemed momentarily disconcerted by the couple in the Jacuzzi, before recovering her composure. She walked over:

"Sorry I am late. What a lovely place. I'm going to start off in the steam room."

The Jacuzzi woman watched Amber walk away and disappear into the clouds of steam emanating from what was sure to be the most luxurious of Turkish baths. She had not missed the silent look directed her way. Maybe it was time to go and get that neck massage from Justin.

Somewhat disappointed at the departure of his prey, especially after the foot brushing, Nicholas hoisted himself out, sluiced himself down and headed for the steam room. He had barely closed the door when two hands were upon him, his shorts were pulled down, and as if by magnetic guidance, Amber Bluett's mouth popped straight onto his cock.

It was steamy. Fortunately the situation had aroused them both equally. This was a relief, because the temperature in the steam room was far too high to allow one to stay in there for too long. They climaxed and rushed straight for the door, gasping for air as they exited, glistening like wet otters, still adjusting their swimwear. As they soaked under cool showers, a tanned, blond pool attendant greeted them cheerily. Nicholas eyed him as the attendant completed a circuit of the room and then left again, with cheerful encouragement that they should make the most of the spa. Little did the dumb blond know.

Nicholas slipped on a robe and lay on a comfortable lounger:

"So, did Skink sort you out?"

Amber stretched out:

"He made me feel rather a fool, actually. He pointed out

how easy it was to wreck someone's career. All you need is access to their computer."

"We lawyers do have some security in place..." said Nicholas pensively.

"Skink thought it was laughable. In any event Ben's secretary has his password on a post-it stuck to her computer stand. Do you know the saddest thing? His password is *k€lly4b€n32.*"

"He's the fool rather than you, it seems. Most satisfactory. So when do you plan to turn yourself into him?"

"Really, Nicholas? Do you have such low expectations of me? Carpe diem, as you always crap on about. It's done. I stayed late last Thursday night and accessed his PC. I had a good snoop around. It's all very dull. Needless to say, there was nothing to truly hang him with. But I bore in mind what I learnt in prison – simple is often best. So I found a document that he had been working on yesterday. It seemed significant, so I deleted a few bits and bobs from it, saved it, and changed the last modified date. I'm no lawyer, thank God, but I think that warranties and indemnities sound faintly important. I took a few negatives out, too. I like a positive – a *shall*, rather than a *shall not!*"

Nicholas guffawed with delight.

Amber grinned:

"He relies on technology so much, that one. I don't know if he could even hold a pen. I heard someone in the deal team complaining about a huge problem with the draft the next day – so I think it worked. Best of all, the document had already been sent out at that stage – not just to the client, either. It was transmitted to the whole project team. I think Ben will be having to explain himself to Hartmut. And Hartmut knows that Ben is not exactly in the best state."

Nicholas pressed his hands together in glee:

"You're devious, decisive and decent at fellatio. Sometimes I almost like you. I have a good mind to let you fellate me again. This is an impressive result. It's almost as good as when I got that partner removed by alleging something nonsensical like *lack of judgment*. You've excelled. I'm developing a whole new faith in the merits of delegation. Enough light praise, though. Get over here."

"Ben's bisexual, actually. Aren't you, gostoso?"

The old Ben would have been embarrassed. The old Ben, however, had gone to hell in a handcart. Ben had a new trip planned, and wanted to take Vicky along for the ride.

"Indeed I am. But if I weren't before, then I would be now, looking at you, Vicky. We all need another drink. For everyone. Where are those waiters?"

Rubens wondered whether he should try and keep Ben under some form of control, but decided that it was neither his place, nor his concern. Let the man do as he pleased. That was a philosophy that had always paid dividends for Rubens. In any case, he needed to pay some attention to Tarquin. His Old Masters expert was looking sweetly put out. Rubens was delighted at this turn of events. He felt that light fluttery feeling as he caught Tarquin's smouldering glance. He wanted to melt those stares into sleepy contentment. This must be love:

"Vicky, I am going to steal Tarquin away from you. Ben

will take good care of you. He's a hot shot lawyer, you know. But he can be entertaining, too."

"Well, I can certainly see he knows how to fill out his briefs. Oh, did I say that out loud?" Vicky laughed easily with the confidence of a woman who knew her power over men, and enjoyed it.

She was just what Ben needed.

Kelly sat in disbelief.

Morten looked at her:

"It's something I must do."

She buried her face in her hands:

"Oh, I know, you big cooyon. I know. I know... I just don't understand why I am so surprised."

He came over and knelt by her, his long frame so lean and familiar now, and comforting. Yet he was leaving. Just like that. Going to Africa to do good things. Of course. The exact aims that made Kelly so proud of him, so in lust with him were now blowing up in her face like Guy Fawkes' plans for remodelling Parliament.

She kissed him. It was strange to think that soon he would no longer be there to kiss. I suppose, she thought, that one day every one of us is no longer going to be there to be kissed. It is the natural course of events. But, from a relationship standpoint, this felt very sudden.

Perhaps not entirely unexpected. Of course, she knew from the outset that there was a risk in allowing herself to love a foreigner passing through Paris, while she was only there herself on secondment for a few months. But parting was still a dismal, daunting prospect – more akin to sending someone to the gallows, than to an appropriate fizzling out of a passing flame. It was so much more of a shock than she could have possibly imagined. Or... was it? It certainly felt permanent. Sad, too, like watching a butterfly die.

She rose, and went to stand by the window:

"It's so far away."

"It's not..."

"It is." She grabbed him. "We are about the physical, here. I need you close. I need to feel you. I am jealous of every glance upon you. And I despise – oh Lord – I despise and hate and refuse to be in another bloody long distance relationship!"

Morten rose quietly:

"Kelly, we have only known each other a short while."

She turned to face him, her eyes accusing:

"That's a little thoughtless and hurtful, right there."

"Kelly, we are good together. But we are both right at the beginning of what we want to do. I am headed out to do what I think is really needed. This is not a time for sentimentality. This is what I have trained for. This is where I am needed most."

She grimaced sarcastically:

"*... and these are my people.* Go on, I know that sort of speech. If you were truly in love with me, you'd be thinking in a different way..."

"Love, Kelly? Really? I know this sounds unromantic, but is this sort of *physical* love all that you think about? Is that the only motivation in your life? Can't you see that sometimes choices need to be made that take you away from the easy way forward? Can't you understand the value in that?"

"Oh, listen to yourself! Of course I understand it. You try understanding this: I need you. I want every inch of your body. And not flattened on a photograph – here, in person. Let me spell it out a little: I want to jump up and down on you, frequently, and I won't be able to do that via Skype."

Morten looked unsure:

"I feel a little used."

"Used?? For crying out loud. Isn't passion important to you?"

"I have passion, Kelly." He looked steadily at her: "I have a strong need to fight injustice, to do something valuable with my life. I don't expect you to understand it. But I want to do good. If that means sacrificing some of the physical pleasures of life, then I'm prepared to do it. There are more important things. Maybe I'm misguided on this. I'm sure you'll think I am. But there is more to life than sex. Even the wonderful sex I have with you."

"Geez."

"I know. I'm sorry."

"You're still here, but I feel as if someone has just come along and vacuumed out my insides."

"As a doctor, I can assure you that they are all still there. Come here."

He hugged her close. She clung to him, but her brain was already whirring. This *hurt*, this was going to be hard, but in a peculiar way, she was already growing used to the idea. It was already nowhere near as hard as she had imagined it might be. The point remained: Morten was right. This was the right thing for him. And *someone* had to be this noble.

Kelly knew from Ben that the glorious days of hot, intense sex had a time limit. She knew that things passed and changed. Even as she undressed Morten for one long, almost final bout of love making, she knew that one thing was keeping her buoyant.

Despite all of the Scandinavian excitement, she missed Ben.

"I remember. It all started when my mother gave me a little pink hippo called Amanda. Well, it was actually a hippo from a children's television show – but I always thought he was more like a little girl hippo, so I renamed him Amanda. In my mind, Amanda was a little hippo actress who just played a boy hippo in the daytime, dear."

Wesley Nest smiled nostalgically at a rather bemused Claudia Barlettano, who smiled back at him, a little nervously. She shot a sideways glance at Piers, Tarquin and Rubens. What was Wesley talking about? *What did all this mean?*

"Anyway, as soon as I had Amanda, then I wanted to have stuffed toys from all my favourite programmes. Or rather, I wanted the little actors that played the characters on television shows. My next pet was a wonderful striped cat called Marjorie. Now in real life, Marjorie and Amanda were the best of friends and were quite inseparable. We had so many lovely adventures together when I was growing up, even though they were ever so naughty at times."

At this stage, it wasn't only Claudia who was left somewhat lost. The silence was finally broken by Piers:

"Did your parents ever worry about you, Wesley?"

"No, not at all. In fact, they rarely showed any feelings at all. They weren't cruel to me. They just saw emotions as a frailty. But children are quite adaptable and I had my own little world to escape to when I needed to get away from them. I would always run to my toys when I was particularly happy or upset over something."

The conversation had gone from odd to faintly disturbing. Tarquin reflected that he had never seen Wesley show anything more than the merest hint of mild emotion. There was always a veneer of patronising joviality covering every interaction that he had. Tarquin wasn't comfortable thinking that Wesley behaved in the way that he did because he had had to substitute his mother's love and settle instead for loving a stuffed pink hippo called Amanda. That was too cruel for words.

"So do you still have all these toys, Wesley?"

Claudia thought it would be impolite not to show some interest in something that was obviously quite important to her host.

"Absolutely, my dear. I couldn't part with them. Besides, a few years ago an old aunt of mine gave me a vintage bear, and that got me hooked on collectible soft toys. There is quite a market, you know. I think it is my knowledge of antique collectible toys that helped me to be so successful in choosing my paintings. You see, I already had an eye for what was genuine. Now, why don't we move along and look at my brass rubbings in the Georgian study? If we're all good, I'll take you to my toys, and show you a good time."

"Rubens. This is hot. But we can't do it here, someone might see us."

Tarquin and Rubens were at the far end of Wesley's garden, standing behind a large rhododendron. Sunshine always made Rubens horny. But being horny reached new levels around the slim Old Master specialist. Tarquin was just *not* like other men. Rubens felt as if his natural lust had somehow upped the ante. It was channelled and directed, in a fantastic firework of feeling and happiness. Someone specific, as opposed to any old cock in a farmyard, was just as good as people used to say it might be. They were right all along! Was this what Ben was always driving at? Rubens looked at Tarquin in disbelief. There was no question about it. Tarquin was a worthy target for unbridled, carefree, intense lust. Tarquin had something unique – brains, personality, and incredible lashes over cool grey blue eyes. How could all this not have been evident so much sooner? This man – this wonderful, beautiful man... Rubens groaned. It would be a very good thing indeed to show Tarquin that he was the only man that Rubens wanted. After some passionate snogging, Rubens' hands were undoing Tarquin's belt and, before Tarquin knew it, his jeans were round his ankles.

Rubens was a little stronger than Tarquin, but he handled him gently:

"Gostoso, no one will come down here, and anyway – who would care? We're in love, remember?"

Tarquin stared into Rubens' brown eyes. These feelings were certainly excellent. Maybe Rubens was right. He should just loosen up a bit and live a little. When did he ever get the chance to have sex in the open air – in the warm sunshine, no less – and with a man such as Rubens? Tarquin knew that he was on private property so, really, risk was limited. Proceeding with dashed enthusiasm was at very least a sign of confidence and freedom – as well as one in the eye for controlling and condescending Wesley, who probably prized the very rhododendron whose leaves were being trampled and potentially ejaculated upon. Tarquin relaxed his grip on Rubens' hands and let the Brazilian kneel in front of him.

Moments later, as they were both locked in a half-clothed embrace, and while Tarquin was fumbling with the condom that Rubens had given him, Tarquin heard the sound of laughter heading his way.

"Rubens, there's someone coming! I do not want to be found like this. Wesley is my client. Quick – hide in the rhododendron."

They had managed to gather their clothing and conceal themselves in the middle of the bush, when Siegfried and Dillon rounded the corner of the privet hedge.

Siegfried sniffed:

"This'll do – right here. I can't take another story of how the supermarket is killing off all Leatherhead's local shops. I need some proper help. Be careful with it. It's good stuff."

Peering through the foliage, Rubens saw Siegfried extract a little plastic packet from his pocket. He expertly tipped some white powder onto the back of his hand, and took a deep sniff through a rolled up banknote.

Dillon followed suit, giggling:

"Oh, Siegfried, it's so much fun hanging out with you. Thank goodness we got our little bonus so we can afford all of this!"

"Quite. Right. Whoa. I think I am ready to endure guests regaling me with stories of their prize-winning sherry trifles again. Let's go and get some more champagne first, though. No point in running the unnecessary risk of being comprehensively bored to death."

As soon as Dillon and Siegfried had walked away, Rubens' hands were all over Tarquin again. Sadly, though, the flame had died down. Tarquin was too spooked to finish the deed, despite Rubens' best attempts to persuade him. The rhododendron was to remain pristine, unsullied by Tarquin's seed.

Rubens sighed longingly. If he had thought Ben was an uptight American, then Tarquin was on a whole new scale. But it was Tarquin – his Tarquin. He looked adorable peering through the leaves like a nervous fox.

They emerged from the bush and dressed in silence, preparing to rejoin the party.

Rubens wondered what Dillon had meant by the bonus. He definitely took a lot of coke for a waiter. His wages were pretty inadequate to match that level of consumption, it must be said...

Wait a minute.

Could Milo and Zahoor have been right all along?

Half an hour and a bottle and a half of champagne later, Ben and Vicky found themselves sneaking upstairs.

Vicky was enduring the usual tussle between her desires and social convention:

"You know, Ben, I wouldn't *normally* do this kind of thing. When Tarquin invited me down here to a suburban gay party I came along for the champagne – and to poke fun at the décor. It has already been a lot of fun doing just that."

She stopped to contemplate an overly ornate gilt lamp. She turned to giggle invitingly at Ben:

"But how could I possibly resist trying to turn a man like you? It's my only chance to help you find the righteous path. You do realise that you will be a card-carrying homosexual when I tell this story to my girlfriends?"

She had made up her mind. Her laughing eyes taunted him. Ben did not put up any resistance. They pulled each other along the landing, and fell through a half-opened door into what Ben assumed would be a spare bedroom:

"Well, would you look at that…"

Ben's impulses had been momentarily stopped in their tracks by the largest bed that he had ever seen. However, it wasn't the bed that had made him freeze. It was the fact that it was covered with dozens of stuffed animals.

Pride of place was taken by a large pink hippopotamus.

"What the hell is this place?"

Ben had had sex in all sorts of unexpected places since arriving in London, but he wasn't sure if he was able to do it in Toys-R-Us.

"Oh, darling, it's just perfect!" Vicky started giggling again and pulled him close, planting a kiss on his lips.

Maybe, thought Ben, he could overcome his reluctance

after all. As his hands discovered Vicky's body, his last doubts melted away.

This time there was no fumbling with fasteners. Within a moment they were both standing naked, his erection rubbing up against her stomach.

Ben had meant to clear the bed of the toys, but they were soft by name and nature, and the combination of the champagne, months of resisting temptation and the utter sexiness of the woman he was with, overpowered any better intentions he had. He just threw Vicky playfully onto the bed and jumped on top of her. Ben had good aim. Vicky started to moan as he entered her skilfully, softly at first, and then more and more vigorously, pumping in and out as his lips paid homage first to one nipple, and then the other.

Quite understandably, neither Ben nor Vicky heard the door open as Wesley entered, intent on introducing his guests to Amanda and Marjorie. Both Ben and Vicky did however hear Claudia Barlettano scream as she saw a bare bottom thrusting with intent between a pair of legs which pointed to the ceiling, still wearing a pair of bright summer shoes. Claudia's scream grew louder as Ben turned around, and she realised that it was her son's behind that she was watching.

Dillon found his voice first:

"Lucky cow!"

As Ben withdrew, he jumped off the bed and grabbed the nearest thing to him to cover his bobbing cock.

The party had just surpassed Dillon Lloyd's wildest dreams.

Another voice sounded:

"Put Amanda down."

Wesley Nest's voice had a cracked tone to it.

Ben looked down and realised that he had seized the pink hippo. But he couldn't release it just yet.

Vicky was in a similar predicament. Rubens looked at her with curiosity:

"That is a very furry pussy."

Marjorie the striped cat was firmly clenched between Vicky's legs.

A dazed silence fell.

Vicky looked apologetic:

"Sorry all. I would have gone for the Brazilian, but he was taken."

It did not take long from then for Ben to find himself being prematurely ejected from Wesley's party.

"It seems you half came on the hippo," sniggered Piers, "I think that was the final straw. Apparently, Amanda was a virgin."

Ben looked at him glumly. Somehow they had ended up walking back to the cars together. Tarquin and Rubens were a few paces behind with Vicky, followed by a mortified and upset Wesley, escorting an equally mortified Claudia. She had hurriedly purchased three pairs of earrings in a valiant attempt to make up for her son's indiscretion, but that was – even she acknowledged – merely papering over the crack:

"Oh Wesley, you showed us so much kindness and then – of all people – my own son does that. I have never been so embarrassed and ashamed in my life. I am so sorry for this. *Che figura di merda!*"

Hearing his mother shout out words obviously directed at him, Ben hung his head. He had indeed shown his mother up. Why had he let himself get so out of control? It was bad enough that he had shown a complete lack of respect for a treasured possession of Wesley's. He now further had to live with the knowledge that his mother had seen him having sex. As had a number of his friends.

Piers looked at his girlfriend's son with a wry smile:

"At least you did it in style. If you're going to get caught having sex in public, then make sure it is with someone that you are not going to be ashamed of being seen naked with. Being caught with an unattractive partner would be true shame."

Ben looked over at Piers, who seemed to have had a permanent sneer on his face since the unintended coitus interruptus. There was much Ben could have said at this point to Piers. But he held his tongue.

Piers continued lightly:

"Your drunken humiliation has at least saved me from one embarrassing situation. I was *convinced* you were gay. I thought you were banging the Brazilian. I was going to ask your mother about you on the way home."

That was enough. Ben's eyes blazed:

"Piers, you may be dating my mother but I am warning you. My sex life is no concern of yours. What I do and who I do it with is my own business, you hypocritical granny-muncher. If you *ever* try to cause trouble in my family, it'll … rear up and bite you right back."

Ben walked off but had second thoughts. He turned to wag a slightly ineffectual finger at Piers:

"You're back in London now – and we don't indulge curtain-twitchers here half as much as we used to. Now, go back to selling overpriced bags to over-aged hags. And stay out of my way."

With that, Ben headed off.

It was all too much, sometimes.

14

Krapwerk

Back in the heart of Elephant & Castle, Surrey seemed like a bad dream.

Despite living nearby, Ben had actually never been to the dark side of the Elephant & Castle Shopping Centre. The south-eastern corner. The Heygate approaches. This was where the Walworth Road disappeared under a railway bridge with the gleaming Strata building standing like a giant sentry marking the end of zone one civilisation, and the furthest reach of the Underground into south-east London. Bus after bus spewed forth from under that bridge, ready to disgorge the tube-less masses onto the Bakerloo and Northern lines. It was another reason for Ben to have taken up cycling.

As he emerged on the far side of the railway bridge, Ben wondered whether he had been somewhat hasty in deciding to leave his bike at home that day. He was on his way to Camberwell to see an installation art exhibition put on by a friend of Hartmut Glick's. Given that he was a little on the early side, he decided to take the opportunity to explore an area that he may not have cause to visit again soon. He had chosen to walk down the Walworth Road. It was much better than sitting on a bus alone. Buses were engine rooms for solitary musing. For sure, he would simply end up brooding yet again over how Kelly Danvers had broken his heart.

He was barely two hundred yards from his flat in The Castle Lofts – and yet Ben felt that he had moved into unknown territory. London could be like that sometimes. The empty hulks of the Heygate council estate reminded Ben of a maximum security prison. No wonder Madonna and David Guetta had filmed there. No one was ever going to disturb them in their gyrations in such a place. The estate made a perfect unattractive friend for The Castle Lofts, boosting the latter's confidence in its own looks. A momentary aesthetic reprieve came with the Victorian charm of Newington Library, the curiously named Cuming Museum and the decent modern blocks on the right, before the street fell victim to a succession of tatty clapboard ground-floor extensions protruding from the buildings lining the street.

They all seemed to house ugly boxlike shops filled with items Ben could never imagine desiring. Cheap take-aways, money transfer shops, pound shops, charity shops, mobile phone shops jostled for Ben's attention, each plainly failing in the endeavour. When Ben caught sight of *Modern Italian Luxury Furnishings* he was stopped in his tracks. In pride of place in the shop window was an enormous bed. It boasted a white headboard with flamingos and elephants carved into the plastic surround, interspersed with mirror shards. He then noticed the matching wardrobe and dressing table, each with its own mirrored menagerie. The suite was a snip at just £2,999. After reflecting that minimalism was clearly an overrated concept in Walworth, Ben then wondered where on earth in Italy they made such items. Who bought these things? What would his mother say?

After passing East Street market, Ben entered wig and nail shop territory. He counted half a dozen of such businesses within the space of a couple of hundred yards, all filled with bejewelled wrists and fingers, carefully coiffured big hair and a dominant number of sparkly lycra leggings. Clearly the Walworth look was as understated as Walworth interiors. Ben decided that he had seen enough, and at Burgess Park jumped on a bus and fled.

He wondered whether he had become a bit of a snob.

"Mind the pubic hair, Hartmut," cautioned Caroline. "It must be part of the exhibition."

Hartmut had already noted the hair on the floor by the side of the toilet as soon as they had entered the room. Black and barely long enough to be identified as pubic, this was clearly male grooming by a man who never let it grow too long. He espied a sleek electric trimmer next to a bottle of Clinique moisturiser on the shelf under the bathroom mirror. A tube of haemorrhoid cream lay half-hidden on the top of the bathroom cabinet next to a packet of condoms. There was an open bottle of Lynx in the shower cubicle and a large black towel drying. A tight Lycra running vest lay in the small laundry basket. A discarded jockstrap had failed to make it in and had been left where it had fallen. An open magazine displayed a picture of a shirtless David Haye. Another cover boasted a picture of a pumped-up Mark Wahlberg and a cameo of The Rock. Underneath were other glossy magazines and the corner of a newspaper.

Caroline stared at the installation:

"This appears to be the ablutions palace of a young gay man who spends too long at the gym and then spends weekends in a club picking up the kind of muscle men he fantasises over. He's probably got a decent job. I say that as I see that he can afford Clinique."

Caroline seemed satisfied with her assessment of the room.

"I would not be so hasty, my dear." Hartmut took his wife's hand. "I agree that we are clearly talking about a man who has a certain pride in his appearance. But if you look at the vest, you will see salt marks. It has actually been used for running and not just for display in a discotheque. The magazines illustrate a boxer's training regime, and also how men in their forties are maintaining the physique of someone far younger. Haemorrhoid cream is the perfect potion for lines below the eyes. The letter "N" one can just make out on that magazine cover I believe to be for "Nuts". Finally, we have a pink newspaper, the condoms, the jockstrap and urine marks almost deliberately left around the rim of the toilet bowl. I say this, taking into account the otherwise pristine nature of the bathroom. My dear, we are looking at a forty-something American male divorcé who is desperately clinging on to his youth in order to attract younger women, before he lets them know about his successful career in the City. It was also a bad break-up."

Ursula Himmelfarb had brought her Berlin show to London, but with a twist. *Krapwerk: Hardly ideal, Holmes* had been designed with the British love of mystery in mind. Each au naturel, carefully curated bathroom scene was accompanied by a folder with the description of the owner or owners of that space. The visitor could test their sleuthing ability. They were asked to participate in the event by awarding themselves points on a self-certification basis for each correctly identified characteristic, marking their card accordingly and being awarded a certificate of detection corresponding to their total score at the exit.

Hartmut and Caroline were rather pleased with their progress. It was a surprisingly enjoyable event. As promised to Ursula, Hartmut had press-ganged many of his acquaintances into coming along.

Eleanor caught sight of her daughter:

"Oh, there you are, Caroline. When you suggested venturing south of your delightful old residence, I hardly expected to be converted by the spectacle of a Camberwell Crapper. I am surprised in one regard, however. I just found myself agreeing with Claudia Barlettano. Never have so many owed so much to so few sheets of cling-film. Miss Himmelfarb's exhibits would be all the rage amongst the stool-studying mediaeval medical profession."

Caroline Napier Jones had never discussed faeces with her mother, and was not about to start. However, shit had brought Eleanor Napier Jones to pronounce the name of her nemesis for possibly the first time. Caroline espied an opening:

"Mother, Hartmut and I would like to invite you over to

Sunday lunch. We also want to invite Piers and Claudia. He seems pretty serious about her. Maybe it's time to proffer an olive branch. And where better to do it than the Glickhaus? You can't argue there, as you might wake up Marky and Sadie."

Eleanor produced a look of disdain worthy of an actress auditioning for the part of a dowager duchess. But she nodded slowly:

"Very well. However, I may subject her to the type of prolonged grilling that you usually reserve for your heavily done meat. Just because you insist on giving a rump a good pounding beforehand does not mean it will remain malleable for the duration if you expose it to such a lengthy roasting. And on that note, I feel it is high time you called me a taxi, if indeed they venture this far south of Father Thames."

Further on in the exhibition corridors, Pam and Lynne were taking in the frank offerings with some incredulity.

Pam had brought her brother Armitage. She was wondering whether this had been wise. He had grown up so fast. She didn't remember him being so knowing and snarky.

He was at it again:

"Oh, look. Swing Out Cistern. It's practically coming off the wall. Pam, looks like one of your gaffs when you were a student."

Pam sighed with some irritation:

"Armitage, your puns don't get any better with the passing years. And I never lived in a *gaff*."

Her brother winked at Lynne who giggled like an

amused five-year-old. She always found the Shank siblings to be so wonderfully mismatched.

Armitage was encouraged by Lynne's response. It helped that Lynne was so pretty. He racked his brain, although that was not where his inspiration seemed to be coming from:

"... or maybe we should entitle the whole exhibition *Cisterns Are Doing It For Themselves*? That would get all the muff divers down here sharpish."

"Oh, Armitage," said Lynne coquettishly, "I wish! You do know that it is many a year since I guzzled Pam's quim. I only ever had the pleasure a few times, lovely though it was."

Armitage was in awe of Lynne. She had just said "quim".

Pam ignored them both, and concentrated on the exhibits. What did Armitage call his speech mannerisms again – banter? What an unreconstructed imbecile he was. He had the wit of a barn owl.

She tuned him out. It was simpler that way.

Footsteps approached. Claudia was not in her element:

"Piers, I am not sure I want to go into that one. My stock of disinfecting wipes is running low. I would certainly not like to touch anything by accident in there. I fear also that the soles of my shoes would exit that room grey or black – but almost certainly not red any more. *Amore*, what a lovely present they were!"

Underneath the old style wall-mounted cistern, hanging on for dear life by two remaining screws, a long thin pipe ran down to a toilet bowl that, although once crystal white, now had a thick brown stain down the back. It was a creamy yellow everywhere else above the waterline.

It was quite revolting. The orange liquid combined with the deep rust of the bowl below the waterline made Piers think of the 2012 Olympic Park – but circa 2005.

The grime continued. The ring around the bath was so thick that you could have put small trinkets there, rather like a dirty little display shelf for forgotten knick knacks from Gran Canaria. The water was a pale greyish colour, with a few lonely suds towards the tap end.

Definitely less Acqua di Parma than Acqua di Manchester Ship Canal.

Although the paint was peeling off the ceiling and the bare plaster walls were faintly dappled with what was once chintzy paper, the room was large, and there were signs of care here and there. The washbasin was stained, but a tube of Sainsbury's Basics toothpaste stood neatly in a clean glass, together with a couple of well-worn toothbrushes. A large vase of wild flowers was placed in front of the broken window as if to mask the missing pane. The vibrant yellows and reds of the blooms contrasted with the washed-out appearance of all else. In a cardboard box near the toilet lay a stack of Big Issue magazines, and a solitary copy of Ideal Home. Claudia needn't have worried about her shoes as there was not, in fact, a speck of dust on the floor.

"Definitely student digs. A couple of girls doing something pointless like law." Armitage grinned cheekily.

"So why is the toilet seat up, then?" Claudia had boldly gone where no Milanese lady had gone before. She approached the dirty bathwater. "Apart from all the encrusted dirt here, this bathroom has been cleaned very well. If they are students, then they can't be English ones."

Piers had guessed Claudia would not be able to resist participating for long. *Cara Claudia Barlettano. Well done, my lioness of the night. You have scored seventeen points on your specialist subject of household cleanliness and bacterial extermination.* She could have been a Mastermind winner.

Claudia was duly carried away by her forensic examination of the exhibit:

"Have you observed those flowers with the little handwritten note saying *Happy Valentine*? There is a man here and also a woman. No, this is definitely a couple. And they are not students. Students have more interesting things to do than aspire to lovely living rooms in their Ideal Homes. But what is that *Big Issue*?"

"Might this be invoking a young, impoverished couple in their first, broken down place? They've met, maybe fallen in love, and are trying to start a new life together. The Big Issues are there to remind them where they are headed back to if they fail."

Piers smiled triumphantly.

"Ten out of ten," said Lynne who had taken a sneaky peek in the folder. "Now let's move on. We've got some points to make up on you two."

Piers waited for them to leave before turning to Claudia:

"You don't often see a female lawyer wearing builder's boots like those, do you, darling?"

The question was loaded. Claudia smiled evenly:

"Do you think I was born yesterday, Piers? They are both lesbians, those two. I have been around, you know. I can read people. I think it is actually rather progressive that

Ben's firm has such a welcoming attitude to homosexuals."

Piers started. So she knew about Ben, then, despite the scene with Vicky at Wesley Nest's party? He ventured an oblique comment to test her further:

"Yes, Ben is very lucky, isn't he?"

Claudia looked back at him as if he were a silly boy who wouldn't wash his hands before dinner:

"What do you mean? Ben could work anywhere. I'm not sure about his present firm – I question if they value him enough. He's not having the best of luck at the moment on any front. That wicked girl who I liked so much has broken his heart. All I want is for my Ben to find himself a nice new girl, settle down, and make me the happiest grandmother in the world."

Realising what she had just said to the younger man, Claudia blushed bright red.

Piers felt for her, and rushed smoothly to her aid:

"I will never see you as a grandmother, Claudia."

The moment was rescued. Piers decided not to ruin it by adding that he never saw her as a grandmother because he still suspected that her only son seemed to be far too interested in cock.

Ben saw a familiar silhouette and wandered over to greet Tarquin:

"It's art, all right, but not as you know it, hey Tarquin?"

Tarquin raised an eyebrow. He had never been a fan of installation art. Of course he recognised it had its place and benefitted from a passionate fan base. But how many wavy trees projected onto walls could you house, in truth?

He did wonder whether the admirers were investment collectors, or simply the nouveaux riches who had no idea of what they were buying unless they had someone similar to him to instruct them.

Tarquin shook his head. In modern art, there seemed to be such a thin line between a work of inspiration and utter nonsense. He was often unsure as to which side of that line the works he contemplated lay on. At least this display was causing him to think about how the works were connected to the underlying ideas. Ursula's precision in choosing all manner of objects had a playfulness to it that appealed to him. He liked her frankness, too.

Come to think of it, he did also rather like wavy tree projections:

"I like this one. This is the first with a clean toilet as well. What do you think that means?"

Ben surveyed the room before them. The room was decorated with a plush, almost fabric-like dark red patterned wallpaper. There was a miniature Louis XV footstool in the corner and a larger chair near one of the many mirrors. The shower cubicle was clean with nary a mark on its spotless glass doors. The dominant feature, however, were the six wigs on polystyrene heads ranged along the top of a long cupboard full of make-up, hairspray and costume jewellery. The pristine WC would imply that the toilet was never used at all. It was there for no other reason than this room had been a proper bathroom before its occupant had started to use it. The bathroom cabinet with its oversized mirror, dressing room spotlights and ridiculous array of products was the soul of the room.

"Seriously, Tarquin? Are you sure you are a gay man? Even I can see from a hundred paces that this is the spare bathroom of a drag queen who wished he had lived a couple of centuries ago. I take it that Rubens hasn't taken you to visit Helena Handcart and Angela Merkin at home yet?"

Tarquin grinned at Ben:

"Sadly not, I'm afraid. I am glad that we have run into each other here. I felt rather silly about the jealous comments that I made at Wesley's party."

"Don't worry about it, Tarquin. I would have felt the same way. How does one ever deal with the ex that your partner is still on good terms with?"

Ben stopped. Perhaps he should find a way of tormenting that damned Scandinavian with his relationship with Kelly? But that would mean having a good relationship with her. That was definitely not the case at present.

Putting his own problems aside, Ben smiled sympathetically at Tarquin:

"You really have nothing to worry about. I don't even see Rubens in that way anymore."

It dawned on Ben that this was true. He understood better now how Rubens and Jamal could be so close, without even a hint of attraction between them. At some point, sometimes, feelings could actually turn themselves off, like motion-activated lighting. This peaceful, even-handed state of affairs could come to pass – all in good time. The torment of feelings could occasionally cure itself. *Awesome.*

A thought occurred to Ben:

"By the way, Tarquin, has Rubens mentioned anything to you about what is happening at the bar?"

It was Tarquin's turn to hesitate before answering. Rubens had told him about Zahoor – and he had heard with his own ears the comments that Dillon had made about his bonus:

"Only in fairly general terms, but I think he's right to be worried. Something is up. I think Rubens needs to keep a very close eye on Dillon. He seems to have quite a lot of power over Siegfried, and Siegfried would not be the first middle-aged man to lose his judgement because of a beautiful young man. Oh, here is your mother, Ben. Mrs Barlettano, how are you?"

"Oh please, Tarquin, do call me Claudia! Now I think I have seen enough untidy bathrooms for one day. Can we all go and get a nice Lavazza and some cake?"

It was late again in the office. Harry was tapping away at his computer. He felt less than stimulated. Everything was so dull, these days.

Lucy had ruined everything. Before her abusive treatment of him, the office was a cornucopia of possibilities, a vast array of possible sexual partners that he could dip into like a flamingo breaking salt. But now the women at work all seemed more alien, more frightening. They were young – too young, these days. They were also alarmingly in possession of their faculties.

A young girl's head used to be easy to turn, reflected Harry ruefully. They were all so insecure, and worried. You just got 'em drunk and moved in there. How hard could it be? You bore no responsibility whatsoever for their moral and emotional wellbeing. Weren't we all liberated from that *rubbish* by the Sixties?

Now he was the one feeling insecure. The ground had shifted. He did not like it one bit.

There was a sharp knock on his door.

He glanced up. Christ. Lucy.

She seemed taller these days.

"Hello, Lucy."

"Hi, Harry."

She reached towards him with a few pages of A4 in her hand.

"What's that?" asked Harry faintly.

"My assessment, you dork. I've reviewed what you wrote. It wasn't a bad effort, but I've made a few suggestions. Please agree them. We can then forward the document to HR."

Harry straightened and glanced at the pages. He put them down for a moment:

"Do you know, there is no need to be so unpleasant. You're actually a good lawyer. We could have..."

"... had it all? Oh, Harry. There are moments when I despair slightly of you."

"No. That was not what I was going to say. We could have worked things through."

She looked amused:

"We have worked things through. This has been the perfect addition to my personnel file. I imagine that you have made many women unhappy in your life. I am sure they got over it – but I sort of bear them in mind. You can't

316

always have everything your own way. Anyway, all sorted now."

She paused on the way out and picked up the framed photo of Sarah with the twins:

"I don't get it. She's lovely. You need to work at these things. Perhaps you lack imagination?"

Harry watched her leave, feeling emasculated.

It never used to be this way.

It had been so perfect with Monique.

It dawned on him that he may never have passionate sex again.

Backstage was a bustle. Technicians came and went like bees, their flight interrupted by PR people, a lone choreographer, gaggles of generic-looking musicians and hangers-on. Of which, mused Monique, I am one.

She loved it. There was such energy in the air. This felt so important – almost *politically* so. The warm-up band was excellent, she thought – but the venue was buzzing for the Fondant Furies.

It was surreal. There were people out there with a photograph of *her* boyfriend on their T shirts.

She clutched distractedly at the lanyard which hung around her neck. It felt weightier somehow. This was the all-important permission that allowed her access to these hallowed boards. It even bore a photograph of her.

Monique Mottin, Joy Division, she thought to herself. Still, who cared? This was fun. This was all the excitement, some of the candles and flowers, and none of the stage fright.

"Hello, Monique. Gosh you look *fabulous* today."

Monique smiled warmly. It was Jenny – not from the block, but from Sizzle! magazine. Even as she greeted her, Monique wondered with amusement at how things had turned out. Where Sizzle! had once marred most aspects of her evenings with Jake, a few meetings with the editorial gang had soon resolved matters to everyone's satisfaction. Sizzle! now largely left Jake alone – although they expected their pound of flesh for charity events and pestered him for quotes and photo shoots. But he was no longer door-stepped. Jenny had warned him that she would be powerless to stop it happening again if he split up with Monique or was caught with his pants down. Meanwhile, though, she gave them leeway. As she put it tartly: "There are enough people begging me for an appearance in the pages of our splendid publication. We'll have you sometimes, but we're far from desperate for content in these intellectually-impoverished days."

Jenny was smart. Monique gained a degree of respect for journalists – even those working on the cartoon representation of life as a famous person that was the raison d'être of Sizzle! Journalists were witnesses. They were at least as valuable as research mice, each important in their own way, as a piece of an ever-emerging jigsaw puzzle of news and views. In popular journalism, the picture represented what concerned people today. Or at least concerned them some of the time. One had to believe that, whether one liked it or not. Harmless fun, Sizzle!

The Fondant Furies stepped up, ready to go on. Monique shrank back, well aware that Jake was not thinking of her at this point. But he saw her, and stepped aside quickly to give her a kiss.

This was the sort of thing little girls might dream of. Fun on tap, and a handsome boyfriend.

Monique felt a little dizzy. To think that she might ever have settled for something less – for a dismal half-life as a young mistress to an ageing, crapulous lawyer. Monique shuddered. It simply did not bear thinking about.

She kissed Jake back with a passion that surprised him. He looked at her questioningly.

She stared him down, calm but fierce:

"I'll take care of you later."

"I might skip this gig…"

"See you soon, you beautiful boy."

Yes. Living in the present. Monique felt her heart lift with the crowd's welcoming roar. You could not plan for this. "I'll keep with this and see where it goes," she confirmed to Sushi the goldfish by telepathy.

Such is life. All about research mice, and men.

15

White wedding

A bride should never cry save to shed a truant tear of joy, and only then because all has turned out for the best on the best of all possible days. But Ben was definitely sniffling.

A crying man dressed as a bride is not a good look.

Rubens looked up:

"What's the matter? I know you look beautiful, but that make up is not waterproof. Gostoso, we had better hurry up, or we are going to be late."

Ben looked down at his clenched hands. He turned away from his miserable reflection in the mirror, and directed a lachrymose look at Rubens, who was just applying some finishing touches with one of Angela Merkin's mascara wands.

They were preparing for Alex and Jamal's civil partnership ceremony. In keeping with the spirit of the occasion, Alex had insisted that all the guests dress as brides. Alex explained that he wanted to make a statement to keep the cause of worldwide gay marriage in the public eye. England, Canada, New Zealand and a few US states were not enough. Uganda was his target now. And the Vatican.

Ben understood and approved that message – but he also suspected that there was an element of shameless publicity-seeking at play. There was no doubt that a ceremony featuring thirty brides was bound to make the local papers, especially as Pam Shank and Lynne Glackett had volunteered to explain what it was all about to anyone who could not run away fast enough. On balance, Ben thought that the aim justified the means – just. And so it was that Ben and Rubens had trekked down to Pimlico, to get ready chez Helena and Angela.

Ben was finding it all a bit too much. Weddings seemed to be temples of misery. Would he ever be able to attend one now, without feeling like death warmed up? They seemed to spell the end, not the beginning.

Rubens was doing his best to lend a sympathetic ear. However, he was baffled by Ben's emotional take on the event. For Rubens, weddings were definitely in the carnival camp. Rubens felt he had turned into the two-faced Janus – juggling exhilaration with tender concern in rapid succession; preening delightedly before the mirror in his vibrant white dress, whilst also tending to his friend.

Ben had slipped into an empire line column dress that suited his height rather well, set off by a cloudy veil atop his black curls. He looked like a Greek sculpture. Alas, he was not as decorously quiet as one:

"Rubens, I had dreamed that I would be marrying Kelly one day. Celebrating the boys' union makes me truly happy for them, but…"

Ben's voice trailed off, as he stifled another sob:

"This is probably the most ridiculous thing that I have

ever said, but looking at myself in this damned wedding dress and veil, it just made me realise that I will never look at *her* dressed as a bride. It's over. It's so damn final."

He wandered over to the window, like a tragic heroine contemplating a swift leap:

"I've been so angry and filled with thoughts of revenge that I've overlooked that. Oh, sure, it's been all about being Jack the lad, and making up for all that time I had wasted on her, but now it just seems that sex, drugs and rock and roll doesn't cut it anymore."

"Uh-huh," said Rubens, refreshing his lipstick.

"I've been spinning tales. I've spun myself into a silken cocoon. But I'm really caught up in a web that a spider of *misery* has lovingly wrapped me up in, all the better to suck me dry later. Everything has dissolved. I am here naked. I'm alone. The truth is shining a cold light on me and it hurts. Rubens, it really hurts."

Ben's face wore a look of utter wretchedness, made more pitiful yet as Angela's cheap mascara mingled happily with his tears to leave sluggish black streaks on his cheeks. Rubens thought about giving Ben a big hug and telling him that everything would be okay, but he reasoned that a hug would lead to more tears, which would lead to cheap cosmetics all over two cheap wedding dresses. Jamal would be appalled.

No, it was time to be firm. Rubens squared up, and caught Ben's gaze in the mirror:

"Gostoso, you are wearing silk, not trapped in it. There is no spider and you are not naked. In that sense, things are looking up already. Look at me. Listen. It will all be fine! Take it from me: you never know what is going to happen in life."

He warmed to his theme:

"Ben, think back for a second. You came to London a couple of years ago with all those thoughts of easy London girls in your head. Then you had your first sexual encounter with a special Brazilian guy in a men's steam bath. Wonderful. So unexpected. So *nice*. Yes, you've now met a bump or two in the road. But who's to say what's around the corner? More importantly, gostoso, we must pull ourselves together. Today is not about you. We are going to honour the commitment that our friends are making to each other and give thanks that they have wanted us to share their special day. So, because of this, man up, Ben. Stop your blabbing, retouch, and let's go for a glass of champagne with the girls."

"Heavens to Betsy!"

Helena Handcart surveyed Ben's slightly botched presentation:

"How does such a beautiful young man make such a hideous bride? Did you lend them your cheap make up, Angela? I keep telling her, it might be okay for the hausfraus of Hamelin, but we're in London now. People are so much less forgiving here. And the dress, the dress! It reeks of market stall. I hope you are proud, Angela. He looks look like a penniless trollop with the physique of an East German shot putter and all the sense of style of a Weisswurst. Oh my! Rubens, you look divine as always. Admiration, my dear. Laced with bitterness and envy, but nevertheless admiration. Now, Angela, four glasses of champagne with a little penthouse layer of Pinkie vodka on top, please?"

Helena was in a class of her own, in a long flowing white gown, a string of pearls, and elbow-length white satin gloves. Her make-up and perfect coiffure would have done justice to an English Oscar winner fresh from recreating her latest royal role. Angela Merkin, by contrast, looked as if she would be ready for a night of passion with one swift sweep of a zipper. Said zipper reached from under her left arm all the way down to the hem of her white PVC ultra mini dress. Flawless, yet dramatic make-up and a raven wig complemented her fine features. Ben had recovered from his earlier crisis, and was wondering how the vision in front of him managed to hide what was by all accounts a pair of particularly bulbous bollocks.

He felt better almost immediately with some champagne and vodka inside of him. He may have lost what he thought now was almost certainly the love of his life, but he was feeling plenty of love from his friends. He was also, all things properly considered, doing pretty well at meeting his emotional needs with casual flings.

The clouds had passed.

Today was all about having fun, and celebrating his friends' commitment. He would not spoil it by being a moaning Minnie.

The registrar had not officiated at a ceremony quite like this one before. It wasn't her first civil partnership and she was very well used to dealing with brides. But not thirty at once. Thirty brides in one room – none of whom was actually getting married – was an altogether new experience for her. She found herself slightly distracted from the words that she had recited hundreds of times, by trying to work out which of the brides were women and which weren't. She wondered if so many drag queens had ever been silent for so long.

As she moved to the climax of the ceremony, she noticed that there was hardly a dry eye in the room. That was except for the two men in front of her. They were at ease, grinning widely throughout, and seemed to find it hard to suppress a laugh, especially when she made them hold hands.

It did seem a little strange – but what alternative could there be? *"You may now bum your chosen partner?"* Of course not. That would be ridiculous. But holding hands seemed a little lame. Perhaps it reflected the fact that English men were really not that physical with each other as a rule? Maybe this also explained why brides were so trussed up in heterosexual weddings – so that touching them would seem as alien as possible, and a simple smooch would pass as an adequate – indeed, as a valiant and conquering – gesture for the occasion.

The men before her were handsome, which softened her. Good-looking is candy for the eyes. They were impeccably attired in decent designer suits, with every clipped hair disciplined. The sunlight streaming into the garden room at Southwark registry office gave them a golden glow that accentuated their obvious contentedness.

Surely, these two would last.

Despite the registrar's occasional distraction, on days like this, she truly loved her job.

"Well it was about time!" Siegfried beamed at his old friend Alex as he posed for photos in the garden with Jamal. Alex smiled benignly at him, his eyes catching on many faces. It was hard to focus on one face in the blur of so many familiar and well-liked countenances. A little slighted, Siegfried's smile died a lingering death on his lips. He felt hollow inside. The momentary happiness that had welled up inside of him listening to Alex and Jamal declaring their love for each other in front of their closest friends was now eroded by the ever-present gnawing envy Siegfried felt for anyone who had what he had never found.

It wasn't an attractive state of mind, he thought ruefully. But it was real. The realest thing Siegfried had in his life was a desire for it to be more like other people's lives seemed to be.

It seemed that Alex had always had it all. At university, he fitted with ease into the trendier-than-thou lefties group, in the way that those oozing with family money and a desire to rebel seemed to manage so effortlessly. Oh, it was all *very well* for them. It was so easy to express concern about the third world when your safe and *opulent* world protected you from any worry whatsoever about what might follow life amidst the gilded spires.

Alex glided like a queenie swan through three years at Cambridge, burnishing his worthy credentials with all manner of charitable endeavours, and never sullying with filthy mammon that glorious physique which he had been honing and cashing in on since his first oar caught a crab in the waters of the Cam.

Siegfried sighed.

It was a rare, lung-deep sigh of utter disenchantment. It seemed to him that nothing had changed. Despite half a lifetime of corporate servitude in the vain hope of reaching comfortable independence, he was still living in the shadow of Alexander the Great-and-the-Good, who flitted around the world doing the right thing, amassing admiration like air miles. To top it off, Alex had now acquired a perfect partner, and even a home-grown business, opened as a side-line. Outrageous Fortune was another success that Alex could notch up. And Alex's side-line had now become Siegfried's main event.

Of course, Siegfried was grateful to his friend. But how could he not feel devilish envy when he sweated forty hours a week in the role of an invisible subaltern, keeping afloat a mere detail of the perfect life of Alex O'Connell?

There was a detail, however, that Siegfried wanted to bring to Alex's attention. Not that Siegfried wished to mar Alex's perfect day – or might it possibly be precisely because of that – but there was a need ever more pressing to tell Alex that something was awry at Outrageous Fortune. And it was going to have a whiff of Rio about it.

He took his opportunity as soon as he was able to:

"Alex," he said with enough urgency to cause Alex to glance up sharply.

"I hope you're not going to talk business to me, Siegfried – today of all days."

Siegfried looked awkwardly at his friend and employer.

Maybe this was a bad idea.

He plunged onwards like a lost dolphin:

"I just want to wish you both the very best in the entire world," he said stiffly, "You have been one of my close friends for so long. Nobody deserves happiness more than you do. You are quite simply one of the finest men I know."

His smile was strained, as he wondered if this sounded as bad as it felt that it sounded.

"Wow, Siegfried. Thank you. All the years that I have known you, I have never heard anything like that from you. That's really nice. Maybe you should dress as a bride more often. But seriously – Jamal and I are so lucky that you agreed to come back and work for us."

Alex had not chosen diplomatic words. Siegfried did not need to be reminded that he was an employee, who could be ordered to do things by Alex and his agreeable partner at any time.

Siegfried caught sight of Jamal and Rubens busily gossiping about something at the other end of the garden. He decided that it was, after all, time to tell Alex.

"There was another thing. I thought we had solved the problem, and I haven't wanted to worry you until I was sure, but I think there is still something going on at the bar. I am afraid that I think it is Rubens who I need to keep an eye on."

"Seriously? You think Rubens is involved?"

"Well, it didn't stop when we got rid of Milo or Zahoor. It calmed down for a while, but now it's back, and I know Rubens always tries to help his family out. I could be wrong, Alex, but it would explain quite a lot. You are very perceptive with these things. May I ask you just to keep your eyes peeled? Anyhow, let's not spoil the day."

Siegfried smiled again, a tad less stiffly, pleased that his poisonous seed had been sown.

"One more, please."

This version of a wedding had indeed been a hit with the press. After numerous flashes, four of the burliest brides had given Alex and Jamal a fireman's lift so they were hoisted above the crowd. They looked like the two little figurines on top of a wedding cake as their white-clad guests formed a circle around and underneath them.

"Connie Coatts, Camberwell Chronicle. What gave you the idea to get all the guests dressed up like this?"

Pam and Lynne moved forward to take care of press enquiries. B.A.D had given its juniors a skeletal amount of media training. It should be enough for them not to make complete tits of themselves – although, given the liberties taken by the press at times, making a tit of oneself is an outcome that one needs to inevitably factor into any conversation with a story seeker. Pam moved with a fair degree of apparent authority towards the small group of journalists and photographers.

Pam, save for the grooms, was the only one in the group wearing trousers that day.

"Ms Coatts, you do of course realise that this is a civil partnership and not an actual wedding?"

The journalist nodded.

Pam continued:

"You will be aware that although marriage for the LGBT

community has been legalized in a number of jurisdictions, it is very far from the norm in the world today. If you look at Mr O'Connell's Wikipedia page, you will see that he has dedicated his life to the pursuit of civil rights for all, and in particular, equality for all. Although this union is a fantastically happy event, the LGBT community is still being discriminated against all over the world – and not only through us not being allowed to marry. We are here to make sure that the plans of governments worldwide – most of whom start with good intentions – are not halted by the bigotry still inherent in the darker recesses of societies."

"Edna Edwards, Elephant Express." Edna fitted in a lightning glare at her rival, pleased to have cut in. "But surely gay rights are becoming so mainstream, especially in London... Is it really necessary to make a stand anymore?"

"Are you homosexual, Ms Edwards?" Pam marched right up to the startled journalist, daring her to obfuscate in answering.

"No, I am not, actually."

Connie had to suppress a giggle as Edna blushed bright red. Edna was well-known in local news circles for being rather appreciative of intimate male company.

"Yet you are a woman, I presume. To be precise, you were born that way?"

Edna nodded in apprehensive affirmation.

"Would you agree with most of my heterosexual male acquaintances, that thanks to endless politically correct legislation, gender discrimination has become a relic of the past in the UK, especially in London?" Pam spat the last three words out, openly mocking the hapless journalist.

"Well, I do think we have made massive strides… but…"

Sudden silence, except for a low-voiced conversation between Alex and Jamal who were standing to one side and were utterly oblivious to the dissection of the Elephant Express's finest, and indeed only, investigative journalist.

"I see. So as a heterosexual woman, you acknowledge nonetheless that gender discrimination still exists, and yet you blithely maintain that discrimination due to sexual orientation has just gone away. I do hope that your journal is more informed than you are."

Edna felt unusually cowed by Pam's aggression. She had only come to cover a bloody wedding, not to grill the council over the latest stalled redevelopment plans.

Pam continued:

"So, Ms Edwards, it is in our view still most necessary to keep the issue of minority rights very much in the public eye in the United Kingdom, and high on the agenda. Furthermore, we also wish to highlight the struggles that our sibling organisations are going through in other countries. In the country of Jamal Qureshi's birth we would all more likely be imprisoned rather than fêted today. On a day of such personal celebration, it is part of the honour of these two that they want to light a candle for equality, liberty and freedom of personal expression for all."

Pam paused. She felt she had made her point.

Lynne saw her chance to intervene:

"Besides, brides are so pretty! I mean, don't we all just look so gorgeous? Not to mention the fact that it might be the only time that most of this lot get the chance to be a bride for a day."

Lynne's jolly smile contrasted beautifully with Pam's pained expression. Edna Edwards smiled back, not quite sure how to respond, before deciding that another picture might compensate for a thousand misplaced words.

"Can we get a photo of just the brides, please? Could we get you, miss, the, er, racy one, right at the front, please? Lovely legs, by the way!"

Angela simpered at the photographer:

"Darling, I know you meant the slutty one, and I don't mind, liebchen. I am very slutty, and I do have fantastic legs, and in fact I can get them right back behind..."

"Angela, we are celebrating a commitment today, and I don't mean in the sense of your ruthless commitment to finishing a bottle of vodka once you open it." Helena Handcart smiled regally. "Please show some respect for Alex and Jamal, who are celebrating the happiest day of their lives."

The first photo was beautiful. But as a commotion broke out in the corner of the garden, the following shots captured thirty brides spinning on their heels as one single body, to find out what on earth was happening.

"You must be fucking kidding! That is total crap and I cannot believe that you could even imagine that could be true. What the fuck, Alex?"

Jamal was staring at the love of his life, to whom minutes earlier he had professed his profound and eternal love, as if he would now like to rip his head off and throw it under the number 12 bus. Even Edna could see how furious he was and how upset his newly minted partner seemed to be. After being on the receiving end of Pam's dressing down, she immediately whispered to her photographer to carry on snapping, thereby capturing a whole series of shocked brides staring at a pair of gay husbands arguing on their special day. How perfect. What an excellent illustration of the underbelly of the institution! The Elephant Express would not be putting out a *Hello* style story on how divine the couple had looked during their sumptuous event. This would be a little more *gritty* and *interesting*.

Despite the exciting twist, Edna still wondered if it were too late to persuade the happy couple that there was another way. They were so handsome. Her last thought matched her very first one upon seeing them for the first time that day in the early sunlight. What *a waste!*

Back home, Ben heaved a huge sigh of relief as he removed his stilettoes, and then the wedding dress that he had been parading around in all day.

On the few occasions that Ben had dressed as a girl, he always rediscovered respect for the trouble that women put themselves to on a daily basis. He was happy to spend an hour in the gym five days a week, but this was another level of commitment. To spend all your life tottering on high heels, wearing clothes that barely allowed you to breathe, and with paint covering your face seemed like a much greater dedication of time and energy to the elusive goal of being attractive.

Was it ever really worth it? Ben smiled. *Of course it was.*

The scene they had all witnessed outside Southwark Registry Office had, however, been anything but attractive. The newly-pledged had quickly realised that their argument was hardly private. Helena Handcart had rushed over to calm the waters, followed by a bouquet of brides and flashing photographers. Alex and Jamal quickly regained their composure, although Jamal smiled through resolutely gritted teeth.

A little later on, all had become clearer. The argument had been about Rubens. Alex, not wanting to keep any secrets from his partner, had told him what Siegfried had said. Unfortunately, Alex had also suggested that maybe they both needed to keep a closer watch on Rubens, because the circumstantial evidence was not looking good. At this point Jamal had erupted. The couple rarely argued over anything serious, but doubting the honesty and loyalty of a person whom Jamal considered one of his closest friends in the world, was not something he could accept – especially coming from the person that he had loved best for the past decade. Alex had apologised afterwards, and there was a need for both to reflect on the poisonous news – but there was no doubt that, for the first time, there was a crack in the façade of the perfect couple. If there was trouble in paradise, Ben reflected, what hopes did *he* ever have of reconstructing his shattered relationship with Kelly Danvers?

He glimpsed a copy of QX Magazine lurking underneath a discarded Metro. Maybe he should just go for a night of sexual gratification and give up on love.

Although he had work in the morning, work that mingled especially badly with the hang-ups of a sexual relationship on the hoof, Ben simply didn't want to be alone that night.

16

Cellar vie

It was a balmy evening and a supper party at the Glickhaus would have ordinarily been a pleasant and low key affair – low key meaning, naturally, that the keys would have ended up stuffed somewhere unmentionable. Tonight, however, felt more like a political summit.

Claudia was nervous like a general marshalling his troops while realising that what worked so well on paper still meant that a great number of them would inevitably perish. She hid her nerves as best she could and chattered away gaily:

"What a lovely street, and such a handsome house. Hurry up and get a promotion, Ben, so you can live here instead of the Elephant and Castle. I don't know how you can bear those underpasses full of litter and beggars. Now, are we on time? I do *not* want to give that woman any opportunity to judge us. She'll only flood us with prejudiced nonsense. Would she have heard about your performance at Bluebell End, Ben? If so, I may die. *Che figura di merda!*"

Claudia insisted that Ben turn up with Piers and her. She needed the support of both men if she were to venture safely on to the home territory of Eleanor Napier Jones. Although, strictly speaking, Hartmut and Caroline were hosting tonight, Claudia felt that she was entering enemy territory. She needed to be fully on her guard against attacks by Eleanor.

Never underestimate your opposing matriarch, she thought grimly.

Hartmut welcomed them with his usual geniality:

"Welcome, my dears, please come in. Ben, Piers... Let me take your coat, Claudia. The ladies are through in the sitting-room. Follow the sounds of conversation."

Hartmut smiled warmly, and gestured them down the hall.

Claudia led the way, determined to show that she was thoroughly at ease, a state of mind helped along somewhat by her appreciation of the utter spotlessness of the Glickhaus. At home in New York she owned a pair of white gloves that she kept especially for the society party finger test. She occasionally delighted in accidentally demonstrating to the host that she would have to put them in the dry cleaners after her visit to their dusty dwelling. Dirt did discomfit Claudia Barlettano. In turn, therefore, she could use it to discomfit her acquaintances.

She strode through the sitting-room door. A fragile look of charmed politeness was pasted on her face. She was intent upon her nemesis, now in sight, sitting on a chaise longue.

Eleanor remained seated.

Caroline rose to greet Claudia:

"Claudia, I'm so pleased you could come." She gave

Claudia a hug. Eleanor reluctantly rose, too, from her chaise longue. The two women shook hands stiffly, each eyeing up the other as if they were about to be weighed and then fitted with boxing gloves.

"Aunt Eleanor, don't you look lovely!" With the exception of Claudia who knew Piers' tastes very well, no one noticed his remark. In fact, Eleanor had a look of domineering Aunt Diana, whom she was growing to resemble more and more as the sisters aged. Piers gave Eleanor a bear hug, noting how she seemed to still be in excellent condition for her age. Claudia fought off the urge to scream.

An attractive young woman whom Ben did not know was occupied with the twins. After the various greetings, Caroline saw Ben's eye falling on the nanny in the way that Piers' had fallen on her aunt. The middle classes could do sexual tension with the best of them, she thought happily.

"Everyone, this is Greta, our nanny. Hartmut and I do not want to turn into one of those couples with whom it becomes impossible to have a conversation once the children arrive. I vowed I would not be endlessly distracted by whatever the little darlings were doing. I used to find that *so* annoying. So I promised myself that I wouldn't fall into that trap. However, as even my iron discipline would wilt at the sight of little Marky and Sadie craving attention, well – Greta has been the answer."

Piers smiled:

"That's a relief, cousin. I would hate to lose you to nappies and baby talk."

Piers had no desire for children of his own. This was convenient, given his taste for women who had generally done all the reproducing that they were going to. He, too, had also noticed Ben's appreciation of the German nanny. Ben obviously liked women, but his violent protestations and threats after Wesley's party had nonetheless confirmed to Piers that either Ben had banged, was banging or would like to bang the Brazilian. He must be one of those greedy bisexuals. Piers shook his head. No one was safe from Ben.

Piers trusted that at least Ben wasn't attracted to the more mature woman. Otherwise, in a world of sexual questions, duelling might have been the only answer left.

Rubens was very much used to being the centre of attention. This was especially so when the weather allowed him to parade around the streets of London wearing cut-off denim shorts, flip flops and a neon yellow vest that showed off his colour and tone to perfection. If you've got it, flaunt it. However, as Rubens walked down Dalston High Street towards the Superstore, he had the odd feeling that not all the glances directed at him were of the admiring and envious type that he took to be the natural way of the world.

The trendy young things of East London were of an altogether edgier feel than the in-your-face body fascists of Vauxhall or the preen-ier queens of Soho. Rubens had not had to make an effort with clothing for so long, he was not sure he would be able to do anything other than fall into something bright and tight. He put his uncharacteristic feelings of sartorial insecurity to one side and stepped into the bar.

"Habibie, what is this cursed vest? *Vamos a la playa*, or what? You obviously don't come here very often, do you?"

Rubens stopped short. He was expecting a private drink with Milo, who had telephoned with a peace offering after Rubens fired him from Outrageous Fortune. Rubens was not expecting company. But Milo was sitting with Lady Gaza, and Zahoor for good measure. Very much on the back foot, Rubens walked slowly over to their table.

Milo was the first to stand up and greet him:

"It's good to see you."

He looked as if he meant it.

Zahoor nodded briefly at Rubens. It was the shortest of greetings, and he stayed in his seat, managing to look wronged, dignified and hurt all at once. His tacit remonstrance was thankfully not echoed by Lady Gaza who planted big kisses on Rubens' cheeks, then wiped off the lipstick marks with the back of a slightly soiled glove.

"Habibie, we are having a cocktail. Let me get you a Hackney Iced Tea. They are great, because they are strong. I think you are going to need it, as we have some news for you about our little darling Dillon, and what he is saying about you."

Drag queens thrive on gossip, and will usually embroider the base material in order to deliver it to maximum effect. Lady Gaza, however, made a distinction between having an audience, and talking to a friend.

She was being deadly serious.

She nudged Milo in one of her less feminine gestures.

"I had no proof when you fired me," started Milo, his eyes flashing with that Balkan *don't fuck with me or one day you will wake up with your balls in your mouth, or at the very least a permanent stain on your most favourite shirt* look, "but since that happened, I have been keeping my eyes on Dillon Lloyd. I don't mean on his butt like everyone else – not that I would touch that lying shit with my bargepole."

Milo looked as if he really wanted to spit for dramatic effect. However, this was the Dalston Superstore, which had a reputation for good food and proper service. It wouldn't really have worked with the edgy retro feel to have installed spittoons. And Milo loved the place, and wanted to return.

He focused on his forensic analysis instead:

"Dillon has been talking and spending too much. He is getting through more coke than he could possibly afford on a barman's salary. I know for sure how little that is. Although I think I was a very good barman, I have always earned much more with my Magic Milo here than from an honest day's work."

The Serb slapped his perpetually convex crotch. Everyone winced companiably.

Lady Gaza pouted:

"Well, habibie, there are a lot of barman out there, whereas there are very few men with an eleven-inch penis and the desire to whirl it around in public as if it were the latest clever invention of that Dyson man. *What does it do? Does it dry your hair with no blade? Oh, how clever!*" Sometimes it fell to Lady Gaza to explain the laws of supply and demand to Milo.

Zahoor wanted the conversation back on track. He was aggrieved, and needed to express it:

"And I did not steal anything," he said with passion, "I have never stolen anything in my life." He gazed at Rubens with big eyes, making the Brazilian feel as if he had just swindled Zahoor's entire family and then accused Zahoor of doing it himself.

"On top of all this, habibie, there is the fact that the little *sharmouta* seems to have your boss, Ziggy, eating out of the palm of his hand. Ziggy seems to be reliving his youth through that boy. He will believe anything he says. You do know that there are rumours about you going round now? This is the point of it all: it all starts with Dillon. Time and time again. Rubens, you have been blind for too long. You have to speak to Ziggy or you will be next. You know, my handsome friend, what happens in life. Once your reputation goes, it is very hard to recover it in this little world of ours."

Lady Gaza drummed her nails on the table for dramatic effect. She directed a sad look at Zahoor and one of reproach at Rubens. She was an honourable, peaceable person, but if you messed with her friends, she was ruthless. Between her and Milo, Dillon had made a couple of enemies. They were determined that Rubens would force Siegfried to see reason at last and send the little cheat packing.

As he surveyed the bustling bar, Rubens wondered if vipers also crawled amongst the über-trendy staff of the Superstore. How had he let himself get into this situation? He had fired his innocent allies, and now was left with a snake – admittedly with a fine ass – who was poisoning his boss against him. No ass was worth this, he thought, with some logic. Rubens was now ready for a fight. This was Rio all over again. He would take the first opportunity he could to have a long talk to Siegfried.

First, though, he had some apologising to do. He pursed his lips as he took in the people before him that he had wronged. Ordering another round of Hackney Iced Teas would be a start.

Going German was not something Eleanor Napier Jones would ever have associated with neutrality. She did, however, see the point in her daughter's reasoning in avoiding either Italian or English cuisine that day. Inevitably, any dish that was either delicious or disappointing would be ammunition for sniping between the two older women. Eleanor had approached the meal with some trepidation, being a fan neither of dumplings which seemed to be second cousins to a shot putt, nor those enormous fatty joints hewn out of a particularly greedy pig. Even German sausages seemed oversized. They so often overflowed with thick, dribbly sauce. It all gave her the collywobbles. German food was so weighty, as if Nietzsche himself were ground into every dish.

She was thus pleasantly surprised when a delicious smelling soup was the first item to make its way to the dining table.

"*Möhrensuppe mit Ricotta-Klößchen*. This is a carrot soup made with German dry white wine, served with a mini cheese dumpling."

Caroline glared at Hartmut. Had he, or had he not, said the word ricotta? An Italian ingredient had slipped the net. Still, at least he had had the presence of mind to mask it in translation.

The soup was delicious. The mini dumpling melted in the mouth, rather than landing with a thud in the stomach.

Eleanor found herself agreeing with Claudia on how delightful the dish was. After a brief pause for more wine, Hartmut absented himself to serve the main course.

"*Rheinische muscheln*. These are Rhineland mussels cooked with vegetables, and served with a small selection of our six hundred types of bread. You will find these accompanied by Joh Jos Prüm 2008."

"I shall never look the same way again at *moules frites*. Once again, simply splendid, my dear Hartmut." Eleanor couldn't quite credit how much she was enjoying Hartmut's cooking. "The Riesling is quite delectable," she added.

"Yes," said Piers, "who knew Germany produced such marvellous dry whites? I thought it was all Blue Nun and Black Tower. They were always the desperation drink at the end of a party when you were too drunk to care anymore." Piers grinned as he watched Ben devouring the mussels.

Hartmut looked pensive:

"My father always said that our country lived through three great calamities in the twentieth century; World War One, World War Two and Liebfraumilch."

Caroline and Eleanor looked mildly shocked, but Piers and Ben sniggered. Claudia opened her eyes wide to feign interest in Hartmut's story.

"Despite the seemingly unending appetite to replay *The Sinking of the Bismarck* on British television, interspersed with new biographies of Hitler, polite British society never brings up the first of those two with German friends such as me. The Liebfraumilch, however, is a different story. It seems not to matter that, for the past twenty years or more, Germany has been producing fine wines that are as dry as the British sense of humour. All the British remember is that damned nun."

A ripple of good-natured laughter spread round the dining table. Caroline winked at her husband. Eleanor and Claudia hadn't indulged in so much as a catty remark. Things were looking up. Now it was time to move to the next stage of the plan: leaving the two women alone to work out their differences. This would be much more testing for them. However, given the irritation their friction had been causing all concerned, the Glicks would thoroughly enjoy engineering their revenge.

Caroline smiled at the gathering:

"Cousin Piers, I have something I need to discuss with you. Let's take a spin around the park before dessert. Care to join?"

"Why of course, Cousin Caroline. One's appetite is whetted. Might one enquire as to what you need to discuss with me?"

"Is this a private ramble, or may I tag along?" Eleanor Napier Jones was not keen on the idea of being left with Hartmut and the two Barlettanos. She was not sure how much longer her enforced politeness would survive, especially if all she had to buttress it were the clumsy New Yorker and his Teutonic boss.

"Oh mother, I did want to get Piers alone. Besides we are going to have a quick stroll through the park and I don't think your heels would cope very well with the mud. Claudia, I'm afraid you're barred too."

Caroline smiled pleasantly to put an end to any discussion of the subject.

Claudia noted a steely tone in Caroline's voice, and decided that she should not attempt to argue. The young woman could be quite domineering when she wanted to, much like her unpleasant mother whom Claudia had been trying so hard not to insult throughout the dinner. Claudia would take advantage of the time to spend some time with her son. It would be fine. Eleanor would probably need to lie down after her meal, given the way she had shovelled victuals into her prissy cake hole. As the walking party left with the twins, the two women couldn't avoid exchanging a frosty glance.

"Ladies, may I top up your glasses?" Hartmut didn't wait for them to reply, and emptied the bottle of Joh Jos Prüm. He had been monitoring their consumption throughout the meal, and had noted that Eleanor was drinking around fifty per cent more quickly than usual, a fact which he put down to the strain off maintaining a dignified exterior when she was obviously itching to score points at her rival's expense. "Not for you, I am afraid, Ben. I do apologise so for talking business, but I must steal young Ben away from you both for a few minutes. We also need milk for the *Kaffee*. Kindly accompany me to the shop, my young associate. *Schnell, bitte.*"

Claudia Barlettano found herself alone with Eleanor Napier Jones.

They faced each other in silent social despair. This soon evolved into frosty small talk about how delightful the children were, and how well Hartmut had cooked, as they both drank ever quicker.

Before they knew it, their glasses were empty and there was no sign of the others returning to rescue them.

Eleanor stared at her empty vessel of happiness:

"Now where did Hartmut put that other bottle of Riesling? Such a charming beverage. Do you know, Claudia – I think we should have some more."

Eleanor couldn't possibly cope with the balance of the evening without the assistance of alcohol. Claudia also sensed that wine would greatly help in keeping her cordiality topped up. Both women rose rather suddenly, before stopping short and smiling at each other, aware of the unseemly haste with which they were seeking another drink.

Sadly, all they found in the kitchen were empty bottles neatly placed in the recycling area. Eleanor wondered whether they should resort to raiding the Glick drinks cabinet. She discounted the idea quickly. She did not want to give Claudia the impression that she was a little too fond of the Bombay. She was, but it was none of Claudia's business.

Then she had an idea:

"Claudia, although it's not a patch on ours in the country, Caroline and Hartmut have a fairly decent wine cellar here. Would you care to come down with me and take a look? I am sure Hartmut wouldn't mind if we fetched another bottle of the same wine. I think he must have intended to fetch it himself, before he left."

Eleanor felt quite sure of this. Meanwhile, Claudia would have happily gone to Lidl in her dressing gown if it were going to procure more refreshment at this point in the evening. She immediately acquiesced to the plan.

The two women stepped down to the basement and opened the cellar door. The light dimly illuminated stone steps. These led down to a small antechamber with two closed doors leading off from it. Eleanor hadn't been to the cellar since her daughter had moved in. She wasn't sure which door to try first.

As it happened, both doors were locked. Eleanor, always resourceful when it came to her interests, had an idea. She reached up onto the top of the frame of the nearest door, and felt along the surface.

Bingo. As she hoped, a key was nestling on top of the spotlessly clean frame. She grasped it and brandished it triumphantly at a relieved Claudia.

"Bravo, Eleanor," said Claudia admiringly. Eleanor acknowledged the approval with a complacent but kindly smile.

The key fitted snugly into the hole. With the lightest of touches the lock clicked open. Eleanor turned the handle and pushed open the door.

Goodness, what a warren this place was. There was a wall immediately in front of her. A narrow corridor about twelve feet long led off to the left. As Eleanor peered into the gloom, lit up only by the already dim light of the antechamber outside, she espied another light switch at the end of the corridor where she assumed the passageway opened up into the main cellar.

"This is quite the adventure, my dear. I feel we shall have earned our glass of wine. Follow me."

Claudia followed her guide meekly, keeping close to her.

She wasn't that keen on dark underground spaces.

Unfortunately, before Eleanor could reach for the light switch, the door to the antechamber swung silently shut behind Claudia, leaving the two women in pitch darkness.

"Eleanor, please switch the light on. I hate the dark." Claudia sounded panicky.

"Claudia, please be calm. We are in the wine cellar in my daughter's house, not Britain's most haunted."

"But we are trapped! We may die here!"

"The way this household binge drinks? Not a chance. We'll be out within the hour. Here's the light switch, now get ready to feast your eyes on…"

As Eleanor flicked the switch, and the reassuring brightness momentarily calmed Claudia's nerves, it illuminated a space that was most certainly not used for storing more of the delectable Joh Jos Prüm.

Hartmut dug his hands deep into his great coat. There was a point to the stroll:

"Is there anything that you wish to tell me, Ben?"

It fell on Hartmut to open discussions about Ben's current wayward behaviour and less-than-stellar performance at work – all as noted by Bartlett DeVere, who had banged on enough about the subject to provoke an informal review.

"This sounds ominous, Hartmut," said Ben, feigning lightness. The events of two years earlier had drawn them together. But Ben was careful never to forget that Hartmut was his boss and, as such, a lawyer, concerned primarily with the bottom line.

Hartmut faced Ben. As the American seemed about as

forthcoming as a Ming Mandarin facing an early Portuguese explorer, Hartmut decided that he would need to spell the problem out:

"Ben, you know better than most that I would be the last person to judge a person's private activities."

The two men looked at each other, both fully aware of the relatively unconventional lives that they both led, with not a little defiance to the ordinary norms of the law.

"I think it is a very healthy thing that you pursue your desires, Ben – especially now that you are regrettably single."

That had not quite come out the way Hartmut intended it. But he battled on:

"Ben, it remains the case for me that it is far better that you have a fulfilling life outside of the office, instead of devoting every minute to climbing the greasy pole. I have observed for many years creatures of all sorts and varying degrees of moustaches getting to the crow's nest. They are fat then, but equally somehow dried out husks of persons. Their main objective then becomes to protect his – or her, in all too rare cases still – perch. They accomplish this mainly it seems by raining *scheiße* down on the poor souls trying to follow him – or her – up. Enjoy the view on the way up, my dear boy, so that when you do actually get to the top you will feel a better person. However, please concentrate on best practice – concentrate, as hard as you can! – that we might better steer the ship together."

Hartmut knew he was not making his point very well. He felt like one of those business leaders who deliver every unconvincing speech in the same way, attempting to inveigle the listener into believing that the speaker was a wise, empathetic person who should be listened to, and followed. Equally, though, Hartmut knew that on these points he was right. Ben needed to listen. Hartmut carried on:

"Too much sightseeing, Ben, and one might lose grip on the pole. The point is that falling asleep in meetings and losing parts of documents will never get you to partnership. Worse, it could damage the firm. Do all you want outside the walls of B.A.D. – but I need you to be fully functioning when you are working. Do you understand?"

Ben nodded, still saying nothing. It was difficult to hear the truth. But he was at least more comfortable with Hartmut giving him a direct warning in straightforward language, rather than waffling on about greasy poles and crow's nests.

Ben knew Hartmut was right. He had taken his eye off the prize pretty badly. He still couldn't understand how he had lost that work in the document. He had never done that before. He must have been so out of it that day. Mind you, on any measure he had been caning it recently. He needed to be careful. Blowing it had to be kept for outside of work – and proper recovery time had to be factored in.

"It won't happen again, Hartmut."

"Excellent. Then let us speak no more of it. The gardens around here are truly lovely. I suggest we enjoy them. It will be quite a long walk."

"Aaaargh!"

Claudia Barlettano rarely screamed. All she wanted

was a nice bottle of wine. She clutched her pearls and staggered back against the wall in disbelief. Calmer, and disapproving of the Mediterranean's overreaction, Eleanor Napier Jones surveyed the scene around her. It looked like Dante's Inferno on stocktaking day.

In front of the two women, there was a chair. It was made of black leather, looked expensive and had a long narrow straight back. Although it probably wasn't the most comfortable chair, Eleanor thought that it would be exceedingly good for one's posture. In fact, the bondage chair came equipped with over twenty separate fetters to ensure no unhealthy, or more importantly unauthorised, slumping or arching of the back. It could prevent any movement whatsoever, given enough patience with its buckles and belts. It also boasted a handy hole in the middle of the seat which made anal probing a breeze.

Beyond that lay what Eleanor thought to be an extremely uncomfortable looking black leather massage table. She recognised the little head recess, although she wondered why one would want to be kneeling in that way, and what was the point of the seemingly omnipresent straps. Near the whipping bench was an item that almost looked like an innocuous piece of gym equipment. However, the spanking horse rather gave itself away with the D-Ring fixing points to which a couple of pairs of wrist and ankle cuffs were still attached.

After the initial shock, Eleanor recovered her composure. She turned to the quivering Claudia:

"My dear, it is all inanimate. Please do not scream again

in such a confined space. I would like to know, however, what the hell this place is."

"Oh Eleanor, you are right." Despite being deeply perturbed by what she saw around her, Claudia did not want to give Eleanor the satisfaction of seeing her any further in a weakened state. It was bad enough that she had not been able to stifle that scream.

Perhaps it was better to overcompensate now and be utterly relaxed. Claudia composed herself:

"Well, these are obviously cages. Do they have pets?"

Eleanor remembered a conversation some time past when Caroline had instructed her on the importance of discipline in a pet dog's life. She ran her hands down the first of four puppy cages lining the walls. The silky smooth black bars and pristine interior told her that these had never been used for animals. She was confirmed in her suspicions by the next item she saw: a cage in the shape of a person. The gibbet cage was leaning against the wall, and was as spotless as everything else in the room.

"I doubt these are for budgerigars, my dear."

Then Eleanor spotted a handsome wooden cabinet that seemed for all the world to be from the same maker of the glass-doored one upstairs, which housed Hartmut's prized collection of Franklin Mint Fabergé eggs. She felt that same frisson of anticipation which sometimes tickled her when walking round a stately home, wondering what treasures she might be about to discover.

How appearances could deceive. She opened the doors and was immediately arrested by the exhibits on the shelves. One object was admittedly stunning, but

Eleanor was not in a state to appreciate the craftsmanship in the beautifully ornamented head cage with oval mouth hole. She was further astonished by a collection of whips, handcuffs, chains and – perhaps most surprising of all – large latex penises that the National Trust would never dream of putting on show to the public.

"Claudia, I think we have seen enough. Let us get out of here."

Claudia was glad to be leaving. However, when they tried to exit, they found the door had no handle. There was nothing but a keyhole. Eleanor had left the key in the lock on the outside.

"*Dio mio!* We are like rats on a sinking ship. There is nobody in the house. Now we are stuck here until they get back. *Mamma mia*, it was bad enough us having to spend any time together, never mind alone, and then in this *Sodoma e Gomorra?*"

Eleanor's eyes blazed:

"My dear, please calm down, otherwise I shall put you in one of those cages. Let us go back into the main room, sit down and wait until we hear a noise upstairs."

"I suppose you are right. I am sorry. No cages, eh? But will they hear us? Do you think they even know this place is here, Eleanor?"

"My dear, of course they know this place is here. This is not the Lion, the Witch and the Wine Cellar. I'm taking the wooden chair, and you can have the leather one."

Eleanor had to admit that the master's shoeshine chair really was rather comfortable, although why it was on a dais, she could not fathom. Claudia did not want to sit on the

353

leather chair, and leaned on the spanking horse instead.

"We love each other, you know."

After the silence, Claudia's words jolted Eleanor as if she had been struck across the bare buttocks with one of the cabinet whips.

Claudia continued, speaking softly:

"I know this must be very hard for you because it was extremely strange for me. I only wanted to compliment him for his exquisite work. I never dreamed that a man young enough to be my son would ever find me attractive, and still less that I would consider him. But your Piers is an amazing person. He brings much credit to your family."

Eleanor held Claudia's gaze, saying nothing, despite the fact she could tell Claudia wanted her to acknowledge her comments.

The Italian weakened first:

"Eleanor, you are in very good company in disapproving of the match. My son, Ben, is absolutely against Piers."

She sighed:

"You can imagine how I worship Ben. He is my only son. I sometimes feel as though he wants me to choose between them. My father never approved of my ex-husband, and now my son doesn't want me to be with the only other man I have ever loved in my life."

This was an unexpected experience for both women. They had both seen enough films to know that when strangers get trapped in strange places, they are apt to tell each other all manner of private things. But it seemed a great leap forward nonetheless.

Eleanor relented:

"You are right, of course. I do disapprove. But then I disapproved mightily of my daughter's choice of Hartmut Glick. I'll share with you that I have disapproved of most of the choices that she has made in life. I also disapproved of Piers choosing to go into fashion. I disapproved of German wine. Sometimes I think that I disapprove of ninety-five per cent of everything I see around me, Claudia. For heavens' sake, I even disapprove of the Daily Mail. That might be the only thing linking me to the real world at this point."

Eleanor paused, wondering if Claudia read English newspapers, or any newspapers at all for that matter. She continued, pensively:

"When I first saw you at Tarquin's gallery, Claudia, my first impression was in fact rather positive. I felt you were like me. But it was also inevitable, once I found out about Piers, that my disapproval would know no bounds. No one will ever be good enough for my family, my dear. I am sure you also feel that no one is good enough for your Ben. Maybe happy families is a circus that we can never join. It goes without saying that Ben *certainly* doesn't think anyone is remotely worthy of the *perfect* Claudia Barlettano."

Eleanor sighed in the master's shoeshine chair, her stilettoes catching on the floor:

"All that being said, I can see that Piers loves you. It certainly won't stop me disapproving of you, for that is what I do best in life. But maybe we can arrange a truce and just get on – rather like I do with Hartmut, despite him evidently being the interior designer of choice for dungeons up and down the finer parts of London."

Claudia was quiet. She identified with much of what Eleanor said. She also enjoyed feeling superior to her peers. She too made the occasional unkind remark to her friends. She too – of course – tutted maniacally over how dirty most people were.

"I think, *mia cara*, that a truce would be a most satisfactory solution."

So well-oiled was the lock, and so involved were the women in the discussion, that they did not hear Hartmut Glick quietly open the cellar door and pad down the short corridor. Their surprise at seeing him was eclipsed by the German's shock at seeing the two women talking to each other. As if on cue, Caroline, Ben and Piers clattered into the room.

Piers was in full flow:

"Have you found them? Oh my God, what the bloody hell is this place?"

All eyes turned to Hartmut, including Caroline's, which were decidedly more alarmed than the others'. Was this the moment she had been dreading for so long? The moment where she would finally have to admit her secret predilection *publicly*? Give it a *name*?

Hartmut waved a genial hand:

"My dears. Please do not be alarmed. After the success of "Krapwerk: hardly Ideal, Holmes", my dear sister Ursula Himmelfarb is now exploring the underground world of sado-masochistic sexual arousal for her next exhibition. This is a work in progress. I do so love installation art. Sorry to have locked you in – but welcome to the Whine Cellar!"

17

Party like no one is watching

Jamal was clear on one matter:

"Let's avoid the subject of the missing money today, shall we? It's Rubens' party. He won't want unwarranted tension."

Alex grimaced, and looked at Jamal. They walked towards Rubens' flat.

"Are you sure you don't want to ask him if he is a thief in front of all the guests?" added Jamal, "I do hope that you haven't worn your expensive watch."

Jamal's eyes were as stony as they had largely been since the argument outside the registry office. The Elephant Express had published an unsympathetic story about attention-seeking and bad tempers. It was all very handbags at dawn. The accompanying photo of Jamal glaring furiously at Alex on the happiest day of their lives was not the media coverage that Alex had aspired to. The aftermath of the ceremony had been less like honey and more like the luminous and distant moon – cold, silent and rather lonely.

Alex swallowed, and decided not to respond. He loved Jamal no less for the cold shoulder. Jamal's unbreakable loyalty to his friends was one of the qualities that had helped to turn Alex's lust into love for the man. Alex was loyal himself, but, being English, he saw most situations in many shades of grey, not the black and white certainties of his Algerian husband.

The silence was broken by a shout.

"My two favourite hunks o' spunk! Hello, your Hotnesses. Are you two ready to *party*?"

The Outrageous Fortune DJ was waving at them.

Alex and Jamal sighed simultaneously. Kel Day was a handful at the best of times. He was accompanied by Javier Bordem, who fitted in the occasional night playing the bar between jet-setting around to play superstar gigs. Siegfried Allcock followed, for once without Dillon in tow.

Javier air-kissed Alex and Jamal dramatically:

"I almost couldn't make it. I was supposed to be playing a massive club in Toronto this weekend – but they wanted me to fly economy! Imagine that. I just laughed down the telephone at them, and here I am instead. Unlucky Canada, lucky London."

For once, Alex was thoroughly glad to see Javier. The presence of a self-obsessed DJ who thought his pulling power was on a level with Angelina Jolie's was just what was needed to lift the mood. Javier's eager jabbering to Jamal about how someone had stolen his Chanel boots from a gig in Istanbul propelled the party to Rubens' door, leaving space for not the merest hint of awkwardness.

Nicholas Casterway hadn't understood the attraction of Skype until he married the technology with Amber Bluett and her collection of naughty lingerie and unlikely sex toys. Such power, such control. He could terminate the conversation and sight of her at any time. No longer did he have to wait those interminable post-coital minutes for her to shower and vacate the premises. Skype was the *answer*.

Today, however, he wanted an update before the relief of pressing the *end call* button.

Amber was fastening a bra that looked as if it were made from lace and scaffolding:

"More news, Nicholas. More news. I think I have inflicted the coup de grâce. Ben's work is staggeringly inept, these days. This time, I removed an envelope he placed in the post tray and put it back on his desk. The twenty-one days for registering the charge at Companies House was up on Thursday. Dear Ben had taken a couple of days off. The date has been missed – purely and simply."

"Excellent."

Failure to hit the deadline to register the charge meant a costly and embarrassing trip to court to rectify the omission. That would reflect badly on the young American.

"But that's not all," continued Amber. "He is so far up that bloody German's arse that even that would not be enough. So the envelope was not the only thing I put on Ben Barlettano's desk. Skink got me skunk, and now the stink will get the hunk."

Amber paused triumphantly. That was a line that had been waiting to find its moment.

"You did what?"

Nicholas Casterway had not been informed of this part of the plot. Although he could see how much trouble this could land Ben in, he was not sure he liked the idea of Amber taking decisions without him.

Amber rolled her eyes. Nicholas was so retrograde, sometimes.

"I hear that when Bartlett DeVere followed up with Ben's secretary, Hartmut was nearby. They checked his office for the letter and found a whole heap of problems. It must have been one thing to find the letter, but quite another to find an explanation as to how dear Ben had seemingly overlooked putting it in the post."

She paused triumphantly, fiddling with her hold-ups:

"I don't think we'll be seeing much of Ben on Monday morning."

Ben was drinking heavily.

He arrived early at Rubens' event, as he desperately needed to tell someone what had happened. Rubens listened with his heart in his mouth as Ben told him what Hartmut Glick had said over the telephone that morning.

"I know that you have been going through a difficult patch, but I warned you to be more careful. What you do outside the office is your business but when you screw up your work and then bring drugs onto the premises I am afraid I can protect you no longer. Bartlett wants you out of the firm."

"Rubens, I don't remember ever taking weed to work, and I swear I put that envelope in the post. But my head has just not been there lately. I'm… I'm not really sure of anything anymore."

Ben looked close to tears. His career was hanging by a thread. Hartmut had told him that the only way forward was for Ben to move back to New York. Hartmut said that he would provide Ben with a suitable reference so that he could maybe start up again back home.

He may have to grow a moustache to get by, but that was the least of his problems at this point in time.

"Rubens, London is my home now. I don't want to leave."

Leaving Europe would mean that Kelly Danvers was definitely out of his life. The thought of being on a different continent to her seemed to make the pain even worse. Ben realised that the course events were taking amounted to the loss of his whole life. The doors that London had opened for him were being slammed in his face. He didn't know if he could go back to the person he had been the day he had arrived on that plane at Heathrow.

"Oh, gostoso, I don't want you to leave either."

The two men looked at each other. As often happens at moments of mutual need they looked at each other as if they hadn't seen each other much before. They both sensed comfort in their common ground, whilst wondering why they had not made it work together the first time round.

"We are a right pair, aren't we?" said Ben, finally. "Maybe we should just run away together and start up somewhere new. Have you ever thought of going back to Brazil? I don't need to be a bloody lawyer all my life!"

As he said the words, he knew that he was talking nonsense. Luckily, so did Rubens. They would both have to face their situations. Ben's would reach resolution in the coming week, one way or another. Rubens' problems, on the other hand, were just ringing the doorbell.

*

Rubens was a dab hand at parties. They were not difficult territory to navigate. They simply required that he have fun with his friends before ending up in bed with the man he wanted.

Today, however, seemed different. The party boasted a minefield of awkward situations. Alex and Jamal were practically not speaking. Ben was alternating between downing vodka and morbidly stalking the cuter guys present. They in turn sensed damaged goods and accordingly looked as flustered as gazelles with an ageing, hungry lion meandering nearby. Time and time again, Ben was sent straight back to Pierre Smirnoff's arms.

Rubens had been trying to speak to Siegfried alone, but he had the distinct impression that his boss was deliberately avoiding him. Even Lady Gaza seemed off her game, watching the goings on with a jaded eye. Thank goodness for Javier who was far too concerned with ensuring everyone knew how important he was to get thrown off by an atmosphere.

Rubens saw Siegfried heading for the toilet. He swiftly followed him and pushed his way into the bathroom.

"Rubens? What are you doing?"

"Ziggy, I need to speak to you. I know what everyone is saying, but it is not me. I would never steal money from two of my best friends in the world. I think it is Dillon. We need to talk about this."

The depth of feeling conveyed by Rubens' beseeching eyes would have melted an iceberg, and yet Siegfried was unmoved. He had seen enough gorgeous boys from all over the world profess their devotion to him one day and then glimpse them looking *happier* with a slightly richer ex-pat the following weekend in Club Whatever. Damn the lot of them. Besides, he really needed to pee.

"Rubens, of course we need to talk. But now is not the time or the place. Go back to your guests. Enjoy your party. We will talk in the bar on Monday. That's a promise."

Rubens looked back at Siegfried as he exited the bathroom. He felt unable to avoid the conclusion that his boss had already made his mind up. Just like Ben's, his job was hanging in the balance.

"Kelly, oh thanks be, you are home." The voice at the end of the phone sounded close to tears.

"Cornisha, what the heck has happened?"

"It's Ben. Don't worry, he isn't hurt or anything, but he has done something really stupid."

The tension in Cornisha's voice was already making Kelly's stomach knot.

"Bertha has just rung me and told me that Hartmut Glick and Bartlett DeVere found a bag of marijuana on Ben's desk."

"What? No way, Cornisha. Something must be lost in translation. Ben knows what bringing drugs to the office would do to a lawyer's career."

Kelly felt as if she had been thwacked round the head with a copy of Chitty on Contracts.

"Kelly, Ben has been behaving out of character since the wedding. He practically fell asleep in a meeting the other day. The whole office has noticed. I should have told you, but I didn't want you to feel, well…"

Cornisha's voice trailed off.

"You didn't want me to feel guilty for breaking his heart?" Tears came to Kelly's eyes. *Oh Jesus, she had lost one man to Africa and now she had dispatched the other one to seek solace in drugs!*

This all felt surreal. Kelly stared at her reflection in the window, which also framed a vision of another Parisian evening. Clouds wrestled in the dusk, like sentiments in a confused soul. Seeing her own ghostly face superimposed on the troubled sky, she felt for a moment that even her apartment was remonstrating with her for being the probable cause of Ben Barlettano's impending downfall.

"I'm not even sure he knows yet."

"What? We're talking about the fact that his career could be over and he doesn't even bloody know? Oh, this is just too fucked up!" Kelly wouldn't usually swear down the phone at Cornisha, but this was serious. Her flat could keep its opinions to itself. Something was mightily wrong here:

"Cornisha, Ben may have a broken heart, but he doesn't have a broken brain. He would never be that stupid. And if he is smoking weed, then why the hell would he leave it at work over a weekend?"

Kelly had a point. Cornisha hadn't thought about that. *She* certainly wouldn't splash out on some Dancong honey Orchid Oolong Tea from Fortnum's and then not take advantage of its delights of a Friday night.

"You said Bertha Cheung told you." Kelly had met Bertha once. She had noted that she was beautiful, bubbly and smart. She had remained favourably impressed until she had noticed that Ben was similarly entranced, and seemed fascinated by Bertha's breasts to boot. "How did Bertha find out?"

"She was out jogging with Amber Bluett and she told her. Amber was there when it all happened."

Kelly felt as if steam were building up inside her like a kettle ready to brew Cornisha's Oolong Tea.

"I should have known. Amber. Always a warning light. That bitch has got something to do with this. Ben would never take drugs into the office. He may be burning the candle at both ends, but he would never burn his bridges like this."

Kelly immediately knew what she had to do. She couldn't contemplate following the Viking to flaming Africa, however long the boat – but this was different. There were no tits or butt about it. She was heading to London to save her Ben.

"Cornisha, may I stay with you for a couple of days? I'm coming over on the next train."

At times like this Rubens was glad of his *espiritu brasileiro*. He had been the perfect host. He had served drinks, laughed merrily, and not given away one iota of the increasing sense of unease he felt. But as the party slowly settled to its end, and he found himself sprawled on the sofa with a vodka-infused Ben and Helena Handcart, Rubens' mask began to slip. Why was Helena giving him that knowing look and asking him how he was?

"I'm okay."

It was not a convincing reply. He certainly didn't believe it himself. But now was not the time to indulge in self-pity and drag everyone else down. He could feel sorry for himself when he was alone. He needed to deflect the attention.

Helena turned to Ben:

"How was your week, Ben?"

Ben couldn't tell Helena the whole truth. However, unlike the Brazilian, Ben was not very good at hiding his problems:

"Well, work has gone seriously wrong. Personally? I miss Kelly terribly. And I hate being alone in my flat in the evenings. So I deal with it. I go out, get wasted, and get laid. It doesn't solve the problems. It makes work harder and has now led to a much bigger issue. Apart from that, everything is just great. Great." Ben pulled a face, and drained his drink.

"My dear boy," Helena looked critically at the American, "you have intelligence and education, and an excellent career. You should be able to retain it. You have a wonderful set of friends. You have decent parties like this to attend, you are young, and money isn't an immediate problem. And then, to top it off, you have looks that make most of those in this room lust after you. Now, if only we could help you to stop feeling so sorry for yourself, just because you're underperforming at work. You should inform them that you have been overperforming in the bedroom."

"Or the sauna, the sex club – or even the street. Or so I hear," Rubens added, helpfully.

Helena aimed a look of reproach at Rubens before turning back to Ben:

"What you need, my dear, is a bloody great kick up that pert and pampered backside of yours."

"Oh, Ben, we do have something in common?" Angela Merkin flounced over. "I too love a bloody great dick up that pert and pampered backside of mine."

"Kick, Angela – kick. Oh, never mind."

Helena had hit home. Ben knew she was right. Nothing is ever quite as bad as it seems. He had to take action. His career must come first for a while. Painful as it was, Kelly Danvers was out of his life. It was time for him to move on, and focus on clearing his name. Ben had no idea how, but he was going to prove to Hartmut that, whatever had been found on Ben's desk, he had had nothing to do with it. At least, he was pretty sure he didn't. Right now, though, it was the weekend and he was going to enjoy this party. He leant over to Rubens and whispered in his ear: "She's right. We're going to get through this. Everything's going to turn out fine."

Although Rubens smiled back, he was not as convinced about Ben's Panglossian confidence. Especially not when he saw Siegfried and Alex disappear off into his bedroom.

Siegfried had felt extremely uncomfortable when Rubens followed him into the bathroom. In fact, the whole party was proving rather painful. The tension which studded the event, rather like cloves in an orange in a vat of mulled wine, was a little too marked for Siegfried's liking. Initially, Javier Bordem's Ibiza stories about snorting with the stars had masked the awkwardness. But there were only so many times that one could hear of how one night a DJ had saved the life of a thousand clubbers, before one wished he would just shut up. *DJs are almost invariably disappointing when they speak*, thought Siegfried. So when Alex beckoned him over, he was quite relieved to join him.

Siegfried noted the opportunity:

"Alex, may I speak to you in private a moment? Shall we repair to Rubens' bedroom?"

The room was compact but stylish, with a double bed flanked by a long low black lacquered cupboard and a matching wardrobe at one end. They sat on the bed and looked around at the décor.

"I do like the no-handle look," began Alex, "but Jamal and I had one of those in the living room at ours and every time we had a party people would lean on the doors and they would open like a market stall holder's mouth. They look good, though."

"Alex, fascinating as it is to discuss bedroom furniture, I wanted to talk about something else with you. It concerns Rubens."

Before Siegfried could continue, Alex slumped back on the bed:

"Oh no. Not now. Listen, Siegfried, there is enough trouble between Jamal and me, and this is Rubens' party. Please can this wait to another day? I really don't want to hear about how Jamal's best friend is stealing our money tonight."

Siegfried looked pained:

"But that's just it. I'm not sure, Alex. Maybe I was wrong. He spoke to me earlier, and he seemed very upfront and straight – I just don't know…"

Siegfried's voice faltered. He grabbed one of the large cushions placed at the foot of the bed and hugged it.

Alex looked at him, nonplussed:

"So, all this time that Jamal and I have been fighting over Rubens, you were not in fact sure of what you were saying to me?"

Siegfried said nothing and buried his head in the cushion. Alex grabbed the cushion and pulled Siegfried's hands away from his face.

"You, my friend, are going to tell me exactly what you think is, and is not, going on. We are talking about someone's reputation. To say nothing of this crisis partly ruining my wedding day and casting the biggest cloud on my relationship since... well, ever, actually."

Alex's eyes were burning. Siegfried cast his eyes around:

"Alex, when I spoke to Rubens earlier, I was a bit harsh with him. I have seen a lot of boys and men protest their innocence, and get away with things just because they look so goddamn good that people want to believe in them. I've been caught out before. I don't want to make the same mistake again, especially not when it is your business that is suffering."

Alex nodded and rose from the bed. He leaned back against the cupboard.

"So. How do you propose resolving the situation?"

Siegfried took a deep breath. He knew that this was not making him look good either:

"I don't think we should take any action yet. I want to go through all the numbers again, with a fine-tooth comb. I also will keep an especially sharp eye out in the bar. I need to watch everyone who comes into any contact with money. I am so sorry that this has happened on my watch, Alex. I feel I have let both of you down."

Siegfried gave Alex a look that pleaded so hard for forgiveness that Alex felt a pang for his old friend. It couldn't be easy managing such a situation. But Alex steeled himself. Maybe they had made a mistake going into business with a friend.

"Listen, don't worry, Siegfried. We'll take it a step at a time. We can't do much more in here. Why don't we join the others and get ourselves another drink?"

Siegfried gave Alex a weak smile. He didn't look reassured. But he couldn't very well hide away in the bedroom all night.

When Alex pulled away from the cupboard on which he was leaning, the door catch released. The door swung open revealing a pile of T-shirts which fell out onto the floor. However that was not all that fell out.

"What the devil?"

On the floor now lay a brown envelope out of which spilled a thick wad of twenty pound notes.

It was definitely the worst party that Rubens had ever thrown. Siegfried had dragged Jamal and him to the bedroom, where like a vengeful blond archangel Alex had demanded to know why Rubens had all that cash in his cupboard. Alex had not believed Rubens' protestations of innocence. Jamal had not said a word, but his face shouted betrayal. Siegfried looked as if he wanted the world to swallow him up. They left soon after. Thank God Ben had been there. He had made the excuses and got rid of all the other guests.

"Do you have no idea how that money got there, Rubens? You weren't saving up to send money back home?"

Rubens hadn't cried for some time. But it was all too much.

"Ben, I have never seen that money before in my life. I swear I did not put it there. You have to believe me. Why would I steal from my friends?"

Ben wanted to believe Rubens. But the lawyer in him had to admit the circumstantial evidence appeared damning. He fought the urge to judge Rubens. The least he could do was offer him support even if he couldn't help but wonder:

"I believe you, Rubens. It doesn't look good, but I believe you. Let's think. Who was in your bedroom tonight? I'm sure I saw Javier come in here to take a line. In fact, there seemed to be a Piccadilly-Circus-load of people who used your room tonight."

"Exactly, Ben. Someone planted it here. Oh Ben, what am I going to do?"

Ben looked at his friend:

"I still suspect that little shit, Dillon."

"But he wasn't here. Maybe he is working with those DJs? I've always thought Javier was a bullshitter. That must be it. That fucking DJ is a liar about everything. It must be him!"

It was as plausible as anything else. Hang the DJ, thought Ben. But where was the *evidence* that it wasn't Rubens? He needed proof to show to Siegfried and Alex.

Dillon Lloyd. The little slut had been lusting after him for ages. Ben pulled out his phone. Dillon's number beamed up at him. Ben had an idea of how he could combine business and pleasure. He had momentarily forgotten his own problems. He knew he would have to do everything he could over the next week to save, it seemed, everyone's skin.

18

Redux

The French may be better at railways but the British now know how to do stations. Kelly's shoes clicked pleasingly on the floor as she rushed through customs. Her spirits soared when she spotted Cornisha waiting for her. The girl from Louisiana felt at home again as she hugged her friend on the St Pancras concourse.

"This may sound odd given the circumstances, Cornisha, but I am taking you for a glass of bubbly to celebrate being back in London. Let's go to the Champagne Bar."

It was a Saturday evening, and Cornisha rarely refused champagne in good company. The women were soon installed in a booth sipping Balfour Brut Rosé under William Henry Barlow's glorious roof.

"I know it's a champagne bar, but English sparkling wine seems the right choice," remarked Kelly. "This is such a splendid place. Maybe the Victorians were building a secular St Paul's, as a monument to their progress and power? Be that as it may. For all its charms, I think I want to forget Paris for a couple of days."

As she surveyed the fastidiously restored structure

around her, Kelly smiled wryly. Her life had become a tale of two cities. She had embarked upon her French adventure with great expectations, some of which had been exceeded beyond her wildest dreams. And yet she never completely escaped the tug back to the island capital. She was truly happy to be back, even if the weekend promised hard times ahead:

"So, what the Dickens are we going to do to save our mutual friend, Kelly?"

Kelly had been going through the options on the train. She was convinced that Amber was not only behind the planting of the drugs, but also had something to do with all those lapses that had led doubting Hartmut to Ben's desk. She had seen Ben work hard and play hard. She had never known him lose work or forget to put important documents in the post. At the very least, he should be given the benefit of the doubt.

The first step was to marshal the troops.

Kelly turned beseechingly to her friend:

"Cornisha, you must call Hartmut and make an appointment to see him tomorrow morning. You are then going to wake up little Hamish and bully him into joining us. Finally, please flush out that ditzy secretary of his. I bet Sissy Sparsit is part of the reason Ben is in this fix. I am going to make damned sure she helps us pull him out."

Unaware that Kelly Danvers had ridden into town on a shining Eurostar to rescue him, Ben sat slumped on Rubens' sofa. The two men looking at each other glumly. So far, so nothing. Ben had texted Dillon Lloyd half an hour ago, but had had no reply. As contacting Dillon was the only plan Ben had, he was currently stumped.

Just then Ben's phone chirruped at him.

Going to Scream. Probably Spartacus tomorrow morning. See you lover. Dillon x

Dillon might avoid Ben if he turned up with Rubens, but Ben didn't want to leave his friend alone. He had never seen Rubens in such a dark place. Maybe Rubens needed Ben to be the Brazilian tonight.

Ben turned to Rubens, decisively:

"OK, here's the deal. You and I are going out clubbing tonight, Rubens. You are going to find that damned *espiritu brasileiro* of yours again. We are going to have fun. You will dance yourself dizzy and pick up the best-looking man in the room. While you are rediscovering your joie de vivre, I shall be off to the sauna to bag myself the little brat."

Hartmut calmly poured the tea:

"Does everyone have tea? Good. Then I am ready to listen, Kelly."

Kelly gathered her thoughts. She eyed Hartmut with some trepidation. She had to get this just right. Ben's future may depend on her convincing his boss that she was right:

"I spent yesterday evening talking to all concerned in this matter. I now believe that Ben has been framed."

She paused to see the effect her words would have on the group. Hartmut looked back at her impassively, waiting. Hamish fiddled nervously with his cell phone. Sissy Sparsit wore the frightened expression of a goose that somehow knew it was the week before Christmas and that its weight loss programme was doing it no favours. Kelly couldn't tell what Cornisha was thinking.

"Hartmut, you were present when Amber Bluett's brothers attacked me. Call me a cynic, but I believe now, and always have believed, that this supposedly reformed character of hers is an elaborate sham. My premise is that she may have been taking advantage of the situation in order to take revenge on Ben. In this sense, I feel responsible for what may be occurring. This is why I would like to get to the bottom of it with you all."

Hartmut eyed Kelly with all the placidity of a man who had made it his profession to listen to accusations:

"I understand why you might think this, Kelly, but the facts unfortunately point to self-inflicted damage. Ben has been seen falling asleep in meetings. He has emailed out incomplete documents replete with glaring errors. He failed to post an important document that was subsequently found lying on his desk. Then we have the anecdotal evidence of his wayward behaviour outside of the office. Let us not of course forget the matter of the bag of marijuana found in his possession, in the office – in a law firm. In order to overturn such facts, my dear, you are in need of some evidence. I hope for his sake that you have not come here empty-handed, for whatever my personal desire may be to believe in Mr Barlettano's innocence, I cannot do so unless you explain away these facts."

Kelly had expected such a response from Hartmut, and was actually grateful to him for listing out all of the items which needed to be dealt with. She took a deep breath:

"I will not challenge the fact that our recent break up has certainly had an effect on Ben, and I shall never forgive myself for causing him so much anguish. I will not attempt to challenge the fact that Ben has certainly been partying hard, and has been letting off a lot of steam. The anecdotal evidence you mention is most certainly likely to be true. Neither will I challenge the fact that this undoubtedly led to the unfortunate fact of him falling asleep in a meeting."

The admission was now out of the way. She had given all the ground that she was going to. Now it was time to go on the attack:

"However, I have known Ben Barlettano for some time. I have seen him play at the top of his game, and I have also seen him at less than full power. Even when he has been having issues outside of work which would have distracted a lesser man, Ben has always brought a relentless focus to his work. He is a very ambitious man. The errors you have cited are simply not part of his make up."

It was a bold statement. She now needed to back it up with fact:

"Let us turn first to the incomplete and error-strewn document. What was Ben's reaction when it was brought to his attention?"

The group were all waiting for Hartmut to respond. Hartmut obliged:

"Ben was in a state of utter confusion. He said he remembered completing it the night before, and had left it to the following morning to email it out as he wanted to have a final check the next day. Then matters had speeded up and someone else had emailed it out from the system."

"Hamish," said Kelly.

Ham started and dropped his phone on the floor.

"You are the person who works most closely with Ben. What did he say to you?"

Hamish's nervousness was not provoked by any mendacity connected to his response. He simply knew the stakes. He had to be convincing. If he wanted some day to be a partner, he knew he would have to face far more repellent adversaries than Hartmut Glick, who was known to be a decent, fair man.

He spoke slowly:

"Ben was mortified, but also incredulous. He swore blind that there were parts of the document that he was certain he had not written, and, equally, that other parts that he clearly remembered writing had disappeared from the document that was saved on his PC."

"So, in effect, Ben told you that the document that was sent out was not the same document that he had written the night before. But surely that is impossible. I mean, we all know that without his password it would be impossible for anyone to access Ben's computer."

Kelly paused to allow the group to reflect on the standards of IT security that were commonplace in law firms:

"I mean, who else could know Ben's password? Do you know Ben's password, Ham?"

Despite the fact that Hartmut's sitting room was kept at a regulation cool temperature of twenty-two degrees, beads of sweat had formed on Hamish's forehead:

"Actually, I do know Ben's password."

Silence. Kelly resisted the urge to stand up and approach Hartmut as if he were the jury:

"So, you are saying that you could have accessed Ben's PC and sabotaged the document in order to make your boss look foolish in front of the firm."

"Yes, I could have. But I did not."

"Well, if you didn't then who could have? It doesn't surprise me that Ben has trusted you with his password, but who else would he possibly trust? Sissy?"

Sissy gulped:

"Ben does share his password with me as well. Although I can never remember what it is."

"So, Sissy you have his password, but you can't remember it. Surely you don't write it down? IT would go mad."

Sissy blushed. This was the moment she had been dreading:

"Well, yes, actually I did have to write it down. I kept it on a post-it stuck to my monitor."

Hartmut sat up in his chair:

"You did what? So basically anyone who wandered round the office could see it?"

Kelly jumped in smoothly:

"Especially a person whose job included wandering round the office liaising with the staff? I think it would be safe to say that, should she have average vision, Amber Bluett might easily have noticed a bright yellow piece of paper with a password written on it."

Kelly paused, fighting the urge to externalise her first victory:

"The document was emailed out on the morning of the 17th. Cornisha, what time did you leave the office on the evening of the 16th?"

"I remember it distinctly, Kelly. I was there until 7.30pm as by the time I got home I had missed the Gardener's World special on Singaporean orchids. Thankfully, Arthur had recorded it for me."

"Were you the last person to leave that evening?"

"Almost, but not quite. Amber was finishing her monthly expenses. She wished me a safe journey home as I left."

Kelly permitted herself a brief smile as she turned to face Hartmut:

"So, I think I have demonstrated that not only did Amber have the motive, but she also had ample opportunity to tamper with the document."

Hartmut Glick tapped his fingers on the arm of his chair:

"Fine, my dear, this could be possible. So how do you explain the letter to Companies House being found on Ben's desk?"

"The letter was found by you on Friday evening at eight o'clock, with Bartlett DeVere and Amber Bluett present. Another late night for our diligent HR Manager. Hamish, did you work on that document with Ben?"

"Yes, I did."

"When was the document completed?"

"The previous Monday."

Hamish was well trained, responding solely to the exact question posed and not offering up any further information until Kelly asked for it.

"What happened to the document when it was finished?"

"As is Ben's habit, he retained the document for a final check on Tuesday morning which we completed together. Then we passed it to Sissy for her to put in the post."

Kelly turned her relentless look on the hapless secretary:

"So Sissy, I assume that you immediately took it to reception?"

Sissy's face turned the colour of an overripe pepper:

"Well, actually, no. I put it in the post collection tray. That is quite usual."

"So the envelope was left in the post tray. The post tray that anyone in the office has access to."

Kelly spread her hands:

"Hartmut, I think I have demonstrated that Amber had the opportunity to remove the letter to Companies House from the tray, ensuring thus that it missed the post, and simply placed it back on Ben's desk. Needless to say, if she placed the envelope there, she could easily have placed anything else there. Such as a small bag of marijuana."

Silence. Kelly continued:

"Now, Hartmut, two options may be open to us. We place a call to Group IT to see if Ben's PC was accessed on the evening of the 16th. If this were a television programme, we would call in the police to take fingerprints on the letter to Companies House. However, that would bring a certain displeasing amount of attention to Beaux, Aspen, Dickerhint. Alternatively, we confront Amber directly with the evidence."

Hartmut had to admit that Kelly had put it well. Bartlett DeVere would never allow such an event to besmirch the firm's reputation. Amber, however, may not be aware of this. He considered the options carefully. He disliked such situations, and yet his heart was gladdened that his protégé already seemed less guilty than had appeared possible just an hour earlier:

"All right, my dear. You have made a convincing case. How do you propose we get the woman to confess?"

"The element of surprise, Hartmut."

Kelly was now more generous with her smiles:

"Cornisha, I think it is time you put in the call in to Bertha Cheung and inform her that the rendezvous with Amber after her run at La Gondola in Battersea Park will take place at 2 pm."

Ben had made Dillon Lloyd squeal, but not in the way he needed him to.

Up to that point, the evening had pretty much gone to plan. Rubens first watched his favourite episode of *Footballers' Wives* on DVD, so that Ben could perfect some scheming skills from Tania Turner. Thereafter, inspired and well prepared, the two men had hopped into a minicab to Vauxhall.

The club was loud, busy and proffered a decent supply of suitable prospective shags for the discerning body fascist. After much flirting, much dancing and an unhealthy quantity of alcohol, Rubens settled upon an enormous blond guy, who introduced himself as *Phil by name and fill by nature*.

Ben left soon after Rubens disappeared with his Poly-Philler. Having benefitted from a strategic power nap in one of the cubicles, Ben found his prey under the showers in Spartacus Spa. Any shyness Ben might once have felt melted away like a late snowfall in springtime. Dillon had never seen Ben naked before, much less in a state of soaped-up semi-arousal and within touching distance. Dillon didn't stand a chance, and within minutes Ben had him just where he wanted him.

The fact that Ben wanted to punish him for what he was almost certain Dillon was doing to Ben's best friend just made Ben drive harder. This seemed to send Dillon to an ever more ecstatic pitch. All too soon it became too much for both men and they gave in to a noisy climax. Ben had to admit that the little bugger was a fantastic shag. However, when it came to exactly how he would get Dillon to spill the beans about thieving from the bar with Javier Bordem, Ben was drawing a blank. He had been most successful in getting rather more than expected into Dillon, yet he had no idea about how he would get anything out of him.

As Ben was about to ask how things were at the bar, and about Javier in particular, there was a knock on the cubicle door.

"Dillon, you in there?"

The voice was quiet but had a tone of urgency. Dillon jumped up out of Ben's arms, wrapped himself in his towel and opened the door a crack. When he saw who it was, he pulled him into the cubicle.

"*Puta madre!*" exclaimed the newcomer.

Ben's timidity was largely a thing of the past. He now revelled in the effect that his naked body could have on people. In fact, for maximum effect, as soon as the door started to open, he had stretched back with his hands folded behind his head, his abs gently tensed, his crotch slightly raised, and his eyes closed, for all the world offering the sexual services of an available Adonis to the nouveau arriviste. Yet as he opened his eyes to enjoy the effect that he was having on the Spanish-speaking newcomer, it was Ben who got a shock.

"Geez, Javier, I didn't know you were here. Sorry, man."

Ben hastily covered himself with his towel.

"*Por favor*, Ben. Please do not say sorry. I think I should say *gracias* to you. I won't be forgetting that view for some time. You lucky little slut, Dillon! Don't suppose you would be up for a threesome?"

Javier Bordem knelt down and put his hand on Ben's thigh.

Dillon pulled Javier back to his feet:

"I don't think so, Javier. I wasn't a lesbian last time I looked and I am certainly not leaving him just yet. We're only at the end of round one, *amor*."

"Well," sighed Javier. "It was worth a shot."

Ben registered that he had not been consulted on whether he would be having sex with the Spaniard. Fairly good looks, tight muscular body? Ben definitely wouldn't have said no. Maybe having them together would bring something out.

Ben realised he was just clutching at straws. This was not the honey trap of the century. He cursed silently. Did he really expect either of them to blurt out the fact that they had been actively framing their manager, to him? They both knew that he was Rubens' best friend.

That being said, the fact that Javier and Dillon were

here together certainly did nothing to demolish his theory. Ben perked up.

Javier waved a hand:

"Anyway, I came here to say that Thiago has got some really good stuff, but he is leaving soon. If you want some, we should go to his cubicle now."

Javier was talking to Dillon, but his eyes kept wandering over Ben's body.

Ben smiled easily:

"I'm good, thanks, Javier. I can't let myself get too wasted this weekend. Busy week ahead."

There was no way Ben was going to fail to obtain any information from Dillon and then further fail to stay away from drugs as well.

Dillon's eyes had visibly widened when Javier mentioned Thiago and his stuff. He loved sex on drugs. Who doesn't? Dillon beamed. The thought of Ben inside him again when he, Dillon, would be even higher was not something he was going to risk missing:

"Babes, do you mind if I just go with Javier for a few minutes? I'll be back before you know it."

Dillon didn't wait for an answer. He reached down for the small bag out of which he had extracted condom and lube earlier. He unzipped it, and pulled out a twenty, almost spilling the entire contents over Ben as he did so:

"Thiago doesn't do charity. Keep the room and look after my bag for me, Big Ben. *I'll be back.*"

As Dillon and Javier left the cubicle, Ben locked the door behind them. His eyes strayed to Dillon's bag and that was when he felt something almost like an electric shock. Amongst the sundry essentials for a Sunday morning drug-fuelled orgy, Ben saw a mobile phone.

It worked when Ben switched it on. Ben's heart leapt into his mouth. He quickly accessed the messages, searching for Javier Bordem. Javier's name was near the top of the most recent received items, and clicking on it revealed a chain several screens long. However, as Ben waded through all the nonsense about where to meet, where to get drugs, and how various shags had been, he was devastated to find absolutely nothing at all about money.

He slouched back against the cubicle wall, looking despairingly at the phone. *Fuck!* He had been wrong about Dillon and Javier. Surely it couldn't have been Rubens all along?

No sooner had the depressing thought entered his mind than Ben's eye was caught by the words in a text written by Siegfried Allcock to Dillon that appeared in the list just under the ones from Javier Bordem:

Envelope trick worked a treat.

Ben clicked on the message chain. Reams of messages told him all he ever needed to know about what had been going on in Outrageous Fortune. Dillon had not been working with Javier Bordem and fooling poor love-struck Siegfried. It was Siegfried. Siegfried Allcock had orchestrated the entire affair, including planting an envelope full of money stolen from the bar in Rubens' flat.

Ben wondered if being a detective would always give him hard-ons of this quality.

*

"Oh Bertha, this is heavenly."

"I don't know why we never thought of using the Millennium Arena changing facilities before? Having a shower straight after our work-out and then enjoying a guilt-free glass of wine and a little Italian amuse-bouche overlooking the lake – well, what could be *better*, Amber?"

"How about being surprised by an old friend?"

Bertha and Amber turned from their lakeside view to find Kelly Danvers standing behind them. She was not alone. Hartmut Glick, Cornisha Burrows, Hamish McDowell and Sissy Sparsit made up quite the committee.

Hartmut positioned himself by Amber:

"Please do not rise, ladies. I am sorry to disturb your luncheon, but we have a small matter that we need to clear up. Amber, I mean it, stay seated, my dear. Listen to what we have to say, and do not even think of walking away until we are finished."

It had been decided that Hamish would take the lead in confronting Amber. Hartmut wanted to see how Hamish would perform. Hamish did want to be a lawyer after all, and this seemed a most efficient way of assessing his potential.

As Hamish laid out the charges against her, Amber maintained a stony silence.

Hartmut took up the baton:

"So, you see my dear, all we need to do is to make a call to Group IT, and another to the local constabulary and we shall have our proof that you were behind all the unfortunate occurrences."

Amber glared at Hartmut. What the German didn't

know was that she had found the plastic sachet in Ben's drawer on a previous foraging trip. True, it had contained a condom, a packet of lube and a drinks ticket from Ursa Major rather than the marijuana that she had substituted those items for, but it would still have Ben's prints on it. Her glare softened into a malicious smile. She clapped her hands, and directed a look of mocking contrition at her adversary:

"Surely the firm would rather sacrifice a foolish young lawyer rather than subject itself to such humiliation, Mr Glick. I admit that I may have been somewhat careless when looking to see what Ben was working on. I may have replaced that envelope on his desk. But there was a dominant reason for all this. I admit I was checking up on him. As it happens, I stumbled across the bag of drugs in his desk. Of course I picked it up, as I couldn't believe my eyes when I realised that Mr Barlettano had brought illegal substances onto the premises. But the fact remains that I did not put it there. Call in the police by all means, but I think you may all be rather upset when you find out what a basic fingerprint examination is likely to turn up."

Discovering that Siegfried was the root of this evil had shaken Ben to the core. That bastard was supposed to be Alex's longtime friend. Rubens looked up to Siegfried. It had never even occurred to anyone that the well-spoken Englishman might have been a thief. It had been far easier to suspect the flighty Spanish DJ, who, although a prize twat for many reasons, was blameless in this current matter. Ben vowed to himself for the umpteenth time that he would not allow himself to be fooled by appearances again.

Laughter outside the cubicle shook Ben from his thoughts. He had to get the phone to Alex and Jamal. It wasn't stealing. It was protection of evidence. He concealed the phone in his towel, and slowly opened the cubicle door.

A few nervous minutes getting back to the changing room and getting dressed passed uneventfully. Ben arrived on the safe grey pavement outside, and immediately hailed a black cab.

Hartmut weighed up the situation. Amber had confessed to some lesser indiscretions in front of witnesses, but had also forcefully denied the main crime. If she had been smart enough to almost get away with it, then she was surely smart enough to cover her tracks in the event of anything going wrong.

Hartmut was reminded of the bags that he himself stored his money in when he attended his S&M parties. Finding Ben's prints on the bag of marijuana would cause problems, to say nothing of the embarrassment caused to Beaux, Aspen, Dickerhint.

He took a decision:

"Very well, my dear. We shall deal with the situation internally. I appreciate your candour in admitting what you did. Kindly come to my office at 10am on Monday morning. We shall leave you to enjoy the rest of this glorious day. Be aware, though, that Mr Barlettano is no longer under investigation at the firm."

Hartmut turned on his heel and beckoned the others to follow, as they dutifully did, Kelly with a steely grin on her face. Bertha also rose. She stared at Amber as if seeing her for the first time. She slung her bag over her shoulder:

"I'll let you pick up the tab, Amber. I don't think we shall be exercising together anymore."

Alex raised a well-groomed eyebrow:

"Right, Ben, so are you going to tell us why we are here?"

Ben gestured at his friend:

"Sure. I need to show you something."

He pulled out Dillon's phone, and clicked on the message chain with Siegfried Allcock. He placed the screen in front of Alex, Jamal and Rubens so all three could read together, and started to slowly scroll.

Alex's face was a picture of mortification:

"Oh, my God. The double-crossing little *shit*. Rubens, I am so sorry. How could I have been so stupid? Oh God. Oh fuck. How can you ever forgive me?"

Rubens put his hands to his face in surprised delight:

"Alex, Alex, you have always been a good friend to me. I know how this must have looked. I am just so *relieved*! Unbelievably so! The evidence didn't look good. I can't blame you for not suspecting an old friend, especially one from Cambridge University. I have no hard feelings. I know how you get all tied up there. Jamal, you must forgive your husband, who made an honest man of you but almost a dishonest one of me. You almost fucked up pretty bad here, Alex – but, *bija*, nobody is perfect."

Alex was aghast. He wasn't sure that he would have been able to forgive so wholeheartedly. He could only make it up to Rubens, starting right away:

"Rubens, I don't deserve a friend like you," he said quietly, reaching out. "Would you consider at least becoming the new general manager of Outrageous Fortune?"

Although Jamal generally liked to be fully consulted before any important decisions regarding the bar were taken, Alex's offer to their friend received a warm welcome in his heart.

Rubens nodded and turned to Ben:

"Ben, I really don't know how I am ever going to be able to thank you. How are you feeling?"

Rubens had asked a very simple but very difficult question to answer. Ben knew he had just saved his friend's job, but Ben's own was still teetering precariously.

His phone rang.

Hartmut Glick. *Oh crap.* Ben was in no state to have a conversation with his boss. Unwillingly he accepted the call.

Hartmut sounded happy:

"My dear boy, I have just had a very interesting conversation with Amber Bluett. It seems she is the person responsible for all the regrettable incidents in the office over the past couple of weeks. I would never have found out about this had it not been for the faith in you that a certain person has shown. To say nothing of some rather clever detective work in unmasking the true perpetrator. I need you to speak to someone. Please stay on the line."

Ben stepped away from his friends. He wasn't sure he had heard this correctly. Then he heard Kelly's voice:

"Ben, darling – it's me. Please don't hang up. I am so

very sorry for being so stupid. Please, please – can we see each other?"

"Kelly," said Ben. "Kelly – just come over."

Magically, or so it seemed, Ben was lying in bed with Kelly in his flat in The Castle Lofts.

He looked around him and simply could not believe what had transpired. Here she was. And everything seemed right again. He ran a hand over her luscious body:

"So you are really going to come back to London to be with me?"

Kelly looked into Ben's eyes with all the feeling of one who couldn't believe that she had been given a second chance at the love she had thought she had lost forever. Morten may have been her Spartacus Spa, but now she knew what she wanted in life:

"You try keeping me away. I love Paris in the springtime, but London is where my heart is."

She meant it.

Ben sighed:

"Do you think we'll be able to make it work this time? I haven't exactly been a saint since... well, you know."

"These last few months haven't been easy for me either, Ben. But maybe it's all for a reason. I'm not going to pretend that Morten didn't sweep me off my feet. If he hadn't gone off to Africa, it would have taken me longer to realise that I was being a perfect fool. But I would have worked it out eventually."

Kelly paused:

"I accept that it may have been too late by then. I think

you don't always end up with those you love best. I think timing is everything. And other bodies get in the way."

She didn't want any more secrets. Ben had to know that Morten had left her. If he couldn't accept it, then so be it, but she couldn't lie any more to the man she loved.

Ben swallowed. He would have preferred it if Kelly had left that damned Scandinavian, rather than wising up to the fact she loved Ben after being left high and dry. But life didn't follow any Hollywood scripts. And he was hardly perfect himself. He may have been physically faithful during their time together, but he had fantasised about more men and women than he cared to – or could – remember.

"I can't pretend it doesn't hurt in some way," he said evenly, "but I suspect that it will pass with time. You could have followed him to Africa, or had that long-distance relationship. Instead you came back to London and saved my career. Actions speak louder than words."

Kelly smiled and softly kissed his lips:

"I don't think our relationship will ever follow anyone else's script. It took me a long time to accept that my big man enjoyed big men himself. We are both highly sexed, and I guess we will just have to live with it. At least we know that if we are together it isn't because there is a lack of options, and that sometimes we might even exercise those options. On a temporary basis, though."

Had Kelly just said she would be ok with an open relationship? Ben didn't care to elucidate just now. All he knew was that being with the girl from Louisiana was everything that he wanted in life right now.

19

LGBT to the rescue

Never had B.A.D's reception area looked so lovely. In anticipation of the LGBT cocktail party, flower arrangements had been multiplied. They were strategically placed to lead the way to the decked-out conference room where the party was being held.

The flaming torches idea had been mercifully scrapped, and no one really minded when the receptionist, a chunky lass from Milton Keynes, sniggered about the "fruit baskets".

"You've missed an obvious requirement!" she cackled, waving a banana from her packed lunch, in what she was persuaded was a witty and original fashion.

Cornisha glided over to admonish her discreetly, fresh from checking the laying out of the name tags and briefing the trainees on the meet and greet:

"No banana jokes, Karen. This is a professional occasion."

Things calmed down, which was just as well. No one wanted a repeat of the long gone – yet somehow never forgotten – scene when a banking partner had been surprised late at night waving *his* banana around at the previous receptionist, whilst she lay prone on the firm's grand piano. That instrument generally remained silent – a classical effigy, capably representing the general lack of creative talent around it – a mere mockery of its potential. Oh, if pianos could sing, this one would be singing the blues so deeply that it would have to be told to shut up, sharpish.

The LGBT party had caused the marketing budget to be diligently tortured so as to yield sufficient funds to hire fine-looking *resting* actors and models as waiters. They were dressed in black silk shirts, proper belts and trousers that fitted. The lawyers were intimidated by such astonishing sartorial know-how. Not to be outdone by the men, the waitresses wore elegant long skirts with vampish slits. There was just the right amount of strain on their shirt buttons, which moulded various epitomies of pertness.

The staff looked cool and composed. This was more than could be said for most of the hosts. Pam and Lynne had decided that a pre-cocktail sharpener had been the way to go. Both slightly red-faced and overexcited, they stomped around like hungry pygmy elephants.

Ben was looking his handsome best. He was elated. He rarely felt sexy in the office. Offices suck sexy out of incumbents. More often than not, sexy is as stifled as the princes in the tower. Or at least Ben thought so. The trouble was that Ben, having a semblance of a life outside of the office, failed to truly understand how confidence, the cornerstone of sexy, gets sapped by office life, and replaced with a variant of any of slightly desperate approval-seeking, or by anger, or by hypocrisy, or in the worst case outright bitterness, which led to the most troublesome couplings and mysterious matches. Ben simply did not see or understand how his colleagues' interests and obsessions grew unhealthily in the otherwise rational surroundings of a large office facility – grew, until strange desires and confused hankerings took on a life of their own. One could not fail but experience awe at the evolutionary process that led Man With Terrible Centre Parting to discover that there was no thing as beautiful in this world as Woman With Twitchy Eye.

That particular petri dish was not evident for the time being. Ben was pleased and proud that the guests would see such an elegant set of surroundings. It contrasted with the chaos reigning in the offices below, where papers were heaped on desks, crumbs stagnated on keyboards, and coffee stains adorned original documents.

Ben smiled as he recalled how people had confidently predicted the advent of the paperless office. Not in law firms, not for the time being. Amateurs of origami need fear nothing yet.

The first guests were arriving.

Ben felt as if he should pinch himself. Gay professionals, out and proud. Why it should feel so trail-blazing, he did not know – but it did. So many people still felt uncomfortable about different expressions of sexuality. So many people would rather not know. So many still disapproved – all over the world.

Cornisha was greeting the speaker. This was exciting. The LGBT group had secured the attendance of what could almost pass for a celebrity. This had seemed an indispensable part of the evening in the planning stages, and, whatever else one might have thought of him, at least Peter Barrowman was on time. His white teeth dazzled as he hugged Cornisha, every visible part of him a perfect brown, like a baked sausage.

It was good to have a celebrity speaker. The link between the anticipated turnout, and the presence of a celebrity, fell to be made. It remained a fact that singer, songwriter and producer Peter Barrowman looked as out of place in a law office as Karl Lagerfeld might in Ikea.

Ben went over to say hello. The privileges of the head of the LGBT group included such treats:

"Mr Barrowman? My name is Ben Barlettano…"

"Ben, it's a pleasure to meet you. Great job."

"I'm – we're all very grateful that you've made the time to come along today. It means a lot."

"Sure it does. I'm happy to help. I'm just going to say a few words about how important it is to stick together. People can't live in fear."

The teeth flashed:

"Mind you, I think it's still not that obvious for you lot. I shared the lift with at least one chap who looked as if he thought I would take him there and then, squishing his face against the mirror."

"You should have," said Ben. "There's nothing like exceeding people's expectations."

Peter Barrowman laughed:

"I'm sure I left him wanting more."

As they chatted, Ben saw a group of people move into the conference room adjacent to the party. That's bad luck, he thought. It's not much fun working within sound of clinking glasses. At that moment a red-faced partner rushed up to the receptionist, and started spluttering.

Here we go, thought Ben. I know your type. You're the kind of person that would slam the phone down on people. A shrivelled little soul, burning with frustration, showcasing incandescent rage over your own inadequacies.

Ben motioned to Cornisha, who escorted Peter Barrowman towards the sanctuary of the cocktail party, while Ben approached the partner to see if he could help.

The receptionist was looking mutinous:

"It's not my fault," she said.

"Oh for fuck's sake!" said the partner eloquently.

"What's up?" said Ben. "Can I help?"

"Oh. You. No, I'm not sure you can. In fact…" and here came a finger jab, "I… I…"

"You?" asked Ben, reasonably.

"He's angry about the room bookings," said the receptionist. "But we can't do much about it. The other rooms are being used in a mediation which looks likely to run late. And room six is currently a data room."

"But what is the problem? Is it the noise?"

"The noise?" said the partner, his face turning a shade of puce. "The noise? Listen, my… friend. I have no beef with your lot. I have no problems understanding that there seems to be an endless need for people to yabber about their particular foibles and preferences. But I'm a little concerned about having a bloody *fairy* cocktail just next door to a closing in present circumstances. I have no problem with diversity – just not when a *particularly homophobic client is around!"*

Ben looked at the partner and felt a strange calm:

"Isn't that," he said quietly, "exactly when you do need to stand up for your values?"

"Values?" said the partner.

"Values," said Ben.

The partner uttered a strangled yelp and stormed off.

The receptionist examined her screen.

"I think I need a drink," said Ben into thin air.

Hamish listened as Bertha dominated the room. Beautiful though she was, he found her to be about as approachable as an angry hippo. Her blouse was straining across her breasts in a most tantalising way, and yet Ham felt as sucked dry as a lemon on a scurvy-ridden ship. Bertha was almost the mistress of events. It was a close call – but she was falling short of achieving control. She betrayed in every strained feature the feeling of utter panic that relative lack of experience nurtures in even the most confident souls.

"Shit," she said. "The Germans are demanding a guarantee because they're nervous about the money."

"What form of guarantee?" asked Ham. This was an area that Ben had explained to him a little.

"They want a guarantee from Norse Bank."

Bertha looked dejected.

Ham brightened slightly:

"Bertha, I think Ben has dealt with Norse Bank. Quite a few times, if I'm remembering right. I think he'll know what sort of terms they're comfortable with. That might help?"

Bertha turned on him like a blazing cannon:

"Of course it would bloody help... Sorry, Ham, I'm a bit tense. This has all been rather more difficult than it should be. When you get a moment, will you go and grab Ben?"

"Will do," said Ham.

He was frowning at the Disclosure Letter.

The Disclosure Letter seemed to be stating that the German sellers had in fact not renewed a licence to manufacture one of their previous generation drugs. Ham thought about this. He was pretty sure that the company would be committing a criminal offence if it manufactured an unlicensed pharmaceutical product:

"Yes. I do think I need to grab Ben. I'm going in," announced Ham.

He left the room like a comfortable rodent alerted to the presence of some decent leftovers – a man on a mission, a hamster on a wheel.

The LGBT party was in full swing. Music was playing and the drinks flowed readily. After a slow start, people were now relaxing. It felt right to get a little drunk. It was a relief that the event had happened at all, and that it did not feel too strange. There was a hint of proper celebration about it.

Ben looked around. It was probably the only time he could remember at work when he could count on those around him not betraying awkwardness about his sexuality. After all the organising, he just wanted to drink it all in, and take comfort that he had not let the side down.

He saw Ham charging towards him, pink faced and determined.

"Ham! I had no idea!"

"Ben, I think we need your help."

"My help? Ham, I'm on my third glass."

Ham looked around, and leaned in conspiratorially:

"Ben, you do your best drafting off your rocker. I know. I've witnessed it."

"That was not my best drafting, I can assure you."

"It was the best of any of us. Look. I wouldn't ask – but I think we've seen an iceberg. The partner is nowhere to be seen. I think he's keeping the client from the meeting room because of *this* party."

"What's the issue?"

"Just come. I'll tell you all about it. I know you'll have some straight thoughts."

"What *are* you implying, Ham?"

Ben allowed himself to be dragged away by Ham. He was strangely pleased to be called upon. Feeling useful is one of life's little pleasures.

As they scuttled away from the warm cheery party, Ham explained about the Disclosure Letter issue. Ben nodded in approval:

"Good spot, Ham. From what you're saying, it would seem you're spot on. And that is exactly the sort of point that you should be looking out for in deals. But let's think through to the next stage. What happens now?"

Ham stopped short and thought the matter through:

"Well… first, they don't have a current licence, which means that they are breaking the law. Therefore, any money they make out of that drug is deemed to be money from the proceeds of crime. That means, as lawyers, we won't be able to complete the transaction until we have informed the Serious Fraud Office, and obtained clearance. God, Ben, this is a disaster."

"Exactly," said Ben.

"Everyone is here and wants to sign, but we can't. This has been dragging on and the clients want to finish it off. How are we going to get clearance from the Serious Fraud Office at this time of night?"

Ben suddenly grinned – a grin so wide that it hinted at resolution:

"Bring on the gays, Ham!"

"What? Who?"

"Enoch Sittikin. Do you remember him? Him from the Serious Fraud Office? Well, in a fabulously helpful way, he happens to be gay, and he is attending our LGBT party as we speak."

"Are you kidding me?"

"Not at all. Networking, Ham – it's all about networking."

"Ben, that could be just what we need!"

"Let me grab him. We'll have this sorted out. Anything else?"

"We also need a Norse Bank guarantee."

"That won't be a problem. They're straightforward to deal with. They won't make a saga out of it."

Ben re-entered the fray and sought out Enoch, who was easy to spot in a crowd, being a very tall lanky fellow in a dark suit with an incongruous red tie. He was complaining enthusiastically to a small audience including B.A.D's court clerk, and a bouffant-haired chap from the Department of Trade and Industry.

"... it's not as if I'm deaf, you know. You don't think that I don't *know* that they call me "the Serious Fraud Orifice" behind my back? ... oh, hello, Ben. This is an excellent gathering. It brings out the revolutionary in me. I am minded to fulfil everyone's prejudices and rock up to work tomorrow in a sequinned suit shouldering a boom box blaring out *I am what I am*".

"I did that once. No one blinked. Sometimes a bit of prejudice is needed to get a proper audience reaction."

Enoch nodded:

"All the world's a stage, but when you're at work you do sometimes feel as if you are chewing your nails in the wings."

He took another sip of wine thoughtfully.

Ben smiled:

"The gays should take over the workplace, just as we have taken over the world of fashion. It needs us, to give everything fun and meaning – and to bring out the best in people. You're only ever productive if you're happy. And – by the way – I am about to be made happy by you."

Enoch looked pleased:

"Anything, Ben, you Italian devil."

Ben took Enoch to one side:

"It's a favour, but I trust it's not asking too much. We're acting for an Arab client who is purchasing some German interests. My trainee Ham has spotted something minor, but obviously notifiable to you. The Germans haven't got round to renewing one of their older pharmaceutical licences. So – technically – they are committing a criminal offence, and it follows that the proceeds flowing from that

403

licence are therefore proceeds of crime. In this case, it's a matter of a few thousand pounds – nothing that should affect the transaction – but technically, of course, we as their lawyers would be assisting them – and therefore unable to act – unless we obtained SFO clearance. So: I would need your clearance. I know this normally takes around three days – but the partner here is having kittens – to make matters worse he is our compliance officer, so is probably cacking his pants as I speak to you – but everyone is here and present, waiting to sign – and I can't even explain any of this to them as *that* would be tipping off."

Enoch grinned:

"Ah. The intricacies of regulation, coming home to roost."

Ben smiled:

"It would mean a lot if you could help. I know it's after hours and I know you're at a party…"

"I like the idea of being useful," said Enoch thoughtfully. "Look – it's quite clear that I can help you. Write me a memo setting out the facts. Given the sums at stake I have authority to give clearance personally on this. Let's get your show on the road. We wouldn't want to put young Ham in the position of telling porkies."

The music was louder. Abdul Ben Ahmad was not familiar with the oeuvre of Cyndi Lauper and he puzzled over the strains of *Girls just want to have fun* as he left the lift and rounded the atrium towards the transaction room.

In the room, Ben was introducing Enoch to the perspiring partner in charge of Bertha's transaction.

"Dominic, without the LGBT group, your deal would have cratered so badly, we'd have been sending lunar rovers to it," said Ben evenly.

The partner looked embarrassed:

"I am very grateful, Mr Sittikin. This has not been an easy deal to pull together."

"We do try to be helpful," said Enoch. "People pulling together is really what it's all about. People of all persuasions, fuelled by goodwill – and by your delicious cocktails, on this occasion, too."

"Once we have signed, I hope you will have a few more. I am in your debt."

"Only doing the job. Happy it can all work out. Ben here is good at getting things done – no doubt about it."

"Thank you, Ben," said Dominic, not ungraciously.

The door to the conference room opened. Abdul Ben Ahmad was greeted by a strong whiff of booze, which he found interesting. He looked a tad puzzled as he surveyed the scene – Bertha as beautiful and fiery as ever, quietly checking the documents, Ham organising the copies for signature, Dominic getting ready to take all the credit, and two men who looked a little pink-faced.

"We're ready," said Bertha.

"This is excellent. I am very grateful."

"Mr Ben Ahmad, this is Mr Enoch Sittikin of the Serious Fraud Office. We had a last minute regulatory question which he has solved for us. Without him, we would not be in a position to sign – so we are most grateful to him for his intervention."

"This is very efficient. I appreciate it."

The two men shook hands.

"Let's go and sign the documents. I'd be honoured if you would all join me very soon to celebrate the completion of the transaction – especially you, Mr Sittikin, whom I understand has somewhat saved the day."

Abdul paused, as if looking for words, and raised his hands palm upwards:

"Please explain one thing, my friends, before we go. I have been seeing these signs all over the building. Please, what is LGBT?"

Also by Tim Brady and Melanie Willems

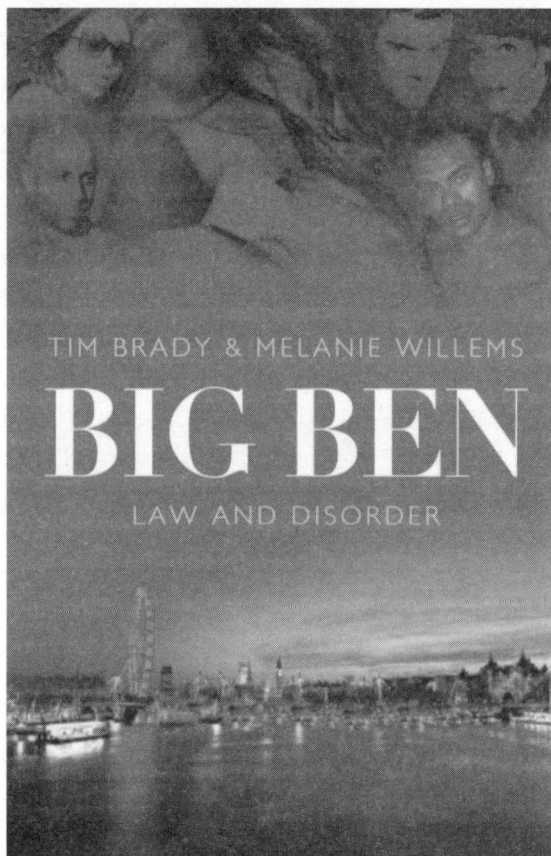

TIM BRADY & MELANIE WILLEMS

BIG BEN

LAW AND DISORDER

London, England. Ben Barlettano, a successful, highly-sexed yet still wet behind the ears 26-year old New York lawyer lands in the Elephant & Castle.

Through a chain of unexpected experiences, Ben discovers his new life. Exciting, sometimes harsh, occasionally extreme, but never dull. Ben meets a number of people, each with stories and secrets. There is the respectable senior partner who is addicted to bondage clubs; the serenely efficient office manager who cannot bring herself to tell her boyfriend she, too, used to have a penis; the statuesque gym instructor hiding his emotions under a perennial smile; and of course the woman Ben falls for, almost on day one, who seems afraid of nothing – until she gets scared.

Uncomfortable encounters in Turkish baths, moonlighting as an escort for charity, violent arguments with a neighbour and thoroughly mismanaging a ménage-à-trois are just some of the things that Ben is utterly unprepared for.

Will Ben survive what London throws at him, or will he end up scuttling back to his Italian mamma in New York?

Contact us:

melandtimbooks.com
melandtimbooks.co.uk